The Poo

Honour Death

The Pool

Honour Death

By

John Michael Coia

Strategic Book Publishing and Rights Co.

Strategic Book Publishing and Rights Co.
12620 FM 1960, Suite A4-507
Houston TX 77065
www.sbpra.com

ISBN: 978-1-61897-448-8

CHAPTER 1

It hung in the air directly in front of him. Steady, rock steady, so steady that it didn't really hang at all. It seemed to be fixed in space as if to something solid, embedded in a perfectly clear glass wall, and yet it was almost two metres off the ground exactly as it had been all the time he had pursued it, or perhaps it was all the time he had been led by it?

The fierce rays made his bare skin prickle, even though he was deeply tanned, and quite used to the "Lion Sun" as the locals called it at this time of year. It was high summer and the strong, harsh light washed out the colours of nature and made his eyes smart as he stared. He began to wish he had picked up his shirt when he first saw the strange thing and cursed himself inwardly when he realised that his sunglasses must still be in the breast pocket of the shirt. The rough, white rocks and thorn plants of the steep hillside cut his bare legs and the sharp gravel trapped in his open sandals irritated the skin; so much so that he knelt down and unbuckled the straps to remove the sandals, never for a moment taking his eyes from the object of his pursuit.

Sweat trickled down his back and the shimmering, dancing air was silent but for the buzz of tiny flies and the background rasp of the cicadas. At this altitude breathing was more demanding and he gasped for breath as his heart thudded after the strenuous climb.

He was fifty-five years old now and very aware of the diminution in his physical abilities. In a way, that was why he was up here. He had left the village that morning, as he had done many times before, to stroll slowly and aimlessly up into the rocky, wooded slopes supposedly for the exercise but in reality he would stop at his random whim and steep himself in the peace and beauty to be found there. A rugged, even harsh world of steep mountainsides and tangled woods beneath the cobalt blue sky from which the great golden orb of the sun beat down mercilessly.

And yet it was so full of life, so full of natural detail and surprise that he often regretted his lack of knowledge of botanical things and would try futilely to remember the names his wife knew of the abundant wild flowers and little creatures that scuttled and rattled in the dry undergrowth.

He had taken off his shirt, he recalled, and had sat down on a large boulder as was his habit, partly to rest, partly to look around, and partly to muse. How long he had remained like that, silently lost in his inner self, he had no idea, but eventually he had become aware of something amongst the dusty, grey stones slightly above him on the slope. It hadn't been very obvious at first; there had been no particular reason to pick it out, but something about it caught his attention and he peered at it, wondering idly.

He hadn't even been able to see the whole of it in the beginning. It might just as well have been simply another rock amongst the many; but still . . . something held his interest.

Finally, after some minutes his curiosity had overcome his indolence and he had risen, a little stiffly, and climbed amateurishly up the slope towards it.

The object glinted dully, like gunmetal or perhaps very dark glass covered with fine dust. Its surface was smooth like a river-washed pebble but much larger and surely far too regular to be natural. It really was odd. It protruded from the ground rather than lay on it, as if it was part of something larger. He stooped to touch it.

Suddenly it rose straight up in the air!

A gasp escaped his lips and he started straight upright with shock, eyes wide, staring. He spoke aloud to the thin air, "What the hell?"

It stopped abruptly at head height, paused momentarily, and then shot back a full two metres. It had made no sound, totally silent, not even small stones rattled.

He felt the little hairs on the back of his neck stiffen and an eerie coldness creep over his skin, despite the blistering sun.

It was quite big, bigger than a man's head. In fact its shape reminded him of a faceless human skull wearing one of those big motorcycle helmets but all made of the same material. Glassy, not quite opaque, dusty as if acid etched and it looked heavy.

For a long time he stood quite still, on edge, wary, watching it, waiting. But after the first shock abated he realised that he had not been afraid, not in the least afraid, and a quiet calm filled him.

If he thought about it, that would have seemed strange for he was not a brave or physical man. Pain and danger Generally upset him. He could be courageous emotionally and mentally but a physical threat always made him uneasy and yet this weird happening seemed detached, somehow curious.

At last he started to move toward it, reaching out to touch it. Searching for some knowledge of it, some sign that it was hot or cold, soft or hard, some means of identification. But at his first forward pace it moved back, back from his touch, his reaching arms, back from his advance.

He stopped, puzzled but not afraid. He gazed around. *Was this a trick? Was someone playing a joke on him?* The tangled, low trees and glaring white rocks hid nothing, no one. Only the little lizards scrabbled unaware among the pebbles. *No, it was impossible to fake this. This was real. This was important.*

He stepped forward again.

It moved smoothly back.

So he started his hard trek after the thing. He couldn't remember how long or how far; surely not too long or too far, though. It was still very hot with the sun still high and the ground was rough and steep and the going slow. He had to scramble for grip at times, the pebbles betraying his step and noisily skittering down the slope. Perhaps he had travelled a few kilometres up and along the wooded mountain slopes; surely no more.

Now it stopped. Stopped in its relentless and maddeningly exact retreat before him. But had it been retreating or leading? It didn't seem to matter much. It was enough that it had stopped. Stopped so that he could move a little closer . . . and closer still. He inched toward it. It didn't waver. He held his breath, heart pounding, afraid that any movement might start the goading retreat again. He was within reach now, could touch it if he wanted to. It didn't move, not a quiver, rock steady.

He felt sure of it now, felt confident that it wouldn't vanish the moment he took his eyes from it and yet he hesitated, took stock.

How many hours had passed since he left home? Perhaps his wife had missed him. She was not given to restricting his movements or demanding detailed explanations of his actions but still she might be worried by now, now that he had not returned. He was not usually away as long as this on these little excursions and she might worry. There was the occasional snake and there was always the potential fall or turn of the ankle.

He was happy here in the hills of the Italian Mezzo Giorno. His adopted lifestyle had brought no regrets. The change from constant and willing participation in the city rat race had brought no unexpected emotional problems. The life he and his wife had led of schoolteacher on her part and engineer on his, coupled with a small business interest had been rewarding financially but sterile. No fulfilment resulted. Their decision to quit working in the conventional sense and uproot their lives from familiar old Scotland had seemed drastic at the time, but it all worked out well.

Their little house, clinging to the steep slopes of the huddled mountain village in this remote province of Italy, had proved to be a spring of happiness and healing to a tired spirit. In the sun and warmth, with the friendship of the village community, its festas and wine; he had begun to forget all the ashes of failure, all the gall of false friends, and the petty betrayals of small men. He was happy.

How strange then to have these fantasies of his childhood awaken here in this paradise, here of all places. *Why had he so readily followed this thing?* He had everything to lose now. His greater family, as he liked to think of the villagers, were dear to him and they would certainly not understand his fascination with an outlandish object like this. How could they comprehend his total acceptance of something so unnatural and potentially dangerous? They would assume it to be madness.

What would he say on his return? How could he explain his actions?

His daughter for sure would laugh and call him silly names as always. She was smarter than ever he had been and that both pleased and dismayed him. The thought of her drew his mind inward. She was working now in Amsterdam and had a bright future. He was proud of her academic and career success though seldom admitted it publicly. *Why had such success eluded him?* he wondered. Was his usual bleating about a poverty-stricken childhood really the root of the matter or had he been, as he secretly feared, simply inadequate?

The glare from the sun made him blink forcibly, his eyes reacting to the strong ultraviolet rays. His train of thought interrupted, he became dimly aware of this fuzzy thinking, his mental rambling. *Was it the heat? Thirst?* He shook his head from side to side, trying to clear his mind, to concentrate.

His gaze re-focussed on the queer, inexplicable object. Glassy black, or maybe a dark bottle green; motionless, silent, menacing. It was certainly aware of him in a very precise sense he decided. It had always faced him in exactly the same way no matter how he had twisted and turned up the slope as if it could see him. It had metered the distance between them with impossible precision.

Again he felt that fog in his head, hard to concentrate, hard to maintain his sharpness. Hunger made itself felt. He hadn't eaten for hours. *What time was it?* But he had given up wearing wristwatches years ago when he had first come to Italy on the principle that they were artefacts of the rat race, a means of enslaving a man's mind, and therefore his body. As always, he shrugged off the pangs of hunger and was grateful for his free-wheeling lifestyle which allowed him to choose when to eat or not. He was getting too fat anyway his wife had said. He knew distantly that his attention was wandering again. It was so difficult to concentrate now. He was sleepy, heavy lidded. Oh! it was so hot. He shook his head again, more violently.

Why had it retreated? What had made it avoid close contact? Was it something he was doing? The notion suddenly grew in his mind that it may be something he was wearing? The idea was absurd, he knew, but perhaps if he took off his remaining article of clothing, a pair of shorts, then it might not retreat. Anyway it was so hot. It was worth a try he decided and slowly stripped, kicking off the well-worn and dusty item without a glance in the object's direction.

He felt foolish suddenly, naked in the sun. This wasn't quite proper, it went against his nature and he felt vulnerable. Glancing from side to side, it somehow seemed the thing to do, oddly right, expected. *Oh why did he feel so fuzzy, foggy?* He rubbed his eyes and face, smearing the dust and sweat, making white streaks on his deep tan.

The thing held his gaze again. He had to touch it, just had to. The urge was overpowering. He inched forward. It didn't move. His fingers reached out . . . closer and closer. He clasped it gently with both hands. It was unexpectedly cool and hard, fixed. Incongruously it seemed to be incredibly heavy for it did not waver by a hair's breadth even when he exerted force on it. Yet it was surely floating or hovering in midair. The weird contradiction of his senses strengthened his fixation on the dusty black, or was it green, object?

Now it seemed to be holding his hands bound to its smooth shape as if glued all over. It was more than a passive stickiness, different from simply being stuck to something. It felt as if even his fingers were being held, being drawn forcibly against its surface. The skin of his palms began to prickle, lightly at first, then more strongly, and then to burn like some allergic reaction. He felt, more than heard, it click several times. He yanked backwards, beginning to feel a pang of fear but the thing held with all the solidity and mass of the mountain itself. Immovable. He felt its surface change, no longer smooth but prickly now. Lurid pain stabbed deeply into his palms like hot needles. *What was it doing? Injecting poison? Sucking his blood?* Fear, naked and raw, welled up in him making him gag with the force of it. Panic swept away any reason and he heaved and twisted with all his strength emitting a thin, wheedling wail from his lungs, rising in pitch. It not so much resisted his terror-assisted struggles as ignored them. It didn't move.

Then it suddenly released him.

He tumbled violently backwards, cursing and yelling, falling heavily on the broken stony surface of the hillside.

At his age a fall like that was painful and it took some seconds for him to regain his breath and take stock. Shakily, using his elbows he got up onto his knees taking care to keep his hands from the sharp pebbles. He hurt all over with small abrasions and bleeding cuts, but his hands hurt most of all. They were red and swollen with what looked like a bad nettle rash and as he looked blood started to ooze from the small puncture marks in his skin. The burning sensation was hardly abating at all and an intense itch had begun. His hands trembled, as much from nervous reaction as from the pain. *What had it done to him? Why had it hurt him?*

He lifted his gaze slowly, fearfully, back to the cause of his pain.

It was gone.

Even as he felt the wave of disappointment and depression sweep over him, he knew that it was an irrational reaction. He should be running from this place, screaming for help. There was something very wrong here. He should be yelling a warning to all who could hear. It was being egocentric to think that he alone could deal with this thing. He should be screaming, "Run! Run! There is terrible danger on the hill." Instead, he stood up and almost howled with the bitterness of his loss. The tears welled and ran down his sweat-streaked cheeks adding to his dishevelment. His dream had gone.

How many times in his childhood had he fantasised of some such encounter; of some magical meeting or discovery of powers beyond the ken of man.

Into his mind came a vivid memory from his past. Again he was a small boy in Glasgow, no more than seven or eight years old. He was sitting on a pew in church on one of those all too rare warm summer days in Scotland. The old fashioned altar was in the traditional Catholic style, large and ornate with statues and big brass candlesticks. God was there, as usual, hanging gloomily from the huge cross at the back.

The Mass had not started yet and, as always, he dreamed great dreams in the dimness. *If God could do it why couldn't he? Why couldn't he do things just by willpower?* As he watched the big candles on the altar burning lazily in the still, hot air, his attention focused ever more closely, more intently on the flickering flame. He would will it to go out, extinguish it by the power of his mind alone; he would make it die. If he could have power over the flame, he would have power over everything. He had thought his brain would burst with the effort. Harder and harder he concentrated, blotting out everything but the hypnotic yellow flicker. Dizziness swept over him, his eyesight blurred, and sweat dampened his palms. Nothing had happened.

The little silver sounding bells announced the entry of the priest and reality came crashing back.

That had always been the way. Even much later, all through his adult life he had carried this fantasy in secret. Only lately, as his life force seemed to be declining, seeping slowly away, had his dream, his desire, faded. Almost without noticing it his need for something bigger, something better than reality had shrivelled and died.

And now it suddenly, unexpectedly, and vividly materialised with such clarity and force that the dry tinder of his ancient dream spontaneously burst into flame. Like a lightning strike in a drought stricken forest, the fire of his ambition had flared again, only to be cruelly dashed and brutally broken.

But no, he blinked his eyes, it all had been a dream. He swayed from side to side drunkenly, feeling sick. Obviously he had stumbled and fallen down the slope. Perhaps he had struck his head on a rock or caught hold of some poison ivy or the like and he was hallucinating. The strong sun certainly wasn't helping and he was now acutely aware of his hunger and thirst. Perhaps that was why he felt giddy and a little nauseated and seemed to have difficulty concentrating. It was all so foggy, so hard to think clearly. He had better get back down the hill he decided, and quickly. Who knew how potent plant poisons might be, some ivy plants were dangerous if touched. He wished he had more of his wife's knowledge of these things.

His hands were a first priority though. They hurt like hell and they were still bleeding. He could clearly see the little puncture marks now, tiny red droplets oozing from them.

Water, he thought. *That's it; water might wash off some of the poison and relieve the pain a little. But there was no water here*. It was high summer and everything was dry and dusty. He felt fuzzy, odd. The sound of the flies buzzing grew in his ears, somehow rhythmic.

Something caught his eye, over there to his right, and a little below, something was glinting. *Was it the thing, the glassy object?* His heart leapt, *please let it be*. With difficulty he focused, squinting in the heat and brightness. *What was it?*

He teetered towards the source of the fractured light, heart pounding. Again the bitterness of disappointment made him sag. It was a pool; small but not overgrown, and seemingly clear. His head swam. He didn't question the oddity of such a find here high on the hill amongst the arid rocks. It was just what he needed.

It was quite close now, only a few more steps. He felt some surprise that he had not noticed it before. Puzzled, he struggled with his befogged mind. *Hadn't he already come this way?* Perhaps he had been deeper under the effects of the poison than he had supposed. *How long had it been since his fall?* It seemed a long time. No matter, "*stop frittering away the minutes,*" he thought. He must wash his hands. It was water, just what he needed.

The surface of the water was below the level of his feet in a shallow depression in the rocks some two metres across. There was no stream entering or leaving, yet the water was clear, cool, inviting, and sparkling in the sun. He was shaking feverishly, a cold sweat beading on his face. "*Perfect,*" he thought as he knelt down, erratic in his movements, and reached to scoop up the inviting liquid in his burning, itching hands. He couldn't see the bottom. The pool was quite black as if of great depth.

Too late he reacted to the dizziness that swept over him as his head bent low towards the water. Sheer blinding terror completely swamped him as he teetered. He had never been much of a swimmer and this dark pool was menace indeed. He screamed and snatched painfully at the rocks as he overbalanced completely and plunged head first into the still, glass-smooth, black liquid.

Down . . . down . . . down. His scream had voided his lungs. He knew in his panic that he had to react quickly, get to the surface, stop his frantic movements and be co-ordinated, purposeful. He forced himself to open his eyes, focus. *Where was up? Where was the surface? Oh God where is up?*

It was cold, a deep cold. He felt his limbs beginning to cramp.

Abruptly he realised that he could see. There was green light. Faint luminescent green all around, but there was no way of knowing up from down. The light was even, lambent.

"*Try to be still,*" he thought, "*keep calm, float to the surface.*" But his terror engulfed him again as he realised that something was wrong. This liquid was not water. It couldn't be. It was too thin. It offered almost no resistance to his thrashing arms and legs.

He was sinking . . . sinking ever deeper into the thin cold green.

Then he knew, knew with utter conviction that he was going to die. Somehow that calmed him and rallied his thoughts. He even had time to feel surprise that his atheism had not abandoned him on the threshold of his extinction. No need for God, he would die with dignity and courage, face death; embrace it.

There were faint, green filaments in the liquid. He could see them clearly now, like surfaces of different densities creating refractive effects, swaying like kelp in an ocean swell. It was pretty in a fairyland sort of way. It reminded him of the cold, clear light from the fireflies that he and his wife would often watch on their evening walks up the hill from the village in the balmy summer evenings.

Were they moving closer? Writhing towards him? Then one of them touched his skin; vaguely leathery, definitely a more dense material. His terror returned. They were touching, more and more of them, crowding. They were smothering his face now; covering his body. Some were growing much thicker, heavier.

Time to die. His lungs were bursting. Then the thick, clogging filaments prised open his lips and slipped slimily into his mouth. He recognised his human weakness as he called in his mind to eternity for succour, *"Oh God, Oh Christ, NO!"*

He did not die. His mouth and throat were full of thick, glutinous, pulsing, thrusting liquid. He gagged. The thick, clear, green, slimy filament covering his nostrils and gaping mouth started forcing itself deeper, past his tongue. Then to his horror it started to force open his gullet. He threw up. Deeper down it went, forcing. He threw up again, more violently. Still it pistoned its way in. First his windpipe. His chest felt as if packed with wool, heavy, clogged. Then his throat. His stomach became distended, stretched. It felt as if his entire gullet and mouth were rammed full of vomit. Yet another filament extruded from the first and forced itself up into his nose and his sinuses. Blinding pain now, his face felt as if it were going to detach from his head. His eyes bulged, feeling as if they were being pushed out of their sockets.

He was rigid now, arms and legs extended, no longer thrashing and struggling.

Something was entering his anus. He shuddered. It felt thick pushing, pushing, forcing in, past his sphincter and up into his bowels. His belly started to bloat, swell, a feeling of great fullness, but not unpleasant.

A thrill of sexual pleasure suddenly tingled at his nerves. Something was entering his penis. His body reacted. His erection grew, seemingly enormous. Erotic sensations swamped him with a force he had never experienced. Every part of his body was being subtly massaged and all his internal spaces being rhythmically distended.

From absolute terror he was now in the throws of a sexual orgasm. His body convulsed with the sheer force of it. *Was he imagining the pale, green swell of heavy breasts? Were there full buttocks pressing against his belly?* No matter, he gave himself over to them as his body writhed and twisted in an orgy of spasms and voiding.

Suddenly he was spent and a great weariness overtook him. He began to relax, slowly at first but soon completely; more completely than he could remember. Muscle by muscle and nerve-by-nerve his body slackened and loosened, becoming flaccid and limp; asleep. The filaments surrounded him in the pale green, silent deep, pulsing rhythmically, and glowing now.

He awoke.

He was alive, in a way at least. *Had he been sleeping?* He felt strange; oddly whole. Homogeneous. Monolithic. He was surrounded by something, something tightly fitting but not constricting. It touched his skin all over, oddly cold and hard.

He too felt cold, cold and still and calm. Everything was utterly silent. He knew it was silence and not deafness, although he didn't know how he knew. But it wasn't dark. Not completely. A faint, endless green luminescence suffused everything.

The pale, cool light gradually brought his mind to focus. He could remember now; the pool and drowning but not drowning, the horrible invasion of his body, and his chase of the mysterious object up the mountain.

What a strange effect the poison ivy was having. This queer dream continued even when he was awake. But no, it couldn't have been that . . . not poison ivy. This was too real to be a dream. He recognised in some fundamental way that he wanted this to be reality.

Perhaps the glass head had drugged him using some kind of hallucinogenic substance or a hypnotic effect maybe? Surely it must have examined him physically too. It had held onto his hands, burned them, and then all those pinpricks. *Needles? Probes?*

•••

The Pool.

The pool? He was in the pool. No, more than that, he *was* the pool. And yet that didn't seem quite right. The pool had to be the key, that strange floating, luring, tantalising object that he had followed had been the tool of the pool. After all it was the pool that trapped him and then kept him alive, prevented him from drowning. It was purposeful, intelligent and it had will. It must also have knowledge of him from the dark glassy, floating thing? *How else could it have sustained him? Known his physical needs?*

A thrill of tension crept over him, "*How else could it have changed him?*"

He felt himself relax again, worry slipping away, his mind loosening, slackening. *Drugged?* Not sleeping, but very relaxed, hovering like a mayfly just above the surface of unconsciousness.

His mind began to expand, his awareness seeming to slowly extend. He was being shown something. His consciousness drifted out . . .out . . .and out. It was big, very big. The pool was vast and yet he filled it. He was vast.

He felt pleased. It wasn't very often that he felt pleased with himself. His mind wandered. Most of his life had seemed to be a series of petty failures. Never quite making it. Oh nothing drastic, no bankruptcies, no prison sentences, not even a decent amorous adventure; always just short of success. Yet, on the face of it, he had done quite well in life he thought, happily married to an intelligent and warm woman, and blessed with a talented daughter. No lack of cash either. Indeed, the master-stroke of his life had been the decision to seek a new way, a way that concentrated on the real values, as he liked to say. In the rural lifestyle lay true fulfilment.

Yet all his life he had ached for something grander, a touchstone to immortality, a wizard's spell for greatness, the alchemist's dream of gold from base metal. He had once, he remembered, experimented with occult practices as a youth, hoping perhaps to tap a source of power that would make him important. The pentangle, the salt, the strange encryptions and incantations; all had served to fuel his childhood dream of power. He would solve the problems of the world, bringing peace at a stroke, and abolish the fear of nuclear war. He would disarm the superpowers in every meaning of the words. Oh, such childish dreams, childishly sought.

This feeling of vastness pleased him. He was at ease.

His awareness snapped back. *"What was that?"*

There was something in the pool! Something big, something alive! Living! Aware.

Fear grew, cold and deep, inside him. *What did he know of the pool? This was an environment alien to him. How could he understand it?* There was more than one. There were many, very many. He strained to identify them, not by sight but by some subliminal sense, some dark awareness.

14

They were enormous, gargantuan, awesome and frightening in their power; and yet, difficult to measure, at once solid yet liquid, enveloping yet penetrating, threatening yet friendly. *Were they close? Were they moving? Were they aware of him?* He reached out, *or was it in?* How, he knew not, but reach he did, trembling in his fear.

They seemed to be proper here, in their place, at home, to belong in some fundamental way. They were at peace . . . sleeping. Somehow deeply slumbering, inert and yet aware of him. They were part of the pool and they belonged to it. He sensed that they had been part of the pool from a time so old that even the rocks might not remember.

He couldn't make them out distinctly. A miasma fogged his awareness, clogged his vision, but they seemed to stretch back and back in serried ranks away to the very edge of existence. His perspective was distorted, *how could he see so far?* Such power. Strength unlimited. His body trembled again, not with fear, but with a physical thrill almost sexual in its immediacy and profundity. They were indeed the pool, the pool was them, and he was the pool.

But it didn't make any sense, dead and not dead? A pool that wasn't a pool, a liquid in the ground with purpose, colossi in a green bath; it was absurd. This was the stuff of conundrum. His mind rebelled with the effort of comprehending, reeled with his sense of impotence. He must have overlooked something, got his wires crossed and yet, undeniably, he was here and he was in some way part of it all. He reached out again to the giants, to the edge of himself, to infinity, and to the borders of the pool.

Suddenly it clicked. This wasn't a pool, couldn't be. It was a vessel, a ship filled with purpose, a sentient living organism, a super intelligent machine. No, it was a dimensionless liquid, formless, how could it be a ship? How could it be anything structured? Yet it had purpose, it had dimension of a sort, it had power, and it had will. Oh yes, it had will! He could feel that implacable will. *A giant ship?* No, that couldn't be correct but

15

it was near, and yet it was no bigger than him, after all he filled it. He had become big, powerful; he had become dimensionless. Oh, he couldn't seem to concentrate, to think straight. It was all so difficult, so confusing.

He felt himself relax again, be led, and be shown. It was very old and yet very new; sort of shiny new. It had waited a long time in the ancient, dark cold rock. *The rock? Was that what was touching his skin? The rock?* All around, close, the rock. Yes it was very big and yet no bigger than he. In some way he was the pool. He couldn't think of it in any other way. It didn't fit, he knew.

It had form. It had purpose. It had strength unimaginable. It had dimension, and no dimension at the same time, both large and small, and it was chaos. It was solid with all the might of invincible power and irresistible force, and yet, only a liquid could be this homogeneous. Like the slow creeping of ice-cold crystals on a windowpane, he felt his fear grow. It was alien. Alien beyond all hope of understanding. Wherever and whenever it had come from, it was not meant for humankind.

What was it doing? Why was he still aware? What was it showing him? Why was he not dead? The pool had not killed him, not ignored him, and not rejected him. It had taken him. It was distorting him, changing him.

Perhaps a foetus felt this way in the amniotic fluid, an extension, and a part of its mother. *Was an unborn child in the womb filled with its mother's fluid?* Fluids could do strange things he knew. An unborn child had no need of air. Oxygen was carried directly in its mother's blood, a fluid, as were all its nutrients. The pool was supporting him in much the same way. *But why fill the other spaces in his body?* he wondered. There were no signs of vomit or body waste. *Had the fluid carried it all away?* The pale green luminescence was unsullied, crystal in its clarity.

Pressure, perhaps that was it. *How deep was he?* There was no means of telling but possibly many fathoms. The pressure might be enormous here and if he were filled with fluid he might be able to withstand great pressure. *Did fighter pilots not have special suits filled with fluids to help them withstand great G forces in combat?*

He was in the green fluid and it in him. They were one. He felt that this was true in an absolute sense. He was the pool.

Deep sagging fatigue welled up as his mind and body struggled with the acceptance of the unacceptable.

He slept.

CHAPTER 2

Where the hell was Cole? It was getting late. The sun was beginning to rim the surrounding hills and if she had counted the church bell chimes correctly as the melancholy sound drifted up from the village in the valley below, it was half past eight, or near to that anyway; the church clock was never quite right. It was one of those things that endeared one to the rural way of life or made it unbearable. She could still hear the last chime hanging clearly in the still, warm air. That was another of the things she liked about this place, it was almost always calm. The lack of wind lent an additional serenity to an already beautiful and remote spot, increasing, she thought, the feeling of detachment from the brutal world of the city.

She had been sewing for most of the afternoon on the balcony of the little house. Basking in the hot, strong sunlight. Her tan was really deep this year and her visitors from Scotland next month would be impressed. Considering she had no Italian blood at all, her dark hair and eyes together with the tan made her as native looking as any of the locals. She had adapted well to this unforeseen turn of events in their marriage. Most of her family and friends had thought her slightly reckless to give up her lucrative job as the head teacher in a goodly-sized school to "disappear" off to Italy, as they put it. After all everyone knew what the Italians were like, didn't they? Male chauvinists, one and all.

Kate was a strong character with a will of her own and a clear view of her role in life. Her childhood had been a little unusual in that her parents had sent her off to boarding school at five years of age. She had spent the best part of each year until she graduated, living in private institutions run by nuns. This had given her a shell of toughness and independence which stood her in good stead in the past, both in her job and in moments of private stress. She had been a sincere teacher with a clear vocation. Her dedication to her career and her deep need to care for young and old alike brought excellence to her job and she prospered, being one of the youngest in her profession to be promoted to head teacher.

Her brow furrowed with a nagging doubt. *It wasn't like Cole to be away quite so long without some warning.* He had gone up the hill on his own, at least that had been his stated intention. Ah, but here nothing went quite as you intended and he had probably met Bene or Amedeo and got sidetracked. Time would tell what mischief the boys were up to. Boys, huh! Cole was the youngest of them all by quite a margin. Still she always thought of them in that way. Always up to something, always jovial. She particularly enjoyed their "university" as they termed it. Proudly they would declaim the difficulty of entry to *"L'università dei Fannulloni"* the study of *loafing* was a science, they claimed.

Everyone in the village was good-natured, kind and thoughtful to the city dwellers, the new comers, and she had never been made to feel like an outsider.

Giannina had passed earlier and called up to the balcony from the steep, cobbled street below, somewhat breathlessly, *"Bella serata,* Kate. I'll hang a bag of piselli and cipolle on the door." She could speak English brokenly from the years she had spent in America. They said that she had liked it there but was forced to return because her husband, Peppine, had been unhappy with the lifestyle there.

"Mille grazie, sei molto gentile," Kate replied. It amused her faintly to listen to Giannina's broken English. Her own Italian was pretty good now and certainly a lot better than most of the locals could speak, although they sometimes teased her by deliberately exaggerating their dialect.

19

She had become an influential and central character in the village and was well liked despite her sometimes authoritarian manner, a legacy of achieving structural authority too soon in life. Kate was a profoundly kind person, sensitive to others' needs, and always ready to help. Already her place as a willing counsellor and comforter of the old and young alike had been established. She would often find herself at the centre of others' family problems, talking things through, and clearly caring for everyone's well being. Many of the younger generation took advantage of her teaching skills and came frequently to the house to study and seek help with their English.

Settling back in her seat, she savoured the warm afternoon. The sky was a pale-washed blue with clouds coloured the faintest of rose pink on the edges as if decorating the ceiling of a grand mansion. Her sewing was going well with the glowing colours of the complex picture seeming more akin to a painting and she knew her daughter, Susan, would be impressed. She had phoned that afternoon from Amsterdam and Kate was always in a good mood after their daughter telephoned. There had been good tidings too. The job in Bologna that she was after was still available. *Where was Cole?* She was impatient to relay the news.

She put aside her work piece and went downstairs, picked up the portable phone as was her habit, and went out into the narrow cobbled street. She didn't bother to lock the door but paused to feed the alley cats from the little dish of scraps she kept for the purpose. It irritated Cole but she kept on doing it despite his protestations, it seemed kind somehow.

Automatically avoiding the sheep and other animal droppings that littered the street, she picked her way along the broken surface of the old narrow lane towards what passed as the piazza for the village.

"What the blazes are the commune doing letting the place get so run down?" she thought. *"Someone should put a bomb under them."*

As she approached the little square, she could hear a number of familiar voices raised in that typically excited Italian manner.

A hoop-hoe called nearby and all seemed well with nature and the world.

She scanned the little group. Cole wasn't there.

"*Ciao* Kate." It was Pietro and no, no one had seen Cole since lunch. No he wasn't at Bene's house. Bene was in Menella with Enzio who had arrived at Rome Airport that very morning from Texas.

"*That's where he'll be,*" she thought with a feeling of relief. In the summer the population of the village and surrounding areas trebled and quadrupled with émigré families returning "P*er le vacanze.*" Cole and Bene were inseparable friends, often invited at a moment's notice to some meal or other, and Enzio was always at the centre of things when he came.

Her brow furrowed for a moment as she strove to recall the telephone number. She dialled from the piazza, much to the amusement of the crowd who still saw such things as "scientific." There was no answer, although she held on for some minutes listening to the tone as it repeated over and over.

A pang of fear clutched at her. He wasn't there. But no, that was irrational. He had to be with Enzio and Bene, maybe in the cantina traversing wine and out of earshot of the phone. In any event, what harm could come to anyone here in this idyllic spot? Here where all was peace and nature ruled. True there were stories of snakes from the old wives and the occasional sheep taken by a wolf but no one could actually name an instance of snake bite in living memory nor an attack by a wolf. *No, no need to worry. Just relax. It would work out.*

She joined in the lively discussion and accepted a proffered glass of wine. The company was jolly and the subjects varied, but never getting very far from politics or football. She laughed a lot, but something nagged deep down.

It became quite dark now, in that sudden way, not like the slow gloaming of Scotland. The stars shone brightly in a spangled carpet above them, like a deep velvet drape with jewels cast across it, heaping beauty upon beauty. The voices of nature changed and the call of night-jars belled in the stillness, mingling with the chirping murmur of crickets.

With a suddenness that stalled the mind, the ground began to shake. Nothing could have been more unexpected and although the movement was small everyone staggered. "Good God the ground is shaking!" she said inanely and immediately felt foolish. But a deep fear welled in her. The ground wasn't supposed to do that. The earth was stable, our support, and the foundation of our lives. She grabbed at the low stonewall on which she sat as if trying to stabilise the earth itself.

At first there was no sound and then a deep, distant, bass rumbling filled the air, seeming to last for several minutes. A couple of bottles of wine crashed to the cobbles spreading a black stain on the stone. Several tiles slid from the adjacent roofs, rattling down the inclines, and smashing noisily on the ground.

"*Terremoto . . . Terremoto!*" several voices shouted together.

"*Madre di Dio salva noi.*" It was Angelina, pale faced and making the sign of the cross, as did most of the women. Everyone was staring wildly around, not sure what to do.

Then, suddenly, it stopped, just as unexpectedly as it had begun.

A different silence descended. Total quiet. No birds, no sound whatever, an unnatural stillness . . . waiting . . . waiting. A dog started to bark in the distance and suddenly everyone started to shout and gesticulate at once; bedlam, no one listening to anyone, all talking at once.

This was an earthquake zone, she knew, but it had been many years since the last big quake, and that was twenty-five years ago, long before she and Cole had arrived in the village. She had never experienced anything like this before. She was pale, visibly shaken, unsure what to do.

"*Non ti preoccupare,* Kate." It was Pietro again, "*Era piccolo.*" They were always like that, quick to help, quick to reassure. It had been very small with minor damage and no injuries. Now everyone was in a rather over-festive mood, it was "festa" all of a sudden. The wine flowed and the conversation became even more animated than usual. Everyone trying to out do the others in their experiences and tales of earthquakes.

Kate's sense of uneasiness had quadrupled now. This was all she needed when she was already worried. *Where was he? Why did he not appear? He might at least phone.*

After a little while, she quietly left the piazza without farewell, slipping away unnoticed by the men and women noisily chattering there.

She walked back to the house unhurriedly, almost reluctantly, scuffing with her feet at the pine cones and other dry debris which littered the narrow street, and pushed open the door noticing that the cats were gone.

Steadily, she tidied up little things in the kitchen, put the phone back on its cradle, and generally fidgeted aimlessly. Then she climbed the steep stairs to the upper floor bedroom, undressed, and slowly got into bed. She lay on top of the sheets in the darkness with her eyes open, perceiving nothing.

Outside, the stars encrusted the obsidian sky and the night-jars called and called.

Sleep didn't come. Eventually, after an hour or more, she rose, covered her nakedness with a thin cotton robe, and walked out onto the balcony.

In the warm still air, all was quiet with no sound from the piazza and softly, gently, as if not to disturb the night, she sat on one of the plastic chairs that always adorned the balcony.

The surrounding countryside was black as pitch, the hills to the south delineated by stardust, more sensed than visible. Her eyes lifted gently upward, unseeing and unseeingly she communed with something deep and menacing inside herself while glory shone above.

CHAPTER 3

Cole felt good, somehow strong and relaxed, cosy and secure, like awakening in the morning after a sound night's sleep with the sun warming the sheets. The warm afterglow of sex filled him like a faint echo of an erotic dream, a dream of power and conquest. He tried to recapture the dream but it eluded his grasp, dissipating and fading like the mists from the hills in winter. His mind, or was it his body? expanded out and out . . . out to the edge of infinity. He knew power then, felt it like never before. Not throbbing or pulsing, not noisy, but still, still as a deep millpond and waiting.

Where was he? It was dark. Complete and utter blackness all around. There was no sky. Not even stars. *Where was the comforting greenness?* His fear had gone and had been replaced by a need, the need to belong, belong to the pool, belong to himself, be the pool, be himself.

Then it was there. He could see it now, the pale, cool green. He was deep in the womb, comfortable, waiting to be born. He exulted and soared with untrammelled ecstasy and limitless joy, seeming to arch infinity. He ached in his heart, in his soul with the enormity, the glory of it. Now, now at last he would be master, master of himself, master of the pool, master of all. He had not seen it before, never realised his power, his dimension. Finally, and at long last, they would know him, respect him, fear him. The mighty would look upon him and tremble indeed.

But it was enough for the moment that he knew himself. Knew that he had power, power to displace space, to bend the fabric of existence. *But how? What was the mechanism?*

He willed a change. Nothing happened. He strained with his mind, the candle, ah yes the candle, he would have power over it if only he could find the mechanism. *Concentrate, make it happen.* His mind felt weak, unclear. It was so hard to do. He couldn't fail, not again. He would not accept failure. Make it happen.

He moved.

Slowly, ever so slowly and smoothly back, back into the night. *"Yes,"* he shouted in his mind, *"YES!"*

The rock felt like fine sand on his skin. Fine but caked and crumbly. It offered no resistance. It fell from him like a flimsy sheet, as a layer of dust would fall from a wine bottle long stored in the cellar. The weight of aeons was as nothing to him. The mighty rocks of ages knew their master, cleaving and splitting, bursting asunder under his will. Opening to him, releasing him and the pool from the timeless tomb. *What was it to him, what was it to the pool, this trivial encrustation? What was it to him who had endured the flowing meld of creation, the liquidity of rock . . . less than nothing.* A towering arrogance, a fierce pride welled in him as he brushed aside the embrace of nature and lifted himself in majesty into another place. "I am made anew," he blazed the words in his mind, thundered them that all might hear.

Above him in the night, the stars blazed and blazed. He had never believed they could be so bright, so multi-coloured, so hard, like magic gemstones showering from a dragon's wing.

In rapture he gazed, in rapture he felt the kinship. These were his. This was his place. He was at home here.

Below him the fires were flaring now. The whole ridge of the hill was ablaze, lighting the night with flickering amber. The tinder-dry timbers leaped into flame as if with joy at his coming. Huge rocks and boulders fell from the great height to which they had been lifted making enormous explosions of flame and sparks as they struck the ground. A pyrotechnic display fit for the pool, fit for the arrival of a new *"Lord of Creation."*

Dust and debris, glowing and roiling with inner fires, climbed high with the smoke and then he heard the echoes of his birth, the screams of mother earth, dying repeatedly from the surrounding slopes.

The mountain had collapsed, fallen inward as if some giant hand had filleted the skeleton from an elephant and the flesh had folded in on itself. The crater must have been more than a kilometre long and nearly a third as wide. As he watched, more rock and burning trees slid down the impossibly steep slopes and disappeared from sight into the depths. Even the stars were becoming obscured now as the cloud of smoke and dust rose ever higher; such destruction just because he moved.

He stopped the planet suspended below him. He held it there. *Was it just a few feet away or hundreds of metres?* It seemed hard to tell. He could just as easily thrust it from him. Hurl it across aeons of time, far, far into the frozen stasis of deep space. He knew the feeling to be subjective but his perspectives seemed to be getting all mixed up now. It was the same with the pool, with his body. *Where was he? Was he in the pool, in the pool and yet out here, here under the sister stars*? But he *was* the pool, not in it, not separate, but of it. It had to be thus.

He felt good, languid, but fatigued, almost exhausted. He lacked strength, the strength to command and control. He would rest now, he would wait for strength. He felt himself relaxing again, slipping down into sleep. It would be nice when the sun, that dragon's gem of fire and abundant power, came up. That would be a new dawn, the dawning of his glory, when all men would see and wonder.

CHAPTER 4

Her cry died slowly in her throat even as the thunderous roar faded from the sky. Then she heard another, howling towards the house, tearing the air with hideous violence. The ugly dark shapes of the jet fighters seemed as if they would rip the tiles from the roof. She clapped her hands over her ears. Those bloody jets, they did this occasionally but not usually so low or so fast. Those bloody Americans at the N.A.T.O. base, she thought.

"You bastards!" she shouted aloud, "Don't you have any respect for anything, anyone?" Her voice was lost in the thunder.

Clammy sweat beaded on her skin. The dream was clear and still terrifyingly real. The great black bird had stooped down from the hot sky and swept Cole up in its terrible talons, screaming horribly. It had rent him apart and dropped his body like a torn rag doll, flopping to the ground in a grotesquely distorted heap. She had run to him, hoping still to save him, to help, to heal. But he had no head and from inside his severed neck a queer green fluid was leaking.

It was just dawn. The sky behind the eastern hill was becoming quite bright now. Soon the warm sun would lift above the ridge and bring life and light to the valley, dispersing the soft early morning mists that clung to the wooded slopes.

She must have fallen asleep on the balcony chair, her back and neck ached, and her legs cramped in painful spasms. *How long had she remained awake last night, waiting in the dark for Cole, waiting for someone she now knew wouldn't come?*

She got up stiffly, groaning quietly with the pains in her joints, and went downstairs to the kitchen.

Nerves jangling, fingers numb, it seemed to take forever to get the coffee machine to operate, but the hot, strong liquid brought fortification and clarity of purpose. From memory she dialled Amsterdam.

Susan answered the phone blearily. "You are not being rational, Kate. How can you say you know something terrible has happened? No news is good news. If something had happened to Cole, you would have been contacted by the police or someone and that earthquake must have been very light, I have heard nothing on the international news."

All that Susan said was true. There was probably a simple explanation for all of this.

"You'll feel much better after a shower and some breakfast. Let me know the moment he shows up. Tell him I shall give him a good 'telling off' for giving you cause for worry. I'll phone from the office in any event, probably about ten." Susan's voice became soft, cajoling, "I'm sure everything's all right, please don't worry." and she made kissing noises as she hung up the phone.

As Kate showered, she determined to set off up the hill herself to search for him if he didn't show up very soon. It was probably futile but what else could she do? The local *carabiniere* were hardly going to react to a complaint that her husband had been out all night. She could see the sly smirks and hear the lewd remarks right now. No, better to put a brave face on for the moment and gather her strength for the trial she felt was coming.

That dream! She could have done without that, it was so real. She was annoyed with herself for dwelling on it now, it was getting out of proportion. After all it was probably her unconscious hearing the jet engines that triggered off the screaming call of the big bird in the dream. Just coincidence that's all.

"Damn those bloody Yanks and damn earthquakes, too." *But it hadn't really been like a bird*, she thought, *more like a skull and a great green hand which swept down from the black hole in the sky, all wet and cold.* "Oh for Christ's sake give it up," she said aloud to the empty bathroom.

CHAPTER 5

Giancarlo Massaro was never going to pass his exams and he knew it. But anything was better than military service right now and a course of university study had much to recommend itself to a lad of nineteen years. Having been born on the lower slopes of Vesuvius, it had only seemed natural to choose a subject which involved volcanoes, and Naples was certainly a prime spot for the study of seismology.

These late evening sessions in the quiet of the seismograph labs were normally pleasant interludes. Keep an eye on the rotating drums, keep the pens free and inked, and do a little research on the computer terminal. Some found it boring but Giancarlo enjoyed the solitude, often drifting off into some private world for long spells.

The winking amber light on the console brought him out of his reverie. He puzzled over its meaning for a moment before jumping to his feet and running to the bank of seismographs. The needles were dancing, scribbling crazy spider scrawls on the drums.

"*Un terremoto, finalmente, un terremoto,*" was all he could think of as he excitedly tried to pinpoint the epicentre and the size with the instruments.

"Not very big and way up on the Apennine Ridge on the edge of the Abruzzi National Park," he muttered aloud to himself, (an unusual place for seismic activity and pretty remote). Still it would be best to alert the authorities. Quakes, even in remote areas could result in casualties.

The standard practice he knew was to alert civil and military authorities by telephone but there was no answer from the *caserma* even though the ringing tone rang and rang. "Those god-damn cops are asleep on duty as usual," he yelled with frustration as he hung up. He hurriedly looked up another number in the log and dialled again.

"Duty Sergeant Walker," the American accent was strong and so unexpected that it overpowered Giancarlo's command of English.

"Come?" *Chi?*" Oh hell, he had dialled the wrong military base, this was the American. Still they were usually pretty efficient. They would notify everyone necessary. The line was really bad, breaking up, and echoing.

"Duty Sergeant Walker U.S. Naval Base Naples here. Who is this?" continued the voice.

"This is Giancarlo Massaro who speaks here. I report *a terremoto,* a, an earthquake . . . " he replied and with much repetition and correction relayed his observations through the mush and static of the line.

"Okay Bud, I got all that," said the heavy southern drawl. "We'll get on it right away. We'll liaise with the police if necessary. Thanks for the info." The connection went dead but the static continued.

Giancarlo felt somehow let down. *Was that all there was to it?* It wasn't every day you were the first to pinpoint an earthquake. Still it would grow in the telling.

If he was lucky he would get extra merits from his professor for his diligence but he couldn't seem to work up much faith in that one. He drifted off into reverie, perhaps he would get his name in the paper.

CHAPTER 6

The sergeant dialled the number repeatedly. Something was wrong with the system. "Jeez these phones get worse every day," he muttered.

When the phone was eventually answered, he drawled through the hissing and howling of the line, "Joe Walker here, lieutenant, we've got an earthquake report, somewhere north of here a bit, near the Abruzzi. Up in the hills near . . ."

Lieutenant Golder's voice was shrill and hectoring,

"For Jesus' sake Joe where have you been? Oh never mind, just shut up and get your ass over here on the double."

Joe made a sour face as he glared at the receiver, "*That young greenhorn is always getting his knickers in a twist. These military academy types couldn't even wipe their own butts without the help of real soldiers*," he thought bitterly and then, hiding his ire, said casually, "What's the problem?"

"Jesus Christ, all hell is breaking loose here. Every fucking alarm in the place is going haywire. Get over here NOW!" Golder was yelling as he hung up.

Joe held the instrument to his ear for another few seconds as the static continued to hiss and pop on the line.

It was only a matter of a hundred and fifty metres to the "ops" room and the sergeant's long stride got him there quickly. He pushed open the door and stopped just inside. The room was a long rectangle with a low ceiling and painted a dull cream colour. Multi-coloured charts on the walls, desks and computer terminals scattered about, usually gave the impression of a slick methodical order. Tonight it was different, the scene inside was complete chaos. Sheets of computer printout and bundles of varicoloured documents were everywhere. Computer operators tapped furiously on keyboards, whilst technicians delved deeply into the innards of others. Jim Golder was shouting instructions continuously but no one seemed to be heeding his commands. The lieutenant spotted the sergeant from across the room and rushed towards him waving a sheaf of pink slips and computer printouts. He was sweating. "Just look at these, Joe. Sweet Jesus what are we going to do?" He was almost childlike in his panic.

Joe grabbed him by the wrist and held it low down so that none of the rankers would see. "Easy Jim. For Christ's sake take it easy. Tell me what's going on." His tone was strong, dominant.

The lieutenant came up short, "S . . .sure Joe, sure thing, sure thing." He took a deeper breath. His voice was steadier when he spoke. "It's the communications. They are all out, every last one. We can't even pick up the God-damn weather report. Something is fucking up radar, radio, and television in a big way. Satellite communication is hopeless. Even the phone's gone out now. We're cut off. It's got to be a hostile action, maybe the Reds. It's just got to be."

He paused, a film of sweat on his brow. "It's point sourced as far as we can tell, up north a bit in the moun . . . wait a minute, where did you say that quake was? The Abruzzi? Jesus, sweet Jesus, that's it. They've dropped a nuke right in the middle of Italy. The war has started. We need communications. Oh Christ, we need them." His voice had been getting steadily shriller till he was almost screaming.

"SHUT UP!" Joe's rough basso boomed out. "Just shut up and do your job. Check, check, it doesn't make any sense. It could be anything, a sunspot, anything."

The lieutenant sagged. The others in the room had become silent, staring white-faced, and nervous.

"ON THE DOUBLE SOLDIER," snarled the sergeant at no one in particular. Men began tapping keys, turning knobs, and riffling through sheaves of papers.

Gradually a pattern began to emerge as the two men studied each monitor and printout. Something was emitting a strong electromagnetic field some sixty-five miles to the north. So big that even the telephones and the satellite links had gone out. "A thermonuclear explosion could cause effects like this for sure," said Joe, " but it doesn't make any sense at all. Still there was that seismic report, the quake." *What the hell is going on?* Sergeant Walker's mind was racing.

"Better get somebody up there, Jim. We need an eyeball." Joe's tone was measured. He didn't want another hysterical outburst.

"But they would have no electronics," replied the lieutenant, "we couldn't even track them on the scope. They would have to fly by ground sightings alone." Jim seemed to have regained his composure. "No, its too dangerous in such mountainous terrain. It's still pitch black and there might be bad radiation, who knows."

Everyone turned towards the sound of a new voice. Several men stood in a small group just inside the door.

"Quite right lieutenant," General George Filshill's gravelly voice was immediately recognisable and the respect in which his men held him, manifested itself in an almost palpable wave of relief flooding the room.

"Quite right. We cannot risk the lives of our men foolishly. It may be no more than a big meteor strike and the civil authorities are already gearing up on the ground. They should be in the area in force in a couple of hours." He gazed around the room, fixing each man in turn with his eyes almost as if he sensed the earlier panic.

The runner had awakened him from a sound sleep but his trained mind grasped the situation even as he listened to the soldier reading the briefing notes as he dressed. His wife said nothing and hurriedly made black coffee, which he gulped down as he went out the door. He waved away the cookies proffered by her as he strode down the little garden path to the waiting car. This was serious, he would have to act on his own until things became clearer and communications improved. It had to be something pretty massive to take out the phones but they would get that sorted out soon. In the meantime he dispatched his aide to set up a net of runners to physically carry messages around the base and to link with the civil authorities. It would have to do for now.

In the short car journey to "ops" he gathered his thoughts. *"War? Not likely. The political situation was far too stable for that. This was the era of détente. The Cold War was history. What then, a terrorist attack with a nuclear bomb? The prospect was chilling but these Arab fundamentalists seemed capable of anything and there had been intelligence reports of possible nuclear capability developing in the Arab world. There were also precedents for Arab terrorist attacks on Italy, mainly due to the large American presence,* he realised ruefully, *but what else might it be? a natural phenomenon? a volcano? a meteor? some space satellite belonging to the Russians crashing to earth?"* The possibilities were endless. Until he had more information to go on things would be tough.

When he had entered the brightly lit room from the warm night air, all had seemed well-ordered, the situation well in hand. He would have to commend young Lieutenant Golder. *Not bad for a greenhorn really.*

"As you were men," he spoke to the room at large. Those standing at attention returned to their tasks. *"And that is good clear thinking on Golder's part, not sending up the fighters just yet,"* he thought, *"it would serve nothing to take risks like that."*

The General's rough tones spoke again, "It will be dawn very soon and there should be enough light to make an initial sortie in a couple of hours. Send up a pair of F16s at the first opportunity." He had directed his remarks to Lieutenant Golder though, of course, Sergeant Walker would actually issue them. His voice was quiet, sounding as if he had pebbles in his gullet, and he made a point of never raising it in command. He felt that to do so would diminish the dignity and grace of his rank. "Bring the base to maximum alert. I want every man on duty."

The telephone rang. "Were back in business."

It was a young, civilian operator. He spoke into the phone, "Sure the General's right here. I'll connect you now." Covering the mouthpiece, "It's for you sir, it's Rome."

The Commander-in-Chief N.A.T.O. Forces in Europe, Field Marshall William Siemens bawled down the phone. "I can hardly hear you, George. The line quality is terrible," hissing and crackling broke up the voice. "Fill me in on the situation down there. There's absolute chaos in the civil section, all aircraft grounded, several accidents and some of them pretty bad as far as we can make out. The trouble seems to be pretty well centred down your way, but it's still disrupting things as far north as Rome."

The General bawled back, "Can't tell you all that much at the moment, Bill. Things are still pretty hazy. All our communications are out, radar, the lot. In short, there is some sort of major electromagnetic disturbance just to the north of here, about sixty-five miles at our best guess, and that's based largely on a preliminary seismic report from the University of Naples. It's on the southern edge of the Abruzzi National Park in pretty remote countryside, but until we can get some of our boys up there or the radar picture stops jumping around, we're literally whistling in the dark." General George Filshill was at his best, calm, slow speaking and oozing confidence. He sounded as if he were conducting some freshers' training exercise.

"I know you've got problems down there, George, but I need hard info right now. The President will be onto this in no time flat and I already have a meeting scheduled in four hours with the other chiefs-of-staff. I think you should get some of your fly-boys up there right now. Get hard info. and photographs. If the *Eye-Ties* beat us to the punch on this one, the shit will hit the fan and make no mistake. Do I make myself clear?" The last sentence was ever so slightly clipped.

"Don't worry. We're right on it, Bill. I'll send up a couple of F16s with full reconnoitring gear as you wish, but you know damn well that it's virtual suicide to send these planes up with no electronics. Are you sure about this? If any of our boys are downed we won't exactly come up smelling of roses. You remember that fiasco in Iran with those choppers a few years back? I'm sure as hell glad that it wasn't my order that sent them out . . . but if you insist?"

There was a few seconds silence. "I am not insisting on anything, George. You're in charge down there. Do what you think is best, but remember the political situation. Things can get pretty tough for a career soldier." Siemens hung up before Filshill could reply.

Filshill's irritation showed as he growled at Sergeant Walker, "Where are those electronics people? Why have they not got this mess sorted out yet? Is it too much to ask, eh? Too much to ask for some God-damn radar and radio? Get a move on, don't just stand there, lieutenant!" he included lieutenant Golder in his ire. "Let me see that seismic report."

For what seemed an eternity the technicians grappled with the innards of every piece of communications gear in the room, testing, replacing, adjusting and all to no avail, while General Filshill paced like a caged animal, to and fro, deep in thought.

Two hours passed like a strange tableau, somehow slow and silent in the cold neon light, silent tension, unspoken fear, cold beads of sweat, nervous drumming of fingers, and endless cigarettes.

"It's Comandanté Di Rollo." The civilian telephone operator had been gesticulating and holding up the telephone for some time, trying to attract General Filshill's attention.

Filshill held up his hand, palm foremost in a halt signal while he took a sheaf of papers from Lieutenant Golder. After a moment's scan of the information, he spoke almost as if to himself, "Thank God, it seems to be lifting a little. At least short range stuff is becoming partly operational. Maybe the pilots can at least talk to each other, if not to us."

He took the phone. "*Ciao,* Rocco." He had an excellent command of Italian but always kept his usage in official situations to a minimum.

He felt that the pre-eminent position of the U.S. in the Mediterranean was best served by the enforcement of English as the accepted language of military communication. "What can I do for you?"

"*Maneggia, Santa . . .*" The string of expletives seemed to overpower the bad telephone line and could be clearly heard in the room. "What do you mean, what can I do for you?" Continued the voice. "Tell me what the hell is going on. That's what you can do for me. I've been trying to contact you for the best part of an hour. Why are your personnel not answering the phone? Are you deliberately being incommunicado? This is too much, you've gone too far this time. We are supposed to be co-operating. What's the use of . . ."

"It's not our doing Rocco," Filshill's voice cut across him. We're suffering as much as you. All our communications went down with the rest of our electronics, including the phones. They've been behaving erratically since . . .since earlier. I don't have any hard information to give you, but I would appreciate an assurance from you that there is no civil air traffic remaining in the area. We are hoping to put some hardware up at first light, with your agreement of course, and they will have no means of seeing what else is up there."

Di Rollo's tone changed completely to one of crisp efficiency, "I see General. Now I understand the problem. I am sorry if I seemed unreasonable but I had no information at all to work on. To answer your question, as far as I know the airways are clear. *Grazie a Dio,* it happened when it did, there was very little air traffic in the area, although there have been some accidents and, naturally, I awaited this contact with you before taking any unilateral action. It may be very risky sending up aircraft before full light and there is no way of knowing what electromagnetic effects may exist nearer to the centre of the disturbance. I would counsel caution, let us get our ground resources in place first."

Lieutenant Golder's voice yelled out, "They're up! Blue wing are off the deck! Now we'll kick some ass." He was punching the air with both fists.

Filshill partially covered the mouthpiece so that the Italian couldn't hear the sudden commotion in the room. "I appreciate your concern, Rocco, but in a short time we should have a more clear idea of what's happening. I'll get back to you as soon as I can. No wait, I have a better idea. Why don't you come over here and bring Comandanté Cocozza and Rear Admiral Forbes with you, he got back from Malta yesterday. We need to get our local team off first base and it'll be much better talking face to face, don't you think?"

"Yes, then perhaps we will avoid any future misunderstandings." Di Rollo's voice was calm and friendly. "We should be with you soon." He hung up.

As Filshill laid down the handset he could barely repress a smile. He'd done it again. Kept them sweet, kept them following his lead, kept them in the dark about his true intentions.

He turned back to the control consoles. The radar screen looked like one of those paperweights with a little snowstorm in it. The two blips from the F16s disappeared almost simultaneously with the loss of radio contact.

CHAPTER 7

Lambent, beginning to scintillate, faint coruscations in the clear
green, so lovely, it was like seeing for the first time, seeing
but not seeing, so clear and limpid. Seeing, yet his seeing was
without understanding, all was strange yet familiar, all was clear
and yet distorted. Did a chrysalis see the outside world like this
before pupation?

It was beautiful. Even the emerald city of Oz could not have
been more breathtaking in its perfection. Like a mighty cathedral
its limits were distant, hazy, and mysterious. Faint yet profound
echoes of unformed sounds seemed to whisper in the vastness.
The stillness seemed almost to have a voice of its own.

The giants were not so profound in their slumber now, silent
stirrings in the deep, deep depths, and deep inside him, deep in the
pool. It was comforting to have the giants. *Were they his friends
or were they a deeper part of himself?* He couldn't decide, but it
didn't seem to be very important anyway. They were still resting
and it was good to rest with them. Languidly and lazily he gave
himself over to reverie, to self indulgent, hedonistic sensations.
He drifted.

"No . . .no, not now," he complained. *It was too soon.
More sleep; more comfort.* He didn't want to be disturbed. It
was always unpleasant being dragged up from sleep, from deep
subconsciousness, unwillingly forced to awaken too soon. *Had
Kate set the alarm clock? What was the rush?* He was irritated.

They were coming . . . tiny, little distant specks, way over
the mountains to the south-east. He tried to ignore them, shoo
them away in his mind, but they kept coming. He came to full

wakefulness, directing his consciousness, clearing his thoughts, looking around him.

His sister sun was full bodied now, low and proud in the eastern sky, pouring forth her bounty, blazing brightly, feeding him from her strength as a mother suckles her child. He had waited so long for this, longer than he had thought it possible for time to span. Now at long, long last, she nourished him again just as her sisters had done in aeons past and infinities away. She distorted his seeing in an odd way, like having forgotten how to focus or as if he was wearing poor spectacles. He was curious.

The dots were coming closer now, from the general direction of the sun, a little to the south, dipping below the tops of the hills and skimming in the valleys. He could hear them, talking on the radio, shouting through the hissing, spitting, static at each other. They were black, ugly things, menacing things of death . . . insects. He resented them, resented their intrusion. *Didn't they know he wasn't ready?* He was impatient with them.

"Full thrust . . . NOW!"

Their speech seemed to be inside his head. "Give it everything you've got." The whisper in the air was becoming a roar. First one and then the other aircraft popped up over the northern lip of the Gallo Matese Mountain Range some ten kilometres to the south, black trails of smoke pouring from the screaming engines.

For all the world they looked like the big, black flying beetles that were so common in the village in summer.

"Great mother of God! Look at that! It's fucking enormous." The voice sounded excited, strained, even through the crackle of the static.

"Cut that out! Cut the chatter. Arm the cameras, infra-red, U.V., the lot, and keep your cotton pickin' itchy finger off the cannon. LEFT! . . . BREAK, BREAK, BREAK!"

Both planes wheeled sharply off to the west to the coast and then turned north again in a great sweep.

He watched, his attention beginning to sharpen as they passed in the distance.

" Commencing my pass in ten seconds . . . keep well to the west . . . record my voice, just in case." The static sparked and spit.

"Breaking . . . NOW, NOW, NOW!"

One of the black specks came round in a big arc towards him, approaching from the north. It came closer. He focussed on it.

"Large aerial object, black, no, blackish in colour; exact size difficult to estimate, possibly more than a klik in length." The pilot was shouting through the noise of the static, ". . . elongated, angular with no visible protuberances."

The fighter was getting very close.

"Making lengthways pass NOW! . . . clock running! . . .Jesus Christ it's big."

"For Pete's sake, don't get too close." It was the first voice, breaking up in the noise." I don't like the look of that mother fucker."

He decided in a flash. He would talk to them. That's what he must do. He must make them understand, make them see that they had awakened him too soon. They were small after all, puny and insignificant, he could hardly expect them to know.

The excited tones of the fighter pilot continued through the static, "Metallic or ceramic looking surface, strangely transparent . . . no readings on Infra re . . ."

"Know me," he spoke to the pilot of the first speck, opening up his mind so that the man might see, might understand, "KNOW ME!"

The plane exploded with instantaneous violence, shredding itself into tiny pieces as if hitting an invisible and immovable wall at the speed of sound. It seemed tiny, almost lost against the enormity of the black cliff beside it. Even the shards slammed against something unseen, breaking into ever-smaller fragments. Like a lopsided, star-burst shell it flared briefly in death and was almost pretty.

His words echoed in his mind, *"Know me, know me!"* Stunned, he barely heard the second pilot.

"Oh no! . . . NO! The motherfucker just killed him. Just like that. It just took him out. He wasn't doin' nothin,' nothin' at all. Come in Blue base . . . Come in Blue base . . .CAN YOU READ ME?" The static sparked and sizzled and the second speck, black smoke belching from its screaming engines, arced away to the west.

•••

The great black, oddly glistening behemoth was still and silent above the ravaged mountain, darkening the earth below despite the already strengthening sun. The death sounds of the plane died ever more faintly in the valleys like the barely heard banshee wail in a dark Irish night.

He felt irritated. *Why? Had he misjudged somehow, not taken enough care? He hadn't meant it to happen. Oh it was their entire fault anyway. Why didn't they keep away? He would come when he was ready.*

"No . . . no, that's not right. WE will come when WE are ready. When the giants are ready we will come." His sister was waking the giants now. They knew her, welcomed her as brothers embrace their sister on her return from a distant land. She in turn touched them, stirred in them the joy of life. He still couldn't really see them, understand them, but they were closer now. All around in the pale green, in the pool, and in him. His humour became harder, almost grim. "Soon, sooner than the world might like, we will make them understand."

He exulted. He laughed. No sound was uttered but the giants heard, heard and understood.

CHAPTER 8

Out of the snowstorm of static on the screens appeared a bigger snowflake.

Lieutenant Golder shouted, "They're back, they're back. I knew we'd show them."

Sergeant Walker, rheumy-eyed, peered for a moment at the screen and tensed. "Only one? Dear God there's only one of them. How far out soldier?" He was shaking the radar operator and at the same time glaring at Lieutenant Golder, who chewed his lip silently.

Some endless minutes later the windows of the "ops" room shook as the plane screamed overhead and the radio loudspeaker crackled into life, "Blue base, Blue base, come in Blue base, request emergency clearance for immediate landing."

Even as the flight controller issued the clearance, the fighter plane could be seen turning low and fast in a tight approach to the field.

"Get him in here on the double, sergeant." General Filshill was already making for the glass-panelled debriefing room. "You pair had better be in on this." No one needed to tell Golder and Walker that it was they to whom he referred.

"Sit down son," Filshill's gravely voice had taken on a fatherly tenderness. The pilot, still in his flight suit was pale and strained looking, his hand trembled, and he seemed to have a little difficulty in lighting his cigarette. He looked very young. "Just tell it in your own words first, then we'll ask some questions. Just the usual drill," continued Filshill.

The watchers from the "ops" room could see the increasing agitation of the group through the glass walls and could sense the crisis even though they could hear nothing.

Sergeant Walker suddenly saluted the General and burst out of the door back into the operations room. "Alert, immediate alert, red and green wings, and second chopper. Get the bastards to the line NOW! Full armament including tactical nuclear weapons."

The effect on the room was electrifying, seeming chaos ensued.

"Recall every God-damn, son of a bitch. The General wants every mother's son on the job, this is NO drill." As he turned back to the glass office, he stopped, drew himself erect, and with a little catch in his voice said clearly, "Post Major Hicks as dead, lost in action." The chaos hardly faltered but one woman stopped what she was doing and sat slowly down.

Half-an-hour later, twenty or so men in flying suits sat in the glass office and listened intently as Lieutenant Golder continued to addressed them:

"We have a difficult and dangerous task in front of us. This object is of unknown origin, Russian, Chinese? Who knows? For all we know its from outer space and I'm not joking. What we do know is that it is hostile. It has already killed one of our men without provocation and may well do so again. So be careful, comply strictly with your orders, keep your stations, and no heroics. You will have full armament including nuclear capability and you may be called upon to use it. As I have said communications are little more than token at the moment but they are certainly better than a few hours ago. We can only hope that they will improve, but in the meantime it will be a severe and dangerous handicap to our operations. I sure hope you all remember your early days and minimum instrumentation drill." He turned to General Filshill. "General?"

"Thank you, lieutenant." The General seemed to take forever before he spoke and when he did he continued to look out of the window. "Please remember gentlemen that we are not at war, least of all with Italy. You will be operating in a civilian theatre against a hostile foe with your full capability, including armed nuclear weapons. The enemy is of unknown power and we are desperately short of hard information, bereft of communications." He spoke very evenly with no emphasis. "Yet we must be ready to demonstrate our own power and resolve from the outset if need be. This is truly the stuff of nightmare, one slip and catastrophe will be the consequence. It is true that we have lost one of our number to this foe, but we must not get carried away with feelings of revenge. We must think first and act later, we must not, I repeat, NOT endanger innocent civilian lives without pressing cause. Good luck and God be with you." He turned sharply and left the room.

The lieutenant turned to the large-scale contour map of central Italy on the wall. There was a red line drawn across the country skimming the northern edge of Naples and a large pin stuck in the dark purple of the mountains to the north. "You will scramble immediately and hold position along this line until the signal to go. You will employ a zero altitude and full throttle approach. This thing is to have minimum warning of your arrival. Any questions?" Lieutenant Golder seemed to be pleased with himself. "Dismissed and good luck."

The men filtered silently out of the room, and soon the building shook to the sound of the machines of war howling their defiance at the sky.

"Go get 'em boys," whispered Jim Golder.

CHAPTER 9

"Comandanté? Rear Admiral? Won't you please come in? We have much to discuss and I have some things to tell you." General George Filshill was at his imperious best, simply radiating authority. But beneath the gold and the braid his heart was ashes, he would have to handle this with the finest of kid gloves. "Jeez, why can't Siemens do his own dirty work?" he thought blackly while smiling radiantly.

The activity of the base pleased Rear Admiral Forbes and worried Comandanté Di Rollo who spoke, "I'll come straight to the point, General. Are you sure that you are not thinking of deploying any nuclear weapons? There should be no need to remind you that there is a strict agreement with the United States about notifying the Italian national government prior to any such deployment and that I am the representative of that body. You will also, of course, be aware of the importance of the Abruzzi region to the Italian State. It is an officially designated preservation area, a European Park and no threat of damage to the ecology there will be tolerated. I would appreciate your assurance that despite the gravity of the situation, you have no plans to allow nuclear devices beyond the limits of the base."

"Relax Rocco, there is not the slightest chance that we would do any such thing. We have Italy and Europe's interests always uppermost in our minds. This problem, as I have stated, is very localised and should be contained fairly easily. Your main task is to seal off the immediate area so that no civilians get hurt, and to keep the lid on any wild speculation. I am sure you are as anxious as we are to avoid any large-scale panic. As soon as the source of this disturbance is clearly defined as non-military in nature, I shall stand down all my people. In the meantime I deem it my duty to keep my forces on alert and the situation under review until your ground forces are in place and have the situation under control." Filshill felt that he was parroting words that he had spouted so many times in his career they were semi-automatic.

Comandanté Di Rollo persisted, "Let me make my position quite clear, George. You will under no circumstances take it upon yourself to act unilaterally in Italian air space. We appreciate the rapidity of your response to what may be a threatening situation but that confers no rights of freedom of action. This is a sovereign, democratic state and even this bizarre happening cannot erase that fact. I want your further assurance that . . ."

"The Royal Navy is in the Med. in some force, as you know General, and we are most anxious to assist." Rear Admiral Forbes cut across the exchange between the American and the Italian, his clipped English accent very different from the open vowels of the others. "Our carrier aircraft are at immediate response and await only the order to go."

Filshill clenched his fist in frustration, "We have enough problems with communications and mixed command structures in N.A.T.O without the Royal Navy sticking in its oar," he retorted testily.

The unconscious pun was not lost on Comandanté Di Rollo who started to snigger.

The irritated response of the British officer set the tone for the rest of the meeting and Filshill fed the flames of national pride and self-interest. Minds arguing were not thinking minds and he needed time before they got the full picture, before the second wave of aircraft returned, before they discovered the first casualty, before Di Rollo realised that atomic weapons had already been deployed.

It wasn't too difficult to get them out of his office and off the base. He watched their respective staff cars move off and turning to Golder made a signal with his hand. The forces he had dispatched would soon be fully committed. In his mind's eye he could see them somewhere to the north, over the wooded hills, raping the natural stillness of the air with the brute violence of their passing.

CHAPTER 10

None of the women had come. She hadn't really expected them to, but still, it was a little strange to be toiling up the mountain with the four men. She was sweating profusely and gasping for breath. The little group was getting well up the mountain now and the air was getting thinner. Every ridge had promised to bring her some sight of Cole, some sign of his passing, but each crest had only uncovered another. She was being driven on by she knew not what, gifted with abnormal strength. The men were beginning to flag and find reasons for going across the slope or worse still, downwards into a gully, behind an outcrop but always she chafed at this, she "knew" he was higher up.

"I wish they'd stop messing about and keep their minds on the job," she thought as Bene stopped and called "Lets have a break. We should be pacing ourselves. It could be a long day." The last was said with a sideways look at the other men. They all grunted agreement and variously found rocks or gently sloping areas to lie on. Amedeo opened his knapsack and soon they were all chewing silently on tough bread, soaked in wine and water from the flasks he had carried. The sun was not yet at its peak, late morning she guessed, but it was already hot. They would make it, find him, she knew, she just knew.

Despite her fretting at the delays, she felt a great warmth and gratitude to them all. They had not hesitated to give up their plans or their work for the day. She had asked for their help and they had given it unreservedly. *How many would have done this in the city?* she pondered. It wasn't as if she had any real evidence that something was wrong or even that Cole was up the mountain, but her fear, her distress had been enough for them. They had come.

Not that she could feel the same warmth for the police. Early that morning she had gone to the *caserma*, just to check if anything had been reported, an accident maybe? But the usually sleepy, helpful place had been chaotic. The normally courteous officers were officious and high handed. "A missing person? Well, yes, we'll attend to that in due course, not a high priority just now you understand. There's been a big accident up in the Maianarde but don't worry, he'll turn up soon enough." She had felt like screaming, but simply thanked them, gave them her name and telephone number, and left.

Susan phoned from Amsterdam as she had promised and they spoke for more than half-an-hour. Her daughter had been very supportive and endorsed her plan to look for Cole. She suspected that it was just Susan's idea of keeping her mother's mind busy, but she had detected the concern in her daughter's voice. They had a closeness born of a mother and daughter relationship that had grown into one of mutual respect between adults and Kate's heart strengthened with the thought.

Rumour was rife in the village. Everyone was agitated and full of speculation. Something was up. The grapevine had it that there had been a big explosion in the Abruzzi, a secret military installation had gone wrong. Hundreds dead. "All shit of course," she said to Bene who had agreed. "They just love this sort of thing. Farmers are the same the whole world over, never content unless there is some disaster or other to complain about."

True there was a lot of unusual activity with military trucks and even lightly armoured personnel carriers coming up the tightly twisting road from the plain below. "Probably some bloody N.A.T.O. exercise. We'll have to contend with the bloody Yanks any time now," she muttered to no one in particular. She was near to hysteria. *Why did they have to start this thing today? Good God, her husband was missing and she knew that something terrible had happened.*

They had left the village by an old mule track just in case the carabiniere objected, or even worse, some snotty-nosed young soldier started playing big boys games with them. She knew for certain, that they would not be welcome in the middle of their silly war game exercises.

"C'mon, lets get started, please." Her voice had a wheedling quality about it. Her desperation was not far below the surface and the men sensed it. Pietro and his son, Mauro, silently relieved Amedeo of the remaining burden of the foodstuff, checking the straps of the backpack over-carefully. Bene, normally always chatting, always near, was silent too and kept his eyes averted from her gaze.

"He thinks I'm being hysterical." She turned half away and pretended that the tears in her eyes were nothing more than dust.

It especially hurt to feel that Bene, of them all, didn't understand. He was a close and special friend, an ex-patriot Scot of Italian émigré parentage who had returned to the village many years before. Indeed he had been instrumental in their decision to come here. He was of medium but muscular build with a merry sparkling aspect which completely belied his years. A bachelor given to boyish pranks and the quintessential handyman, he was known to almost everyone for miles around, and still a prized catch in the minds of many a widow. A kind man, he was discomfited by her distress, she knew, and had no means of dealing with it. If only she could articulate her feelings, her certainty that Cole was close now.

In silence they turned once again to the mountain and the little group toiled ever upward in the increasing heat.

Then they all stopped, cocking their heads, listening. What was that noise? Away in the far distance a faint sound of thunder, air being torn . . . engines. "Not more of those bloody jets. God won't they leave us alone? Let us get on with solving our own problems?" She had muttered the words through her gritted teeth so quietly that no one reacted. They returned to their self-appointed task even more subdued as if the distant rumble was some ill portent.

The next crest was very close now and she suddenly felt afraid, her heart leapt, thudding violently in her chest. *He was here! But how could she know that?* He was here and so was the hole in the sky, that black menace. A cold sweat mingled with that of exertion. Her mind stalled, how could she know, be so sure?

The scrubby brushwood was quite thick as it often was on the southern slopes and they had to push aside the low, twisted, branches as she strained to see ahead. The dream came back, overwhelmingly, overlaying reality, and swamping her vision. She began to tremble, hands shaking, sobbing gently, her strength ebbed away. The great black bird was again rending his body. Green slime was everywhere.

"You feeling all right, Kate?" queried Bene in a fatherly tone and coming towards her. "We can stop if you like, take a rest for a bit."

"NO!" She rapped it out like a slap. *Cole was here, just over the ridge, couldn't he see that?* But she was afraid, more afraid than ever before in her life.

"Jesu!" Pietro's voice was low and awed. Both he and Mauro had stopped, standing erect, quite still, just a few metres above them on the rim of the ridge.

Bene, startled, looked up. "What is it? *Che cosa?*" but neither replied, their silent backs unmoving.

"Is it Cole?" in a small voice. "*È' Cole?*" she screamed, hurling herself up the slope.

The hill dropped away, almost sheer, scree and boulders intermingled with tough scrub. A wild and hostile wilderness of barren grey rock and about half-a-kilometre in front of them, a horse-shoe shaped valley, thickly forested, forked around a lower central ridge with a little clear lake at its foot.

The view, beautiful as it was, was not even glanced at. All their eyes were fixed on the gigantic object in the sky. It was immense, an ebony Everest hanging above the central ridge. In front and slightly above them, it filled the horizon, fixed in the air; glassy black. Its size was staggering, numbing the mind, and making the breath falter. It was not quite in line with them, but seemed to be at an angle of thirty degrees or so, angling away to their left. No one spoke. The awesome scale overpowered all efforts to fit it into the landscape, kept making them reassess what they saw. If the mountain had been in the air and it on the ground, perhaps it would have been easier.

The shadow from the object darkened the entire valley floor and much of the central ridge which had the form of a double hogback with a broad longitudinal valley, reflecting the shape of the behemoth, running its entire length. The ground was charred and blackened as if some great fire had raged there and wisps of smoke still curled lazily upwards in the still air. The sun glistened oddly from the great angular facets and unexpected planes of the giant. It might have been a rent in the pale blue sky, a hole in the fabric of the universe. It made them want to cower, to shrink away from it lest it crush them.

A keening, sibilant hiss was coming from Kate. Her teeth bared in an animal grimace, eyes staring fixedly at the colossus in the sky, breath coming in great gulps, she seemed to be in some sort of trance.

Her cry of pain as she was thrown to the ground was stifled by the soldier's hand across her mouth. She twisted savagely catching him completely by surprise and wrenched free from his clutches. Scrambling to her feet, she could see that there were eight or nine of them, all in olive drab, faces smeared and painted, grim, implacable, frightening. These people meant business. The others of her little group lay quietly among the rocks and gnarled branches, each closely held by an armed soldier.

"There's a hole in the sky! Cole is there. Let me go." She frantically scrabbled for footing, clutching at roots, fiercely trying to regain the ridge. But this was no young boy fresh from conscription. The man with lightning reflexes and athletic strength was on his feet immediately and with cruel force knocked her to the ground with the heel of his hand.

Then the deafening scream of the jet fighters as they hurtled low overhead, completely drowned out her own howl of pain and frustration.

"*Fermati! State zitta! Non ti muovere.*" Hissed the soldier, hand raised for a second strike. But she lay still and quiet as he had instructed. Her mind ignored the pain, the trickle of blood, and concentrated on the planes. They were so low, so fast, that they shredded the air, pounded her ears with a violence that took her breath away. They howled in savage glee, their murderous ululation directed towards . . . towards . . .Cole? *What were they doing?*

"Stop!" she yelled, the sound lost in the wake of the engines' howl. It was no use. She could no longer see over the ridge. Could not resist being dragged away.

None too gently, they began their retreat from the mountain. She recognised the insignia of the Alpini troops, crack soldiers she knew and legend in Italian military history but there was nothing chivalrous about their behaviour now. They might as well have been herding sheep off the slopes for slaughter. Pushed and bundled, never letting up, the grim taciturn men carried out their task.

All of the group of civilians were silent. After Bene's first protestations had been cut short by a heavy slap across his face, they knew that further pleading for release was useless.

The descent of the rocky slopes took what seemed like forever, with no respite for drink or food. The grim tension of the soldiers rasped on the already stretched nerves of the little group.

At last they reached the road and were rudely pushed into the back of a covered truck and brought into the village. They waited a long time in silence in the hot and stuffy room at the *caserma*, while policemen and soldiers shouted and cursed and seemed to rush around aimlessly.

The interrogation, when it came, was short and not unkind, more of a lecture on the restrictions now being placed on movement. No unauthorised traffic was to be allowed beyond the village. All personnel had to carry their identity cards even within the village until informed otherwise. A curfew was in force with immediate effect.

Then they were examined by military doctors. Blood and urine samples taken, skin smears, Geiger counter and other unidentifiable instruments passed over their bodies, and photographic records made.

One doctor, a tall American who questioned Kate, listened attentively to her story, showing considerable interest in her conviction that she had to return to the mountain to save her husband, to try to rescue him from some terrible catastrophe. He questioned her closely but kindly on the timings of her feelings in relation to actual events, making copious notes, and speaking into a little tape recorder from time to time. All through the interview she wept inconsolably and every time another plane came over she would shout, "Go back, go BACK."

After a time the doctor said, "Enough for now, you're tired and distressed. We can finish this later." He then administered a sedative and prescribed a period of rest and relaxation.

Kate left the room to find Bene waiting in the corridor. He said nothing, but took her arm and the pair made their way silently into the bright sunlight and slowly up the steep roadway to the little house. The peasant women of the village crowded in, sympathised, made camomile tea, brought flowers, and constantly fussed.

CHAPTER 11

He began to grasp in his mind, consciously, clearly, the change in him and began to articulate his power. He had grown, oh, how he had grown. His limits were still untested, unplumbed. In some way he was not yet whole; yet he was, he existed, he commanded. It filled him. The power and the glory of it blazed in his brain and in his heart.

He was aware of himself still, his old self. He pondered on his existence before power. It seemed somehow unimportant, just like these creatures all around in the woods and rocks below. Insignificant things of the surface, chained by gravity, and impotent against him, they had gathered skulking and dodging in the rocks and trees. *Did they not know that he saw them, watched them? Like he used to watch the bugs on the pavement far below their balcony.*

Their balcony. He thought of his wife, somehow distantly, detached. He thought of her and turned his awareness outward and southward in the direction of the village. It required an effort, an act of will to look out. There had been happiness, he was sure of that, but it seemed to elude his mind's grasp. His memory was vague, distorted like so much else. Still, it was important. He began to feel a need to identify that memory and make it clearer. She was important to him. He missed her odd mixture of sentimentality and practicality, with her kindness. She would understand and help. She would reassure him and help to clarify things. *Was he making a mistake, should he go back, could he go back? Kate?* He directed his mind southwards.

Beyond the ridge lay the village, his wife, his past, and perhaps reality. Perhaps she would hear him, listen to him, understand him, heal him, and make the distortion go away. He reached out . . .

There! There on the ridge just beyond the lake, creatures, people, small in the distance. Someone, not just people, but someone, someone in particular, someone special, he could feel it. *Who was it? Kate? His wife?*

"Kate . . .Kate?" She was there, he could sense her, feel her distress, her reaching out to him, searching. He began to reach out to her, bridge the distance between them.

But wait! Awareness re-focused! What was that, far beyond, far to the south? Aircraft? Low. Several, perhaps six, were making a sweeping, wide arc from an easterly heading and beginning to bear north, towards him. He sensed their urgency, the straining of the engines to the limit. He became aware of others now, much closer, lower, skirting and skulking in the wooded ridges to the west . . . helicopters, big and ugly.

Again he could hear the static and focussed on it. The pilots bawled into their microphones trying to cut across the hiss and mash of sound.

He watched them almost sleepily, as yet unconcernedly, stretching in the warm, strangely fierce sunlight. He was feeling stronger. His mind wandered, he could commune with some of the giants now. That was good, that was all that seemed to matter.

What did the puny want with him anyway? He could no longer be of them. They must realise that. How could he go back? Back to his wife, back to being powerless, and a non-entity. He had been dreaming when he thought of his wife, his destiny lay on other paths, on the paths of might, and in the halls of wisdom. The affairs of men were for men, not for him. He pushed his earlier sense of unease away.

The radio transmissions were closer now, still mangled and fragmented by the static. He listened idly to their communications. They were associating the radio wave distortion with him, accusing him of causing it. He mulled that over slowly. Perhaps they were having greater difficulty in understanding him with all this interference from the static. He relaxed his mind, disciplined his thoughts, and reigned in his expansive, vague, fantasising.

"Comms are back!"

He heard this with absolute clarity. It pleased him.

"We have clear scopes, come in Naples, Can you read me? Come in Naples, red leader to Red base, come in . . ."

"Red base, reading you loud and clear, red leader. Thank God for that. Wait! Message from Top Dog, Message from Top Dog. Abort previous, repeat; abort previous . . . revised directive . . . make direct approach . . . make direct . . . repeat DIRECT approach. Do you read?"

"Understood, Red base. Make direct approach –direct approach. Over and out. Red two and three hold, hold your station, the rest, on me . . . break . . . break . . . BREAK!"

Four specks dropped down into the big valley to the south and turned, first west and then north again, streaking low towards him and suddenly popped up skimming impossibly low over the near ridge.

"*Kate*?" It was a blow, like someone had struck him, suddenly and unexpectedly. He felt momentarily stunned. He seemed to reel, stagger. Anger budded in him.

He felt the savage passing of the low flying planes stripping the leaves from the trees. He felt the force of their passing as if they were only meters from him and not a kilometre away. He felt her fear, her alarm, and frustration. Rage flared suddenly, inexplicably in him.

He concentrated on the planes, "Go away. STOP!"

Pretty, pale, blue light, barely visible in the strong sun, coruscated gently, briefly, and silently. All four aircraft blossomed like a hellish flowering of some infernal orchid, its incandescent petals lurid and bright, the black, smoking exhaust trails of the engines making ephemeral stalks, drifting gently in the slow breeze. White and yellow and deep red, the flames billowed.

Fragments large and small arched and spiralled in the clear sky trailing incandescent smoke. The ugliness of destruction gave birth to beauty of a kind. The death screams of the planes died again and again in the hills.

Then all was silent. Only the faint steam and vapours drifting and dissipating slowly in the currents of the upper air gave any hint of the deaths of men.

Deep in thought, he didn't even hear the frantic radio calls back and forth, back and forth, repeating the same thing again and again.

For the first time he felt troubled, empty, lonely. There was no going back now and even as he thought it, he knew that he did not want to return. He had all his life yearned for this, known that with power he could do good, could erase the mistakes of man, and lighten the burden of mankind. His childhood dreams flooded back. He would be the harbinger of peace. He would force the dictators to open up their countries and peoples. The Americans would get out of the Middle East and stop bullying the world. The French and British would retreat from Empire and all nuclear testing would stop. He would arbitrate in disputes, absolutely.

Childish fantasies. All passed now, faded and tattered like the toys of childhood, overtaken by events, and his own maturity. It was just so disappointing and heartbreaking, such missed opportunities and he was all alone.

But no, he wasn't alone. The giants were awaking now, soon he would know himself more clearly. Then he would act. Oh, how he wished he could awaken them completely, know them fully. They perhaps would help him find himself, help him find purpose.

He needed purpose, a reason to be.

In an instant it was clear in his mind. Of course! He had spoken of it for years, had debated and argued futilely with all who would listen. It had been, still was, his crusade. The world was dying, dying in its own excrement, gagging in the filth from its loins, choking in it's own stench. He would save it and turn man from his headlong plunge into oblivion. Stop without quarter those who fouled and stained the earth.

His mission shone like a Holy Grail before his eyes. His purpose was clear. Without him mankind would die. Like some knight in shining armour, he had come in his strength at the eleventh hour. Nothing would stop him now. The global ecological disaster could be averted through his implacable will. He had always known that drastic measures were needed and only immense power, properly wielded, could hope to succeed. Now he was mighty, powerful, menacing. He would succeed, he knew it. He only had to work it out, find the fulcrum, learn to control his strength, and deploy his resources wisely.

He pondered in still, silent reverie, the newly dead already forgotten. *How would he go about his sacred task? Who could he enlist as his pawns?* He needed a global lever. The Americans were the obvious choice. Once he had demonstrated to their President his will and power, the national government would follow his wishes obeying his commands. The military strength and administrative organisation of the U.S. would forward his plans, easing the process.

But the Americans? Liars and cheats, self-seeking, self-motivated, grasping at power and dominance. In all history he could only see their isolationism and self-interest. Americans above all loved Americans. Americans confused wealth and power with wisdom and they had sinned more than most in the destruction of mankind, and the crippling of the environment. They were a greedy, self-centred culture unlikely to accept self-denial. No, he would have to influence pivotal people the world over and few indeed would see wisdom in using America as an intermediary. To ally oneself with the culture of consumption would be madness. America would not do.

The Russians then, the communist block or the Chinese? Too adventuresome, too dangerous, too much was happening in the communist world now with too much instability. How the communist megalith had fragmented and fractured since the days of his childhood, *did anyone take them seriously now?* Nowadays in the lands that lay behind the torn remnants of the Iron Curtain people died in the name of freedom without ever having known that it was an impossible dream. His plans called for controlled, purposeful action, carefully and precisely delivered. He could not permit chaos, random slaughter, or muddy thinking. If he were to attempt to use the communist or ex-communist states, who knew what might follow; runaway nationalism, destabilisation of many sensitive areas in the world, civil wars . . . anything was possible. No, much too risky.

Britain? He was, had been, British after all, he knew the British. He smiled grimly. He knew them only too well; the arch double dealers in the history of the modern world. Truly accomplished in the arts of diplomacy. *"Why do they not call it lying?"* he thought. Always promising, always betraying. He was aware of a small nagging fear deep down. He must not leave himself open to betrayal, to the turning of his own power against himself. He could be outwitted and led to the unknowing service of an individual state, ultimately be the tool of unscrupulous exploitation. The British were truly dangerous.

Europe? The EC? Not as silly as it first seemed. Not as yet a political unity certainly, but culturally and economically stable. An outward looking polyglot; perhaps symbolic of a future world union under his aegis, a new force in the world bringing new ideals, new objectives? But Britain was now part of Europe, a canker at the heart of his stratagem, a worm eating at the very timbers of his bridge to hope. So dangerous, so convoluted, a quicksand of lying minds. No.

The United Nations then, it seemed obvious. But no. *Why should he deal with the pomp and trappings of formal government dissembling? Would that not appear to give them status?* In some way lend his authority, his approbation to their foppish puppet? The United Nations was weak and their weakness would reflect on him, his plan, and his resolve. No, perhaps better to find a podium without the accepted political stage.

That only left the Muslim world. Everything else was too fragmented or too disorganised to be useful. Yes, perhaps a religious base had much to recommend it. Enormous credibility if he could harness the faithful, worldwide communications and dedication to his leadership. *Was not his cause a world renewal, a new dawn for mankind, a holy cause indeed?* But surely even here there was danger; too much fanaticism, too much blind righteousness, and too much politics. The rank and file of the Muslim world murdered each other for reasons so subtle that he doubted if any other than the most fanatical sons of Allah could understand the reasoning. He needed something less strong, less rigid, more malleable, but just as big.

With whom would he deal? From which platform could he address the human masses? It would need to be carefully chosen. Not so powerful in its own right that his message would be seen as an extension of existing policy and yet with worldwide exposure. Something that he could bend to his purpose, perhaps something that could claim authority in both the temporal and the spiritual worlds . . . the Vatican?

Of course, why had he not thought of it before? He was already here in Italy, worldwide attention must already be turning this way. Awareness of his arrival, his coming would be touching the common consciousness of mankind. It would be easy, quick to set up worldwide communications, and make his wishes clear from the start. Papal involvement might give his presence a less threatening aspect encouraging more rapid acceptance of the inevitable. There were deep forces in the minds of men already tuned to religious dogma, W*hy not turn them to his own use? Such possibilities, such rich seams of obedience and respect.*

"*Yes, just let me work out the finer points.*" He felt the slow, languor creep over him again drifting . . . drifting in the cool, cool green depths. In the pool, in him, he could sense more of the giants now, not clearly yet, but they were awaking, soon he would know and command them all.

CHAPTER 12

Something resembling chaos reigned in the White House. The Presidential press secretary, Bill Simpson, yelled above the clamour of the assembled pressmen, "Gentlemen, I assure you that there is nothing further to say on the subject. The President and Vice President are having private discussions on a matter which they have not as yet deemed themselves ready to reveal."

"*Washington Times,*" shouted a small man, "why was the Vice President called away so suddenly from his engagement this morning. Is it true that there has been a major incident in Europe, a N.A.T.O. base attacked by terrorists?"

"*Herald Tribune,*" called another, "the President has cancelled his trip to the western White House and sent his family on unaccompanied. He never does that. What is going on?"

"I know no more than you do," yelled the press secretary over the hubbub. "You can be sure that you will be notified immediately when there is anything to be released."

"Where is Mister Clarke?" several called together.

"The Secretary of State is in conference with the President and Vice President and that is all I have to say on the matter," the press secretary's voice betrayed his irritation. "Please await the announcement of a formal press conference."

Despite the rain and the heavy overcast making the daylight dim, the curtains in the Oval Office were completely drawn making the room almost dark, so much so that Vice President Borrhim was using the light from a small table lamp to read the flimsy in his hand. It was early afternoon and President Albero had been closeted with his Vice President and the Secretary of

State for an hour. Apart from the occasional phone call, there had been virtual silence for all of that time, no evidence of the noisy clamour elsewhere penetrated to the three men. They would alternately read intently and then gaze blankly into space, lost in deep thought. In the darkness each man could only be seen dimly by the others, simple block outlines in the gloom . . . silent shapes in the silence.

When the President spoke, he did so at little above a whisper, as if he were in a public library, afraid to be overheard. In the shadows he seemed to be speaking to no one in particular, "No matter how many times I have read and re-read these reports, I keep coming up against the same conclusion, absurd as it may seem. We have a non-terrestrial object staring us straight in the face, and it could hardly be in a more awkward location." He paused. Borrhim and Clarke said nothing. "We are going to have to do something about it before someone else does."

Borrhim's deep voice came out of the gloom and silence, "Thank God you're taking that view, I was afraid you might want to talk to it, or make a deal of some sort with the little green men."

There was no humour in Albero's voice, "Green isn't my favourite colour this year, and bug eyes are definitely out." He continued in the same low whisper, seeming to speak more to himself than the others. "Let's just run through the obvious possibilities."

"Number one: that it's a product of Russia or some other foreign state. That is clearly a non-sequitur, no technology could put something that big in the air without us knowing something about its development and even if they could, they would not put it over Italy. They would place it over their own territory as a demonstration of power, or if hostile to us, over U.S. territory as a threat."

"Number two: that the unthinkable has happened and an alien technology has somehow come to earth. The facts fit that scenario very well. It's unlike anything ever seen before, it arrives from nowhere, and it behaves in a hostile manner making no attempt at communication. The only difficulty for me in accepting that conclusion is that we had no sightings of any kind as it approached from wherever it came from, but I am sure the scientists will come up with some explanation for that. After all it did screw up telecommunications in a big way after it arrived. Maybe it can cloak its movements from our radar?"

The President sat up in his chair and looked straight at the Vice President, "Okay Arnold, what are we going to do about it?"

Borrhim seemed to chuckle slightly, "It's kind of funny you know, but I don't feel at all frightened by this thing. In all the books we should be panicking and running into the streets shouting about the end of civilisation as we know it. Instead it seems to be more problematic than frightening."

"Speak for yourself, Arnold," said Clarke, "I have no doubt that the reaction of the public will be exactly as you have described it when this gets out." He looked straight at Borrhim, "Well, answer the question, what are we going to do about it?"

Borrhim shifted his position so that his face was clearly lit by the table lamp, his features set hard, "Get rid of it."

"Get rid of it?" Clarke's tone was light, querulous.

"By whatever means at our disposal. I believe that the best possible course of action is simply to dispose of the thing, and quickly at that." Borrhim had become matter of fact, crisp, "What is there to gain by any other action? Nothing beneficial to us can come of this object. In theory, we might communicate with it, gain new knowledge and technological advantages that will advance mankind's lot."

"Just think of the potential benefits," Clarke interrupted, sounding excited.

"Oh, yeah?" Borrhim sneered, "Like shut down the fossil fuel industries, mining and oil refining, wipe out the automobile industry, and render obsolescent all our computer and electronics' achievements. Do I need to go on?"

Secretary of State Earl Clarke was silent.

"How about out-dating our armaments and reducing us to equality with Libya, or Tierra del Fuego?" his tone took on a sarcastic acidity. "Perhaps the total dissolution of the world monetary system would be a good thing . . . make the dollar worthless, eh? No, Mister Secretary, no single developed state can benefit from this, at best the third world countries could gain world parity, not by being made equal to us, but by us being made equal to them."

"Go on, Arnold, I'm listening." the President poured himself a cup of coffee from a flask on a side table.

"What is much more likely to be the case, and a best possible scenario at that, is the complete disruption of world economic, social and religious systems, for absolutely no useful return at all." Borrhim spoke in an emphatic manner, modulating the emphasis on key words.

Earl Clarke was a slight, small shape in the gloom, almost womanish in his proportions, his voice a light tenor. "Perhaps they would bring wisdom, a new philosophy to the world, enhance the causes of peace."

Borrhim had an air of strained patience, "Why do we tend to assume that an alien civilisation would be benign, and bring us presents? At best they might be missionary and bring us their way of life, and that did a lot for the natives of Africa and South America didn't it? I wonder how many Incas enjoyed the arrival of the Spanish, or how many African slaves rejoiced in the aftermath of Dr. Livingston."

Borrhim got up and poured himself a coffee. Albero said nothing.

"Let's consider the down side now. Suppose this is a hostile race, warlike and imperial, what then? Slavery, exploitation or even worse, we've all read some of the more lurid fruits of science fiction writers' minds. In every possible scenario the United States stands to lose everything, I repeat, the United States stands to lose everything," he enunciated the last word syllable by syllable. "Are we going to let that happen? Are YOU going to let it happen?" Borrhim addressed the last remark to the President.

Albero continued his gentle tone, "but how do we get rid of it?"

Clarke interjected, "It's as big as a mountain and right in the middle of Italy for God's sake."

Borrhim was on his feet now, pacing to and fro. "It's big for sure and we have to presume pretty powerful, and no pushover if it came to a battle. We cannot take any risks with it. We must try to make sure of a first time victory, using the element of surprise to best effect." He paused for a moment in his pacing. Peering through the gloom at the President, he bent over his desk, pausing for dramatic effect. "We let it have it right in the ass with a nuclear missile, shortest range, no warning."

"In Italian air space?" Albero still spoke in an even, gentle manner.

"In Italian air space?" Clarke's tone was incredulous.

Borrhim smiled acidly, "Perhaps we should invite it to meet us on the plain of battle, or behind the cathedral at dawn. You never know, it may be full of knights in shining armour or chivalrous cavaliers. What would you prefer, pistol or epé?" He returned to his seat and slowly sat down.

Albero smiled widely, "Sometimes talking to you, Arnold, is like talking to myself, listening to my own echo. You have overlooked one thing though. Suppose there are others? Others we don't know about, either in remote spots of the globe or out there in space somewhere waiting for a signal from the first."

Borrhim took a few seconds before he replied, "Fair point, Robert, but everything I have said still stands. One or many, the effect upon us is the same. If we fail to destroy it we are no worse off than if we did nothing. It, or its friends, will still wreak havoc on the world as we know it. If it is a solitary object and we succeed in destroying it, then the problem is over and done with forever. If there are others then they may well be warned off and choose an easier target. It always comes back to the same conclusion. Destroy it NOW."

"Earl?" the President looked piercingly at his Secretary of State.

The light tenor voice was so quiet that even in the silent room it was difficult to hear, "There is no denying the logic. We have a duty to the people of the United States of America to protect their interests first and foremost even at the expense of others." He paused, lost in thought for a few moments and then resumed, "I was taught to believe in the right to life. I grew up in the Christian ethic and tried to promote a way of living that abhorred murder and the abuse of others' rights. Oh hell, I believe in God and believe that he created us, but no one ever talked about creatures from outer space. Perhaps as far as aliens are concerned, what must be done must be done. But dear God, to detonate a thermonuclear device in Italian air space . . ."

Albero tapped the desk with his pencil for a long time while complete silence reigned in the room, then lifted a phone on his desk, "Get me Moscow, the Chairman himself, maximum security." He turned to Borrhim and Clarke, "This is going to be bad enough politically without the Russians mistaking our intent. By coming clean I believe they will go along with us, help to control the aftermath."

Borrhim was crisp, businesslike, "You're right of course, and it will allow us to explore the possibility that they may have received information about the location of any others. We would need to mount simultaneous operations if there were more than one."

The phone rang. Albero lifted the handset and after listening for a few moments spoke, adopting a formal manner in his voice, "Mister Chairman, it is good to speak to you again. I trust that you are in good health? Please excuse my lack of an interpreter as this call has been precipitated by an unexpected and very urgent matter, I am very willing to accept your interpreter alone if you are happy to do so."

Borrhim and Clarke could hear the reply from a small speaker on the President's desk. It was a woman's voice which partly overlaid the rich baritone of the Russian Premier," I am very happy with the arrangement you propose and, yes, I am in good health. How can I assist you?"

Albero looked at his aides for a moment, then said in slow, clearly enunciated words, "Can I presume that you are aware of the developments in southern European air space in the last two days?"

Despite the strange tongue, the humour in the Russian's voice was evident behind that of the interpreter, "Yes, we of course have been observing these developments and have been wondering when you would take some action. Can I take it that you wish to consult with us over possible eventualities?"

"Indirectly Josef that is correct. May I speak frankly, man to man without prejudice?"

Josef Sergei Christof did not hesitate and spoke directly in slow, heavily accented English, "Of course Robert, we are old enough in politics to, how do you say, 'know the score'."

"Then I will come directly to the point Josef. We intend to remove this object and wish to be certain that there is no misunderstanding on your part when we initiate the . . . shall we say, unusual measures. These measures will be of the strongest possible nature. Do I make myself quite clear?" Albero looked strained, listening intently for the Russian's reply.

There was an audible exchange between the two Russians on the open phoneline. Then the interpreter's voice sounded clear and precise. "The Chairman understands exactly and wishes you good fortune. He further states that the unpredictability of certain wind born by-products may prejudice areas of Russian sovereignty. He expects this problem to be carefully considered in the action you propose."

The Chairman's heavy accents intervened, "Robert, do we not have time to discuss this jointly? Even get our advisers to consult?"

"You know as well as I do Josef that time is of the essence and that political niceties would make such a discussion extremely difficult and potentially very embarrassing for me. No, we must proceed at once, but there is one question I have for you and I am sure you understand the risks for both of us if your reply is not absolutely frank. Do you know of the existence of any more of these objects?" Again Albero looked strained as he awaited the reply.

The Russian Premier spoke personally, "I am always frank with you Robert, you know that." Borrhim smiled, his teeth gleaming in the light from the tabletop lamp. "There are no other objects known to us."

"Thank you Josef, I am sure that out of this in the end, will come good for both of our countries. Good-bye." Albero gently placed the phone on its receiver.

"That's that then," said Clarke, distantly.

"I might have guessed that they would acquiesce readily," said Borrhim. "I suppose that they have the additional problem of worrying about any clever tricks that the thing might teach us if it were not destroyed. I am sure we would not be in a hurry to share them with our Soviet brethren on earth."

President Albero nodded, "Just the chiefs-of-staff and the Europeans to deal with now." He poured a second cup of coffee. "Better get Field Marshal Siemens on the phone and the British Prime Minister too. It will be useful if we can get her to tag along with us on this one."

Borrhim stood up. "I'll attend to all of that but I'm worried about our lack of knowledge about the object's defences. Can we upgrade what Filshill is doing?"

"Better let Siemens handle the details; but yes, a closer encounter with the object might give us valuable clues, but no shooting. We need a few hours yet to arrange this and we don't want to shake up the Italians too soon."

CHAPTER 13

The driver cursed and honked his horn at the elderly truck which was hindering his passage as it ground up the steep winding road. There were many trucks such as these in southern Italy and this one was no different from the others in that it completely ignored his complaints. In the back of the fully air conditioned Buick, General Filshill and Field Marshall Siemens were comfortably cool in the deep, leather seats despite the blinding sun outside and were deep in earnest conversation. Only rarely were they aware of the rugged beauty of the countryside through which they passed; precipitous rocky slopes intermingled with terraces and olive groves, and all capped by the cloudless, copper blue of the sky.

"There can be no doubt that it's not Russian or Chinese or any other government's doing that we know of. Our intelligence in this matter is pretty hard. Ever since communications cleared we've been in touch with every son of a bitch this side of Hades and them with us for that matter. We are even getting pretty good data from satellite surveillance." It was Siemens' voice, light and cultured. "Bizarre as it seems, there can be little doubt in my view that we are dealing with an alien presence and a hostile one at that. But in all probability, it is simply testing us at this time. I have to say, George, that you have done a good job on this one. Costly perhaps, but the lives of those airmen have bought us valuable information."

"I'm glad you think so," there was an edge to Filshill's voice. "Was it really your idea to make a direct approach? Was it some sort of trade off, lives for information?"

Siemens behaved as if he hadn't heard. "The films taken by the ground forces are still to be analysed in full but I have preliminary reports which suggest it's using a powerful ray of some sort, not a laser, and clearly of very limited range, possibly no more than two or three kilometres. Our technical people believe that they may have a lead on the technological basis for such a weapon. The static seems to be import . . . " He broke off, "Is this the place?"

The village had come into view as they rounded a sharp bend with a high stone wall. So steep was the terrain that it nestled high to their right, against the wooded hillside with the houses seeming to be built on top of each other.

For a moment Siemens seemed to drink in the natural beauty of the place, then he turned to Filshill, "I would like to interview the civilians who were up on the mountain when we lost the air crew before we go up to look at the big bastard for ourselves," his voice was calm and even, businesslike.

"There's no problem with that Bill, the locals are scared shitless and will do anything to co-operate. But the Englishwoman may be another kettle of fish. Her husband was lost up there sometime just before our visitor arrived. By all accounts she's well educated and used to dealing with the modern world. I don't think she will be bullshitted easily. She maintains that he's still up there by the way, dining out with the Martians or something."

They both chuckled at the joke.

The big, dusty, pale blue car skidded to a halt on the smoothly polished road surface and the driver quickly got out and held the rear door open for the two senior officers.

At first there appeared to be no signs of life, strong sunlight contrasted with deep shadow, and the air shimmered in the heat. Cicadas rasped continuously, but otherwise all was still.

Both officers doffed their braid-covered caps and wiped the sweat that had formed on their foreheads. "Whew! It's even warmer than usual this year. I'll be glad to get back to air conditioning and Coke machines, preferably in the 'States'."

Field Marshall Siemens was well known for his urbanity and his extreme dislike of rusticana.

At that moment several soldiers, both American and Italian, together with a number of senior *carabiniere* hurried out of the large square, green shuttered house at which the car had stopped. Both Siemens and Filshill replaced their caps hurriedly and returned the several salutes of the reception party.

Siemens cut curtly across the rather over florid greeting of the senior *carabiniere*. "Let's get on with this, shall we? The General and I intend to go up the mountain and see this thing for ourselves as soon as we can. But first we want to have an informal chat with the locals who saw it first hand from the ridge. I believe that two of them speak, indeed are, English. Perhaps you can arrange something to drink in the meantime?"

A rapid-fire exchange in Italian resulted in four Italian soldiers leaving at the double. "They will all be here in a few minutes General. The village is very small and there will be no trouble finding them." The senior *carabiniere* spoke with a pronounced accent but good grammar. "Would you prefer coffee or whisky?"

They entered the old house through a large and ornate wooden door with a coat of arms carved above the arched stone entrance. It seemed no time at all when the soldiers returned with the small, untidy, group of civilians.

The room the local forces had provided for the interview was cool enough, and at first seemed very dark, but the shafts of sunlight penetrating the dusty interior from the ancient wooden louvred shutters was quite adequate once their eyes adjusted. The two senior Americans and sundry other officers, both Italian and American, sat behind a long trestle table and the group of five villagers arranged themselves on a motley assortment of old chairs in front. Two hard looking *carabiniere* with machine guns stood at the door.

The three Italian civilians were obviously very nervous, fidgeting and continuously turning to Bene and Kate for noisy explanation and translation as the interview proceeded. But after a period of questions and answers, in which the group was caught out in various petty inventions and contradictions, things quieted and some minutes passed in the stuffy air with very little said. The villagers were acutely aware of the eagle-eyed observation of the military men.

Kate raised her hand slightly, like a child in a classroom, trying to attract the attention of the teacher, "You must understand, sir, that what you have been doing is very dangerous and it must stop." Kate had not spoken unprompted before. "You can't keep this a secret and you have no right to keep us virtual prisoners."

"Oh. You don't say? And what makes you think that you know more about this than the U.S. Air Force . . . Ah, I mean N.A.T.O. and the Italian government?" Siemens' confusion was either unnoticed or those present were too polite to comment. "We have the situation completely under control and there is nothing to worry about. No harm will be allowed to come to you or your families. So don't lose any sleep, just have patience, stick to the things you understand, and we'll get on with the job, just trust us."

Kate's face distorted and she leapt to her feet, "Don't bloody patronise ME, you trumped up chocolate soldier. Who do you think you are?" Her voice was hard, hectoring, "I KNOW that my husband is IN that thing. I have told you so, till I'm blue in the face. I can sense it with all my being and I think he can still, in some way, communicate with me. I can feel his presence. He's still alive. I KNOW it. How many times do I have to say it? I knew something was wrong before the earthquake even started, I saw the thing in my sleep a full day before I saw it in reality. I saw it attack him. I KNOW he saw me when I got to the top of the ridge. If your bloody gung-ho soldier boy had not intervened, all this might not have happened." She paused for breath looking drawn and pale with dark rings around her eyes despite her tan. . The outburst had taken them all aback. No one spoke.

A full minute passed in awkward silence.

"Are you bloody deaf or just stupid?" she yelled, "Well?"

"Easy, easy Kate, take it easy," Bene was on his feet, hand on her arm, trying to make her sit down, "don't get so worked up." He turned to the table, "She's had a bad time since her husband disappeared, has hardly slept at all. Please excuse her gentlemen."

"Oh, dear Christ, don't you start now Bene. You know better than that, you know me better than that." Tears were flowing freely down her face and her voice was starting to crack. She sat down abruptly, heaving with silent sobs.

Siemens seemed at a loss, his mouth partly opened but no words came out. He looked from one to another of his aides.

"Gentlemen, General." One of the Americans seated behind the foremost row at the table had leant forward and was speaking in a low voice. "My name is Crawford, I am a psychiatrist, a civilian working on research into psychic phenomenon in military environments. I was posted here as M.O. when this thing broke because I happened to be handy at the time, working as I was at the base at Gaeta."

He stood up, smoothed his uniform jacket, and spoke in an authoritative manner, "I have to tell you that I have medically examined this woman and interviewed her immediately after the event. She is well educated, intelligent and articulate, emotionally stable, and well adjusted psychologically. In short I would not lightly dismiss the possibility that she is in some way, unconsciously or otherwise, in possession of relevant information. It is my experience that feelings such as have just been expressed often have a firm basis in reality." Crawford stopped and sat down almost sheepishly, as if regretting his uninvited interruption of his senior.

Filshill spoke, "What are you talking about, 'firm basis in reality?' Since when did hysterical imaginings become reality?"

Crawford seemed to weigh his words carefully, "since the Department of Defence saw fit to consider such a possibility and invest resources in just such research."

"I see," Siemens spoke very slowly and so quietly that only those at the table could hear. His brow puckered as he struggled with his thoughts. "There is something very odd about this situation, of that there is no doubt. This thing is quite abnormal, quite bizarre, and it is my duty to make sure that I do not deprive myself of the slightest advantage, no matter how remote the chance." He seemed to decide on his course of action and turning his gaze on Kate, raised his voice in a lighter than usual tone, "I would like you to accompany us back up onto the ridge madam, today, this afternoon. I wish to see your object personally. Please make yourself ready." With that he rose and strode out of the room followed by his retinue.

Kate stared after him, wide-eyed. She stopped crying.

Crawford, last out of the door, turned and, catching her eye, winked.

An hour later the call from the White House set the entire company alight with speculation. Within seconds everyone had known that Field Marshall Siemens had received a direct, most secret, call from the Presidential Chief-of-Staff.

General Filshill sipped his whisky, looking into the amber liquid while he spoke, "It's too bad, just too bad. I really did want to see it first hand."

"When the President calls you, you shift your ass, George." Field Marshall Siemens was stuffing a salami roll into his mouth in a most unseemly manner. "We'll be in Washington by tomorrow and I ain't complaining about that. God this backwoods bashing makes me spit." He sipped from his glass, "Is there never any ice in these places? I don't care what the Scots say, I like my whisky cold. Are you sure your people can keep the lid on this for another couple of days?"

Filshill seemed to relish the full flavour of the fiery liquid, savoured it for some seconds before swallowing, and replied, "They're a good team, don't worry and Di Rollo is very competent. The Italians sure as hell don't want any panic reaction. It's bad enough for them with all the disruption to travel and business in general. I think they can handle the political heat of a big, secret, N.A.T.O. exercise for a while longer and they don't have a choice anyway. What are they going to do? Hit it with pizzas?"

Siemens laughed out loud, "I like that, hit it with pizzas. You never know, maybe it likes pizzas. Do you think it's got any ice?"

•••

From the balcony, Kate could see the square house on the edge of the village clearly. The air force blue car was still parked out front. There was a lot of activity, Jeeps lined the road and men gathered in the little flat meadow behind the building.

She thought, "*It's strange how every important event in the history of the village involves that house.*" She recalled that a distant son of the village, a very famous entertainer of some years ago had stayed there on a visit when he came to Italy to make a film. It was even said that General Kesselring of Nazi Germany had slept there during the Allied invasion of Italy during the Second World War. But today it would surpass itself. Today it would witness something tremendous. She was more keyed up than she could remember. This was going to be important. Somehow today she would play an important role in these affairs and Cole would come back. The thing in the sky would be dealt with forever.

The intimidating, slashing sound of the big helicopter's blades as it approached brought Kate from her dream state and the villagers running out of their homes to watch. It came over the hill to the southeast, where the old quarry was and lost height until it settled in the meadow behind the big house. It had accomplished its task with surprising speed and now sat, blades chopping the air, like some great beast of prey awaiting the chance to sate its hunger.

Kate shuddered at its deadly, unabashed ugliness. She bit her lip, suddenly even more nervous than before. "Surely this isn't going to delay our trip to the ridge. Maybe it is someone even more important arriving. Maybe it is someone who will change the soldiers' crazy stratagem, someone who will listen to me, believe me." Her knuckles were white as she clenched her fists with tension.

The senior American officers who had interviewed her were easily recognisable from this distance. They exited from the square house onto the meadow and stopped below the slashing blades. They shook hands with the group that had accompanied them into the open and climbed into the belly of the helicopter. The great blades slashed with ever-greater fury and like some enormous, over-heavy insect, it lifted into the air, spun slowly round and made off to the south.

"No! No!" She cried out in despair. They were leaving, had left, without her, without going to the ridge, without even explaining. She watched the black speck till it had faded completely, till its sound had died away, and the cicadas regained mastery of the air. Her heart was ashes.

She didn't even cry.

CHAPTER 14

His torpor felt quite natural, almost like daydreaming under the warm sun, but the sun was much stronger than he had ever felt it before. As if he could see and feel more of it. Its colour was different, less golden, whiter. It brought strength, strength to him and to the giants in the deep depths of the green. More of them were stirring, not purposefully, but more alive than before like chrysalis nearing pupation. Most of his attention was fixed on the giants now, he needed to understand them and somehow he knew that their awesome strength had to be brought to full awakening. But how? There were so many and all of unimaginable size, of such power and might that he feared that he could never encompass them, never address them all.

Still, it was good that no one disturbed him now. All was strangely quiet in the surrounding countryside. An odd inactivity, no traffic on the local roads stretches of which he could see between the hills, even the autostrada far to the east seemed to be empty. No aircraft were evident except the low flying, military helicopters hovering on the fringes of his vision, peeping cautiously above the ridges and between the hills. Only the little creatures of the ground far below moved and they did so on seeming tiptoe. *Had they understood his need, awaited his contact, his instructions?* No matter, the giants were more important than all their petty doings.

He turned his awareness inward into the cool, comforting greenness; such mightiness within himself, incomprehensible, yet his to command if he could only awaken it, direct it. *What did he have to do?* He felt like a newborn child might feel, knowing yet uncomprehending, aware yet unable to communicate, in command of a body yet without the mechanisms of control. The giants, however, knew him, they were aware of his presence, his attention to them but they seemed somehow indifferent, detached from his purpose. He felt frustrated, irritated with himself.

His heart ached with the desire to begin, to bring his power to the service of the world, to call the giants from their slumber, and with them return humankind to the age of sanity, drag the species back from the edge of self-extinction.

His reverie drifted on, his power and strength ever increasing. He opened himself to the sun, to the warmth, to its boundless energy, sucking it to himself, draining it as a drunkard greedily swigs the contents of his glass.

Outside, above the mountains, the sun shone down with the savage power of high summer in southern Italy but the slopes of the hills below the black behemoth and all the trees for a kilometre around were strangely white, silvery, cold, rimmed with a hard hoarfrost. The surface of the little lake was glassy still, a sheet of ice.

CHAPTER 15

There was a good deal of shouting and cross talk going on as Siemens and Filshill were ushered into the Oval Office, a remarkable amount considering the few people actually present.

"Good morning, gentlemen. We've been awaiting your arrival. Had a good flight? Not too jet lagged I hope? Coffee?" President Robert Albero was a slim man of middling build with an untidy shock of thin hair and unbounded energy. He walked round his desk and greeted Field Marshal Siemens warmly "Good to see you again, Bill. How's the family? Kitty married yet? And without waiting for a reply turned to General Filshill. "General? I don't think we've met. Good to have you on the team. Let's get the show on the road, shall we? You kick off Arnold. Get the formalities over quickly." He was speaking as he walked back to his seat. The room quietened and attention turned to the newcomers.

Vice President Arnold Borrhim indicated seats to Siemens and Filshill and stood erect facing the attentive audience. "You all know Field Marshal Siemens of course, but some of you may not know General Filshill, Commander U.S. Forces, N.A.T.O. Mediterranean. Both he and the field marshal have had the closest contact with the object, and have of course been co-ordinating our actions to date." Borrhim was a sweaty, fat man with an extremely deep and resonant voice, given to grandiose political ventures and frequently in the thick of U.S. foreign policy. A "hawk" by inclination and with very powerful economic connections, he was a politician to be respected. "For myself I must say that they have done a good job so far."

Both Siemens and Filshill acknowledged the compliment by a slight inclination of their heads. Filshill noted that apart from the President, Vice President, Secretary of State, and the military chiefs-of-staff, only two others were present, neither in uniform. He did not recognise them.

"Our purpose today, gentlemen, is to arrive at a firm policy for dealing with . . . shall we call it, *the ship*? You have all been briefed and I presume read the reports, so let's begin." He paused and drew a deep breath. When he spoke his voice was even deeper, more commanding than usual. "Now that the cat is out of the bag and our efforts to keep this thing quiet have failed, the military and political implications of this, ah, . . .*ship*, are almost incalculable. Just think, it is sitting right in the heart of the most developed part of the world, large population centres all around, excellent communication structures, and crawling with free press. Its very presence is screwing up every imaginable economic and industrial interest on the globe. Every industrial, financial, and administrative organisation of note has virtually frozen all activity. In addition it has effectively shattered our military heart in Europe. In short, each and every day it remains up there is a disaster of unprecedented proportion. We need a policy, a plan to remedy this situation, and fast. We don't want to hear about ideas that involve months or even weeks."

He spread his arms, palms open, "Gentlemen?"

Field Marshal Siemens glanced towards the President who nodded slightly. "I am disappointed to learn that the, ah, *ship* has become public knowledge," he glanced briefly at Filshill, "when we left Naples everything was still under wraps. I had hoped that the Italians would have had more success in keeping the news restricted." Borrhim made a sour face. "Can I take it that the *ship,* has not moved or attempted contact in the last few hours?"

"No, not a thing, not a God-damn thing, Bill," the President turned his back on the group and was leaning back in his chair gazing out of the window. "That only makes it all the more infuriating. It's doing nothing and yet it's screwing us up. Every weirdo organisation and cult ever known and a few more besides are crawling out from under their rocks. And that's in only the few hours since the news leaked. This is going to explode. We've got to react, got to deal with it, NOW!" He turned back to face the meeting, "What have you technical boys got to say, can we blow it up?"

"What? Really Mister President!" one of the civilians said, "you can't seriously be considering such an action?"

"We need to examine every possibility, doctor," the last word was pronounced more heavily than the rest. "We don't need your philosophy, just your expertise. Humour me. Can we blow it up?"

The scientist spoke carefully seeming to weigh each word. "Well that depends on what you mean by *blow it up*. You would need a means of delivering the explosives first of all, and *the ship*, we know, has short-range defensive weapons at least. Perhaps rockets would be fast enough to get past the ray that the ship seems to deploy, it's hard to say. Having overcome that difficulty we still need to establish its mass to make some estimate of the weight of explosives necessary to destroy it, and with the thing floating in the air like that, how do we make such an estimate?"

The scientist fingered his ear. "Perhaps it's full of gas and quite fragile, quite light. On the other hand, perhaps it's armoured and massive, although if that is the case how does it stay up in the air? Whatever, it clearly needs power and controls; on balance yes, I think modern weaponry would have a good chance of damaging it, at least if delivered in sufficient quantity. Its defensive weapons could be saturated by simultaneous multiple attacks and its armour, if it has any, overwhelmed by sheer weight of fire power." He stopped and an empty silence ensued for several seconds.

"What about a thermonuclear device?" Borrhim's deep rumbling voice graced the words with a kind of beauty. "One of our M.I.R.Vs. would that get through, be fast enough, saturate its defences?"

This time the silence was heavy, pregnant with tension. "You know as well as I do Mister Vice President," the scientist made the title sound like an insult, "that nothing can withstand a direct strike with a thermonuclear warhead, you are joking I presume."

Secretary of State Clarke slapped the table with his hand, "Just answer the questions doctor, please."

The scientist started at Clarke's action, "Its defences seem to be very short range and even if activated in time to prevent surface detonations, the fusion reactions would be quite close enough to include the vessel in the fireball. The multiple warheads would obviously improve the chances of penetration. It would undoubtedly be completely destroyed . . . and much of the surrounding countryside along with it . . . you can't be serious?" The man's voice had risen almost to a shout.

"Take it easy, just examining all the angles that's all." Borrhim's tone was placating, friendly.

At that moment an aide came into the room, "The President of the Italian Republic is on the phone, sir."

"I'll take it here, on the open speaker." President Albero flicked a switch on the console on his desk. "Good afternoon, Signore Moretti, or is it evening there? I am in conference with the chiefs of-staff and have the phone open. What can I do for you?"

The clear, cultured voice sounded close over the speaker. "*Buon giorno,* Mister President, I am pleased to speak to your meeting on this matter. The situation here has deteriorated further in the last few hours and my position and that of the government is becoming untenable. Ever since it has become open knowledge that there is an alien presence over Italy and that there never was a N.A.T.O. exercise, the credibility of my government is almost zero. I can no longer protect the role of the United States in this matter. I am forced to make a public statement later today, and unfortunately I will have to admit to the military intervention by your forces in Italian airspace without full parliamentary approval from Rome."

"Now hold on there. There's bound to be some alternative open to us. We need to confer further on this matter," President Albero was sounding agitated.

"I am truly sorry, Robert but the matter is out of my hands now. There is only one further thing that I have to say. I need your absolute assurance that nuclear weapons were never deployed in Italian airspace and never will be." Despite his use of Albero's first name the Italian's tone was decidedly formal.

"You have my unreserved guarantee on that, Mister President. The United States has the closest regard for her European allies and every respect for Italy's non-nuclear policies in particular. We would never consider such a possibility. Please reconsider your plans. Do we not have time to try to work something out?"

"Goodbye, Mister President." The line went dead.

"See! See, what did I tell you, this God-damn thing is screwing us. God knows what will happen now that this has gotten out. This administration will be dog meat." President Albero banged the desk with his fist. The others remained silent. "Oh, get on with it." His tone was irritable in the extreme.

"Do we know its origin? Perhaps it's from outer space, perhaps there are more of them, more of these ships just waiting to come in?" It was one of the army chiefs present. "We can't know that it is alone."

"We have thought about that," the by now quite unsettled scientist spoke with a nervous catch in his voice, "it is our considered opinion that *the ship*, as you call it, did not come from outside the atmosphere. There were no radar sightings, no radio traces, and no interruption to our satellite monitoring systems. The ground damage certainly could be interpreted as a massive impact crater, but the seismic reports don't match, they are too light. A more attractive hypothesis is an extraction from beneath the surface. The geophysical characteristics of the crater give that conclusion a ninety percent probability."

"You mean it comes from deep under the earth?" The army officer continued eagerly.

"No. Not in the sense you mean. It may, however have been, in some way dormant, sleeping if you like under the earth's surface and something activated and continues to activate it if our latest observations are accurate."

"Explain that please, doctor, if you will." Borrhim's excessive emphasis on the 'if you will' clearly irritated the scientist even further.

"Well unless the device had some remote or automatic timing device, it would not have become active and would have remained dormant."

"Doctor," Borrhim's tone was menacing, "explain, if you will, what you mean by 'continuing to activate it'." The Vice President's eyes looked murder at the scientist.

With some difficulty the man steadied his voice and with clear precision enunciated as if to a student class, "*The ship* is currently absorbing energy from its immediate environment in such quantities and at such speed that an approximately circular area with a radius of well over one kilometre is below zero degrees Celsius despite an ambient temperature of near thirty-five degrees." He stood quite still.

"Whaaat?" several said together. Utter astonishment was on every face.

"How long has it been doing this?" Borrhim's tone was censorial, "Why were we not informed of this sooner? This could change everything, time may now be of the essence." His voice was rising.

"Ah, well you see, we have only received this update in the last two hours and no accurate measurements have yet been made, at least as far as we know." The scientist was speaking rapidly, quite unhanded, "We are very short of hard data . . ."

"AS FAR AS YOU KNOW?" Borrhim's face was purple.

"Let me get this straight, doctor" It was the navy Chief-of-Staff cutting across and speaking rather over-loudly, "You are confident of the effect of massive fire power upon this *ship*? That a diversified simultaneous attack would succeed in penetrating its defences, and a thermonuclear detonation would surely kill it?"

"All the information available to us suggests a very short range defensive capability." The first scientist conferred briefly with the other, obviously glad of the respite, "and we have reason to believe from detailed analyses of the various film records that its weapon may not be rapid response. A type of induced reaction perhaps. Rockets may indeed be too quick for it, especially if delivered in rapid succession."

"Thank you doctor." The admiral sat back in his seat with a knowing glance at his colleagues.

"There can be no question, surely, of attacking this *ship.*"

Both scientists were on their feet, "We must take time to study, to communicate . . ." Borrhim's wave of impatience stopped them in midstream.

"Are we fully deployed in the area, Bill?" Borrhim's question was directed at Siemens.

"Yes. We've been on maximum alert for two days. The *Fer-de-Lance* should be on station by now." The last sentence was pronounced a little more carefully than the rest.

General Filshill spoke. "The *Fer-de-Lance*? What's she doing in the Med.?"

"That's all for now gentlemen." Albero's voice interrupted, staring at Siemens. "Navy chiefs remain, all others, thank you for attending." The dismissal was couched in a tone, which brooked no appeal. "Bill, you and General Filshill, please remain behind as well."

When the reduced conference had re-seated itself, the President signalled to his second in command.

Borrhim was clearly angry and addressed Siemens gruffly, "Jeez what made you do that Bill? You should know better than that. We've enough problems without all these do-gooders knowing that we've placed a nuclear missile submarine in the area."

"I'm sorry Arnold, I wasn't briefed. I presumed the meeting was square." General Filshill smirked at Siemens' discomfiture.

"Okay, okay boys, don't bicker. It's all history now. Those *Eye-Ties* will blow us out of the water in a few hours anyway." President Albero's tone became conspiratorial. "Listen to this, it's part of a tape of a conversation I had with the British Prime Minister in the early hours of this morning." He indicated the console and Clarke flicked a switch.

". . . .as I was saying, whilst we appreciate the delicacy of the diplomacy, we fully understand the hard reality and we would fully support a military solution. The Italians won't like it of course, but the greater need must take precedence over the local issue." The female voice was clipped and cultured with a slightly ingratiating tone.

Albero's tenor cut in. "Do I take it that I can count on upfront support from the British Government, clear and unequivocal? I need to know for certain."

The female voice was even more ingratiating in tone, "Indubitably Robert. You can count on me. Europe needs strong leadership and we can provide it with strong action at this time."

There was a click as Clarke switched off the speaker at the console.

"Well? What do you think of that then? We wouldn't be isolated politically, wouldn't appear to be acting arbitrarily. With the British openly supporting us and with the . . . *the ship* destroyed, we could come up smelling of roses, be the heroes." President Albero cast his gaze around the meeting. "That clinched it for me even if that God-damn frost business hadn't come up."

"Excuse me, sir," General Filshill spoke with a deferential air, "but am I to presume that you are contemplating a nuclear strike against this ship from the *Fer-de-Lance*. A nuclear strike in Italian airspace?" A faint note of incredulity had crept into his tone.

President Albero leant back in his chair, fingers making a bridge. "Just consider the reality George." Filshill noted the use of his first name, "this thing has shown up from nowhere and in two days has paralysed a big chunk of Europe, completely undermined the military situation in the most important military sector in the world. It massively disrupted communications, and destroyed without provocation or warning, several aircraft and their crew. It has destabilised the money markets in Europe and is already having similar effects on the other money markets of the world. In short it's poison. And now we know it's growing, getting stronger. We don't need it, in fact we need it like a hole in the head. Yet what are we to do? Talk to it, ask it to go away, please? Pretty please? It doesn't even move. It could be there for weeks, months. Its very presence would soon completely undermine our way of life. God knows what the political and social consequences might be even if all it did was only hang in the sky."

He paused for effect, "We have no option but to take immediate action and since there is no way of knowing its physical capabilities, or its strength, we must act with the maximum force at our disposal."

Filshill said, "Nuke it?"

"Not to put too fine a point on it, yes," the President smiled grimly.

"The plan is this George," Borrhim was wiping the sweat from his ample neck with a pure white handkerchief, "we will launch a M.I.R.V. from the *Fer-de-Lance* with every warhead targeted on *the* thing, the *ship*. Nothing could withstand such a blow, it will simply be vaporised. Okay, the Italian environment will suffer some damage and casualties will be inevitable but there is no other way. The situation will only get worse the more we delay. The difficult bits will be keeping everything secret till the launch and mopping up afterwards."

"That's where you come in, General," the President was now issuing an order, "it is your task to evacuate all American personnel from the blast area without arousing suspicion. We must maintain absolute secrecy. There is no way of knowing *the ship's* ability to monitor our communications, always assuming that it understands them, but take no risks whatever. And last but not least, you will take the brunt of the political reaction afterwards. We will do what we can to defuse the situation after the destruction of *the ship* but I intend to present the motives for our attack as military in nature. Have I made myself clear?"

"Very clear, sir," Filshill had a sinking feeling in his heart. *Why the hell did he always have to do Siemens' dirty work?*

"Nice meeting you General, good luck and good day." The President's dismissal certainly left no doubt about who was in command. As the Secretary of State escorted him to the door of the Oval Office, the conversation was already intense between Field Marshall Siemens and Vice President Borrhim. He had been made the fall guy and the knowledge made it no easier to bear the twisting hurt in his gut.

He got very drunk on the plane back to Europe.

CHAPTER 16

From the balcony Kate could see the approaches to the village clearly and had learned to recognise the assorted vehicles, cars, Jeeps, and trucks which came and went with increasing frequency. The upsurge in activity in the village disturbed her. There were many more troops now, sealing off the roads and patrolling on the hillsides with dogs. It had been two days since the helicopter had taken away the American Generals or whatever they had styled themselves and she didn't like it. There had been no jets since then either. No air activity at all except far away to the south and sometimes she could hear engines over the hill to the west. What were they up to? It was strange that she hadn't seen an American soldier since yesterday. Perhaps they were leaving it all to the Italians, but that didn't seem likely. The Americans never left anything important to the Italians, or anyone else for that matter. They were up to something that much was clear.

It had taken all of her inner strength to weather the psychological blow she felt when the expected return to the mountain had not materialised. Yet it had been a turning point, a fierce tempering of her spirit. Never again would she show her innermost feelings, her fears. All her efforts to get an explanation for her disappointment at being left behind by the Generals had been politely brushed aside. Every ploy she had thought up to get an expedition mounted to find Cole, had been calmly and politely ignored. But in her heart she knew that her demands had really been for show. She had changed, had grown in her belief in herself, and in her inner knowledge. Above all she knew he was alive.

She had been sleeping well. The dream had changed and was no longer terrifying. The big bird had gone and huge, friendly, creatures from the hole in the sky cared for Cole in deep, soft, cool, healing snow. She felt less worried about him now, maybe she had been mistaken, perhaps he was just lost after all. It was all so mixed up, confusing, but no longer frightening. Still, for her own peace of mind, she would like to discuss it with that American psychiatrist, the one who had interviewed her after the soldiers brought her down from the mountain. She felt he had understood her more than the others. He had been kind and patient with her and she already felt a strong empathy between them. Perhaps he would help her back up the mountain.

The television was full of it now; mysterious object from outer space, bug-eyed monsters, the lot. Air, rail, and road travel were being badly disrupted. For reasons she couldn't really understand, there was an increase in industrial disputes, and strikes were threatened all across industry. Movement in the Abruzzi and surrounding areas was completely controlled. There was no denying that the government had acted with great speed, almost as if they had been prepared for such an eventuality. She wished that Cole had agreed to buy a television of their own, instead of insisting that it was simply bringing a mind control mechanism into their home, so that she could watch the reports by herself. It was very stressful to see the fuzzy, long range, camera shots of the object which haunted her in the presence of the neighbours who gathered to watch the latest news in one house or another.

The government was having increased problems with civil disorder and other parts of Europe were beginning to react as well. Britain had called for positive action, *What the hell did that mean*? Queer religious cults were springing up all over America and Asia. It was just silly, there was nothing to fear from it if they only let it alone, gave it time to release Cole. She shook her head trying to block out the reverie, bring herself back to the unpleasant reality of her lost husband, her feelings of loneliness and isolation.

The doorbell chimed and when she looked over the balcony railing she didn't recognise the strange man standing there. She turned, entered the house through the balcony door, walked down the hall and hurriedly descended the stairs. It was the American psychiatrist. She stood for a long moment, quite taken by surprise.

Eventually he spoke in his calm voice, "Hello Kate, Doctor Jim Crawford, from the army base, have you forgotten me already?" His voice had a quizzical quality and he extended his hand in greeting.

"Yes, yes of course, I'm, I'm sorry, it's just that I was thinking about you a few moments ago," as she returned his firm handshake, "please come in. Can I offer you anything? Something to drink; wine, whisky, or perhaps you would prefer coffee?"

"Coffee would do splendidly," he said fanning himself with a sheaf of papers. He was sweating in the heat. He loosened his tie a little and unbuttoned the first button of his shirt collar, "Do you mind? It's so hot at this time of the year."

In the village situation where everyone wore the minimum of clothing and often rather tattered at that, his formality seemed mildly incongruous to Kate.

"Please do," she said, "a*rmy protocol I suppose*," she thought.

In a short time they were sitting in the cool dim of the lounge, deep in animated conversation. "It's just that I felt I had to have one more chat with you before I left, see how you were keeping. It was obviously a harrowing experience for you, your husband disappearing in such an unfortunate way." His manner made her feel relaxed, at ease with the subject.

"Leaving? You are leaving too? All the Americans seem to be leaving? Why?"

He smiled, "Astute observation on your part. I'm not supposed to discuss it but yes, we have all been recalled. Leaving this business to the locals. But, please, I didn't come to discuss my problems. Tell me more in your own words about your experiences on the ridge, before and afterwards. As I think you know, I have a professional interest in these things. It's my speciality."

She smiled, "Huh, don't give me that. You think I'm nuts like all the rest."

"Not at all, you would be surprised at the body of knowledge surrounding psychic phenomena, especially in moments of great stress like in battle. It is not all that uncommon for individuals to have accurate visions of events and situations when they are far from the locus of the event, or well before the actual fact. If we can learn to understand and to control or even to simply observe these events objectively, we might be able to put the knowledge to good use. Yours is a good case in point. Your awareness of the object over the hill, by the way, did you know they are calling it *the ship*?"

She nodded.

" . . . is much deeper than simple observation can explain. Much of what you claim can only be explained by para-normal mechanisms." His manner was almost that of a schoolmaster, authoritative yet caring, teaching as well as listening.

"Are you telling me that you believe that Cole is alive – alive inside that thing. That you believe me?" She was guarded.

"No, I am not saying that. I cannot judge the reality but I can say that I know that you are not lying, and are telling the truth, your truth. I am saying that there may be more to this than meets the eye. I do not know how much more but I have to keep an open mind."

"Oh, I see," her disappointment was obvious. "Very well get out your notebook, that's what you're going to do isn't it?"

"Yes," he smiled sheepishly.

They spoke for some time, around and around, often going over the same ground several times, often discussing some point or other in painstaking detail. But she didn't mind, it helped to talk about it with someone who seemed genuinely interested.

Suddenly he said, "What? What did you say? Giants taking care of your husband in the snow? Did you say snow? That's an odd image, don't you think? It's very hot where *the ship* is, just as hot as here. What made you think of snow?"

"Yes, I'm sure of it. It is snow all right, cool and white. I don't know what it means, I suppose I've never thought that much about that part of the dream before, but I'm sure. It's bright or sunny but very cold where they are." She realised that he was reacting strongly, becoming deep in thought.

"So these giant creatures are your husband's keepers?" he was speaking slowly and carefully, making every word seem important.

"No, no I don't think they are his keepers, that's the awkward part, they seem to be more like his slaves, subservient to him in some fundamental sense." Her eyes were glazed now, unfocussed, as she looked with her mind's eye at what he could not see.

"Can you see them clearly?" he spoke very softly as if trying not to disturb her inner seeking.

"No. They are in something which makes it difficult to see, at least for me, they are huge though and immensely strong. I think they are sleeping. Sounds silly, does it not?"

"No, it's my business to treat everything seriously, no matter how silly it might sound," he said, matter-of-factly. "I expect to be posted to Rome shortly, perhaps if I give you my address there, you will come and see me when this is all over and you are feeling better. I would like to use your experience in my research." He pulled a page from his notebook and scribbled on it, leaving it on the table as he stood up.

He looked at his watch, excused himself and as he left, carefully putting his notebook into one of the many pouches in his trousers, said, "There may be a lot of military activity here soon, I am not party to the plans of Generals, but there is a lot going on. It might be a good idea if you took a vacation, got away for a while, went back to Scotland for a holiday."

"Thanks for the concern," she said, inwardly pleased at his remembering her homeland was not England, "but I am quite sure that this is where I should be."

He paused for a long moment looking into her eyes, then he gently took both of her hands in his and kissed her lightly on the cheek. "Take care," he whispered and turning quickly opened the door, walked briskly down the steep street, and out of sight. He didn't turn around or glance back.

A little later she watched from the balcony as he climbed into the foremost vehicle of a small convoy at the front of the square, green shuttered house and soon they had driven off down the winding dusty road.

"*What a nice man,*" she thought, unconsciously touching her cheek, "*so simpatico, it's a pity there are not more like him.*" She felt saddened by his departure and stood a long time gazing across the valley.

A strong sense of foreboding grew in her and she turned to look up at the crest of the hill behind the village, northward towards *the ship* and a feeling of chill invaded her body despite the hot sun.

"Cole?"

A great, black rent began to open up in the sky above the mountain behind the house, ripping an ever greater hole till it was above her and the sun went out. A cool wind sprang up. The colour drained from the countryside almost as if nature herself had become afraid. The hillside became quiet, still, waiting. No bird sang. Even the cicadas were stilled.

She became aware of the screams, the shouts of warning. All over the village people were running, calling for their children, their husbands, and their wives. Terrified people and silent animals.

Calmly she returned her gaze to the sky. She could recognise it now, it was *the ship*. Impossibly huge, seeming to be quite close, low above the village. But it was impossible to tell. There were no marks, no seams, no lines, or projections. Just the smooth, dull glassy blackness or was it green?

How fast was it moving? Again it was impossible to tell. Silently, smoothly, irresistibly it moved across the sky, across the sun. Soon there were no sounds even from the villagers. All was unnaturally dark and motionless while it moved above.

"Cole?" she whispered. She was still, like a phantom listening in the dark, but nothing answered her faint call. Only the soughing of the unseasonably cool wind gave any hint of hearing.

At last the sun returned, light and colour came flooding back to the hill, to the village. The blackness receded west, still filling the sky. Voices began to be heard, tentative heads seen in the doorways, scuttling movements as life returned to the narrow streets.

She turned and went indoors while the great black object still filled much of the western sky. In the bedroom she began to lift little things, laying them first in one spot and then another, distractedly. She wondered if Jim Crawford had been afraid of the great, black object. If he had truly believed her then he would have remained calm knowing that there was nothing to be afraid of.

Suddenly as if spontaneously incandescing, the room was filled with a searing, blinding light. So bright that she could see no details at all. There was no sound, no motion, only the light transfixing her.

CHAPTER 17

It was just like lying in a warm, soft bed in a sunny room after an illness, idly staring at the ceiling, and letting time drift past as his body healed itself. Well, but not strong, the illness conquered but the aftermath still being felt. The giants were awake now, alert, communing with him, part of him. They seemed to be many and yet one. He had stopped trying to analyse them now, they defeated his ability to rationalise. There didn't seem to be the words to describe them. He no longer liked to think of them as giants, it didn't fit. Yet he had no better word.

His body was whole but he was not yet its master. The giants told him so, just as the doctor would admonish him, tell him to take it easy, rest for awhile, let his strength return. But he was impatient to walk again, to get out of bed and into the sun, into the world. Oh, the doctor didn't know everything, the giants were too cautious. He would be all right.

It was time to do something, time to start his great task and awaken the world but he felt wobbly, his body not quite responding. "Relax, just relax, take it easy, it's just a matter of concentrating." *Was he speaking to himself or were the giants communicating?*

He let his awareness turn outward and saw the beauty of the place again, dallied in it. The forested hills were in full leaf and the sun dappled ridge after ridge as they marched away to the heat-misted horizon. All was quiet and tranquil, "Just as it should be when one has been ill."

The gentle stretching of his muscles felt good, it stimulated the nerves, tingling, invigorating; he moved. Oh, it was good to move. It had been so long, *how long?* He couldn't say. Time was different now, both longer and shorter, like the distorting mirrors in a fun house. He stretched, extending his cramped muscles, aware of each in turn, feeling the lifeblood coursing, hearing the giants sing. Their song was low and quiet, a basso chord dying and dying in a great cathedral.

Did the masters of steam listen to the sounds of their great engines with such pleasure? Did they hear the hiss and sigh of the pistons and valves as a song? He remembered long ago on the river Clyde when his father would take him down to the engine rooms of the paddle steamers where the smooth, oiled motion of great pistons and wheels held him entranced in the clouds of soft steam. Sighing and sobbing like living colossi they had called to him and spoken of power.

There was an alto now and another, the choir was building slowly. Oh, the music! The giants were calling now and they too spoke of power but power of a different magnitude. They spoke of an immense and terrifying might. He trembled. When his strength returns he would make them sing, direct them as one, coordinate their song and help them vault the universe with the sound of their power.

What was that? Feathery touches brushed his skin like cobwebs in the attic of an old house, impossibly light yet felt. Again, and again, more cobwebs, more touches. Now he could hear them, distant muffled voices in the back alleys of his mind on the very edge of hearing. They were shouting! An explosion of radio transmissions, deafening now that he listened to them. An avalanche of radar cobwebs showered him from the spider dens all around.

Intense activity burgeoned in the hills. He listened, tuning his mind to the mechanical voices.

"It got bigger, are you deaf? No shit, it got bigger! Just like that, it fucking got bigger, it stretched. Oh Jesus, I don't like this. Things like that aren't supposed to happen."

Whoever was speaking was frightened and alarmed, communicating an incipient terror with the tone of his voice.

"Time to communicate," he thought, *"no sense in letting them panic, get the wrong impression before I get started."* He opened up his mind, reached out towards them, directed and focused his attention, "Know me!" The radio traffic stopped. There were no communications at all as if they had been stunned into silence. He waited, open to them, receptive, searching for their reply. Nothing happened. Silence. *"What were they up to?"* The radar cobwebs had gone, nearly all had vanished, only faint, slender filaments from far spiders touched him now.

The giants sang of rest, of gathering strength, but he did not have the time, he needed to move, to go to the puny, to explain his will to the little creatures, to save them from themselves. He turned ever so gently towards the southwest. He felt groggy, giddy as if he had stood up for the first time after a long time in bed. In the direction of Naples lay authority. He would go there, show himself and then turn to Rome, begin his mighty task.

If he wasn't careful he might bump into something. Moving was difficult so slow and steady was best. The ruggedly beautiful terrain passed slowly beneath in silence. Nothing stirred, neither in the air nor in the ether.

The giants' song was still a little discordant, out of key, out of synch, and he knew that he was not yet whole. He needed a stimulant or a tonic. *Why had the doctor not given him one?* In time all would be healed, patience and a little care was all that was needed. The giants and his sister, sun, would make him whole.

Something important passed below, important? What could it be? He tried to fix his memory, It called to him, dimly, from out of the long, long past. Kate? *Was it Kate?* From a distant green vortex he felt her call him, tug at his awareness but the cobwebs were stronger now, all around; and out there, far out over the sea to the west, a different spider cast its malicious cobweb towards him.

CHAPTER 18

In the dim red glow of the command centre, it was impossible to know that the submarine was well below the surface of the sea. Everything happened smoothly and efficiently with a minimum of sound. Voices were pitched low, orders and responses crisp, clipped. The many consoles glimmered with little specks of vari-coloured lights and a gentle hum suffused the cool, dry air.

In his cabin Commander Jonas Christensen sat quietly on the edge of his bunk examining with seeming care the many little personal objects scattered around the tiny room. On his desk the silver framed photograph of his wife held his eyes. He spoke to her in his mind, "*Is this what it has come to after all these years of training, of dedication, of sacrifice? That I . . . I should be the bringer, the herald of Armageddon.*" For the first time in his life he was glad that she was dead.

He lifted the simple sheets of white paper on which several columns of alphanumeric were tightly typed. These plain lists of letters and numbers seemed too ordinary to be the last trump. Surely Gabriel would sound a more imaginative tune. They had been received only hours ago, quite unexpectedly, and had not seemed to be very meaningful at first, despite the extremely rare occurrence of an instruction to re-target the missiles. He couldn't decide what had made him look more closely at the codes; the unusual nature of the order itself or his nagging puzzlement at being instructed to enter the western Mediterranean in secret. In any event he had, quite against proper protocol, made an analysis of the destination ciphers. The truth the codes proclaimed had staggered him, central Italy. It was not possible and yet he had done it, had aimed all the destructive might of his deadly wards at the heart of a friendly, non-nuclear nation. Soon he would be on station, waiting. *Waiting for what?* He knew the answer. He had been at sea too long not to recognise the telltale irregularities which distinguished drills from the real thing. Something terrible was going to happen and he knew it.

He rose slowly from the bunk, checked his watch, and walked out of the door feeling as if he carried, Atlas-like, the very world on his back. "Duty officers proceed," he said flatly.

The two officers looked at each other, synchronising their movements, and together inserted their keys in the duplicate locks. The safe opened and Commander Jonas Christensen lifted the sealed, brown envelope from the interior, placed it on the table in front of him, and opened it. "Ready?" he looked at Captain Wilson who stood close beside him. He removed a sheet of white paper and another envelope from the first. "Cipher decode," he spoke clearly, enunciating carefully, "Apple, Hotel, Golf . . ."

It took some thirty seconds to complete the series and silence reigned until Captain Wilson called "Decryption complete, sequence valid."

Commander Christensen moving quickly, took out a fresh sheet from the second envelope, spread it on the table so that Wilson could see, and then seemed to take a long time to read it. Suddenly he straightened. "Battle stations, bring missiles to launch readiness, secure the bridge." His clear voice galvanised the crew, a Klaxon sounded, watertight doors swung closed, and a senior officer started to call out a sequence of action checks.

Christensen was not a young man, looking every year of his service, grey headed and wrinkled; more like an old sea dog than the commander of a nuclear submarine, and in stark contrast to the youthful, fresh-faced Wilson. But the two men knew and respected each other, were friends in a way. Christensen mused, "There's something I don't like about this Brad. Why are we to maintain launch readiness? We haven't had a drill like this for more than eighteen months." He spoke in little more than a whisper.

"It is strange, Jonas, and the western Mediterranean is an unlikely spot for us. Do you think those new targeting ciphers we fed the missiles yesterday are connected with this exercise? I've got a bad feeling about it." Captain Brad Wilson's voice dropped even lower, "I know we're not supposed to do this but I took the trouble to work out the approximate location of the new targets."

"You what?" Christensen's voice was a hiss.

"It's just that I noticed they all had the same suffix and I've never heard of such a thing before. My curiosity got the better of me." He was looking Christensen directly in the eyes. "They are all targeted on central Italy!"

The commander's eyes opened wide "Wha . . .? You must be mistaken, Brad, you've got to be mistaken." He couldn't tell if his mock surprise was fooling anyone.

"No mistake Jonas. I've double checked." Wilson put his hand on Christensen's arm. "Can't we do something to confirm these new targets? Check the orders? There is always the chance of something going wrong. You know as well as I do that you never point loaded guns at friends,"

Jonas Christensen ached to tell the younger officer that he already knew the significance of the codes, had already accepted their authenticity, was in complete agreement with Wilson's sentiment. But that was not why he was here in command of this terrible vessel. He was trained, as all men of war throughout history had been, to obey his orders both in letter and in spirit. He would not, could not countenance the least deviation from duty, for all he knew the lives of many men hung on his actions. Not his to reason why.

"Battle ready!" The officer's words brought a silence. Only the machinery ignored their significance.

Then . . .

"Signal Sir, Immediate attention. Decrypting now," the radio officer was already feeding the enciphered message into the computer.

"You can't be serious Brad, this isn't a game we play. We do as we are ordered, it's not for us to question, or to decide what's right and wrong, to pick and choose our actions. You could be courtmartialled just for talking like that at this time." The commander turned away from the young captain and fixed his attention on the radio officer who pulled a flimsy from the console in front of him and handed it to the commander.

He read, and re-read it, then clasping the paper behind him, paced to and fro while the bridge waited expectantly. He stopped, facing the radio officer, "Send 'Battle readiness confirmed: guidance systems reconfigured: communications fully functional: end message." He turned and looked at Wilson, a long and frank gaze, that seemed to bore into his soul, such was its intensity, and then he turned again to the radio officer. Again he said nothing for many seconds, the intensity of his inner struggle clear for all to see.

"Send: Require confirmation of targeting. Extant ciphers follow. Append the target ciphers; full encryption; at the double."

Captain Wilson visibly relaxed.

Jonas spoke in little more than a whisper, "I hope that I do not regret this Brad. I am putting my life's work, my reputation on the line with this." the commander's tone was not harsh, but rather sad, resigned.

"Red code, red code," it was the radio officer again, "Launch code transmitting."

Wilson literally snatched the flimsy from the operator staring at it with disbelief as he compared it with a sequence from the envelope on the table. "It checks, it's valid. Dear God it's a valid launch." He looked at his watch then at the chronometer on the bulkhead, "Six minutes. . . launch in six minutes." His voice was barely audible in the hum of the machinery.

"Get me Gaeta Base NOW! Open channel. Commander-in-Chief. Combined Forces, General Filshill; AT THE DOUBLE SAILOR." Christensen's voice bellowed in the confined space.

They watched the sweep hand of the chronometer gliding smoothly across the white face. One minute, two minutes passed.

"Filshill here, commander," the static hissed and crackled, "What's happening, why are we in open? Is there an emergency? Be discreet in what you say."

"Commander Jonas Christensen, General, I need immediate confirmation of target ciphers, I fear that there's been a terrible error. Permission to delay initiation urgently requested."

The crackle and hiss of the static rose and fell fluctuating randomly. ". . . . . . ats all you have to know commander. Proceed as . . . irected . . .you understand? Obey . . . orders with . . .estion. Time is running out. Execute your ORDERS!" The last was spoken with a terrible finality, a tone that brooked no denial.

"He can't be serious, there's some terrible mistake." Captain Wilson had his hands spread in appeal. "Make them understand, please Jonas, we must make them understand."

Jonas spoke into the microphone ignoring Wilson's pleas, "Aye, aye, sir. Received and understood, over and out."

Christensen was standing erect as if at attention. He swung round, faced Wilson, and in a moderate voice said, "Launch in two minutes and counting. Proceed Mister Wilson."

Wilson turned stiffly to face the command centre, "Confirm missile readiness on my mark . . . mark, launch confirm on my mark . . .mark."

A seaman's voice somewhere started to count backwards and a clear, almost musical chime started to sound every second.

"*The bells of hell,*" thought Commander Jonas Christensen.

Every man stood still as if rooted to the spot, pale-faced and wide-eyed. They all knew what was happening, they were going to unleash upon the world all the devastation and fury of a multiple-warhead, nuclear missile and there was confusion among their commanding officers about the act.

"God have mercy upon our souls." Captain Wilson's words were echoed by many of the men making the sign of the cross.

"Amen," Commander Christensen's head was bowed.

"Launch Initiated! Hatches clear. Missile clear." Despite the amplified sound from the address system, the words were not distinct amidst the deep shuddering of the ship. "Ignition established, guidance established, TARGET ESTABLISHED." The last words carried a hint of triumph.

"Carry on captain," Commander Christensen saluted Captain Wilson formally, holding his posture till the captain had returned the salute. "Maintain station as directed until further orders," and then he turned and slowly left the command station. He walked slowly, heavily towards his cabin, entered, and closed the door behind him.

"Aye, aye, sir." Captain Wilson couldn't think of anything else to say.

Christensen sat wearily on the bunk bed, flopping like a rag doll, bereft of all will, all energy. He took off his wristwatch, laying it carefully on the little table beside his bed and opened the drawer below the table. Slowly he lifted out the heavy, calibre pistol that he kept there and laid it carefully beside the framed photograph of his wife. He gazed silently and intently at the well-known face, his own distorted by near tears.

On the bridge men waited silently and still. Then, in a flat tone, the syllables carefully enunciated, a sailor turned from his console and said, "Detonation confirmed." Moments later a gunshot rang out. Commander Jonas Christensen had killed himself.

CHAPTER 19

The sea was visible as a faint line away on the horizon to the west, as were the coastal plains and some of the holiday towns, hazy in the distance. Below and all around were the hills and in every elbow and niche a tiny hamlet basked peacefully in the sun. Away to the south a brownish, spreading cloud, the signs of dense development and activity, a city, Naples.

Still they were silent. No effort had been made to respond to his query, his invitation to communicate. The aircraft on the periphery of his vision to the west, had gone, turned away abruptly, hurried out of his sight. *What was going on? Why did they not answer? Were they still afraid?* He turned to the giants, Why? Why? But they were not responding properly although he knew that they heard him. He felt them looking, seeking, feeling for an answer. They had turned their attention in some small way outward, towards the west, the sea.

What was *that to the west; far, far to the west over the Sapphire Sea?* A strange cobweb this one, different, not sweeping over him like the others, but steady, clinging to him, ominously tenacious. Its source? A spider he had not seen before, low on the water over the horizon but rising now, high and fast on its silken, flaming cord. It rose higher and higher, higher than he could imagine. It seemed to rise higher than the very atmosphere to the edge of space. *How could that be?* The spider arched the apex of the parabola in the cold borders of the void and almost paused before it turned down, down towards the earth, its multiple eyes fixed implacably upon him. Faster and faster with manic intent, pouncing at its prey, slavering for the kill.

There were no voices, he suddenly realised, nothing emanated from it. A drone or a remotely controlled probe? *But why?* Distant and tiny as it was he felt troubled by it. Unease stirred in his heart, it seemed menacing.

A giant awoke! Then another and another, calling to each other, hurrying, suddenly urgent, desperately urgent. More and more sprang to wakefulness, to purpose.

What was happening? Why were they so agitated, hurried? He had asked for nothing to warrant this. *Was it the spider that motivated them?*

Transfixed, he watched the spider's belly swell and split apart, saw it spawning its young into the thin, thin stratosphere and felt all its hellish brood cast their cobwebs upon him.

Danger leapt, alarm jangled, fear trembled, and deep dread clawed with a clammy hand into his bowels. All too late he recognised his peril. Death was now assured, violent and terrible.

The giants were singing now in tune, harmoniously, but low, too low, too slow. Something was wrong. Where were the altos? The seraphim needed the cherubim and both needed the master, both needed HIM. NOW! NOW! He must bring them together, marshal their might. He commanded, he beseeched, he implored, and he called them to his baton, screaming in his terror. "NOW! Sing, SING! Oh, Christ, SING!"

A wall, a cliff of sound engulfed him, a *Dies Irae*, to shatter the vaulting span of heaven, to ring in the ears of infinity. The entire chorus of giants gave vent, uttering their secret hymn of power. Reverberant, pulsing, surging energy threatened to unhinge his mind. Intense light, vertigo, nausea, heat, pungent burning, all assailed his overloaded senses.

Was it all too late? He felt a bitter resentment, not at the prospect of his extinction but at the timing. Not now, please not now, death would be too bitter now; life too precious to relinquish now, so much to lose now.

The spider brood pounced and there blossomed a fire as if the very gates of hell swung wide and the legions of perdition spewed and vomited forth. "All hope abandon!" he screamed in agony. Despair and fear and dread swamped his every fibre. Flaccid with terror, he wailed an ululation of surrender. "Stop, oh Christ, sweet Jesus, stop, oh stop."

Something in him snapped, burned through, and changed in the infernal furnace, alloyed into something different, something new. Anger and defiance welled up. "Fuck you," he yelled with maniacal glee, "Fuck you . . . you bastards." With masochistic ecstasy he opened himself to the furnace of fusion, embraced the burning death of matter, the disruption of existence, the very essence of the stars themselves.

The giants roared and roared their mighty *aria* till all of creation echoed with the basso booming such that their song might be heard in the endless reaches of space, across the deep dark, light years from whence they came.

His skin blistered and boiled, flesh seemed to bubble away, exposing the raw intestines, his bowels dripped like candle wax in an oven. Could eyes see, imagination conceive, mind endure such torture?

Still the giants sang and sang, at first in rage and fury, hate filled, venomous and desperate. Then as the balance of the colossal struggle equalised, they sang in defiance with steely control. And finally as the furious fight tipped at last in their favour, they crowed in glory and arrogant triumph. Oh, how arrogant!

Their ultimate chord seemed to hang in the pale, green void, dying by degrees with almost indistinguishable steps; diminishing in strength, and dropping semi-tone by semi-tone to a barely audible rumble in the far, distant corners of his mind. At last all was quiet, quiet and dark.

And in the dark he knew that He commanded them.

"And in the darkness bind them." he shouted the words and felt the power like a physical sensation. A sensation over-spilling his physical bounds, swamping his mind.. sending his senses reeling, his body convulsing in spasms of delicious pain and sagging release.

The giants rejoiced with him and in him. They were one. At last they were one.

The little creatures had erred, had tried to kill him. They had thought to pit their puny strength against him, strike at his lack of readiness. That was truly a mistake.

He felt emotion building from irritation at first to righteous indignation, then a cold hard anger which turned to poisonous rage, and then finally, blind, irrational fury. As he would swat a wasp that stung, he would show them, demonstrate their folly to them, make them gag with fear, and wish that this had not come to pass. Death was too good for them. Only agony would suffice.

Time was passing, the seconds, *or was it hours?* or just nano-seconds ticked away. He was healing, the green was healing the burns and the fissures, and the scars were fading. Ruptured matter regained its whole. The giants licked their wounds, held their hurt. The giants would recover. He knew instinctively that his uncertainty had been near fatal. Grimly, he re-shaped his mind, hardened his resolve. He would not be unready again.

At last he looked outward, tentatively, fearfully.

The warm Italian sun still shone and all around him the countryside lay fair and fertile. Away on the horizon he could see the glint of the sea, sense its nearness, its freshness. The beauty of it all swept over him, diluting his inward hurt, softening the razor's edge of hate.

The land had not felt the fires of fusion. He was pleased at that, only he could leash the hounds of hell, only he was their master.

It did not occur to him to question the awesome significance of his observation.

Revenge filled his heart. He burned with hate for these fools who thought only of desolation. *Had they no thought for others? Did they not care for their own world, their own future?* As fury cooled he increasingly refined his objectives, realised that undisciplined destruction would prove nothing. It would only shock and numb, producing a catatonia in the nations of the world. *How could he demonstrate his power, punish them and bring them unresistingly under his hand?* He would need to be disciplined, structured. A clear yet contained action was needed. His objective would need a fulcrum, a pivotal action through which his power could be demonstrated to all.

But what, where, when? At least he knew the answer to the last. Soon, it should be very soon, clearly a reply to his attackers, a warning against further stupidity.

Where? The capital city of his attacker? But he had no idea who *they* were. Italy was out, they didn't have nuclear weapons and surely even the most arrogant state would not inflict such damage on its own citizens, or would they? No, not Italy.

America then or Russia, even China, all of these had the capacity. Britain? He almost wished he could convince himself of that one, but the fact was that he hadn't a clue. No, he would have to settle for a less specific target.

An island? Perhaps. Yes, an inhabited island would be perfect. If he were to deliver some of his power to an island, a small island, there would be no mistaking his intent. The deliberate and calculated nature of the action would be evident. This would be a clear signal to all of mankind, not just the politicians. The politicians had already tried to kill him, almost certainly in secret, like so much of what they did. This reply would speak to the world, not just one nation, not just one strata of society.

His *hammer blow* would need to be located where all the world would see, not some distant Pacific atoll, but inhabited and close to the developed nations in the midst of commerce and communications.

The landscape continued to drift steadily past while his mind raced. Madagascar, Sicily, Long Island, Taiwan, the list was endless and yet none appealed to him. All were too big or too remote or in some way unsuited to his needs.

Gibraltar! Of course, it was perfect. Not very big but famous the world over and right in the heart of the developed nations. The entire island was a military base, every square inch developed, and the subject of international dispute to boot. It was ideal. Gibraltar would feel his might, his wrath. The world would watch and wonder, look upon his works and tremble. It fit perfectly. *Why had he not thought of it at once?* He smiled inwardly, satisfied, resolved, his way forward, his pathway to dominance illuminated.

He relaxed his inward struggle and gazed in wonder at the beauty of the Bay of Naples spread below him in a great, sweeping arc. It lay just to the south, the Islands of Ischia and Capri set like jewels on an azure cloth and painted with all the colours of nature's palette. The earth was too beautiful for humankind.

Slightly to the east, the torn, beheaded cone of Vesuvius in all its majesty protruded above the brown fog, above Naples. It seemed to survey with haughty disdain, the sprawling, swarming metropolis spreading like a mouldering fungus along its shoulders and down to the very edge of the life-giving sea. His mood hardened. *No, this was intolerable, it had to stop.* Man had to stop his headlong plunge into the midden.

Nature had done her best, even Vesuvius had played her part, had killed thousands in her time. Yet man had not learned from Pompeii, had not accepted that nature knew better, knew that too much, too many, was always disastrous. *Runaway population guaranteed extinction, couldn't they see that?*

The earth was too fragile for mankind.

CHAPTER 20

President Albero looked unusually tired with red-rimmed eyes and clear signs of lack of sleep. Vice President Borrhim was no better as he slumped in a chair before the President's desk in the Oval Office. He looked not unlike a bag of potatoes badly tied in the middle. His face was puffier than normal and he sweated profusely. Both men drank from large steaming cups of black coffee. Only the slight figure of Secretary of State Clarke seemed fresh, betraying no sign of the night-long session.

"Better bring them in Earl," the President spoke as he buttoned his shirt collar and straightened his tie, "we don't want any of them to miss this. We will need to react quickly to international opinion."

Clarke looked at the wall clock, "I never could fathom why these things are always scheduled for such ungodly hours. 3:00 a.m. for Pete's sake, and I don't *care* if it is afternoon in Europe." His complaining was cut short as he opened the door and ushered the waiting uniforms in. "Please be seated gentlemen."

President Albero waited until the hubbub from moving chairs and folders slapping on the table had subsided, then signalled for silence. "I am sorry gentlemen that not all of you were privy to the decisions which led to the action you are about to witness. I deemed for reasons which I think will become clear later that speed and secrecy were the paramount factors in ensuring military and political success. The action of which I speak will commence very soon and therefore I will make this introduction brief."

There was a quiet murmur of surprise and excitement around the table.

The President paused for a long second and when all attention was focused on him he spoke. "In a few minutes the U.S.S. *Fer-de-Lance*, currently lying in the western Mediterranean will launch a nuclear missile strike against the alien *ship.*" He stopped speaking as the ensuing uproar made it unlikely that anyone would hear him.

"GENTLEMEN, gentlemen, please." Borrhim's deep bellow brought silence.

"As I was saying, this strike is imminent and will be reported live from Naples by General Filshill via the usual satellite link. If you will, gentlemen." Albero indicated the large screen television to the side of the room which Earl Clarke had just switched on. "It was our considered opinion that any delay whatsoever in dealing with this object would have resulted in enormous political risk to all of our endeavours in the world and even threaten the sovereignty of the United States itself." He paused and sipped from the glass in front of him.

"We are convinced of its solitary nature and have taken note of its unwillingness to make clear its peaceful intentions. A demonstration of which we would of course have met with goodwill, despite its earlier hostile behaviour. In addition, the British and Russian governments were consulted in this matter, informally of course, and they have pledged their support for this action." Again he sipped from the glass, betraying his edginess to the more astute among his audience.

"In the event, all further debate and consultation would be cut short by *the ship* commencing further dangerous and potentially hostile activity . . ." he paused for a moment, letting the assembled brass hang on his words, ". . . it lowered the temperature of the surrounding countryside to below zero degrees despite an ambient of above thirty-five degrees and then, without warning or communication of any kind, started to move directly on our bases in Naples and Gaeta."

A gasp of surprise came from several of the assembled officers.

"Any questions at this time? Briefly, please." Borrhim's question was clearly rhetorical as the President had already turned his attention to the clear picture on the television screen.

Everyone else had done the same and no questions were asked.

The coloured image of the great black shape was clearly visible above the distant hills, glinting dully in the sun, and at this distance seemed to be stationary.

General Filshill's voice came through, thin and metallic, "We are fortunate to be transmitting this at all as the telecommunications blackout imposed by *the ship* has only now lifted. The communications disruption was very complete over a radius of some fifteen miles and most troublesome over a further sixty-five. I have to report that *the ship* is now moving slowly but steadily towards the shoreline and in the General direction of Gaeta."

The voice stopped abruptly and the transmission continued in vision only. The group in the Oval Office continued to watch intently in silence, a feeling of tension filled the air.

Earl Clarke's light tenor broke the silence, "Something's gone wrong, there must be a problem. What's keeping them? Why can't we hear anything?"

"Hello! Hello! Are we on the air?" the General's voice could be heard.

"Hello? I am sorry gentlemen, but I was just in urgent communication with Commander Christensen of the U.S.S. *Fer-de-Lance.* We will have a launch in less than two minutes."

Filshill's Gravely voice was strained. Other voices superimposed: technical data, readouts, timing and countdown.

Filshill's voice came in strongly again. "Launch! Missile launched and clear, target acquired, strike in one hundred and twenty seconds."

Every eye fixed on the elongated, strangely glinting like dull glass, shape of *the ship* seemingly hovering above the wooded ridge. The camera zoomed in until *the ship* occupied nearly half of the screen, the hot atmosphere made the image dance and waver.

"Ten seconds, nine . . ." the anonymous technician who spoke could not have known the weight of officialdom which hung on his every syllable, ". . . two, one, detonation!"

The ship became incandescent, a green sun, its light shining with such strength that it completely blotted out the camera image, turning the screen to an incandescent pale green. An impromptu cheer rang through the Oval Office.

The camera lens came back to a more wide angled view, the dazzling light diminished, and the image returned. The fierce light from *the ship* still shone like a false sunrise above the ridge. There was no sound, no thunder, and no fire. just a great green sun hanging in the sky. Something was wrong.

The green incandescence dimmed, became an iridescence, and quite suddenly *the ship* was black again, glinting dully in the natural sunlight.

Silence reigned in the Oval Office.

"Oh my God!" it was Filshill's awestruck voice, metallic over the speaker. "It's still there, it didn't even move. Jesus Christ it didn't even move, it's still there, still there."

The screen went blank.

Bedlam broke out. Everyone speaking at once, arms waving, fists clenched, aides running to and fro, bringing reports, delivering orders, and all the while President. Albero sat slumped in his chair, absently tapping on the desk with his pencil. Then he stood up.

He was completely silent, unmoving. No one seemed to notice for some seconds and then all stopped and turned to face the grim-faced and pale President. He gripped the furled Stars and Stripes flag behind the desk in his right hand.

"Gentlemen," his voice was a hiss, "we have seriously underestimated the strength of this adversary, we have been ill advised." He glared with venom at the two scientists, "We may not have much time to redress the situation. There is no way of knowing how *the ship* will react now. At this time I consider our bases and personnel in the Mediterranean to be at risk, not to mention the civilian population, of course." He drew himself erect. "I propose to initiate immediate communications with Moscow in order to mount a massive and co-ordinated strike which will overwhelm *the ship* before it is too late."

Several of the chiefs-of-staff started to protest. "That is complicated, we will need to re-target, locate all operational units precisely, synchronise launches, calculate yields, evacuate whole areas . . ."

Albero raised his hand and held it aloft until complete silence reigned. "Gentlemen, I expect a full scenario on my desk within twelve hours; all forces available and all possibilities examined. I am sure our Soviet friends will manage it." He turned slightly, "Get the Kremlin on the line, Earl." The President now spoke crisply, clearly, and confidently. A man in command and happy to be there. "Initiate a nation-wide and world-wide maximum alert for all our forces with immediate effect."

The chiefs broke free of their imposed silence,

"Such an action will prejudice our strategic situation," said one.

"It may be impossible to keep sensitive locations secret in such an exercise," said another.

"It would be much better to do this on our own. We have more than enough fire power," yet another.

Albero leapt to his feet and bellowed, "And how do you propose to launch a nuclear strike of such dimensions as to guarantee the destruction of a target which has withstood a direct multiple warhead strike without involving the Russians? Better that they get involved by invitation rather than by interference. Do you suppose that they are going to sit back quietly while we blaze away with ballistic missiles in the heart of Europe?" Albero's tone was almost sneering.

The verbal exchanges continued for some time, the exalted members of the military of the greatest armed power on earth behaving like a rabble of undisciplined renegades. Finally an aide called across the verbal melé, "The British Prime Minister on the phone, sir."

Albero turned towards him, anger still on his lips, "Put her on, but keep that line to Moscow hot."

The female voice was clear. "I know you must be in a pickle right now, Robert. No one could have foreseen such an outcome, but I wanted you to know that Her Majesty's Government is ready and willing to assist. Unfortunately there are none of our Polaris submarines within useful range but I continue to pledge my political support and such conventional arms as you deem appropriate. We must stop this thing right now. Who knows what it will do, where it might go?"

Albero composed himself. "Thank you Marjory, we are reacting with all the speed we can muster. The situation is still unclear but I value your support and I am sure that the British forces on the ground over there will be invaluable. I am awaiting connection with Moscow, right now and hope to mount a joint operation with the Reds." He was speaking rapidly. "I am sorry to be brief but things are moving fast. I really must go, I will keep you informed."

"Of course, Robert, may God be with you. I await your update and in the meantime we are mobilising every available resource that seems appropriate. Good-bye and good luck." The line went dead.

"Field Marshall Siemens, sir." The aide held the phone towards the President.

"I'll take it." He snatched the phone and spoke hurriedly. "What's the news, Bill? What's happening over there, for Christ's sake?"

Siemens sounded panicky. "The thing is making for our bases, straight for them. It's no more than twenty miles away right now. Filshill is trying to get stuff in the air but he doesn't have a chance, he has nothing as big as the yield we've already delivered. What are you planning? The thing will be too near Naples and our other bases for another strike if it keeps moving as it is now. In all probability all we've got here couldn't even scratch it. It's not even hot for Jesus' sake and after the belting we gave it, it's uncanny."

"We're trying to get organised, Bill. No messing about this time. We'll fry it for sure, if possible a joint effort with the Russians. No discussions, just action. We'll worry about the niceties after the event. Local casualties will have to be accepted, there will be no delay on account of evacuation procedures. This is confidential Bill, secret, do I make myself clear?"

Siemens still sounded edgy, "What about Filshill, he's still . . ."

Albero cut in, "Secret, Bill, top secret, do you understand? No prior notice to anyone," he was addressing the field marshall like a recalcitrant child.

"Understood, sir, clearly understood. Top secret, no advance notice." Siemens sounded as if he were standing at attention.

"Wait," Albero read from a note scribbled by the Navy Chief-of-Staff. "Get Filshill to keep the *Fer-de-Lance* on station and missile launch readiness just in case we need some diversionary action."

"Understood, sir. By the way, the Italians are going berserk, I think President Moretti would lynch me if he could. It's a good job in a way that the warheads behaved the way they did. It's easier to keep denying the use of nukes when there was no radiation or blast to speak of."

"That's a point," said Albero, his brow creasing, "were there no casualties at all on the ground?"

"It's difficult to tell for sure at this time, it's still very early," Siemens' voice had lost its panic and was back to its usual cultured level, "but apart from reports of very localised heat injuries and eye damage from the light, I don't think so."

"Good God. Ah well, at least that's one less thing to worry about. We'll keep you posted, Bill, goodbye."

Albero slammed the phone into its cradle. "Where the hell is that Moscow call?" he screamed, "are all you bastards asleep?"

The aide looked as if he might be sick. "It, it's the Italian Prime Minister, SIR," he said holding up the phone.

"Oh for Jesus' sake, that's all I need. Earl, find out what's the problem with Moscow," he snatched the phone from the aide's hand.

"Hello? Signore Moretti? How are you? What can we do for you?" Albero might as well have been inviting the Italian Prime Minister to tea.

"Mister President, I have instructed my ambassador to deliver our note of protest to you in the most formal manner. You will no doubt appreciate the need for form and etiquette in such communications; however, on the telephone I do not feel constrained by such niceties." Moretti's anger could be heard through his carefully enunciated speech. "Your use of missiles in Italian air space is unforgivable, and before you deny the nuclear nature of the missiles, I have already had all that shit from your Mr. Siemens. You have no rights whatsoever in our country and your unwarranted, undeclared, and callous act will surely prejudice forever our future relations. In short Mister President, you are a LIAR!"

Albero didn't appear to turn a hair, "Really Mister President, you must appreciate the international nature of this threat. No one nation can be considered above the welfare of all others. It was and is imperative that this threat to world stability, even world survival, be stopped at all costs."

Moretti's voice rose in anger, "When you explode nuclear bombs over New York, I will listen to you. Goodbye, sir." The line went dead.

"I don't have to put up with that shit from anybody," Albero said to no one in particular and threw the phone onto the desk.

"Moscow, Mister President, the Chairman." The aide seemed glad to deliver the news and proffered a red coloured instrument.

Albero smoothed his hair, "Good afternoon, Josef, please excuse me if I proceed directly to the point, but speed of action is imperative." None of President Albero's irritation was evident in his voice. "Further to our last communication, we have now concluded the action as we discussed and I regret to say that we have not had total success."

The Russian voice replied without an interpreter, "I am now receiving our own agents' reports and it would seem that you understate the case Robert, no?"

Albero's tone did not waver although his face betrayed the gall he felt, "The important fact upon which we must focus is that of the lack of total success, Josef. We deem that a much more concerted effort is required to eliminate the problem and that is why I have called you. Not to put too fine a point on it, are you prepared to undertake a joint operation with our forces?"

There was a brief exchange between a female voice and several male Russian speakers. The interpreter then said, "We have anticipated the possibility of American failure and are already retargeting our resources. What is your anticipated time scale and the degree of support requested?"

Albero visibly relaxed, "We would anticipate that one thousand kilotons from each of us delivered simultaneously by multiple warheads from diverse directions would ensure success. I would stress that this is a minimum delivery. It would be better if we could deliver more. We further believe that the chances of success are heavily time constrained and therefore suggest a zero hour, fifteen to sixteen hours from now."

The interpreter replied after a few moments, "We can be ready much earlier than that, say in five hours. We suggest delivery then."

The flush on Albero's face was a give-away of his embarrassment at the Russian point scoring. "Fifteen hours is better we feel. Do you agree?"

A pause, "Very well, provided there is no further deterioration in the situation such as the object turning east." The interpreter had hardly finished speaking when the Chairman's rich voice said, "Do not misunderstand us Robert, let me speak clearly. We will not permit this craft in our airspace or even near our borders.

We will take unilateral action if it turns east. Please understand that. I hope your people are ready in time." This last was spoken with just a hint of humour. "Goodbye and good luck to us both." There was a click and then silence.

"Jesus, I didn't think about that," it was Borrhim, "of course, they won't let the problem become theirs now. It's too easy for them to blow it away in our backyard or anyone else's for that matter, we would have to go along. Hell, I sure hope they don't get trigger happy and give us time to prepare politically."

President Albero brought the meeting to order with a rap on his desk. "You are all in the picture now. You all know your opposite numbers in Moscow. Get on with it. We'll firm up on the exact delivery time a little later but I want this show on the road in ten hours. I've eaten enough Russian shit for one day without being late against our schedule."

Albero remained standing for a long moment and then said, "I want that bastard fried, fried, do you HEAR?"

The most senior officers of the U.S. armed forces filed silently out of the room.

CHAPTER 21

Ever since Cole's disappearance, normal life in the village had ceased. Kate's usual social contacts had been disrupted, her English classes stopped, and even her dutiful visiting of the elderly interrupted. It had become her habit to keep herself busy with little things about the house, trying to keep her mind calm, objective. She had been in the kitchen when she heard Giannina's scream.

Rushing from the house, she nearly knocked her neighbour over. Giannina, white and shaking, stood in the narrow street pointing frantically to the mountain behind the village. Kate spun around and froze, her eyes wide. There, ever so slowly, the giant black hulk of *the ship* was creeping into view. Kate stood, like Giannina, rooted to the spot, her mouth hanging slightly open as more and more of the sky became obscured by the blackness. It towered into the clear sky making her feel queasy. In the end she had had to help Giannina back to her home where she had immediately fallen on her knees in front of a little shrine to the Madonna and started to mutter incomprehensibly.

She patted the stupefied woman tenderly and returned to her own home, glancing warily upwards. From the balcony she watched, frozen as a statue as the day turned to night, the heat drained from the air, and a deathly stillness descended over all. At its peak the light had been reduced to a wan twilight. "Cole," she had called in a small voice but at no time was a sound heard from the crushing weight above.

Slowly the centre of *the ship* had passed and bit by bit the light and warmth returned as the blackness receded until she could see its full extent hanging in the air against the sun. Movement came back and she started at her unconscious wiping of the tears that ran down her cheeks. Slumping her shoulders, she drew a deep breath and turning from the bizarre sight went indoors and sat on the edge of the bed in the dimness, lost in reverie.

She had no idea of how long she sat there when suddenly the room filled with light. Even through the partly shuttered window the light was blinding. She lifted up her hands, covered her eyes, and still she sensed the light. It had a greenish quality, unearthly, unnatural. She stumbled to the balcony door and out into the dazzling brightness, brighter than the day. The light was in the sky where *the ship* had been. She could see it clearly through her closed eyelids. *The ship* was shining. Shining with ferocious brightness in the sky like a new dawn. But this was no dawn she knew. Her heart was bitter ash. This might be the last dawn. Armageddon, the beginning of the end. She sensed that there was pain here; fear; titanic struggle. She could feel his pain, his terror. He was being attacked, tortured, they were trying to kill him.

The sound, great crashing tidal waves of sound, felt rather than heard, made her reel. The sound of hellish voices, baying, screeching, and bellowing defiance. Then the brilliance began to slacken, imperceptibly at first, and then quickly until it finally dimmed and went out. But the sound still hung in her consciousness, terrible and implacable. Foreboding filled her.

"Why, but why?" Her voice was small, frightened. *They shouldn't have done that,* she thought. This has changed everything. Fear welled in her. *Now there is danger, danger for us all,* the thought hammered at her mind, *terrible danger. Something dreadful is going to happen.*

She opened her eyes and focused on *the ship,* still huge in the sky to the west. It sparkled now rather than glinted, with little shards of clear, green light spilling from its sides and angles, black with green sparks. It showed no signs of damage. It filled her consciousness and she began to tremble, gripping the balustrade rail with clenching fists, eyes wide and fixedly staring. Her breath began to become shallow, catchy, quick with little twitching motions occasionally tugging at her eyelids. She was rooted to the spot, unmoving, while chaos reigned all around.

The vision in her mind seemed to overpower her other senses as strange sights and sounds overlaid reality. She could see him running, running in the snow, running from the snow, shouting out in fear as the towering white cliff avalanched down on him. The great creatures were trying to hold it back, protect him, protect themselves but they seemed overwhelmed by the sheer mass of the white hot snow. White hot, searing and scorching snow, she sensed the contradiction in her dream, the wrongness of everything. It seemed to last forever even though she screamed in her mind for it to stop, desperately seeking escape from the horror, knowing that she needed to regain control of her mind. But she was powerless, impotent in the grip of her inner hysteria.

High-pitched wailing filled the air, screams and shouts from men, women, and children. Animals fleeing, dogs barking, and livestock running amok. Many villagers held their hands over unseeing eyes, moaning in fear and incomprehension. But she neither heard nor saw any of it. Even the Jeep as it roared up the narrow, cobbled street to the door of the house went unnoticed.

Jim Crawford leapt out, looked up to where she stood and called, "Kate,Kate, are you alright? Can you hear me? Answer me."

She remained rooted to the spot.

He ran to the door which opened to his touch, and up the stairs to the balcony. Grabbing a hold of her wrists, he wrenched her hands from the rail, spun her around, and with pain in his face, slapped her soundly on the cheek.

"Kate, Kate, listen to me. Can you hear me? Answer me."

He raised his hand for another strike but she said quietly, "No, no, there's no need." Her eyes were quiet, beginning to brim with tears. She started to sob silently and he took her in his arms, gently holding her to him. Reassuringly he pushed back her hair, cradled her head on his shoulder, and felt the trembling of her body. Her gratitude for her rescue, her release, was plain as she sagged slightly in his arms.

"Easy, take it easy, don't cry. Come inside the house and we'll try to sort all of this out," his voice gentle, steady, authoritative, "Get away from it Kate, come on."

"No." She replied with a still small voice, "I want to be able to see it. It's not finished yet."

"Not finished yet? What do you mean? What do you know?" There was an edge to his voice now, but he continued to hold her, touch her, as she turned back to face the south, to face *the ship*. She felt comforted by his touch.

"I don't know exactly." She didn't turn to face him, didn't even appear to be addressing him directly, always keeping her entire attention directed towards *the ship*. "I just know that there has been a change. Something has gone wrong and there is terrible danger now. Something terrible is going to happen, I can feel it. Cole has been changed now. I am frightened."

He gently tried to turn her to face him, but she resisted, holding onto the rail.

"Why do you feel that?" he asked, "Do you feel personal danger?" His head was close to hers, his voice low and sounding sibilant in her ear.

She said in a distant voice, "Why did they do it? What did they hope to get by attacking him, attacking his friends? They have ruined everything. Didn't they know his friends would protect him?" She turned slowly to face him, looking directly with a discomfiting frankness into his eyes. "You understand, don't you? I know you do. You don't think that I'm crazy?"

He returned her gaze steadily and in a whisper, "I don't think that I am truly objective any longer. I, I want to believe you now and not for very scientific reasons." He felt her unspoken response and knew that it was not a complete rejection.

After along moment she said, "I'm glad you came back."

The commotion below intruded into their private world and both started to look around, Kate calling to some in the street below. "What has happened, who is hurt?" In her anxiety using English and of course getting little response. "I should go down and help them," she said, "but I don't want to leave here. Have many people been injured?" She directed the question to the psychiatrist.

"I can't say, I don't know, it all happened so quickly and I rushed back here to see if you had been hurt. I somehow don't think that there has been much damage done. There is no sign of blast damage but the big fear must be radiation. I am no physicist but a discharge of energy on that scale must bring some risk of unhealthy side effects." He knew he was deliberately fudging the issue in her mind and felt guilty about it. After all she was quite able to deal with such concepts, both intellectually and emotionally. Still that could all wait until a quieter moment.

She came closer to him, instinctively seeking comfort. He drew her to him, conscious of his awareness of her body, soft against his. Her perfume, sweet and heavy in the still, warm, afternoon air was intoxicating. He inhaled deeply and slowly, letting his tension slip away, surrendering to the chemistry of his body; feeling the subtle encouragement of hers. He lowered his head to hers, lips brushing her ear, he started to speak in a low whisper, "Kate . . .?"

"Yes," she replied, quietly but distinctly, "Yes."

She was plucking gently at his lapel, pulling at the material in a distracted way, dry eyed but sorrowful, vulnerable.

He did not know what to say. Silently he reached for her, drawing her close again, burying his face in her fragrant hair, feeling her body respond.

They turned together and went indoors.

The noisy clamour from outside was little heard in the dim interior of the house. Shafts of sunlight slashed the dust-hung shadows and myriad tiny motes swam in the warm coloured light. It was quiet, almost silent. Only the most vague of sounds penetrated from the street, not enough to mask the heavier than normal sound of their breathing. In the hall he halted her slow progress by the gentlest of drawing on the sleeve of her loose dress. She stood quite still in the gloom, a halo of golden light illuminating one shoulder and the side of her face, making her eyelashes and the little fine hair of her skin glow. Again by the gentlest of pressures, he turned her to face him. Her eyes were lowered and lips slightly parted, her breathing seemed to be over-controlled, a little too heavy to be so steady. Her breasts rose and fell with the steady rhythm of her breathing.

He suddenly realised that his own breathing had slowed, his heart pounding. He was taken aback by the awareness of his sexual arousal. He felt her sexuality like a blow.

She called to him, stimulated him, provoked him without so much as moving a muscle. He reached out; hands trembling to feather touch her well-formed and heavy breasts, the nipples swelling, protruding through the fine gossamer material.

She reacted. Eyes raised to his, full lips parted further, the slightest of forward pressure. Her arms hung by her sides, loosely but invitingly.

He cupped her breasts in his hands, kneading them gently, using his thumbs to touch her nipples. Her sexual arousal was clearer now, more demanding. With the practised skill of a mature woman, her fingers unbuttoned his shirt, and pulled it gently apart to expose his chest which she noted distantly was hairless, not like her husband's. She bent her head forward ever so gently, ever so slowly.

He felt her breath on his skin and then with a start her tongue as it played over his skin, dallying on the nipples, teasing the soft tissue.

He pulled her close to him. His hands explored her back and slowly, sensuously, crept down to her buttocks, probing, reaching.

128

She could feel his erection now, strong and hard, urgent. The familiar warm melting sensation grew in her belly. She gradually bent her knees lowering herself and him to the floor. She wanted him, needed him. Needed to feel the strength of his penis, wanted him to penetrate her, thrust himself into her body, make her forget.

As his passion grew she prepared herself, letting the deep sensations grow, encouraging them, feeding them with her mind and body. Her little squirming movements to assist his removal of her clothing became exaggerated, became sexual writhing. She looked and felt pleasure at his nakedness, his unashamed penis, hard, engorged. She spread her legs, raising her buttocks slightly as he lowered himself onto her, into her. She met his deep thrust willingly with vigour. He was a much younger man than her husband and athletically fit.

Their couplings were long and varied, energetic and enthusiastic. His endurance belied his slimness and she responded beyond her normal, quiet manner to his imaginative demands, vocally orgasming repeatedly.

At last he was spent. As she slackened, her body relaxed, becoming flaccid, she drifted up from the deep, dark places within herself. She felt her skin, warm and sticky with his fluids, and began to see again the dim, sun-streaked interior of the house; hear the faint sounds from the street. The air, heavy with the cloying, musk smell of their sex, seemed to echo her body's sated state, chide her, remind her.

She began to cry, quietly and softly.

He, with infinite gentleness, caressed her neck and cheek and said nothing.

Like a whiplash, she stiffened and spun around, out of his arms. Leaping to her feet, she rushed naked onto the balcony, pointing with rigid arm and finger to *the ship*. "Look, LOOK!"

"Wha . . . "? He started to exclaim, hurrying after her out into the sun and turning his startled attention to the great black object.

It looked just the same, unchanged, unmoved. For some seconds there was nothing to note, then it started to change colour, get paler,; more green.

It disappeared! Winked out! A long momentary streak of bright light arched to the west out beyond the mountain to the sea.

Then came the sound. Thunder had never been so cataclysmic. A wall of crashing, rumbling noise as the air, rent and tortured by *the ship's* passing, struggled to fill the vacuum tunnelled in the atmosphere. It was physical in its impact, making them shrink away, open mouthed from its violence.

Eventually the rumbling echoes died away to be replaced by unnatural quiet. Kate's voice seemed out of place, "He's gone. I am afraid of him now. I am afraid for everyone."

Quiet sobs convulsed her bare shoulders as she turned and sagging slightly went into the dim interior of the house, shrugging off his consoling caress. "Please go now. I'm sorry, please go," she said as she turned into the bedroom and closed the door silently behind her.

Jim Crawford, after a few moments of silent, still, waiting, slowly dressed, and left the house, making no sound.

CHAPTER 22

President Albero was awakened from his fitful, dream-filled sleep by an aide shaking him by the shoulder. He was lying on top of the cot in the little room he used as an emergency bedroom next to the Oval Office suite. He had decided to snatch some rest while he could, let the commanders get on with it. He felt wretched, his biological clock rebelling against the European time zone of events. It had seemed an eternity since his last sound sleep, why could he not be left in peace? Even as the thought formed, he knew that he had left firm instructions to waken him if anything unexpected happened.

As he splashed water over his face and head to freshen up, he tried to bring himself up to date with developments, but all the aide would say for certain was that there had been a major change in *the ship's* disposition. He seemed reluctant to say anything more.

Albero barged into the Oval Office proper, slurping noisily from a cup of black filter coffee, his tie and clothing still maladjusted. He gloomily observed the light from a vehicle's headlights as it turned onto the Presidential grounds, scattering sparks on the rain-bespattered window. It was raining heavily, constantly, a miserable night.

"Bring me something to eat," he grumpily instructed a junior military aide while mentally logging the people already present.

Vice President Borrhim and Secretary of State Clarke were there, deep in conversation and several military chiefs-of-staff, strangely quiet, turned to stare, pale faced as he crossed the room.

"Something has gone badly wrong," he thought darkly and addressing the Vice President said, "George, fill me in, what's the . . .?" He looked up at the big clock on the wall and noticed that little more than an hour had passed since he left. "Have the Russians detonated a bomb prematurely?"

"It's moved Robert. Blown all our plans right out of the window. We'll need to re-calculate all the target co-ordinates. The Reds ain't looking so smart now. They want to delay the attack, say they too need more time now." His voice was edgy, strained.

"What do you mean it's moved?" Albero asked, irritated by Borrhim's understatement. "Where to?"

"An hour or so after the strike, it took off like a bat out of hell, seemed to plain disappear from sight. It took us a little time to find it." Borrhim's reply was flat, free of emphasis.

The President interrupted him, "What do you mean took some time to find it? Something that big? Didn't radar keep it under observation, no planes followed it?"

Borrhim looked straight at Albero, "No. It moved too fast. The acceleration it used must have been bordering on the theoretically impossible. It simply vanished from sight without warning."

"Jesus Christ! What the hell shit are you giving me?" Albero's exasperation bordered on outright rage. "Nothing that big can move so fast that we can't keep track of it. Someone has screwed up."

The Secretary of State's voice cut irascibly across that of the President's, "You don't understand, do you? You haven't got it at all. *The ship* crossed the entire western Mediterranean in LESS THAN A SECOND." The last words were spoken loudly and slowly like a schoolmistress instructing a particularly dull child.

Albero blinked. Then, in a quiet voice, "where is it exactly?"

It seemed that every voice in the room spoke in unison, "Gibraltar."

"Gibraltar," he inanely echoed. "Gibraltar?" His mind seemed to have stalled.

"The British Prime Minister is waiting to speak to you." Borrhim's demeanour was little better than the President's." She's been waiting for some minutes, seems to be very agitated."

The unconscious understatement brought a snicker from one of the Generals.

Albero visibly straightened, cast off his mental torpor with the slightest of shrugs, and galvanised the room with his ringing authoritative voice, "I'll talk to her, but connect me with the Chairman right after I have finished speaking to her. Get all the chiefs-of-staff and those God-damned scientists back in here on the double. We need a full briefing."

"Robert," the clipped female voice said over the clear line, "This is a terrible turn of events. We will have to rethink this thing through. There is no way that a nuclear strike can be contemplated over Gibraltar. We need to find another way."

"You bloody hypocritical bitch," thought Albero.

"Our people are suggesting an attempt at communication using computer-based fast switching techniques or something. They say it has a good chance of working. We should give it a try. After all *the ship* didn't retaliate after the attack, it may even have run away. Maybe it's ready to talk. Whatever, I must insist that you take no unilateral action in British territorial airspace. Her Majesty's Government will not countenance such an action. Do I make myself clear?"

"Perfectly," he made no effort to disguise the dryness in his tone, "have you been in touch with the Russians?"

"Yes, I was going to bring that subject up. I need your cooperation there. It is my view that they do not seem to be inclined to change their plans. I fear that they may still consider striking at *the ship* at its new location. I do not need to spell out to you what such an action would mean to international relations. Do you agree? Will you support me in this, make it clear that we stand together in this matter?"

"I have a call in hand to the Chairman and hope to speak to him in the next few minutes. After that I will be in a better position to comment." His tone was even, businesslike.

There was silence for some time. Eventually the woman's voice in carefully measured meter replied, "Do not try anything clever, Robert, there is no room for negotiation in this one. I hope to hear from you within the hour." The phone went dead.

"Who said a week is a long time in politics," he thought, *"an hour is a long time."*

People were filing in, milling around, looking for seats, noisily discussing, and arguing. All were pale-faced and tense.

"Well?" said Borrhim and Clarke in unison. Both had been listening on extension earpieces.

"It's all come down to the Russians," said Albero, "somehow it always does. No point in looking for political support in Europe any more. If we can keep the open participation and support of the Reds then we will be able to live with the political consequences."

"Yes," said Clarke thoughtfully, "I am glad I'm not in the British Parliament right now.

"Call them to order," said Albero brushing aside the proffered bread rolls and coffee from the over-brisk aide. He sat at the head of the long, beautifully polished conference table, beckoning to the others to be seated. A much gold encrusted naval officer placed a slim sheaf of papers in front of him.

"Okay," he said with an effort at lightness," who's going to speak first?"

The naval chief stood up and beckoned to an aide who unfurled a hanging map of Europe on the wall. "Mister President, gentlemen. In front of you is a synthesis of what we know to date. It's not much but our intelligence is improving by the minute. If you will turn your attention to the map, you will note the two large yellow pins. These locate the initial and current location of *the ship*, almost directly over Gibraltar. The smaller blue pins indicate the present position of our submarine strike force and the red pins are our best guess at the Russian positions. Much of our force, which had already approached within maximum range, is now no longer close enough and presumably that is also true of the Russians. The situation is further deteriorated by the need to retarget the missiles. It is my opinion that we should accede to the Russian request to delay our strike."

An army chief said gruffly, "What the hell, why not re-target the I.C.B.M.s, let *the ship* have it from here. It would be much quicker to do that."

Borrhim's bass cut across the General, "We've been through that already. We need absolute accuracy, relatively short range is our only guarantee. If one of our land-based missiles went astray, struck Lisbon or Barcelona," he shook his head, "the consequences are unthinkable. We have no alternative open to us."

The navy chief continued, "It is the majority opinion of the military chiefs-of-staff, that *the ship* moved in the fashion that it did in order to escape further punishment. If we keep a low profile, avoid any action that might seem threatening to it, then it is our belief that we still have time to retarget."

The President addressed the scientists, "What do you think of that? *The ship* seemed to be unharmed by the warheads."

"Seemed to be, yes, but it is inconceivable that it was completely unaffected," replied the first scientist.

The second continued, "It reacted by moving away and that signals some gross effect, albeit not a visible one. We can be reasonably certain that it didn't like what it got. Perhaps it is quite badly damaged and its movement impaired. Why else move to its current location when it clearly has the ability to travel at incredible velocities, to go anywhere; the South Pole, some deserted area, even off the planet, who knows? No, we think that it has been damaged, that it stopped where it did involuntarily." He sat down.

"Hmm," said the President, "at least that's an upbeat thought. I like it. Sounds like pretty solid logic, but we still can't take the least chance. We need to act as fast as possible, destroy it beyond all doubt." Turning again to the navy chief, "When will we be ready?"

"We need to delay the launches at least another ten hours," he started to say but on seeing the Presidential reaction, "or perhaps we might do it in eight. Say eight hours from now; 8:00 a.m. central European time."

"Are we still in synch with the Russians? Have we been able to co-ordinate the new position of the target with them?" Albero was addressing Borrhim.

In a rumbling bass he replied, "Yes, they are of course keeping the thing under as close a surveillance as we are. I believe that we are still in good order and that a co-ordinated strike is still possible if we stick to the revised schedule outlined by the admiral." His puffy face was puffier than usual with the dark rings around his eyes declaring his lack of sleep.

Albero's tone was preoccupied, distant, "I have a bad feeling about this. It doesn't ring true somehow. I can't put my finger on it but I don't like it." He turned to gaze at the map on the wall. "Why has it stopped there? What is so special about that spot? Gibraltar? The Atlantic? Spain, Africa, what?"

Clarke spoke for the first time. "Perhaps all these scientists have got it right, maybe it is damaged, unable to proceed any further or unable to control its movements well enough to risk further flight. Even the English say they think it's damaged."

"Perhaps," said Albero.

An aide leaned forward towards the President, holding out a red telephone handset, "it's the Russian Premier on the line, sir."

Beckoning an aide to his side, Albero, in a brisk tone said, "Good to talk to you, Josef. I will hand over to my interpreter now so that we have no possibility of misunderstandings. Is that to your satisfaction?"

The Chairman's rich, thickly accented English could be heard in the room over the speaker, "Very well, we understand the need for accuracy at this time, proceed."

The interpreter translated as Albero spoke, "I understand that our military personnel are still in accord over the new target co-ordinates and timing. If you are happy with that statement then I would like to move on to the primary purpose for my call?"

A different voice spoke in clear English, with the Russian Premier's voice in the background, "I am happy that the military effort is responding as quickly as possible and that our joint action has not been prejudiced so far. But please allow me to reiterate, we will not accept any approach by the vessel toward our territorial air space. If it does so we will act unilaterally."

Albero replied, "Understood. I believe that you have been in communication with the British and that you may have been less than frank concerning our joint intentions. It is my considered opinion that the situation has not changed materially from its earlier gravity and that we should pursue our original goal in seeking the total destruction of *the ship* as soon as possible. To this end I commend your caution with the Prime Minister and suggest that you keep it that way."

"We have never been easy bedfellows," replied the clear voice, "and that is as true now as ever. Our motives are widely divergent in this matter but our resolve to destroy this *ship* is implacable and such dissembling as is necessary to facilitate our task will be undertaken unhesitatingly. Do not underestimate our resolve Mister President, we will strike at this *ship* decisively wherever it lies, irrespective of sovereign airspace."

"Let us hope that we achieve our aim soon and that there will be no further complications in the next few hours. I suggest that we communicate again in person one hour prior to the attack," Albero's voice was over carefully mannered, so that the interpreter could not mistake the warning tone.

"Very well," it was the Russian Premier in person who spoke, "till one hour before our strike." The connection was broken.

Everyone stared openly at the President as Clarke turned to him and asked, "suppose it moves over U.S. territory?"

"We'll worry about that if it happens," Albero turned to an aide and continued in the same tone, "I thought I asked you to get me something to eat?"

The meeting broke up after some further inconclusive speculating, leaving Albero alone with Clarke and an aide.

The phone rang and the aide, answering it, said, "it's your call to the British Prime Minister, Mister President. Do you want it on the open speaker?"

Albero nodded, laying aside the hamburger roll he was eating.

"Good day, Marjory, I am sorry about the delay but I took the opportunity to seek the views of my advisers prior to returning your call, The news is good. As far as we can tell the Russians have no intentions of striking at *the ship* whilst it is over Gibraltar. The political ramifications are too great even for them. I hope that you are satisfied for the moment at least."

"I am delighted to hear that Robert," the female voice replied, "and I hope that your assessment is a sound one. In the meantime we are taking no chances. I have sought the co-operation of every European head of state in bringing pressure to bear on the Russians. With the exception of the Italians, I think that we have solid support. One further thing, as *the ship* is now in our air space I have taken the liberty of authorising the initiation of trial communications with *the ship*."

Albero blanched, "Whe . . ., when are you going to start these experiments?"

"We should be ready for initial trials in about forty-eight hours."

Albero visibly relaxed, "Ah, well, yes, good luck Marjory. Do keep us posted." He hung up.

Turning to Clarke, "Keep the pressure on. Make sure that the military get it right, we need to get it first time now. There will be no second chances."

"Of course," replied Clarke, but he was addressing Albero's back going into the adjacent bedroom.

CHAPTER 23

Reaching out, beyond the ship, down to the earth's surface, he wondered how far away it was; difficult to tell. He could feel it turning beneath him. The planet moved, rotated on its axis, orbited the sun but he was fixed. Fixed in existence, all other points took reference from him. How long had he been like this? His sister was still high, strong.

They were silent now, the puny. *Were they waiting in catatonic fear, in absolute astonishment at his prowess? Wondering at his silence, his inactivity?* Well they would not wait much longer.

"West is there, there in that direction. That's where Gibraltar is, where my voice will be heard." He thought the words clearly, articulating them in his mind.

He had no idea how much time had passed but he knew he was healed, strong again, in command. The pain, the damage had been to another part of him, to the pool, *the ship*, his friends– the giants. But they had won, controlled the energy, and turned it to their own use. Grown stronger by it.

With the barest hint of will he called to the giants deep within him. Their song was raw beauty to him. As the master engineer of a great ocean liner might pause before deploying the full might of his charge, savouring that moment of peace, the eye of the storm, knowing that his will would unleash the engines' towering strength, so he sipped at the cup of power. Delayed a fraction, sensed the giants anticipation.

"Now!" he commanded.

He gagged with the pain, feeling as if he were being split apart. In his mind he screamed. Things were breaking, bursting, and crushing inside him, the very cells of his body collapsing. His awareness dimmed.

It stopped. The force abated. The pain receded. *The ship* stopped. The giants were still. He shrank. Again he was in the pool, not it in him. The perspectives were fixed again. He was leaking into the green, his blood making a dark, spreading stain. He knew that he was mortally hurt. Important parts of him had been badly damaged. He wanted to breath, to cry out, but there was no mechanism left to him. Again the filaments, leathery, probing, urgent, entered. Sleep crept over him.

His mind idled. Thoughts came and went, randomly at first but gradually more structured. Odd sensations not unpleasant, filled him. He dreamed.

He awakened, became aware again. He was the pool, it in him and he in it, one again. The giants sang a mournful song. They got it wrong. His pitiful body could not take such battering. Even fluid filled, it lacked essential strength. Acceleration was his enemy. The giants sang of gentler ways. They had reacted instantly to his agony but still too slowly to avoid damage. They had danced to an older tune, to a master greater than he; a god, or a demon, of a time before time.

He turned his mind to the exterior. *How to proceed now, how far to go, how long?* He was hurt. He hoped it wasn't far.

It was there! Directly in front of and below him, clearly and easily recognised; Gibraltar, a topaz jewel in an azure sea clinging to the dun-coloured mainland. It made him think of a pendant hanging from the golden collar of the beach. But the motion, the acceleration had lasted only a fraction of a second; he was sure of that, so far so fast. *How could it be possible?* It must have been almost instantaneous. Again he marvelled, stretching to comprehend the power of the giants.

The filaments filled him still, he knew that he needed time, time to heal properly. Let the pool heal him as it healed itself. He knew it would not take long. The delay might suit his purpose anyway, giving them time to focus on him; turn their cameras

140

and microphones in his direction. Give them time to speculate, to wonder, and to fear. Let them rally their crude defences, prepare another sneak attack. He was ready now; saw their treachery, their perfidy.

"*WE are ready,*" he recognised the plurality in his thought, "*Their time has passed and ours is come,*" a sense of unbridled power swept over him.

He drifted in and out of clarity. Hours passed and with deep, boding reds his sister sank in splendour into the black ocean. He slept.

In the night the sister stars shone warmly over him like a well-loved and oft used duvet; comforting and friendly.

His sister sun, awoke him as she rimmed the globe, showering him with her abundant bounty; coddling him as a fat mother enfolds her baby in her flesh, soft and safe, giving strength. He was well, he felt fresh, invigorated, ready. The pale green was clear, no dark stain, no filament to spoil the crystal clarity.

His clarion call rang in the cathedral of the giants. "Awake! Awake and muster to the task." They responded with joy, leaping into sonorous action, seeming eager, eager to begin his great opus. Again all perspective was lost; high and low, great and small, near and far, all seemed the same. The giants were in him, the pool was a part of him, he commanded them all, and he bound them all to his will. The song of power began to build. Chord on chord, voice on voice, and the deep, deep shuddering bass supported a richly woven harmony above. All was well, all was healed, and all was unity.

He looked at the island, lovely in the dawning sun. The voices of men were clamorous now, filling the ether. They shouted in his mind. "*Why was it here?*" they said. "*What did it want?*" The puny were afraid, very afraid. Aircraft were leaving the ground, flying low in the distance. He sensed the warships with their radar cobwebs clinging; their spider broods deep in their bellies, nervous and ready, fidgeting. And high above in the cold borders of the air, eyes watched from afar. There was a sense of urgency, great panic in all that they did. He sensed the greater engines of destruction, far, far away still, toiling towards him. They were gathering their strength.

"Did they think to defeat him?" He laughed in his heart. The giants sang with joy. He rounded to them, holding their attention like a great conductor holds a mighty orchestra teetering on the edge of a long quiet bar, awaiting his signal to unleash, *fortissimo,* the final crescendo. The feeling of immeasurable force awaiting his will tingled deliciously at his senses.

The land below swarmed with people, like a dank fungus clinging to it. He felt no sense of identification with them. They were worse than useless, a malaise actively polluting the planet. Forever betraying, forever untrustworthy, forever self-seeking; mankind had become a self-consuming organism. It was time for surgery.

As he unleashed the first bolt of energy, he felt his skin tingle as if under a hot sun in the village. He halted, only partly seeing the living rock geyser erupt in hideous fury as it was struck.

The village? He suddenly felt uneasy, something was wrong, distorted. A bitter feeling welled, deep inside. *What was wrong in the village?* It had never betrayed him. *Or had it?* He sensed, felt, the betrayal. The ashes of bitterly dashed trust were alum in his mouth.

He knew then that she had turned away from him. Kate, sweet Kate, he remembered her now, so soft and gentle, so understanding. Now so distant, dim, and yet somehow still close at hand, still in his heart. No, this was folly, he could not allow this, he was truly alone now, none might share his Olympian task. Alone he was mighty, in sharing there was weakness. He felt the isolation. Anger flared.

The smoke and debris of the first strike rose in a great column high into the air. He could still hear the last of the terrible sound. His anger focused, became icily directed. With glee he shouted aloud as his energies vomited forth, hurled with demonic fury. Wildly arching, coruscating, writhing, they struck and struck again. Earth and sand, lake and sea boiled and vaporised. The heart rock flowed and spouted, running like brightly illuminated waters in a fountain. In a few instants all life was extinguished but he cast his bolts again and again. Dazzling, flashing pyrotechnics leaping into the multi-coloured clouds of thick smoke and steam that now enveloped the island. Snapping back and forth like fiendish whiplashes, the spewing energy rent the very atoms of the air.

At last he stopped.

Silent and watchful *the ship* hung in the air, the uppermost fog swirling around it. Slowly the atmosphere began to clear. In time the vapours and steam drifted in the strong ocean breeze eastwards over the sea. The heavier dust and gases settled back to earth and formed long, broad, stains in the waters where breakers, multi-coloured and dirty, broke over the shallows where the island use to be.

It took him a moment to identify the sight, comprehend what it was that he saw. ***"Gone. Completely gone?"*** He was shocked, taken aback. How could it be, so little effort, so easy. He had removed something the size of the Rock of Gibraltar from the face of the earth in a few moments. Nothing remained. He felt numbed, distant from the fact, the reality . . . he felt no remorse.

All was silent. No radio voices spoke, but up, up in the cold, cold stratosphere he knew the eyes watched. They had seen it all.

"Away, away!" He thrust the planet from him, fleeing from the sight, from the ugly fruit of his power; suddenly claustrophobic in the poisonous clouds.

Blackness, still and deep, bright with starlight filled his vision. He felt the deep, unyielding cold but was warmed, felt the sharp, brittle, hardness of the place and was comforted. Stunned by the awesome beauty of infinity, its endless purity, unsullied, crystal, limpid, he thought of the pool. He knew he had travelled at mind numbing speeds, endured crushing accelerations but they had got it right, allowed for his frailty. He was whole and unhurt. The giants shouted in joy. Freed from the bounds of stultifying gravity and the thick cloying air, their song seemed even more sonorous.

Yes he would wait here amidst beauty, wait for wisdom, and reflect on his purpose away from their pitiful voices. Let them look upon his work and shudder. He had much to consider, much searching of his soul ahead. He needed to summon all of his courage and determination.

From behind the great, blue-marbled orb that shone above him, his sister sun rose, clearer than he had ever seen her, scorching him with her bounty, blazing a triumphant welcome to her domain. Oh, it was good to be here, here where the pool belonged. He sensed that it had been a very long time since he had been here, so long that it wearied his mind to think of it. He drifted deep, deep inside himself, deep into the pool among and with the giants.

In the cold, light-less vacuum, the great black object was barely visible. The faintest of pale green swirls flickering and dancing over its surface.

CHAPTER 24

No one had slept well that night, Borrhim's pallid flabbiness seemed exaggerated and Albero's neat and formal manner just ever so slightly dishevelled. Only the dark rings around Clarke's eyes gave any hint of his fatigue whilst his voice belied all concern as he almost cheerily greeted the assembled brass in the situation room which had been set up in the White House.

One end of the long table was vacant so that all could see the large television screens positioned on the wall. Each displayed a different picture but in the centre were a couple larger than the rest. The lower screen of the two was split horizontally, the upper half with a clear close up of the British Prime Minister, strained and tired looking, and the lower with a wide-angle view of the cabinet room in London. The other bore an aerial view of Gibraltar with *the ship* seemingly disproportionately large, obviously much closer to the lens.

Albero achieved a measure of silence with a gesture and facing the screens spoke clearly, "Marjory? Can you see and hear me?"

The Prime Minister's eyes focussed into the room. "Yes Robert, we are ready at this end. The pictures from the spy plane are very clear, you can go ahead."

"Marjory, I have requested this somewhat unusual method of discussion as I feel that the situation is now so complex and urgent that there is no room for error or misunderstanding. As you know, we already have an understanding with the Russians over *the ship*. Granted the situation has developed since then into one in which your government is much more sensitive;

but notwithstanding, our best efforts to dissuade the Russians from our earlier agreed policy have failed." He paused.

Two or three seconds passed before the British head of state began to speak. In a slow measured tone she said, "Are you suggesting that the Russians intend to make a nuclear strike against *the ship* in BRITISH AIR SPACE?" The last words were heavily stressed. "You must be mad. Under no circumstances will we permit such an outrage." Her next words were almost drowned out by the outbursts from every member of her cabinet around the table. "This folly must be stopped at once."

"Marjory, Marjory, please think about this," Albero had to raise his voice to be heard. "I understand the difficulty you face but there is no alternative. The Russians cannot be dissuaded and if they strike unilaterally with insufficient fire-power the situation could be degraded beyond all hope of recovery. We MUST cooperate in this, lend all possible assistance. *The ship* must be destroyed NOW."

"Forget it George," the woman's voice was shrill, sharp, losing its usually cultured roundness. "If you go ahead with this, you threaten a much greater disaster than this *ship*. I am warning you, Her Majesty's Government will defend its sovereignty with every means at its disposal." The voice got even harder, "Just in case you don't understand the Queen's English, that means we will retaliate!"

You could have heard a pin drop. Silence gripped both scenes. The faces in London lit by the evening sun staring warmly from the screens into the pallid lamp lit room in Washington seemed to reinforce the sense of conflict.

"Madam," Borrhim's deep tones were even and calm, "Surely there is some room for discussion, some flexibility in the situation. If I may remind you, it was not so long ago that we were jointly party to a similar course of action over Italy. Then, as now, the greater need overshadowed the lesser, the need of all must override that of the few. I am sure that the international community would assist with damage repairs after the event."

The woman's face filled the upper half of the screen as she leant closer to the camera lens, her voice dropping lower, becoming more intimate and menacing. "If I have to target Washington to stop this, then I shall do so," she paused, then, "Do I make myself clear?"

"Please, please, this type of threat and counter-threat will get us nowhere," Albero was waving his arms in a placatory fashion. "What are you suggesting that we do, attack the Russians, ask *the ship* to go away? Look at it. One thing is for sure, its not going to go awa . . .a . . .ay," his voice trailed off.

Every eye focussed on the lower television screen. The lack of sound heightened the image, made more graphic at the sight of the land spouting up as the first energy bolt struck.

Bedlam broke loose, voices clamoured, "It has fired on Gibraltar. What the hell is it doing? What is it using? Its like lightning or something."

The clamour grew for a few moments then waned to a hush as they peered at the glowing crater from which a huge column of thick boiling gas and smoke arose. No one seemed to be able to speak. The seconds ticked by in silence. *The ship* appeared to be jet black, menacing in its size and stillness far above the land.

"Oh! dear, God, No . . . no," the Prime Minister's voice was the only sound that greeted the next bolt of energy. Eyes wide, mouths agape, they watched in stunned silence as Gibraltar ceased to be. The bright, coloured TV image remained clear and steady. The rising clouds of virulently coloured smoke, filled with inner flashings and flickerings gradually obscured the isthmus and eventually partially hid even *the ship* high in the sky.

No one spoke. For a long time they gazed as the scene slowly cleared and the utter destruction became visible. It was no longer possible to identify the scene with the previous view of the isthmus. Roiling swirls of thick colour and muck, steaming and smoking like some colossal witch's brew above the stained, soiled, sea was all that was to be seen.

The ship, which had been completely immobile and utterly silent throughout, suddenly vanished with a flash of lightning. A few seconds later the TV image began to rock and shake as the shock waves of its passing struck the camera aircraft high above the now non-existent island.

Those who had been standing, slowly and silently sat down; then, white faced and drawn, with a haunted look in their eyes, the men of power gazed at each other not knowing what to say.

The President placed his hands palms down on the table and slowly lowered his head until his forehead touched the polished wood. In a small voice he said, "Sweet Jesus what are we going to do?"

No one answered.

CHAPTER 25

Idly he pushed the planet further from him. It somehow disturbed his tranquillity, rippled his calm. Absently he gazed as it diminished in size, smoothly and steadily till it was no bigger than a golf ball, shining brightly as if lit from within. The sister stars were even more glorious now, feeling thick in their abundance. He wanted to scoop them up like diamonds from a hidden dragon's lair and cast them again and again across the inky black. They drew him, pulled at his consciousness, seemed part of him.

The big, dull, leaden planets seemed so useless in comparison. Much closer than the stars, closer even than his sister sun, they crowded his view. Like mud stirred up by the propellers of a boat in a clear river; they somehow sullied the universal beauty. *Why did they have to interfere with him? What had he to do with such ugliness? Just forget it, leave it alone, let them die.*

He wallowed in the comfort. Luxuriated in the warm cosseting deep of space. *What would the giants tell him? What strength and power might they impart?* Now that the clamour from that foul place was distant, faint; he could seek oneness, wholeness. He had eternity to do it in.

They spoke gently, in low reverberant tones, never hurried, never discordant, always supporting, always obedient. But understanding was difficult, just out of reach. Comprehension would seem to loom and then recede. It was as if they understood him but he was unable to encompass them. As if they had a quality, a dimension that exceeded his own.

Time passed as he watched, detached, a turgid river flow beneath a bridge. It was no longer a matter of great significance to him and with the passing came a slow competence, a shallow control of the pool. Like a schoolboy might produce clever effects on a computer screen by tapping the keys and yet have not the faintest concept of the physics which he invoked, so he too gained a more detailed response from the giants. With will alone he would modify the pool, change its shape, its position, its colour, even its mass. Crude and inadequate as he was compared with the masters of long long ago, the giants never allowed him to overstep his competence. They seemed somehow to govern his commands and his will, such that he did not damage himself. He knew their patience was endless, that they had already waited an eternity. Surely he could wait for their gift, a gift beyond riches; the gift of power. He felt giddy and trembled with the feelings that swept over him.

The ship flashed and sparkled, scintillating with green fire in the stygian blackness, such beauty and none to see it.

In time, he turned his attention to the bright golf ball far away. *What called him? What disturbed the slow, absorbing river of knowledge? After so many aeons had passed what possible interest could lie there?* He reached out. *What was it?* A deep and distant force welled in his mind. Warm, sunny, friendly, reaching to him from the long ago of his past, from another time when he was another being.

Time collapsed around him like a house of cards. With a suddenness which caught him by surprise, a different universe overlaid that of the pool. A coarse, animal feeling invaded the purity of his isolation, sullied the crystal vacuum in which he dwelt. The universe of mankind that of the stupid, doltish louts who could only procreate and squabble, forced its way into his mind. The brutish, squalid world of the puny, the world of those too stupid to manage their own affairs. He recoiled.

Only a few days had passed, so much in such a short time. *Was it possible? He had amassed so much in such a little time.*

THE POOL

The Grail still lay before him, his mighty *opus* hardly started. Sharpness flooded back with the memories; such destruction, such betrayal, such a need for the surgeon's knife.

Now *the ship* was black again, a deep glassy black with only the faintest of green slowly moving swirls on its surface.

With the slightest exercise of his will he began a slow steady movement back towards the earth.

His mind fixed now on his mission, he again turned deep inside himself; down, ever down into an unpleasant place in his soul. *What had he done? Murdered; annihilated thousands of innocent people.* Without warning or explanation, he had in anger, simply removed them from the face of the earth. *What had he become?* His thoughts tumbled ever downward. *Yes, it was true. All that he had done was horrific, but not inexcusable, not without a great purpose, the greatest purpose of all. How else was he to protect mankind from itself if not by the death of many?*

Would it be beyond his powers, he wondered, *to wreak havoc and destruction on such a global scale that it might be effective in stemming the uncontrolled flood of that greatest of all pollutants, humanity?* But that was an inadequate solution. The very act would create great, global atmospheric disturbance and perhaps exacerbate the already deteriorating situation. *Might such an act not precipitate the very calamity he sought to avoid?* No, the solution had to lie with mankind itself. Mankind had to be taught the folly of its outmoded thinking. Mankind must cull itself.

He must return, he knew, in such a manner that all would fear, all would watch, and listen. The more he considered his options, the more he fixed on his original plan. He would cow the great powers by a further display of might and then, using the Vatican as a pulpit, (the analogy made him smile thinly), he would articulate his message.

Implacably he sloughed off all remaining doubts, cleared his mind and will, and let a cold, calculating, grim purpose fill him.

The golf ball was larger now filling his forward vision becoming blue and white, pretty. *The ship* was utterly black.

CHAPTER 26

She stared into space, absently stirring her coffee even though she never used sugar. The little kitchen was tidy enough but she herself looked just a little dishevelled, her hair slightly mussed, and her clothing uncoordinated. The events of the last three days had been almost unbelievable, occurring so rapidly that "normal" life was left behind. The disappearance of her husband; the coming and then the departure of the ship; the unexpected development of her relationship with Jim Crawford; and her betrayal of her husband; had swept aside the old, quiet, routines.

As these happenings were reviewed in her mind, she felt somewhat detached, unemotional. There was no escaping her conviction that Cole was in *the ship* or connected with it in a profound manner. She had felt his presence again, his awareness of her when it had passed overhead. The desperate sense of loss and hurt that propelled her into the arms of Jim Crawford and his puzzlement and hurt at her reaction to the departure of *the ship*. But she hadn't really meant it, hadn't meant to seem to reject him, for he was a kind and extremely sensitive man. He had sought to understand her, see it from her point of view. He had been kind when she had called him, had come back; if a little hesitantly, and listened patiently and with wisdom to her words while she worked it through.

In the end he had stayed with her that night and all the next day till late. But it had been a different interaction, more tender, more tentative, almost as if they had never made sexual love at all. But he helped her and their relationship had grown. She gained knowledge of him too, his work, his background, his life of study in America, and his research into psychic phenomena. Unlike her he had a sad personal life of childhood romance growing to marriage and then withering into divorce. Childless and really rather alone, she felt his need of companionship and warmth. She knew now that he had a place in her life and it disturbed her. *But what of Cole? What would happen when he found out? Perhaps that was all over now, what had happened at Gibraltar was frightening and confusing. How could Cole have anything to do with such death and destruction? He wasn't like that, he was kind and gentle. He had never killed anything bigger than a fly in his life.*

Jim had phoned her from Rome when he got there, primarily to let her know how to get in touch with him; but of course, they had talked long and in detail about *the ship* and its actions. Not that there was anything to marvel at, the entire world was obsessed with it. There were riots and civil disturbances breaking out all over the place. The police and armies of every nation were being hard pressed to maintain even basic services. Jim kept pecking away at the fact that she had seemed to know that *the ship* would leave before it had done so.

But all she could do was repeat her conviction that Cole was in *the ship* and in some way she and he were aware of each other. He had pressed her to come to Rome, stay with him. She had been tempted but the village was quieter now with few soldiers and she felt safer here than in the city with all the violence that was endemic now.

He persisted but in the end had given way to her wishes, yet said that he would dispatch a travel permit for her use in case she changed her mind. It would arrive tomorrow by military courier.

Her memory of the conversation brought back the deep feeling she held for him and she felt warm and content. With any luck the telephone lines would be better and she would phone him tonight just to chat.

The doorbell rang and Bene pushed his head around, "*Permesso.* Anyone home?"

She quickly gathered her thoughts, straightened her hair with her hand reflexively, and called, "In here Bene in the kitchen."

Bene was his usual breezy self but she could see by his eyes that he was observing her closely, trying to gauge her mental state.

"Any coffee going?" he said as he helped himself to the filter brew that all of the Scozzese preferred. "How are you feeling today? Better I hope now that all those military types are leaving. Leaving us to our own devices and to solve our own problems. It is bad enough for you without all that jazz going on."

They chatted for a long time in general, trying not to mention Cole or death. She set the kitchen table, prepared a simple *sugo* for the pasta and they sat down and ate, all the while chatting amiably. Of course their main topic was the destruction of Gibraltar and its terrible aftermath. It was difficult to know what was happening elsewhere in the world because of the clamp down on press and television reporting, but they agreed that Italy was unlikely to be worse than anywhere else.

"I hear they have banned all mass gatherings," said Bene, "that's an end to the football for now, I suppose."

Kate smiled, "Sometimes I think you believe that football is the most important thing in the world."

Bene laughed, "Of course it is."

The flask of wine emptied and another took its place. Perhaps it was the alcohol or the fact that for years now this had been a normal evening scene except that now Cole wasn't there; slowly her thoughts turned more and more to Cole and *the ship*. Her conversation began to drift in that direction and Bene, seeing her need, let the subject develop.

"You know, Bene, I still firmly believe that he's alive," she spoke in a soft voice but calmly and unemotionally. "I still think that terrible *ship* thing has something to do with him. He moves when it moves although sometimes it feels the other way around. It moves when he moves if you see the difference."

Bene leaned back in his chair, slowly sipping from his glass and said, "Kate, I love you dearly, like my daughter and I don't want to hurt you, but you really must give this thing up. It is simply not rational. Cole may well yet be alive, it's not so very long after all, but *the ship? The ship* is another thing alltogether."

"Oh! Bene," she said leaning over the table to take his hand in hers, "I know you too well to ever think that you would be anything other than kind to me and I understand and value your opinions, especially now. You and Cole were so close and shared so much. He was always talking of your help and friendship. I wonder if he is thinking of us now." Her eyes brimmed. "Its just too bad. Cole disappears and no one in authority cares a damn. All they can think about is curfews and permits and roadblocks. Why can't they spare a few men to search properly? Oh dear, it's just too bad, just too bad." Her voice was shaky now and she felt that she was about to burst into tears.

Leaning back in the chair, she lifted her glass and stared into the ruby liquid, blinking until a tear escaped and ran slowly down her cheek. Very, very quietly she whispered, "I can reach him if I try, you know? I am sure I can." A far away look came into her eyes and she seemed to drift away almost into sleep, closing her eyes to a slit.

Bene leant forward, closer to her and asked in a low voice, "Kate . . .Kate are you all right? Don't think about these things, it's bad for you, this is unhealthy."

She seemed not to hear him, not to see him, not even to be present. Her hand began to tremble, the wine rippling and overlapping the glass. "Cole? Cole? Where? Where are you?" in a little voice, and then louder, "I can't hear you, I can't hear you."

Bene leapt to his feet, "Kate," he said sternly, "Stop that, stop that at once. Kate, speak to me."

She started and spilled some wine on her skirt, "Oh dear, look what I've done. What a mess." She got quickly up and went to the sink and with a sponge doused the wine stains with cold water.

Turning, pale-faced and stern she said coolly and deliberately, "Bene. Please don't speak of this to anyone. Something is going to happen. Cole is coming back. *The ship* is coming back, do you understand? *The ship* is coming back."

Bene blanched and stood up, "If you say so Kate, if you say so," and with a light touch took her hands in his and squeezed them, looking straight into her eyes. After a long moment he seemed satisfied and with no further comment turned and left the house.

Unusually, she locked the door carefully behind him and turning to the phone, dialled the number in Rome that Jim had given her. "Jim? Is that you?"

"Kate? Its good to hear your voice. Are you okay? Is everything all right?" His voice was calm and welcoming, "Have you changed your mind? Are you coming to Rome?"

"Yes. I'm fine Jim and I miss you but I haven't changed my mind. I phoned for another reason and I want you to promise that you won't lecture me when I tell you."

His chuckle was clearly audible and she smiled. "Well, Bene came to visit and after awhile we started to talk about Cole and *the ship.* Then something strange happened, I felt as if I could in some way contact him and; oh I don't know, a queer sensation crept over me. I felt him, his presence quite strongly. He was sleeping or something and then he thought about me and became angry. He's coming back, Jim. I think *the ship* is coming back."

There was a long pause. Jim's voice was slow and careful. "Are you sure? Do you realise what you are saying? No one even knows where *the ship* is. For all we know its blown up, self-destructed, gone back to where it came from."

"Now you're lecturing," she said.

"No, no, don't take it like that, Kate. It's just a natural reaction for me. It's my training. You've got to remember that I believe you. I believe that something strange is happening between you and Cole, between you and *the ship,* if you insist. But please do not speak of this to anyone else. They will think you are over-stressed and prescribe tranquillisers and the like. If what you say is true, then it might be enormously important some day and you must remain a free agent just in case. Do you get my drift?"

"Your so sweet Jim, I don't know what I'd do without your support, I really don't." Her tone was childlike, cooing.

Crawford's voice followed her's becoming soft and tender. "You can rely on me, lovely lady, you know that. There is nothing anyone can do to test your statement anyway, so don't worry about it. I will endeavour to find out if there are any recent developments known to the army in the meantime." He paused, "Kate, I think you should come to Rome, come to me, you'll feel safer and I can look after you better if you are here."

"No Jim, I don't want to do that. You know my feelings and this experience, contact, call it what you will, has disturbed me. I will wait here for whatever to develop, but please keep in touch with me, I miss you." Her voice was soft, warm towards him. She gained strength from his support and felt her feelings for him strengthen.

He tried to persuade her but to no avail and kept prolonging the conversation, coming back repeatedly to her story about Cole and *the ship.* Eventually they parted with sweet nothings and Kate waited till she heard his phone hang up before she replaced her own instrument.

Returning to the kitchen, she over-cleaned everything, tidying fussily, then went upstairs to the balcony, and sat quietly down on one of the chairs. All was quiet and still in the warm night air. She turned her gaze upwards to the obsidian sky ablaze with starlight. She knew she would sit there until she fell asleep.

CHAPTER 27

Professor Tils Larsen, head of the New Mexico Radio Astronomy Laboratory, was one of the world's most respected men in his field. He had more years of studying the cosmos than he cared to remember. Long past retirement age, he was a small, frail man with thick eyeglasses and a pronounced stoop, much given to chain-smoking long, thin cigarettes. He had witnessed, and indeed contributed, to some of the most famous developments in his discipline, but today was different. Today the world of science as he knew it would change forever.

All evening he and his two assistants had been labouring over a new sighting.

"There can be no doubt about it. It is emitting random radio noise over a wide spectrum and it certainly wasn't there yesterday." The young, strong, baritone voice came from a tall, slim man garbed in a white coverall. Both of Tils' assistants were agitated, shuffling scrappy pieces of paper on top of the big bench.

The other, a woman, seemingly barely older than a teenager replied, "I'm sure your right but we must double check, perhaps we missed it in yesterday's pass. Perhaps its a glitch with the equipment, after all it's not very big."

Tils inhaled slowly on a cigarette. *How many times had his team detected a new radio source?* "*It must be thousands*," he thought. All of them had filled him with delight and excitement. But this was different, he felt it deep in his guts. He felt very old, suddenly the years weighed heavily.

With an air of vague disinterest, he thumbed the slim sheaf of computer printout. Like a man reading and re-reading a letter bearing news of the death of a loved one, the implacability of the truth began to make itself felt. Extinguishing his cigarette, he sat down rather unsteadily. There was something very queer going on. All the signs indicated an object smaller than almost any interstellar type except perhaps a small asteroid. It had not been in that position twenty-four hours ago and it was very close to the earth, inside the orbit of the moon in fact. It must be moving; but if so, it was not following any of the possible orbital trajectories. It simply didn't fit. It didn't belong in his world. The implications were terrifying.

"Are you all right, Tils? You are looking very pale." It was the younger of the two assistants, blond and slim, she tended to mother him. "Would you like a cup of coffee?"

The old man stared at his thin fingers as he lit another cigarette, "No, no coffee, thank you." He still had quite a strong Scandinavian accent. "How about a good measure of Lagavulin instead please, Helen?"

Helen puckered her brows, walked over to him and taking the cigarette from him, took both of his hands in hers.

"Would you get it, George," she said to her fellow assistant and leaning close to the old man said quietly, "what's wrong Tils? You are very pale and your hands are shaking. Do you feel unwell, should I call a doctor?"

The old man didn't answer. He remained silent for a long minute slightly shaking his head from side to side. Then he sighed and brushed away the tear that brimmed his eye.

George appeared with a large glass, well-filled with a dark, amber liquid and silently handed it to the girl. The pungent odour of the malt whisky seemed to bring the professor to himself and in a thin voice he said, "I'm sorry, Helen, I just feel so old, so old that I have lived to see this day."

"What on earth are you talking about?" said Helen and George in unison.

Helen continued, "I think you should call Doctor Kerr, George. I think Tils should be looked at right away." She was looking very troubled.

"No, no, don't do any such thing. I'm quite all right, it's passed now." Tils stood up a little unsteadily, took a big swig from the glass, and lit another cigarette from the still burning stub of the last. He removed his glasses, cleaned them meticulously, and then said in a brisk manner, "Right, this is what I want you to do."

They unhesitatingly followed his instructions, setting up measurements, realigning the relevant antenna, and bringing others to bear on the object. In an hour it was becoming clear that here was indeed the impossible, an independently powered interstellar radio source. This was no stray asteroid falling towards the earth under the gravitational pull of the sun. This object was defying the orbital laws of nature.

Then George's baritone, "Tils, Tils, quickly, I think, yes it is, it's changing course. Just like that, it is changing course. My God what the hell is it?" George was speaking loudly, agitatedly.

Helen, wide-eyed turned to Tils, "You don't suppose it has anything to do with that *ship?* Could it be another one coming?"

Tils said, "It doesn't bear thinking about but it has been my hunch all along that is exactly what it is. Get the pentagon on the phone and Jodrell Bank as well. Wait, get me Jodrell Bank first. We must be sure."

The connection was immediate and the line crystal clear. "Hello Ronald, Tils here, how are you, is it still raining in England?" He and Professor Ronald McKenna of Jodrell Bank radio telescope in England had been friends and close collaborators for many years and he felt no need for formalities. "I need your help to confirm some readings we have been making . . ."

The Irish lilt in the voice as it cut across that of Tils was unmistakable, "I bet a crock of gold you're referring to that new radio source nearby. We have just picked it up. What's the problem?"

Tils' voice became deadly serious, "Listen carefully, Ronald, we have been observing the thing for some hours now and we are about to lose it below the horizon. Perhaps the signals are becoming distorted but I believe it to be independently powered. I mean it is capable of independent motion and I don't think I have to spell out to you what that might mean?"

"You can't be serious, Tils? Just a moment, some new data is imminent." The phone went silent and at the same time a computer printer began to chatter in the laboratory. George tore off the first sheet and began to read it with Helen peering over his shoulder.

"Tils? Tils? You still there?" the Irish voice sounded urgent, "Your right it has changed course and it looks as if it's slowing down. Mother of God this is awful." There was a momentary silence and then in a quiet voice, "It must be another one of those *ships*." The soft Irish tones seemed to mock the devastating significance of the statement.

Tils looked across the laboratory to George who slowly nodded his head and said quietly, "That concurs exactly with our data Tils. What's going to happen?"

"Ronald, we confirm your data. I'm sorry but I must hang up now, there are things we need to do." Tils tone was dead flat.

"Me too," said the Irish voice, "Me too. Good Luck Tils, good luck to us all." There was a click as the line went dead.

The big clock on the wall ticked away the seconds as the silence hung heavily. No one spoke. The old man lit another cigarette and absently drained the whisky.

Tils' voice did not betray his tension, "Helen, please make a précis of our findings for me, and George, bring in the rest of the Lagavulin while I make the coffee. This is going to be a long night."

In less than half an hour they were seated together at the big bench, papers and printout spread before them. The laboratory had dimmed to utter darkness with the setting of the sun and only the pool of white light from an angle-poise lamp illuminated their workplace. A long curlesque of pale cigarette smoke spiralled up into the dark. There had been little talk and the huddled group of three figures silhouetted against the cold light, hardly seemed fitting to announce what might be the last trump for mankind.

"Okay, I think we're ready," said Tils. "It's time to let them know the worst," he paused, "do you realise" he said to no one in particular, "I don't even know who I should speak with? This is so potentially explosive that it will need to be handled with kid gloves." His accent was stronger than normal giving an almost comic, Dr. Strangelove-like sound to his words.

Helen's nasal soprano contrasted strongly, "Tils, perhaps it would be better to speak to the politicians rather than the military, the White House maybe. You could try to speak to the President. You never know."

The old man thought this over for a few moments. "That's a good idea. I don't imagine I will get to the President, especially at this hour. But surely, someone in authority will speak to me. Okay, let's try it, go ahead, dial the number."

It had taken a lot of emphasising Professor Tils' position as a senior scientist, and much persistence on Helen's part but eventually she handed the instrument to Tils. "They are going to connect you with someone in the Secretary of State's office."

Placing the phone to his ear, Tils straightened his tie. A woman's voice said, "I am connecting you with Vice President Arnold Borrhim, professor, hold the line please."

"Good evening, professor, what can I do for you?" The deep rumbling bass of Borrhim's voice sounded regal, "I am informed that you have information of the greatest urgency and importance to the United States and since the Secretary of State is unavailable at this time, I shall be pleased to receive it on his behalf."

Tils stuttered, "M . . . mister Vice President, this is indeed an honour, I did not expect to reach such a high office."

"Come, come professor, the views of a man of your standing are not taken lightly in Washington." Borrhim's tone was slightly jocular. "But please, let us come to the point. What is it you wish to say to me?"

Tils mustered all the authority he could in his voice. "Mister Vice President, I fear that I have the gravest of news. I believe that this evening, we have positively detected the approach of an independently powered object from space. From such measurements as we have been able to make of its size and mass, it could well be another one of these black ships. It may, of course, be the original returning from wherever it went, we have no means of knowing, but it is undoubtedly manoeuvring and is on course for the earth. Tils stopped and waited for a response.

"I see," the voice was inexpressive, "do you have any details on how far away it is or how soon it will get here?"

"It is well within the orbit of the moon, Mister Vice President, and so is quite close in interplanetary terms. Clearly if it is the same type of object as that which destroyed Gibraltar then it is capable of very rapid travel indeed. But it is impossible to say when it will arrive as it is now varying its velocity and direction in an unpredictable manner." Tils' manner had become very precise.

"Very good, professor, I shall have the appropriate personnel contact you immediately. You will treat this information as classified, top secret. Goodbye." Borrhim's speech had been hurried.

Tils took the instrument from his ear and looked at it. "Goodbye," he said weakly.

CHAPTER 28

Despite the sweltering heat of Rome and the milling throng outside, it was cool and quiet in the back of the stationary air-conditioned car. Jim Crawford was glad of the deeply tinted windows, which hid him from view. If the crowd realised that the car was carrying military personnel, there would be trouble. Everyone was blaming everyone else for the recent happenings and the military were certainly getting their fair share of blame. He checked his uniform yet again. This would be an important meeting and he needed every ounce of help he could get.

Suddenly he was pitched sideways as the car rocked violently. The crowd had suddenly become much denser and was beginning to get ugly. People were banging on the roof, heaving and shoving each other, and whatever else they could find. A chant began to form from the furore *"Va via, Americani,"* repeating over and over again.

"Go home yanks." *How often had he heard that before?"* But this was no longer funny and he slid down the partition between himself and the driver.

"I don't like this," he said, "do we have a radio? Can we summon assistance?"

Turning slightly the driver, grim-faced, shook his head. "I'm afraid we're on our own, sir. But don't worry the *carabiniere* will soon sort these sons-of-bitches out."

Jim Crawford sat back and tried to put his more unpleasant thoughts out of his mind. It had been quite difficult getting through to General Siemens at first. After all, Jim Crawford was hardly top brass, was he? It wasn't everyday that a medical officer wanted to talk to a General urgently and with the crisis situation developing, he felt pleased that his persistence had paid off in the end.

When he had heard the General's voice on the phone, he had felt like dropping the instrument back onto the receiver. *What would the man think of him with his crackpot ideas?* Telepathy, a hysterical woman in a remote village, *the ship* coming back, the General would surely laugh at best and maybe get him thrown out of the army as unstable. "It's a good job I'm really a civilian," he said under his breath to himself.

"Beg your pardon, sir. I didn't catch that," said the driver turning towards him.

"Oh, It's nothing, nothing at all. I was just thinking aloud. Sorry about that," he said, a little abashed, and slid up the glass partition again.

The mob were more agitated now and fear gripped him as he realised someone was pressing his face against the window, trying to see into the dim interior. "Dear God, this is going to get nasty. Where are the police? Why doesn't someone stop all this? This is Rome not Baghdad." He suddenly wished he had a gun.

The face turned abruptly away. Bedlam broke out; people cursing and screaming, falling to the ground, and being trampled. A tear gas canister whizzed by and landed some distance behind the car. The whinny of horses mixed with the yelling voices, suddenly the throng lessened, the press of people loosened and started to run. *The carabiniere were magnificent in their flamboyant uniforms*, he thought as the riders came abreast of the car, batons flailing. But the hard-faced and grimly-dressed riot squad police who followed closely were the ones, which gave him the most comfort. There was no mercy shown; men, women, and children were summarily dealt with. The street cleared in seconds and the stalled traffic began to move forward slowly.

The driver turned and gave him the thumbs up sign.

Wiping his brow, Crawford closed his eyes and forced himself to review his position yet again. He would need to be word perfect if he were to stand the slightest chance of convincing the General of his plan.

His mind drifted back to the phone call. Siemens had remembered him after a few moments and to his surprise indulged in a little social chat before asking him to come to the point.

"Well General, perhaps you may recall an Englishwoman," he had deliberately used the term *English*, all British were English to the Americans, "who lives in the village and whose husband had disappeared coincidentally with the appearance of *the ship*. You asked her to accompany your party on your intended trip up the mountain to see *the ship*." He had tensed as he heard another voice address the General. *That was all he needed, something to distract the man just at this moment.*

"Yes, I think I do. But we left early, got called away and we never saw *the ship* or the woman again, if I remember correctly. What's this got to do with anything?" His light tenor didn't reflect his authority.

"What I have to say will sound crazy I know, so if you will bear with me I would like to ask you a straight question. I believe that you will want to listen to me afterwards." He was having difficulty controlling his breathing. "Is *the ship* coming back? Do you have any information which would support that view?" His jaw muscles were so tense that he had problems with his articulation. Heart hammering he waited tensely.

There was a long pause. "That is classified information, son. Why do you ask such a question? I advise you to think carefully before you answer."

"General, I believe that *the ship* left this planet. It is no longer anywhere on earth and I further believe that it is returning, and that it is on its way back right now. This is not speculation on my part. This information came to me from what I believe to be a bona-fide source." He wondered if the General could hear the tension in his voice.

Again there was a long pause. "Son, get yourself over here right away. We had better talk face to face." The phone went dead.

He knew instantly that he had hit the jackpot. He had been right, there must be something happening and it fit with Kate's story.

"How long to get there?" he wondered. *"God-damn this traffic."* The car progressed in fits and starts through the congestion. Looking out into the bright, sunlit street he saw the graffiti everywhere, fresh and ugly. *"This is not the way to treat Rome,"* he thought, *"Where has our appreciation of beauty gone? Why is it that stress and fear always brings out the worst in mankind? Things were already going from bad to worse in society without this global threat from God knows where."*

The car turned and stopped at a red and white barrier. He lowered his window to allow one of the American soldiers on guard to peer in and identify his papers. The soldier saluted casually and signalled to another in the little sentry hut. The barrier lifted and they drove into a dim passageway through the building and out into a bright internal courtyard. There was a lot of activity with uniformed and civilian personnel crossing to and fro.

Presenting his papers at the desk, he was ushered into a large and beautiful room on the first floor. It was empty so he sat down on one of the antique divans. There was virtual silence but he could faintly hear voices from behind one of the pairs of huge doors leading from the room. Suddenly General Siemens' voice, raised almost to a shout, could be clearly heard, "I don't give a God-damn, I want to hear his story first. Bring him in."

A few moments later one of the doors opened and a woman in uniform came out. She closed the door behind her and walked over to where he was seated. As he stood up to greet her she asked, "James Crawford?" He nodded. "The General will see you now, follow me."

She swung the big door wide and said in a clear voice, "Lieutenant Crawford, General."

The room was as beautiful as the first with the same high ceilings and tall elegant windows but half the size. The General was seated behind a huge, ornately-carved desk completely bare of any papers or telephones, only a single white carnation in a slim crystal vase decorated its surface. Seated around the room in a seemingly random manner were three uniformed men. None of them stood to greet him.

He drew himself to his full height and trying not to look too rigid, strode over to the desk and came to attention. "Lieutenant James Crawford, sir."

The General's eyes were like lances, open and fixedly gazing deeply into his own. "Sit down lieutenant," he said, indicating the single, beautifully upholstered chair by the desk. His tone was steady, formal but not commanding.

"We will dispense with the formalities and I shall come straight to the point. These officers are from army intelligence," he indicated vaguely around the room, "and quite frankly, they are here to interrogate you. You are under suspicion of obtaining classified information irregularly and distributing it in a manner prejudicial to the national interest of the United States of America."

Crawford gulped involuntarily, "But, General . . ."

Siemens waved his hand in a gesture of silence, "Let me finish. In normal circumstances you would not be sitting here at all but would be the guest of our counterespionage colleagues. However, I clearly recall your speciality and your advice regarding the woman and her para-psychic experiences concerning *the ship*. That was at the very beginning of course, long before we had any information at all; and therefore, could not be a matter of illegal knowledge of classified data. You have this opportunity to clarify your position and justify my time on the matter. If you fail to convince me then I will have you arrested."

Crawford was wide-eyed and pale. His composure, so hard won, had vanished. His thoughts raced. *How could he have foreseen this turn of events, had he made a mistake?* Suddenly he realised just how thin his theory was. He began to tremble slightly, sweat beading on his brow.

"Well lieutenant, we're waiting," Siemens' voice was harder now.

Rising to his feet, Crawford stood erect and swivelling to survey all in the room he faced Siemens. "General, gentlemen, I have never done, am not doing, and have no intentions of ever doing anything which could be construed as prejudicial to my country. My entire motive is to help and assist in this crisis. To bring to bear all my skills and knowledge in whatever way I can. I am acutely aware that my expertise lies light years away from the hard pragmatic world of military reality, but would remind you that it is the U.S.army that pays me to carry out research in this field. There are clearly some elements of military thought which are prepared to consider the veracity of para-psychic phenomenon in battle."

His voice was becoming steadier now and he began to consciously modulate his tone to further his ends. "Ever since I first met the Scotswoman, of whom I am sure you are all briefed, I was struck by the complete fit of her claimed experiences with the theoretical model which I was studying. At first, I admit that was as far as it went. However I took the opportunity to maintain contact with her and have gotten to know her quite well. In the time that has elapsed since her first being aware of *the ship,* she has displayed some graphic examples of pre-knowledge of *the ship's* behaviour."

One of the others present interrupted, "Are you telling us that you know someone who can anticipate what *the ship* is going to do? You can't be serious."

Siemens waved him silent.

"Gentlemen, I have personally witnessed *just* that fact."

He raised his voice slightly, adopting a school-masterly manner. "You will recall the day *the ship* seemed to overheat, the day it incandesced, just shortly after it began to move from its original site. Well, whatever it was that caused it to glow, I have no means of knowing, but the woman claimed that it had been attacked by us." The General stirred in his seat and looked uncomfortable. Crawford's trained eye caught the subtle movement and realised that he had again struck home. "I was in her presence when she anticipated its movement to Gibraltar. She ran out of the house and pointed to *the ship* some seconds before it moved or exhibited any visible change. From the very beginning she has had psychic experiences, which, although sometimes couched in strange words and images, have proven in the event to be correct. She knew of the freezing effect. She anticipated *the ship's* change from passive to aggressive behaviour. She . . ."

Siemens interrupted, "You have not come to the most important point. Was it she who told you of this 'return'?"

Crawford hesitated a little, *what was he letting Kate in for?* This might not be pleasant for her, and yet he had no alternative. If what she had said was correct then disaster beyond imagining would occur.

"That is correct, General. This lady told me that *the ship* is somewhere far away. She describes the place where it is, as dark and empty, silent. It is bright, yet cold, where the stars are more abundant. There is a giant, bright blue orb hanging above the vessel." He spread his arms in a gesture of appeal. "It doesn't take a genius to see this as a subjective, non-technical description of space and of the earth as seen from space. She further says that *the ship* has decided to return to earth and that it is returning with hostile intent. She told me all of this yesterday evening."

Turning around slowly to face each man in turn, Crawford said slowly, "Only you can know if my statements are accurate. And if they are, you must realise that the possibility of my obtaining information of this type by stealth is unlikely in the extreme. As for the woman . . . how could she, isolated in a remote mountain village, have received it? In addition, if I had stolen it, what could I hope to gain by presenting you with information that I already knew you possessed? It doesn't make sense."

There was silence.

"I tell you again, gentlemen, by some mechanism which I cannot define, this woman is in touch with her husband or whatever remains of him and in some way that gives her knowledge of *the ship* and its intentions." This last statement was delivered in a quiet voice.

There was no response from anyone.

Then one of the seated soldiers got slowly to his feet and with cold, grey eyes looked Crawford straight in the face and said, "The General is right, you're not a spy. You're a nut, a raving lunatic, you should be locked up."

The others got to their feet collecting briefcases and papers as they did. The most senior spoke, "General, we have no further interest in this matter. Perhaps the medical core would be better suited to the investigation of the lieutenant's statements." All drew themselves erect, faced the General, and saluted.

Siemens, still silent and without rising, waved them away. They filed quickly out of the door and Crawford turned to follow, so crestfallen that he looked pitiful.

"Not you, lieutenant. Sit down."

Crawford, like a small boy awaiting punishment from his headmaster, sat down on the edge of the chair.

Siemens put his elbows on the desk, made a peak with his fingers, and leaning his chin on them looked directly at the shattered man in front of him. His face was inscrutable, giving no hint of his emotions.

"Listen son," he said quietly, "I believe you are sincere in what you are trying to do and I am prepared to admit to a certain sneaking feeling that there might just be something in what you claim, but I cannot give you any official support. The army doesn't act on hunches." Crawford seemed to slump even more.

"I once told you that I always keep all my options open as long as I can, no matter how remote they may seem, and that is precisely what I intend to do now. I want you to keep in touch with me and let me know of any developments that you feel are important. I will give you a telephone number, which will bypass most of the administrative layers when you need to speak to me. You will use this means, and only this means, of communicating with me. Always verbal, nothing is to be written down. Do you understand?"

Crawford, eyes downcast, nodded.

"I hardly need to say that it is not in your best interests to talk about this arrangement with anyone." He reached into a drawer in the desk and flicked a visiting card across the polished surface towards Crawford. "Dismissed."

Crawford took the card, stood to attention, saluted and left without a word as Siemens swivelled his chair back to the window.

CHAPTER 29

"Get me the President, the Secretary of State, the Chief of Staff and the press secretary, and quickly." Borrhim's voice brooked no denial.

His secretary said, "But sir, the President and Mister Clarke are both at the reception for the Gibraltar Disaster Fund."

"Didn't you hear me? Are you going deaf? I said get me the President and do it NOW. Get him here on the double." When Borrhim yelled, the room shook. He stomped off into the Oval Office, leaving the secretary furiously dialling.

Half an hour later, Borrhim had finished briefing the press secretary who had been in the building. "Remember Bill, nothing, absolutely nothing of this matter is to be published. Make sure that every editor gets that message loud and clear." At that moment the door of the Oval Office opened and Chief of Staff Armed Forces, Clay Robeson came in.

"Okay Bill get on with it but stay close at hand in case we need you again." The press secretary got up and left with a passing gesture to the big dark man in uniform, "Good luck Clay, it's going to be a long evening."

Borrhim was hurried, impatient in his manner. "Come in Clay, come in. We have a problem, a big problem. Sit down."

The soldier eased his bulk into one of the easy chairs dotted about the room. He was a huge black man well over six feet tall and well built. His well-cut uniform did not hide his brawn, if anything it emphasised it. He was strikingly handsome with an aristocratically held head and chiselled features. His years had given him grey temples, which contrasted starkly with his shock of dark curly black hair and lent an air of urbanity, an air of refinement. "What's going on, Arnold?" he asked, the voice dark and deep with that huskiness typical of most black men.

Before Borrhim could speak, the door opened again and the President, followed by the Secretary of State hurried in. They were both dressed in dinnerwear with black ties and white silk scarves.

The President threw his scarf and jacket onto one of the chairs. Turning to Clay Robeson he said brightly, "Hello Clay, you too?" and turning to Borrhim, "Get right to it Arnold, what's happened?"

Borrhim looked at the President directly, "*The ship* is coming back Robert, it's on its way back to earth right now."

The Chief of Staff stood up momentarily and the President sat down, suddenly ashen-faced, "Back to earth? What do you mean back to earth . . . where is it now? Is it . . .? Where is it for Christ's sake?"

"Professor Tils Larsen of the New Mexico radio telescope has located it in outer space. He says it is somewhere closer to us than the moon and it's heading this way." Borrhim was still speaking quickly.

Earle Clark interjected, "In space, near the moon, how do we know it's *the ship?* It's too small to be seen at that distance. How can they see it, how can we know it's *the ship?*" Turning to the seated soldier he asked, "Have your people picked it up, Clay? Can they verify this?"

Clay spoke first, "We don't normally look into space Earle, at least not beyond our satellites. There has never been any reason to do so, at least until now."

Borrhim continued, "It's true, New Mexico can't see it yet but they can measure it in different ways and Larsen says that if it isn't *the ship* itself then it's another one approaching."

"Another one?" all except Borrhim spoke in unison.

There was a loud crash from the adjoining room. Albero spun round, "What the hell was that?"

"The boys are checking out our comms." it was Borrhim, "I expect we'll need them very soon."

Albero sat down behind the big desk, "Okay Clay get your boys briefed by this professor, whatever he calls himself, and see if your people can get a bead on it as well. We will want military surveillance at the earliest possible moment. Let's schedule a briefing in, say, two hours, let's say midnight."

Robeson got up like an earthquake thrusting up a pinnacle of rock, "Right on it, Mister President." He turned to leave.

"Get right back as soon as you can Clay, I want you in on this every step of the way," Albero's natural command was evident.

The big man turned and in three strides was gone.

"Any ideas Robert?" Borrhim was sweating.

"Yes, I sure as hell do," the aggression Albero displayed was hard and determined. "If it's true that this is *the ship* we're tracking and it's coming back to earth then I damn well know what I'm going to do. We will make it so fucking hot for the bastard if it comes over the U.S. that it will take a hike and pick easier targets. It sure as hell won't like what it gets if it fucks with us."

Earle Clarke sucked his teeth, "But how, there's nothing short of a nuclear bomb that . . . just a minute, are you suggesting that we shoot at it with nuclear weapons over the U.S.? Surely not?"

"I told you, if that bastard comes into our air space, I am going to let it have it and no mistake. Huh, it soon moved its ass after we made it hot for it in Italy, didn't it?" Albero was becoming a little high pitched.

"I protest. I most vociferously protest. This isn't a dictatorship yet, and no one will accept the detonation of nuclear devices over American soil." Earle Clark was angry, losing his usual composure. "I intend to block any such move."

"Oh, shut up Earle," Borrhim's anger matched that of the Secretary of State's, "You're at it again, what do you propose we do, run away and hide? Hide the entire American continent?

I am with Robert. There are plenty of places it can go other than here. Let it go play with the Reds."

The bickering continued until the door opened and Clay Robeson came back in. "All under way Mister President. We don't have much that looks that far into space but when and if *the ship* gets closer, we'll have it under a microscope. Until then I am confident that our scientists will fully co-operate. The snag is that at the present time it is on the other side of the world and our Pacific facilities are not up to state-side standards."

"Who else has information on *the ship*?" asked Albero to no one in particular.

Borrhim replied, "The English know, their set-up at Jodrell Bank is monitoring it at the moment. I do not know if anyone else is picking it up. But you can be sure that it's only a short time before the Australians notice it. Maybe the Japs will be in there too. We can only hope that they keep the news tightly under wraps. God help us if this gets out raw, there will be mass panic for certain."

"Can we count on their full co-operation? Will the British give us everything they've got?" Albero directed his question at his Secretary of State.

Clarke snorted, "Huh. Now that they know we lied over our intentions in mounting a nuclear attack over Gibraltar? You've got to be kidding?"

Borrhim's anger no longer showed in his voice, "Take it easy Earle, they need our help with this. What are they going to do alone? This is a global issue now and they know that only the combined resources of the developed world will stand a chance of stopping this thing. Anyway, look what happened to Gibraltar, perhaps if we got our shot in first, none of that would have happened and *the ship* as sure as hell isn't about to hang around for a parley, now is it?"

The thick bass of Clay Robeson seemed even deeper than that of Borrhim, "It is my information that the English are co-operating fully at this time and I am confident of the armed forces sharing information on this. The political scene is another bowl of beans, but we only need this night. After that we should be self-dependent. There is the option of repositioning one of our orbiting satellite probes so that it can scan that part of the sky."

Eventually the discussion was interrupted when an aide opened the door and said, "The incident room is ready, sir."

Albero checked the wall clock. "The meeting will commence in forty-five minutes. I am going to change out of this carnival outfit. See you all then."

In a few moments the Oval Office was empty.

CHAPTER 30

"How pretty?" he thought. The huge, bright orb hanging against the speckled blackness of space was stunning in its majesty. "From here it seems so clean, like something brand new, just out of its wrapper. Like a gargantuan version of the luminescent globes that hang on Christmas trees."

He remembered his childhood long ago. He would walk with his mother along the dark tenement streets of Glasgow in the days just before Christmas with their breath hanging in plumes in the keen, cold air. The serried ranks of bay windows glittered with the tiny lights on the trees. Almost every window had a tree. They were never big, just little trees in little windows but it had all been so beautiful, tantalising, and distant.

Every evening he would creep quietly into the parlour at home to gaze in silence and wonder at the frosty mystery of it all. The tree always sat in the window, raised on a little box, outlined against the dim light from the street. The pinpricks of light had seemed so cold, so pure, so lovely, the lambent glass globes picking up and reflecting their enigma. He had wished that it would always be like that, peaceful and strangely quiet. It seemed that somehow peace was found in the tree.

Now at last, at long last, the reality was his. The fairy lights were real stars and the earth was his globe. He could do with them as he wished. No need of symbols now.

He spoke quietly and assuredly to the giants, those mighty engines at his command. No discord now, no hesitation, no lack of syncopation. All was harmony. He rode on a carpet of sound, deep and sonorous, yet quiet, peaceful, steady. The lambent green was everywhere clear, limpid. All was ready. The overlaying of place, time, and perspective no longer troubled him. Internal and external were the same. He was inside and at the same time outside the pool. He was old and new, both huge and tiny, somehow it seemed that it had to be this way. He exulted in his powers and the huge black object began to flicker and scintillate with green, sparkling light in the darkness.

He sensed the siren call of his fiery sister, her subtle beckoning. The call spoke of life for the giants and also of their death. He knew he could use her strength, her savage dragnet to let himself fall in an elegant parabola to his goal.

Her embrace was leviathan even at this distance but he resisted, he cut his own crude path, ignoring nature, defying gravity. He would arrow an unmistakable, direct line to his target, displaying to all who might see, his sovereignty over the vast emptiness. Dimly he realised the immensity of what he was doing but the giants merely sang their sonorous song, happy, and at ease.

Soon the enormity of the planet dominated everything, blotting out most of the universe beyond. It filled all forward vision and sang its own siren song, beckoned with its own power, but there was nothing here to threaten the giants.

He aimed a tangent to the great globe, to the outer reaches of the skin of turgid air that thinly cloaked it.

"Fast, but not too fast," he whispered, "so that all may witness our return." The giants knew his wish as soon as it was formed.

The gasses of the uppermost layers of the stratosphere, scant as they were, began to burn and incandesce. He sensed the friction, the resistance, and revelled in his easy dominance over it.

"A long, curving descent." The giants already knew.

Below, he saw the sea, flat, blue, besmirched with white streaks and great swathes of cloud. Ahead, the east coast of South America and the globe spinning slowly as it turned towards him.

"Perfect," he thought, "A near complete encirclement of the planet, slicing down through their precious atmosphere will awaken their dread." He smiled. The glassy black sparkled and glinted with green.

The air burned and fused. The static leapt and arched, the lightning snapped at his heels miles and miles behind. The thick gasses grabbed and snagged at his passing, screamed in outrage at their rape, but the giants brooked no delay. He hurtled ever onward, ever downward, ever closer to his goal.

CHAPTER 31

The room, dimly lit from concealed strip lights, was already heavy with cigarette smoke when the President entered. What little talk there was, was strangely subdued. The television screens glowing pallid, but showing no picture, added a strange flickering quality to the light. The bulky form of Clay Robeson stood in a corner examining a report together with the Vice President. They were talking in not much more than a whisper and the combination of their plummy basses provided a dolorous background to a scene that had already reminded Albero of a grotesque funeral parlour. Scanning the others present, he identified Earle Clarke and Bill Simpson in close conference among the dozen or so officials and aides.

"Bill," he called softly, obviously influenced by the atmosphere, "have you had a chance to sample the foreign press for any reaction yet?"

The press secretary excused himself and came over to where Albero was standing, "Not completely, sir. We are still working on it, but what we have been able to glean so far makes no mention of anything remotely connected with our latest information. It would seem that we might be lucky that the news has not yet broken."

"That's a relief at least. We need all the edge we can get to control public reaction. Keep a tight lid on it Bill, and I mean tight."

Before the press secretary could answer, Albero turned away and sat down. "Let's get this show on the road," he addressed the Vice President. Then in a louder tone, "C'mon Arnold, let's go."

As soon as everyone was seated and had turned their attention to the head of the conference table, Albero leaned forward onto his elbows, a pencil held lightly in his fingers. Nothing in his demeanour betrayed the momentous weight of what he was about to say.

"Gentlemen, you have all been briefed regarding our latest intelligence from New Mexico. As you can see this sighting may, or may not, be *the ship* returning, or indeed be one of its kin following in its footsteps, either way it makes no difference. We have no option but to act upon the information at hand. Until we know for sure that this is not *the ship*, we must treat it as a fact that the object currently being tracked is indeed *the ship* and that it is returning to earth from wherever it fled after our attack upon it and its subsequent retaliation upon Gibraltar. In addition, we must view its return as a hostile act and a potential threat to the United States of America. Do you all understand the significance of my words? This is no longer a matter open to discussion or opinion. This sighting will be treated as if it is a positive identification of the craft, or one of its kin, in the course of a hostile return to earth and we will react accordingly."

He stood up a little theatrically and looked around the table at each and every face in turn. All hung on his words. "It must be clear that the recognition of such a belief must have the inevitable consequence that we are duty bound to take each and every action necessary to ensure the protection and defence of our nation."

He paused to sip from a glass on the table in front of him, clearly using the few moments' silence to focus everyone's maximum attention on his words. "To this end and from this moment, I declare the United States of America to be in a state of emergency and under martial law!"

Again he sipped from the glass, all waited in silence. "I am assuming to myself, and with immediate effect such powers as I deem necessary without grace or favour. I intend to act upon decisions made here in this room and that will include possible military action. From this time on, and until further notice, all military and civilian authorities will deem themselves to be subject to such decrees issued by me, or my authorised delegates in person." Albero's voice had become clearer and harder as he spoke.

There was a stunned silence, as the President sat down.

Then Earle Clarke spluttered, "B . . . but Robert, that is unconstitutional. You may not declare a state of emergency, assume unlimited powers, and take unilateral military action. You know you may not do any of these things without the agreement of the Senate. You can't be serious. This is the U.S., not a banana republic. This is a democracy for Christ's sake."

Murmurs of agreement and General incredulity erupted all around the table, " he must be mad . . . who's he kidding? . . .it won't work . . maybe in Nicaragua . . ." but no one addressed the chair directly.

"Of course, it's unconstitutional Earle." The President cut across the hubbub, looking directly at Clarke. "I think I know what is constitutional and what isn't." His voice dripped with sarcasm.

"Let me spell it out to you in monosyllables. This *ship* is a hostile enemy with the demonstrated capacity to destroy the whole of Long Island in a few moments. It's coming this way, perhaps into our backyard. We can't communicate with it. It'll be here in a few hours. What do you suggest we do?" His voice rose to a shout, "Wait for a vote? Carry out a public opinion poll, have a televised debate?"

Clarke opened his mouth to respond but Borrhim interrupted, "Jesus, Earle, you know damn well that we need all the help we can get to have even a remote chance with this thing." He slammed his fist on the table." I have had enough of your legalistic nit picking. We need to be forceful and united in our purpose to be effective, immediate in our reactions. This is no ordinary threat. In case you haven't noticed, this isn't the

Viet Cong or some other rag-tag army on the other side of the world. We have no time for your niceties, no time for political protocol, and public opinion. For all we know the thing might attack us tomorrow. And if we do nothing, by the day after, there might not be any public left to complain about 'unconstitutional behaviour.' Can you say I'm wrong? Can you? I am with the President, I support him completely. Do you get the message? There is no time for all of this shit."

The Secretary of State leapt to his feet, glaring angrily at the Vice President. "Arnold," he said loudly, "be careful what you are suggesting. This is getting very close to treason. Do not let your loyalty to one man override your oath of allegiance to the Constitution of the United States. I don't care what your perception of the danger is. There remains the inescapable fact that no one in this room can ignore the constitution, not for any reason. Do YOU understand me? I mean NO one."

"Earle!" The President's voice was even, controlled.

"Hear me out," Clarke cut straight across the President, his face drawn, white, "when I said no one, I meant NO one. Not even you, not even the President is above the constitution, above the law I can't believe this, you are behaving completely irrationally. My God, how far can you go? On top of this announcement, you have openly stated, in front of witnesses, that you are willing to use nuclear bombs in our airspace, to explode thermonuclear devices over the landmass of the United States. To even consider the detonation of fissile material over populated areas of our own country is the act of a madman. I ask you, beg you, withdraw your last statement."

Albero sat, unmoving, steadily observing Clarke's performance. He said nothing.

Clarke focussed directly on Albero's face for what, in the silent, electrified atmosphere of the room seemed an eternity. Finally, he drew himself up to his full height and said in measured tones, "Mister President, sir, if you persist in this folly, I shall have no option but to have you removed forthwith from the presidency and by force if necessary, on the grounds of mental instability rendering you unfit for office." He stopped speaking and held his gaze firmly fixed on the President.

The room was dead silent. No one moved, all eyes switching back and forth between the two men.

Albero was still for several seconds, returning Clarke's stare unflinchingly, and then he signalled to an aide who opened one of the doors into the hallway allowing two immaculately uniformed marines to enter. They stood rigidly at attention just inside the room, sparkling, chromium-plated bayonets fitted to their rifles which were held at the port arms position.

"Earle," the President grated, "to quote one of my predecessors," he paused for a long moment and his voice became steely hard, "if you don't like the heat, get out of the kitchen."

The silence was unchanged, the tension heightened, the eyes of the onlookers wide, anxious expectancy evident on every face.

Clarke's expression betrayed nothing, not even an eyelid flickered. It crossed the mind of more than one onlooker that here was a clash of redoubtable men in a moment of significant and historic importance. None predicted the outcome of the titanic struggle.

Clarke turned slightly and addressed Robeson and Borrhim together. "Mister Vice President, Chief of Staff, in my capacity as Secretary of State and in the interests of the national security of the United States of America, I require you to do your duty and remove this man from office. He is clearly mentally unstable and pursuing a course of action which endangers the lands and peoples of the United States of America. An action which he himself has admitted to be unconstitutional and therefore a negation of his oath. I call upon you, Mister Robeson, in your capacity as Chief of Staff, to have this man removed and you, Mister Vice President, to now assume the office of President of the United States of America until such time as the due process of law under the constitution allows the democratic election of the next President." Clarke was pointing rigidly at the seated President.

An audible gasp came from one of the aides. The assembled brass remained seated, rooted to their positions as if in shock. Borrhim was sweating profusely, his handkerchief forgotten. His eyes turned to meet those of Robeson. They seemed to commune silently for a moment.

Albero pushed his chair back and slowly stood up. Never taking his eyes from Clarke he pointed at him and said in a clear steady voice, "Arrest that man."

The marines by the door hesitantly took two paces forward and stopped.

Robeson turned his head towards them and nodded ever so slightly.

The soldiers paced forward smartly and took position either side of Clarke, standing rigidly at attention. The Secretary of State stared, wide eyed at the President, the slightest of twitches in his jaw betraying his tension. He said nothing.

A slight signal from Robeson's hand and the marines took each of Clarke's arms and walked him, head held high, unresisting from the room. The silence remained unbroken.

As the door closed, Albero, white faced, surveyed all at the table and in a clear challenge asked, "Anyone else?"

No one spoke.

Albero sat down with an air of weariness which his voice belied, "Right, lets get on with this. Clay, what's our military situation?" His voice was brittle, full of nervous energy, edgy.

Robeson, blinked, "There is not much to report as yet Mister President. We are still relying on the English for our tracking of the object, ah, I'm sorry I mean, *the ship*. The latest report indicated that it was approaching on a steady course at a steady speed, but it is still far out of range of any weapon in our arsenal."

Borrhim cut in, "Do we have any E.T.A. or approximation of its likely location when it gets here?" He was still pale faced but seemed to have put the crisis of a few moments earlier to the back of his mind.

"No, mister Vice President I'm afraid not. It has only recently begun to follow a steady, and I might add, artificial trajectory, but I'm sure we will have the information shortly." As Robeson said this he looked at an aide who got up and left the room.

Albero looked straight at Robeson and said, in a slightly raised voice, as if he wanted to be sure that all in the room would hear and remember, "Under my assumed emergency powers I am instructing you to arm and bring to immediate launch status, every operational, land based, nuclear device capable of being brought to bear on the landmass of the United States."

Robeson's dark voice placed subtle emphasis on his words as he replied, "As you instruct, sir."

"I further instruct you to re-target these devices and all other appropriate long range platforms capable of being brought to bear on the territory of the United States in such a manner that they provide best possible cover of that territory. I want to be in a position to instruct an immediate nuclear strike against this *ship* if it enters our air space. Do I make myself clear?" Albero had spoken as if reading a speech already prepared.

"Perfectly, Mister President." Robeson got to his feet along with his aides on either side. "I shall attend to it immediately, sir." The three men turned and proceeded towards the door.

"Wait," said Albero. Robeson stopped and turned to face the President.

Albero got up and walked towards the Chief of Staff until he stood directly in front of him. He looked very small beside the big man. He spoke softly but clearly, intimately, "Clay, are you with me? Can I count on you, one hundred percent?"

Robeson returned the President's gaze steadily, his black eyes bright. He did not respond immediately but seemed to weigh his words in his mind before uttering them. "We have been friends a long time Bob. We've been through a helluva lot together, both good and bad. You can count on me. I think you know that." The gentle smile on his face was reflected in the warm tones of the dark voice.

Albero visibly slackened. "I am very glad to hear that Clay, very glad. We'll see this thing through together." He took the big man's hand in his and shook it warmly then, pursing his lips he, in turn, seemed to be choosing his next words with care. "I am putting you personally in charge of the state of emergency. I want complete military control of the country; martial law, curfews, restricted movement, identity documentation, the lot. I am not interested in Philadelphia lawyers screwing us up, any dissent or non co-operation is to be silenced. We must prevent civil disorder at all costs. We will be lucky to keep this out of the press for very long but you can be sure that when the news breaks, the shit will really hit the fan."

Robeson's reply was pitched calmly, evenly, like a discussion of the weather. "Let me get this straight Bob, I don't want any misunderstandings. When you say silenced, I take it you mean 'by force' if necessary?"

"Whatever it takes Clay, whatever it takes."

"I'll need to mobilise every mothers' son including the National Guard." Robeson spoke as much to himself as to Albero.

Placing his hand on the big man's arm, Albero was almost reassuring in his manner, "Like I said Clay, whatever it takes."

Robeson nodded and led the soldiers out of the room. An aide closed the door behind them.

Turning to the press secretary, Albero was a little more relaxed in his demeanour, "Bill, I'll leave it to you to handle the details but I want this thing kept out of the public eye for as long as possible."

The press secretary was out of his depth. The events he had just witnessed left him unhanded. "But Mister President, there is only so much that we can do. This will be so big that I can't see us stopping it for more than a few hours. Maybe a day or so at the most, and even then satellite reception from Europe is beyond our control." He was speaking rapidly, wringing his hands.

"Get this straight Bill," Albero's tone was hard. "We are taking control of the media. Nothing is to be published without our direct consent."

Simpson started, as if pricked with a needle, "You can't do that Mister President. Freedom of the press is crucial, sacrosanct. Only by that means can we get their co-operation. How else can we prevent them from publishing?"

"You still don't get it do you Bill?" Albero was becoming angry. "If they step out of line by so much as a semi-colon, they will be SHOT. Do you understand, SHOT! Fucking shot in the head." Simpson looked as if he might be sick. "You will instruct the press that as of now they will do exactly as they are told. They will announce the state of emergency and do it in such a manner that it will be seen as acceptable and necessary. There will be no discussions, no objective views, no analyses, no editorials published. The press will become our mouthpiece and do exactly as we say. Jesus Christ do I have to do the job MYSELF?" Albero was snarling.

"N... no SIR, I'm on it, don't worry. I understand perfectly, just as you say Mister President. You can rely on me, just as you say, sir, just as you say." Simpson's voice had become so high pitched it was cartoon like.

"For Christ's sake get out of my sight you moron." Albero's shout propelled the press secretary out of the room followed by his quaking aides.

Albero angrily waved the remaining officials out of the room with the exception of the Vice President.

When all had gone, Borrhim stood up with arms spread wide and a smile on his face and said, "Fucking ace Bob, positively brilliant. What a performance, truly magnificent. I hate to admit it but that was the stuff of greatness, you do this office proud." He beamed his pleasure.

Smirking slightly, Albero put an arm as far around the fat man as he could, "We'll see, Arnold, we'll see. History will be our judge." The two men walked into the Oval Office.

CHAPTER 32

Two hours had passed with little more than the odd telephone call being made and received. Albero and Borrhim had spent a lot of the time variously huddled together over the Presidential desk or pacing to and fro in the room, all the while wrapped in deep conversation.

"I am still not convinced that we are right to go it all alone," it was Borrhim who spoke, tired sounding. "The Russians and the British between them have as much fire power as we do. Don't you think we should at least try to establish some sort of communal strategy?"

Albero, lying back in the big chair was hidden in shadow. "You may well be right and later on we may try it. But no one, not even the Russians, is going to go along with us until the political situation is clearer. Our actions were hardly normal political practice after all. Everyone is going to be as cagey as hell until they see which way things are going. In any event I believe that in our own interests we must strike the strongest defensive position possible. To hell with the others. There are plenty of easier targets than us in the world and they can stand up for themselves for once."

Silence descended on the room. The two men hardly moved as some minutes ticked past, lost in their own thoughts.

The door opened without a knock and Robeson strode in, indicating to his retinue to remain outside.

"What news, Clay?" Albero sat erect in his chair.

"Everything is under way Bob. It will take some hours yet to be fully effective but every army, navy, and airman is on full alert and mobilisation is gearing up at maximum speed. By mid-morning the streets in every city should be secured and I have begun the occupation or closure of all major newspaper, television, and radio stations in the states." Robeson was slightly breathless.

"*The ship*, what update is there on *the ship*? Arnold and I are blind until we know what it is doing."

"We are not a lot firmer on that, I'm afraid. It has maintained a very regular course for some hours now, but it is slowing down, so when it will reach us is just guesswork. If it continues to lose speed at the current rate, I am informed that it won't reach the earth till the morning eastern standard time, probably coming into the southern hemisphere, or at least near the equator. We are still dependent on the British for a lot of our information. In fact my latest information is a lot colder than I would like. It is more than an hour old, but we should have *it* under direct surveillance very soon now." Robeson's voice trailed off as a Presidential aide entered the room.

"Excuse me sir, sorry to intrude but as you ordered . . ."

"Oh shut up soldier, what's the news?" Robeson's irascibility was clear.

"Its in range, sir. *The ship* is in range and on the scopes."

Albero, Borrhim, and Robeson exchanged glances and simultaneously headed for the adjacent incident room.

Half a dozen men in uniform were already watching the television screens. They all got up as the Presidential group entered and stood at attention.

Robeson, with barely a glance, said, "As you were."

Albero noticed that the door to the corridor was open and two marines in full battle fatigues, weapons at the ready, barred the opening. He could hear the sound of other soldiers as they moved into the Oval Office behind them. He turned quizzically to Robeson.

"Better safe than sorry, Mister President. You cannot tell to what lengths some crank may go. I have taken it upon myself to fortify the White House. We are ringed with armour in the streets and have continuous helicopter surveillance as well as double sentries. I hope you agree to these measures." Robeson was very business-like in his manner.

"Yes, I'm sure your quite right, Clay and the public sight of our precautions will strengthen the acceptance of martial law."

Albero turned his attention to the television screens as he sat down. "What is happening? Where exactly is *the ship*?" He addressed no one in particular.

Robeson nodded and one of the uniformed men close to the screens got to his feet with a long pointer. He indicated each screen in turn as he spoke, "Each picture is a graphic representation of a part of the surface of the globe and we hope to simulate the path of the vessel as it descends through the atmosphere. At this time it is still some thousands of miles away, well into space, but at least we can detect it on our own military equipment with reliability now. If *the ship* maintains its course, we should expect to see it on this screen quite soon," he then indicated a monitor displaying an outline of the South American continent. "However its time of arrival is uncertain as its velocity has not been constant. It has in fact, been slowing down. There remains the possibility, of course, that it will select an orbital path and remain outside the atmosphere. It is too early to say."

Borrhim addressed the man. "Do we know if it is the same *ship* or another, or indeed if there is more than one?"

"With our equipment it is impossible to tell as yet sir, we are tracking a radio source, not a radar target. *The ship* or ships, as you say, are still too far away. When we pick up the signal on radar we should be able to see more than one blip on this screen if there is more than one vessel," he indicated the monitor with the outline of South America.

"What do you mean by a radio source?" it was Albero, "is it trying to communicate?"

"No sir, at least not as far as we can tell. The object is simply emitting radio noise, not unlike some stellar sources already observable by radio astronomy. The emissions are far from steady and vary in a quite unpredictable and indecipherable manner. An interesting fact is that they can reach immense power from time to time, powerful even to the stage of disrupting telecommunications. It is not trying to sneak up on us, that is certain."

At that moment a quiet 'beep' sounded and a single red blip appeared on the monitor for South America. It was off the green line indicating the west coast of the continent, over the Pacific Ocean. "It's here," the man said, somewhat awe struck. "My God it's here."

"Steady soldier," no voice could have carried more authority then Robeson's deep basso. "Do your job, interpret what is happening."

Without taking his eyes from the screens the man snapped to attention, "Yes SIR. *The ship* is now entering the upper atmosphere over the equator to the west of the South American coast. I would say somewhere over the Galapagos and is proceeding in an easterly direction," his voice trailed off. No one spoke as all eyes followed the little red spot as it etched a steady elongating line onto the screen. The man swallowed. "It's moving very fast."

"How fast, God dammit?" Robeson betrayed irritation for the first time.

Consulting other screens filled with scrolling letters and numerals the soldier spoke softly, "I, I'm not sure of the exact velocity but it must be in excess of twenty-five thousand miles an hour and maintaining. It is descending slowly into denser air now and it's not slowing up. It's incredible."

"Spare us your incredulity soldier," Robeson was sarcastic, "what is its course?"

Again the soldier swallowed, "As far as it is possible to say at this time, it is bearing slightly northeast."

Silence descended as all eyes became hypnotically fixed on the ever-lengthening red line. It inched a ruler straight path across the ocean and crossed the green screen outline of South America into Columbia. Inexorably it traversed Columbia and Venezuela and then Guyana until it eventually exited the South American landmass somewhere over Georgetown.

On an adjacent screen they watched it begin its slow traverse of the Atlantic. Without deviation it crossed the vast, empty distance in a matter of minutes, passing to the south of the Cape Verde Islands and into Africa.

"It's still losing altitude, and still maintaining speed," the soldier seemed to be speaking to himself.

"God preserve and protect us," said one of the soldiers seated at the table and made the sign of the cross.

Albero without turning to Robeson said, "Are we prepared Clay? Can we hit it if it comes our way?"

"Not a chance at that speed Bob, but if it slows enough or stops over the mainland of the U.S., then I promise you that we can let *it* have it with something big at short range." Robeson's big black fist clenched and came down softly on the desk. "It will know it's been hit for sure. My boys are just waiting for my signal. You just need to give me the word and it will get hell."

"What's our response time?" Albero had not taken his eyes from the screens.

"I have had all fail safe procedures stood down. All weapons are armed and at immediate launch readiness. No decryption, no double keying, just plain language instruction on my voice." Robeson had focused intently on the President.

The intake of breath from a number of those present could be clearly heard.

Albero turned, white faced, from the screens and looking directly into Robeson's eyes said, "Excellent. We need speed, we may not get two chances."

"Jesus, Bob." A little twitch beside one of Borrhim's eyes betrayed his tension, "That's a helluva dangerous risk. One slip, one misunderstanding and we could immolate half a state." He turned to Robeson, "How are you going to selectively launch?"

"I'm not, Arnold. When I get the word from Bob, all warheads within a five minute trajectory will be launched against *the ship,* no matter how many that means." The use of the first names sounded incongruous.

Borrhim's eyes opened wide, "Dear God, that could . . ."

"Arnold!" Albero's voice was sharp and reprimanding.

Borrhim shut up.

The thin line was creeping across the screen. It looked so slow, it seemed to be taking forever to bridge the few inches of glass, but everyone knew only too well the significance of those millimetres in reality. It was all too easy to imagine the howling fury of its passage. In less then a half-an-hour from its first appearance on the screens, it had reached the western coast of North Africa.

"What's its speed now soldier?" Robeson's voice showed no tension.

"No change sir. As far as we can tell it's holding course and speed."

The line inched agonisingly slowly across the screen across Senegal, Mali, Nigeria, Chad, Ethiopia, and into Arabia, across the Arabian Sea and the Indian subcontinent and into China. No one spoke; all remained still, mesmerised by the implacable advance of *the ship.* In the harsh artificial light they might have been zombies, pallid and lined. Only the tick of the big clock on the wall punctuated the silence, time seemed to stand still.

The red line, unwaveringly, crossed China exiting into the East China Sea to the south of Japan and began to inch across the Pacific, slowly passing well to the north of Hawaii.

Then Albero spoke, flatly and slowly, "It *is* on its way here."

Robeson lifted the handset of a telephone and in almost a whisper spoke into it. "Confirm immediate launch status."

The reply couldn't be heard. Robeson replaced the receiver.

Eventually the line neared the west coast of America. No one breathed.

The soldier with the pointer spoke, "*The ship* is still losing altitude."

It crossed into California.

"Shoot Clay, let it have it," Albero's voice was strained, speaking quickly, "Let it have it now, right now . . ." Never turning his head from the screens.

"Impossible Bob, it's still going too fast." Robeson's big hands were spread wide, fingers trying to grip the table.

The line began to inch across the continent, straight as a die, time was suspended.

Across California, then Arizona, New Mexico, Texas, Oklahoma, Missouri, Illinois, and West Virginia.

"My God it's coming this way, it's heading straight for us." Borrhim's voice was thick. He was sweating. No one spoke.

It reached Washington DC. Robeson's voice, strained and husky, broke the total silence in the room, "Sweet Jesus, it's going to pass directly overhead!"

A colossal shock wave hit the building. Windows shattered, spraying shards of glass into the room; the lights went out; sirens wailed amid the thunder; plaster fell from the ceiling as the whole structural fabric shuddered; the television screens imploded into smithereens; the noise was physical in its violence.

Everyone screamed and fell or dived to the floor, covering their heads and crawling under furniture or crouching into corners. The force of the blast threatened the collapse of the building making the walls and floors vibrate heavily and stunning the minds of all inside.

Suddenly it was over.

Utter silence descended like deafness and in the darkness the air filled with a white talcum fog of plaster powder. No one moved. Then the big wall clock crashed to the floor with an explosion of shattering glass. A woman screamed somewhere in the darkness.

It seemed like minutes later, the dim emergency lights flickered on and the indistinct forms of the men began to stir and rise, groaning and covered with dust from the debris.

"Everyone okay, anyone hurt?" it was Robeson's voice, hushed, muffled by the thick dust.

"I, I think I'm bleeding," it was Albero from the floor.

Borrhim struggled up from his supine position beside the President, wiped the clinging white plaster dust from his mouth, and with disgust in his voice said, "You've shit yourself Bob."

Albero shakily got to his feet and looked down at himself, "Oh," he said inanely.

A marine, bleeding from the nose and breathless scrabbled over the rubbish into the room. "It's right on top of us, sir, *the ship* has stopped directly overhead."

There was a stunned silence as everyone turned and stared at the marine, blank amazement on every face.

Robeson pulled himself erect and futilely tried to dust his uniform. He straightened his tie and then, snapping to attention and grim faced, turned to Albero. "Mister President, shall I instruct an immediate launch?"

After a long pause, Albero, eyes downcast said, "Ah . . . no, not just yet."

CHAPTER 33

The menacing presence of the ship, its mind numbing, gargantuan black bulk, stationary and silent above the White House was devastating in its effect. Hard, professionally trained men, the cream of military academies, many seasoned in battle, were reduced to mere shadows of their former selves. They spoke in hushed whispers, moving slowly and carefully picking their way, noiselessly, among the light rubble. Many of the younger staff, typists and clerks, huddled in corners in a foetal position, clasping their knees against their chests and staring unseeingly. Some, who had become uncontrollably hysterical at the savage fury of the returning ship, now staggered drunkenly from the effects of heavy sedation.

In the hours that had passed since its cataclysmic arrival *the ship* had done nothing. No movement, no sound, no communication, it just hung there in the air not more than fifty meters above the cupola of the famous building. A black flying mountain, immeasurably heavy, impossibly close, defying all reason, all logic. Its very presence choked the breath from lungs, bowed the heads low of all who had the misfortune to be under it.

In the dim, half-light of the street outside, beyond the grounds, there was little movement. The light had an eerie, greenish, almost moonlight quality as it filtered weakly in from the sun at the distant edges of the vessel. That, together with the odd distortion of sounds, which had an echoing quality, gave everything a sense of unreality, almost as if the White House and its surroundings were in a cave or deep canyon.

The two men at the shattered windows of the Oval Office struggled to hide their almost overwhelming claustrophobia, a claustrophobia that the huge object imposed on everyone. They felt dwarfed, crushed by the immensity of the object that reduced the once proud buildings to dolls' houses. Both were white faced and strained, dark bags under their eyes, looking dishevelled despite the fact that they were freshly dressed in crisp, clean suits, free of the white plaster-talcum that pervaded everything and still rose in little choking clouds from the carpet when walked on.

Borrhim spoke first, "Jesus, that thing sure is scary, I don't mind admitting it." He shakily put a cigarette in his mouth and futilely searched in his pockets for a means to light it. After a few moments he stopped rummaging but didn't take the unlit cigarette from his lips. It trembled ever so slightly. A full minute passed. No one spoke. "What are we going to do? What the hell are we going to do?" His voice trailed off quietly and, for him, was high pitched, ragged.

Albero seemed not to have heard and idly picked shards of glass from the window frame while glancing repeatedly at the distant line of sunlight away at the edge of *the ship*. He couldn't decide whether *the ship* extended beyond the monument or not. "It's a big bastard," he muttered. They were directly under the centre of the colossus and he dismally realised that it stretched an equal distance behind him.

Robeson arrived, his shoes making crunching noises on the glass and rubbish scattered on the floor. His uniform was still covered in white dust and he looked quite bedraggled. His deep voice, on the surface controlled and calm, nonetheless managed to convey a sense of unease. "As far as we can establish, there is no problem with communications beyond the physical boundary of *the ship,* some static, that sort of thing but no big deal. Underneath it's a different matter. No radio communications are possible at all, not even short-range, walky-talky stuff. The phones are okay though and as long as we use them as far as the edge of *the ship* then we are able to communicate as normal."

He waited for some response but there was none. He continued, "The trail of damage from the airborne shock wave as the ship arrived has left some populated areas badly hit. Injuries from flying glass, fires, that sort of thing, but apart from that it doesn't seem to have done anything else. No rays, no wilful destruction, no attack as such." He paused again.

Borrhim spoke, "What's our position on the outside, is the situation still under control. Do we still have government?"

Robeson sagged slightly, "It's very bad. There is mass panic in the populated centres all along the areas that the ship passed over. People are looting and rioting and religious fanatics are springing up at every corner. We are not yet fully in control, although I have authorised a shoot to kill policy. It's hard to know if it will work, people are behaving so irrationally.

Bill Simpson tells me that the worldwide reaction is terrifying. Social order is breaking down. People are running amok in every nation as soon as the news arrives. It's the same here. Our suppression of the media wasn't completed in time and inevitably the word is spreading. Our problem is that we are not dealing with some extremist minority but the majority of the population, ordinary men and women. It is getting very ugly out there. I am sorry to say that we are even having some discipline problems with the troops."

Albero shook himself slightly and turned to face Robeson, "What is our situation here underneath the thing? Is there any increase in radiation or other hostile change in ambience? What effect is *the ship* having on the local environment?"

"None at all. *The ship*, apart from blocking out the sun, is doing nothing that we can detect. It just hangs there giving everybody the creeps. Apart from a natural temperature drop due to the lack of sunlight, our situation seems to meet the predicted parameters. It is totally inanimate. We have tried everything in an effort to communicate with it including some pretty crackpot ideas but nothing, not a squeak from it."

"Albero pondered for a few moments, "Exactly how long has it been there now?"

Robeson consulted his watch, "Four hours and twenty-three minutes."

Albero pondered this for a moment, "What are the chances of getting an aircraft, a fast helicopter under *the ship* and getting us out of here, out to the open?" Albero indicated the distant line of sunshine.

Robeson expressed puzzlement, "But we can drive out in a car, you know that. It's already been done several times, *the ship* doesn't react at all to our movements."

Albero calmly continued, "Just answer the question, when can you do it?"

With the slightest of shrugs Robeson replied, "I honestly don't know but I'll find out. There are fast attack 'copters just on the periphery of town, I'll order one in right now."

"Wait!" Albero suddenly seemed his old self, confident, authoritative, "I want all three of us to ready ourselves for departure in fifteen minutes or as soon as it is possible to do what is necessary, and I want it to be done secretly. You Clay, will have the fastest helicopter available make a dash to the White House lawn where we will be waiting. Do not use radio or telephone communication, do it all by runner. The copter will pick us up and leave again immediately. It is to be fully fuelled and will carry us without stopping to a nuclear shelter at least twenty miles distant or to a distance of fifty miles if there is no shelter available within that range."

He paused waiting for their total attention. "I will then instruct an immediate nuclear strike against the ship. Do you understand?"

"Yes," Robeson seemed at a loss for words.

"I repeat no one is to know what we are doing, not even your closest aides or secretaries, absolute secrecy is vital."

Borrhim and Robeson spoke together, "But our families are here in Washington."

Albero looked at each man in turn, steely eyed, "So is mine."

Borrhim continued, "But why? Are you really being serious Bob? Are you asking me to condemn my entire family to death without making the slightest effort to save them?"

Albero's voice became soft, cajoling, "Don't you understand? *This ship* has come here for a purpose. It is no accident that it is right on top of the White House. Why is it here? That is the question. Why not Moscow or London or Paris? I'll tell you why. Because WE are here, the heads of the government of the United States. The men who control the mightiest military machine in the world. Perhaps we are the only men who can threaten it. It wants us neutralised, out of the way, unable to initiate another blow against it. If it keeps us here, we are hostage to its every move. What chance of effective organisation against it if it has so easily captured our entire seat of power? You know as well as I do that we have been caught with our pants down. There is no one outside this complex who can initiate a nuclear strike. The United States is impotent at this moment."

He continued as if talking to himself, "I am also convinced that it is aware of our movements in some way, able to monitor our communications. Jesus anything as technically advanced as it is would have no problem tapping our phones and cracking our codes. We cannot take the slightest chance that it will discover our flight. If we start moving families and friends, organising evacuations, it will suspect something is up and then who knows what it will do. No, we need to move fast and light. We need speed and surprise." Albero looked up at both men, "I am sorry but that is the way it is."

For a moment there was silence, then Borrhim reached out and gripped Albero by the shoulder. "Bob, I never thought that the day would come when I would say this to you," he took a deep breath, "No! I refuse to follow your instructions. You can do what you like but I am not coming with you. I could not live with myself if I did what you are asking of me. I cannot and will not leave my family to die at my hand. I choose to die with them."

Albero snapped back his voice heavy with sarcasm, "And what of all the others here? Don't they have families? You'd be quite happy to sacrifice them wouldn't you. You were prepared to let thousands of others die when you supported the strike over Italy. Oh yes, you're such a bleeding heart. You're a hypocrite Arnold, you haven't got the guts when it gets personal, you make me sick."

Borrhim's face, hardened and he seemed about to speak. Then, without making a sound, he let go of the President's shoulder and turning on his heel walked quickly from the room.

Albero stared after him, venom in his eyes. Then he turned to Robeson, "Clay?"

Robeson returned Albero's gaze silently, his dark skin ashen, the big man's dark eyes seemed over liquid, his voice over husky. "Bob, that was unfair, what you are asking is not courageous, it's cowardly. I know you are supposed to be protected, come first, carry on as the figurehead, and maintain the integrity of the state. I know all that, but to knowingly flee to safety without so much as lifting a finger to help others; to condemn thousands of our own citizens to certain death while we run for safety, that's too much." His voice dropped to a hoarse whisper, "It's too much to ask of me."

Albero's eyes dropped and he turned to the window and began picking at the glass again. He was silent for a long time. Several times he made as if to speak and each time seemed to think better of it.

At last, he turned, and looking Robeson directly in the eye said quietly, "This is a last ditch stand Clay. This is our Alamo. We must prevail with this attack or it will surely be our last. What will follow if we fail? I cannot imagine, I shudder just to think of it. Perhaps it would be better not to know. Perhaps we and our families would be better off dead."

He fell silent again, turning to gaze at the distant sunlight. He lifted a corner of the furled flag behind the desk in his right hand, stroking it with his fingers. When he eventually spoke his voice was steady, calm, assured, "Very well Clay, I don't seem to have any options left. I suppose no one is indispensable, not even us. Perhaps Borrhim is right."

He turned and with a soft, almost distant expression on his face, said quietly, "Immediate launch against *the ship* Clay, maximum delivery, strike it with all we've got."

Robeson drew himself erect. Smiling grimly, he saluted and said, "Yes sir!" He turned and picked up the red phone on the Presidential desk. "Hello, this is the Chief of Staff, connect me with General . . ." but before he could say another word, he stopped. "The line's gone dead. Hello, hello . . .?"

"Wha . . .!" both men exclaimed together. A queer creeping feeling grew on their skins, the little hairs standing stiffly, goose bumps, like something occult. A strange odour began to pervade the room.

Faxes and flimsies, computer printouts, began to jiggle and move, eerily dancing to some silent tune. Paper clips, pencils, and other small paraphernalia skittered and rattled on desktops. Suddenly most of the paper in the room shot upwards into the air, and stuck nervously to the ceiling.

The emergency lights began to flicker and pulsate. A ticker machine in the corner started to chatter. A deep, deep, almost subliminal hum, powerful and resonant, began to be felt more than heard. Little things around the room started to make sizzling sounds. The hands on the clock in the Oval Office began to spin round at a crazy speed.

Then the paper on the ceiling began to move, slowly at first and then more rapidly, towards one end of the room.

"What's happening?" Albero directed the question at no one, "Aaagh " He clasped his mouth as sharp pain from a metal filling shot into his jaw. "What the hell is happening?"

Both Albero and Robeson turned and leaned out of the broken window, staring up at *the ship* and then wildly all around the grounds. Every piece of paper and light rubbish on the lawn and in the street seemed to be imbued with a life of its own, dancing and leaping as if to some nightmarish Pied Piper.

Robeson yelled, "Jesus Christ it's moving, it's moving."

Soldiers and civilians were rushing out of the building onto the grounds, running hither and thither, shouting and gesticulating, the clamour of their voices sounding hollow and indistinct. Some cursed and others called on God. All were clearly terrified.

Little by little, with no sound other than an ever-strengthening breeze, the sky began to lighten. *The ship* itself was so smooth and featureless that movement could not be discerned by watching its surface alone. The even, glassy, black of its underside defied the eye to fix on it. Only the gradually widening strip of sunshine and light gave the clue.

But move it did. Gradually, as more of the sky cleared, the sense of movement became more evident and, paradoxically, the feeling of claustrophobia strengthened. The awesome size and impossible weight of *the ship* was shocking. Everyone fell silent, craning their necks, agog at the spectacle.

Albero sagged back, sinking down onto the big dust covered chair behind his desk. He still held the corner of the flag in his hand. He was shaking.

Robeson continued to stare out of the window. Absently, he lit a cigarette and inhaled deeply.

Slowly, the room filled with sunlight and warmth returned.

CHAPTER 34

Bill Siemens flicked the switch on the desktop speaker, his secretary spoke with her usual soft Italian accent, "General Filshill is here, sir."

"Send him in." He flicked the switch again and turned back to the television screen.

A moment later he heard the door open and without turning his head indicated a nearby seat, "Sit down George, glad you could get here so quickly."

Filshill lifted the heavy chair and pulled it closer to Siemens so that both men were sitting almost side-by-side facing the television. On the screen in the foreground, was, by now a familiar sight, the shallows and rocks of what had once been Gibraltar. The picture rocked slightly, confirming the impression that the camera was on board a small aircraft. The wide-angle view made the outlandish black shape of *the ship* floating low above the land seem quite small. As they watched, the view telescoped and the camera lens closed in on *the ship,* helping to give a sense of how far away it was in reality. Neither man spoke for some time as the camera alternately zoomed in and panned back, sometimes focussing on the military aircraft and helicopters that were clearly shadowing the huge slow, moving object. There was little commentary from the commentator, the scenes seemed to say all that could be said.

Filshill spoke, "What broadcast is this Bill, one of ours?"

"No, this is *RAI Uno* and, as far as I can tell, it's being uplinked by most other public channels in the world as well." Siemens sounded irritated. "It never ceases to amaze me what the press will do for kicks. What good on earth is being served by showing this? Already we have mass panic and near complete breakdown in civil order and all they do is fan the flames. It makes me want to puke."

"You are right of course Bill, at least the President had the guts to try and curb our own people, but these *Eye-ties* are just undermining the whole thing."

The screen darkened as Siemens switched off the set and pushed his big chair back on its castors without getting up. Filshill pulled his seat back in front of the desk and sat down. "What's up Bill?" he asked.

Siemens slouched back in the chair, "George, I called you here to discuss likely developments with *the ship*. Up until now we have had little idea of where it was going or what it was going to do. No contact of any kind has been made, as you know, so we really are guessing, groping in the dark," he paused, "just consider the facts for a moment. It barrels in from outer space and circumnavigates the globe at some God-awful speed. Stops plumb on top of the White House scaring the shit out of every one, and then calmly cruises, low, across the Atlantic at a hundred miles-an-hour or so. It just doesn't make any sense."

Filshill interrupted, "Why didn't we have another go at it while it was still in mid-Atlantic? It was a sitting duck, well away from anywhere."

Siemens smiled thinly, "I am not privy to the President's inner thoughts. Especially now that we have the imposition of martial law in the States, but as far as I can work it out, the current thinking is to interpret *the ship's* behaviour as conciliatory. Apart from the damage from its passing it has behaved in a passive manner. We, in accord with most of the international community, are prepared to let the thing have some rope. To wait and see what it is trying to do. After all, it is making itself very visible and behaving in a cautious manner like it was being careful not to start anything accidentally."

"Are you kidding, 'not start anything?' By behaving cautiously as you put it, by making itself visible, it has brought most of the civilised world to near chaos. Much more of this and it won't need to do anything at all."

"My instructions are to maintain a state of readiness but to do nothing until we know what it intends." Siemens was brisk in his manner.

"Huh and when might that be?" Filshill sounded sarcastic.

"No need to be flippant George. At first, of course, we thought it was threatening the United States and now, that it is returning to the site of its attack on Gibraltar." Siemens leaned forward, "for my money it's not going to do that."

Filshill looked puzzled, "What makes you say that?"

Siemens tapped the desk with his fingertips, "It has been travelling at the same slow speed and low altitude for nearly thirty-six hours now without wavering by a millimetre in speed, altitude or course. It is now nearly over Gibraltar, or what's left of it, but it's not directly over it, it's to the north. It's been obvious for some time now that it would pass some way to the north, over the southern tip of Spain. You have to admit that act is at odds with the idea that it is returning to the site of its attack. And further more it is still showing no signs of slowing down."

Filshill interjected, "That means nothing. We know it can stop on a dime and turn in the same space. So what, that it has not arrived directly over Gibralter. It doesn't need time to slow down and turn, indeed it might be stopped right now for all you know."

Siemens switched on the T.V. with a remote control. They both watched the screen in silence for a few minutes until eventually Siemens spoke. "It hasn't stopped George. It is still moving, still following the same course."

"Well, where do you think it is going?" asked Filshill.

Siemens looked straight at him, "I'll tell you where I think it's going. It's going home, back to its hole in the ground, back to your patch George."

"What, you can't be serious. What makes you think that?" Filshill seemed agitated.

"It's simple, just extrapolate the curved line of its present course beyond Gibraltar and you arrive as near as dammit at the place from which it came." Siemens paused.

Filshill blinked, "You don't say?"

Both men turned back to the outlandish image of *the ship* on the screen. Siemens waited quietly while the notion sank into Filshill's awareness.

Filshill spoke, "Why would it do that?"

Siemens' gaze unfocussed, looking inward, "It's my bet that the thing is a machine, a robot. Some nightmarish device, unmanned, from God-knows when or where and is following a programmed response. It's on a sort of autopilot, if you get my drift. We interfered with it when we attacked it and it retaliated reflexively but it's now back on programme and having finished whatever observation or measurements that it needed, it is going back to standby status. It's my belief that it will nest itself back into that hole and go quiescent."

"That's one hell of a speculation," replied Filshill, "I grant you that much of its behaviour is machine-like, no communication, reflexive responses to our, how shall I say, approaches, and no discernible sentient activity but it must be one hell of a machine to know where Washington is from outer space . . .and why would it go there anyway?"

"How the hell would I know? It did nothing there, nothing at all." Siemens seemed irritated. "Have you a better idea? It's coming this way and until we know more, I am going to act as if it is returning to its starting point. That's why I called you. We need to prepare. The President's plan to destroy the thing is much weaker now. He believes that the effects on world affairs from its presence are now too deep to reverse and that is the consensus view in NATO also. The original motivation for quick destruction is much reduced and the latest policy is that we are going to have to face the consequences of its appearance on the world scene whether we like it or not. We are going to have to live with it for the moment."

Filshill interrupted, "Are we to let it peaceably do what it wants, make no attempt to stop it? Accept its authority?"

"Hardly." Siemens had become quite conversational in his manner, smiling slightly, "In fact, it is unlikely to come to that. But publicly at least we will roll out the welcome mat and attempt to communicate with it, learn from it, and all that crap. But there is one big fly in the ointment. The Russians have made it clear that they are not prepared to let it get into their air space. If my prediction is wrong and it overshoots Italy on its present course then all hell is going to break loose. The Reds are going to hit it with everything they've got and we will be forced to participate. We better be ready George and by God if I have anything to do with it, we WILL be ready."

He leaned forward, his face lined and hard. "I want you to pull out all the stops on this, no delays, no excuses. You will withdraw all senior American personnel including civilian scientists from the Abruzzi area immediately and prepare for a nuclear war. Even at the speed *the ship* is travelling, we don't have much time. If it over-shoots Italy, it's my bet that the Russians will let it have it as soon as it gets over the Adriatic." He paused, "Well? What are you waiting for?"

Filshill got up from the chair, then stopped and leaned his hands on the desk, "What's our chances with this thing Bill? Do we have a shot?"

Siemens didn't answer immediately. He turned to the image on the television screen first and then with a heavy, tired quality in his voice, "Son, if it comes to a shooting war, I don't think we have a chance in hell."

Filshill stood up and left the room.

After a time Siemens rose and went to the big window and looked down into the street below. It was chaos, traffic at a standstill, an unruly mob gesticulating and waving placards, and heavily armed riot police everywhere.

He spoke aloud to the empty room, "How bad can it get? Every day it gets worse." He looked up as the helicopter came into sight from the roof. He waved his hand half-heartedly, "Good luck George, I hope to see you again some day."

The sight and sound of the ugly machine was like a signal to the mob. Fighting erupted with women screaming and men shouting as they clashed with the police, driving towards the heavy gates at the entrance to the courtyard. Bedlam ensued as the conflict swayed back and forth below. It was a full half-hour before the mob was routed and the street cleared.

He was still gazing out of the window some time later when the door to his office opened. He turned to face the aide, "Yes?"

The aide crossed the room and stopped in front of the desk, proffering a sheaf of papers, "We think it has changed course, sir."

Siemens started, "*The ship*? It has changed course? Where to, what is it doing?" He seemed unhanded.

"It's a minor alteration, sir, but we believe that it has adjusted its path. It is holding a slightly more northerly direction now." The aide spread one of the pages onto the desktop. "Here is the adjusted projection if it holds its new heading."

Siemens leaned over the desk, staring at the outlines of the northern Mediterranean clearly identifiable on the sheet. There were two dotted lines in red, very close together, but one slightly north of the other. He traced the more northerly with his finger until he touched the coast of Italy. "It's going to pass over Rome." He looked up at the aide, wide eyed, "It's coming here. Why would it do that?"

The aide didn't answer.

He sat down, "Where is it now, has it changed speed or altitude?"

The aide indicated a position on the map, "Just here sir, to the east of the Gulf of Almeria, it will be clear of Spanish territorial waters soon and it hasn't altered altitude or speed."

Siemens dismissed the man with a wave of his hand and swivelling in the big chair, gazed at the television screen where the huge, black shape dominated the picture. He plucked at his lower lip, *"This is all wrong,"* he thought, *"Why is it changing course now, here in the middle of Europe? It has nearly completed one and a half circumnavigations of the world without wavering and now it has changed heading."* A heavy sense of dread and foreboding bore down on him, *"I don't like this, I don't like it at all."*

The speaker on his desk buzzed.

"What is it?" he asked curtly.

His secretary's voice said, "It's Washington on the line sir, the Oval Office, the President in person."

He shuddered involuntarily, *"This is it,"* he thought and picking up one of the phones said, "Put him through."

CHAPTER 35

Apart from the slightly-clouded, plastic sheets which passed for glass in the windows, the incident room at the White House was barely changed by the arrival of the ship. All was clean and orderly and even the big clock had been replaced. The room was crowded and noisy, smoke filled, with several aides running in and out of the room servicing their seniors who ringed the big table. Everyone was haggard, tired looking, and tense.

The bank of televisions had been replaced with the majority displaying an image of *the ship*. The remainder had various outlines of the globe including the Mediterranean Sea with the position of *the ship* indicated by a glowing red dot.

All eyes were fixed on the President as he laid the telephone receiver down, the Russian Premier's thick accent still ringing in the room.

"Well that fixes that," he said wearily., "You all heard, Christof cannot be dissuaded from attacking *the ship*. The Russians won't let it anywhere near their territory and now that it has changed course, I can't really blame them. What's our status, Clay?"

Robeson, flanked by his Generals and admirals, exuded military authority. His eyes fixed every member of his team as if seeking final assurance before speaking. "We are ready, sir. We have been tracking it closely and upgrading our strike capability ever since it left our shores. I believe that we can deliver a yield that at least equals the combined Russian, British, and French forces, and we can deliver it right now."

Borrhim, looking pallid and somehow flabby, spoke, "How many kilotons is that?"

Robeson hesitated before replying quietly, "You don't really want to know Arnold. I can't speak with any accuracy for the Russians or the others but the total will be enormous."

A hush descended on the room. Only the quiet background chatter of the commentators from the televisions broke the complete silence.

Borrhim wiped his neck with a handkerchief and speaking in a whisper to himself, "Truth sits upon the lips of dying men."

Albero spoke to the assembled group at large. "Gentlemen, it grieves me that we have come to this. Our hope that an alternative strategy of conciliation, of wait and see, has come to nought. *The ship*, as you know, cannot be contacted and will not contact us despite our best efforts. We have all witnessed the all too horrific effects of its passage over land. Massive, near hysterical reaction on a scale that threatens to overcome our peacekeeping forces. Many of our cities are still marginal, and now Malaga looks like it will take days to be brought under control. We are on the verge of complete civil disorder in every developed nation in the world. Trading in every stock exchange world-wide is suspended, industry and commerce is grinding to a standstill."

Borrhim's deep voice cut across the President, "But do we need to use so much force? The effects of nuclear detonation on such a scale must be incalculable. It might poison the entire globe."

Robeson replied, "We do not know that. The first attack on *the ship* was in some way absorbed, there were no fission products at all. This makes it impossible to assess how much radiation will result."

Borrhim persisted. "But so many. There will inevitably be a massive residual tonnage as soon as *the ship* is destroyed."

"We believe that we can abort most of the remaining warheads as soon as *the ship* is killed." Robeson surveyed the assembled faces, staring back at him, wide-eyed and silent. "Our hope is that if we attack by surprise and rain down warheads from all directions, its defences will be saturated and it will be forced to take a huge number of direct hits. It is inconceivable that it can sustain what will be tantamount to unlimited nuclear detonations." Again he looked around the table and lowered his eyes, staring at the paper in front of him. "However, it is certain that there will be a number of excess detonations. How many we cannot say; but clearly, considerable damage will result to the local environment."

Albero broke the ensuing silence, "In any event, with France and Britain siding with Russia to strike as soon as it is clear of the Spanish mainland, I do not think that we have any alternative but to go along." The semblance of a smile escaped his lips. "I intend to give our allies in this affair, our wholehearted support. We will not hold anything back. This time we will fry it. Any comments?"

There was a nervous fidgeting around the table, some glancing uneasily at the armed marines stationed at both open doors.

Borrhim spoke, "Better let Siemens know. There is nothing he can do with this short notice but it is his patch, and we should inform him."

Albero seemed brisk, almost bright in his manner, "Okay if that's all, lets go." He turned to Robeson, "Clay, it's up to you now. Co-ordinate our effort with the others, we don't have much time." Robeson followed by all the uniformed men, left the room.

The remainder turned to watch the television screens where the strange black object could be seen from every angle.

"Right," said Albero speaking over his shoulder to an aide, "I'll speak to Siemens now."

CHAPTER 36

"Perfect," he thought. His skin felt as if it was crawling with cobwebs. The eyes of the world were fixed on him, following him every foot of the way. The surface of the earth passed slowly and beautifully below as he tugged leisurely at the planet's skin, making it spin. He had noted the distant touches of the eyes high in the sky, in the cold pure reaches of space. These would help him he knew; these would be his tools when the time came.

Somehow the giants sensed his readiness, his mental preparation for the test ahead. Feeling their kinship he collapsed within himself, deliberately telescoping his perspectives like playing a game with a kaleidoscope, deep into the lambent green. Here was his power, his communion with the great ones. They ignored him and yet saluted him, aware and yet unaware, always the enigma of simultaneous singularity and plurality.

The colossal symphony hummed its overture, pregnant with power, awaiting his command. He spoke with them, he knew not how, but communicate he did. They replied, calling the roll of giants. Oh it was faulty and incomplete but still they recognised his will. He ached for perfect oneness, though he knew it could never be so. They would always know more of him than he of them. Their ancient masters had been greater then he, only those timeless magi truly knew the giants. But he was happy, satisfied. Here was a completeness greater than he had thought possible, not perfection but near. He had grown in them and they had found expression and purpose in him.

Again the twisting distortion of place and he looked down on the shoreline as the planet brought the sea to him. He looked ahead over the calm blue water to the distant horizon, he must be precise in his actions, arrive with purpose.

In his mind's eye, he recalled, behind him now, the place of destruction, the symbol of his wrath, the bones of Gibraltar. "*Was it enough,*" he thought, "w*ill they require another lesson?*"

The giants interrupted his inner wanderings, whispering to him of their tiny shift in direction. He was pleased. Yet again they knew his will.

He reviewed his actions so far. All had gone well. The world was already reeling from his presence, running from him in fear, or toward him in worship. Yes, soon they would listen and do as he instructed. The great cleansing would begin. He drifted into reverie as the sea rolled beneath him.

He started violently, wrenching himself back to alertness as a giant bell tolled, the thunderous concussion shuddering in the green. Great voices boomed distantly, deeply resounding chords. Accompanying sounds rapidly and majestically swept up the audible spectrum until a huge sotto-voce curtain of harmony hung in his mind. The giants sang of warning.

"*What is it?*" He snapped his focus outward, out beyond the horizon. "There, there, far away, and there, and there, all around," he could feel them now, the cobwebs, clinging. More and more of them, suffocating, scores, no, hundreds of them.

Now they climbed above the limb of the earth, higher and higher, clawing their painful way up the ladder of gravity, scaling the slippery funnel of the earth's mass to near escape velocity.

He knew then that man had not surrendered. The puny were challenging him, throwing all their might against him. He felt the giants observe and measure. The thrum increased, doubling on itself. The giants were watching attentively with care, great care, and with caution. This was not a threat to be ignored.

He felt a snag of fear. "*Was it possible? Could they, the puny, by stealth and numbers undo him?*"

The giants watched and waited.

218

He felt his fear grow gnawing at his confidence. He called in his mind, "Do something, do something." The giants held their harmony, long, breathlessly long. On all sides the deadly creations hauled their venomous children like brightly glowing blooms on stalks of smoke and fire, up and ever upward to their frigid spawning ground. He gazed, transfixed with a cold dread as they climbed for what seemed like an eternity. Then at last in the still dark depths of space, the myriad spiders paused, hanging against gravity. He felt their robot minds, simplistically fixed on their deadly purpose, fix on him. He watched as their bellies swelled and ruptured parting their hellish broods.

He shivered as he felt the thick, cloying webs they threw towards him, thick like a carpet. "So many . . . so many," his mind stalled, there seemed to be hundreds of them. *"How can they do this? In order to destroy me, they will destroy themselves."* He knew instinctively that they had simultaneously unleashed more nuclear destruction than any man could imagine, perhaps enough to render the earth a wasteland. He quailed, shrinking from the memory of the first attack; the pain had been excruciating, unbearable. Now his dream, his great goal would never be achieved, all was undone.

The giants checked, their song faltered. Dissonance, a lack of syncopation, confusion.

"Wha...?" fear galvanised his purpose and cleared his mind, the giants had mistaken him, confused his momentary weakness with a desire to surrender, to flee, or perhaps even to die.

"NO!" He screamed in his mind, frantic, *"NEVER!"* He flung his arms wide, embracing them, melding with them, burying himself in them.

"KILL! KILL!" with all his heart he implored them, willed them to respond.

He felt fiery tears well up in his eyes and his throat close in joy as the colossi rallied to unison and harmony, roaring their challenge.

He choked with emotion screaming, "KILL, KILL, oh, kill them all."

Ever closer, the warheads began to fall like icy hail from space while others still climbed on tails of fire from every horizon. All funnelled towards him, ravening to consume him with their own maniacal death. Rage filled his breast, his heart pounded, and he clung precariously to awareness as the thunder of the giants threatened to overcome him.

His skin grew hot, prickling with fire like fierce pins and needles. Blisters bubbled, itched, and burst. Thick shafts of pale, green light flickered and flashed outwards, stabbing again and again into the firmament. Bolts of shimmering brightness, whiplashing the air, each one finding a warhead and consuming it in a great splashing ball of brilliant whiteness. Quickly the entire sky filled with blinding flashes, incandescent showers of leviathan sparks, and volcanic fulminations like some pyrotechnic festival for the gods. "Festa" in Valhalla.

Amidst the fury and confusion, he sensed the concussions, felt the air rip and shred with the violence. He saw the upper atmosphere cloud and thicken, fill with foulness; here indeed was Armageddon. And still the deadly weapons rained in like a monsoon from hell, threatening to overwhelm the giants by sheer numbers, and by sheer weight batter a hole through the lances of green.

The giants' roaring intensified, seeming that it might split his head, pounding at his senses till he felt that he might never hear again. The warheads crowded thicker and thicker, closer and closer to victory, ever onward. The mighty concussions hammered at him now, the searing heat bathing his skin. The lances flashed and flicked, dancing a madman's nightmare in the lurid sky. Any moment now they would be in range, start their self-detonation.

The first got through and pounced. The slobbering spider lanced him with its fusion fangs. Agony flared. *Another, oh Christ, not again!* His mind recoiled from the memory of his agony, a dolour beyond enduring. *And yet another!*

He sensed fear, the onset of defeat. He braced himself for the crushing acceleration of flight. The giants heard, sought an opening, an escape in the midst of chaos, a back door from Hades.

Then, suddenly he knew it was over as he felt the climax pass. The bombs still rained in, but their numbers were reducing now, the press was slackening, the attack was spent. The heat and concussion receded till at last the final group flared balefully in the high thin air of the upper atmosphere. The brilliant light of their passing illuminating the thick, boiling clouds and the thunder of their destruction, dying by degrees, stifled by the intense putrescent rain that fell.

The world was dark and gloomy, lugubrious. The seas rough and whipped to frenzy by the high, shrieking, winds. But he felt joy. He had won! They would come now, on bended knees, begging mercy.

The giants sang a quiet song and tugged at the skin of the planet.

CHAPTER 37

Pope Michael the First raised his right hand to give his blessing to the dense crowd below the balcony. Thousands were crammed into the huge, near circular piazza of Saint Peter's Basilica. The overall impression was of a dark carpet, speckled white with upturned faces. He was acutely conscious that this enormous gathering represented only a tiny fraction of his worldwide audience. Television was bringing his face and words into millions of homes and churches all over the world.

His sermon, delivered in several languages including his native English tongue, had been difficult for him. How to reconcile the seemingly devilish manifestation of *the ship* with the Christian concept of God, and of his chosen people, had not been easy. *How could he include something possessed of seemingly supernatural powers and capable of such destruction within the teachings of Christ? Was this Armageddon, the end of the world? Was this Gabriel sounding his last trump as so many had claimed?*

His strong Irish brogue had revealed itself in his voice as he delivered his impassioned call to the faithful to reaffirm their faith, to pray for deliverance and salvation in this time of darkness and despair. He had to call on all of his deep-rooted Irish Catholic convictions in the hours of private and silent agonising that he had endured since the first appearance of *the ship* in order to maintain his own strong faith.

"This is the will of God," he had proclaimed that afternoon, "God who moves in mysterious ways. We have to accept this as part of His divine plan. From this sorrow will come good in the end even though we cannot see it. In God's own way, when He is ready, He will reveal His purpose to us."

He had despaired at times in recent days, especially when they pointed out that he was English speaking. He knew only too well the gutter prophecy that the world would not end until an Englishman took the crossed keys, the golden Keys of the Kingdom of Heaven and was chosen to be "The Servant of the Servants of God."

"Why, oh, why me?" he had cried to God in his despair. "Make Your will clear to me, give me the strength to understand." He had implored, beat his breast in his mental struggle but there had been no insight. The images in his tiny private chapel had remained as enigmatic as ever.

"This is a test of our faith in the Lord, Jesus Christ," he had intoned to the attentive millions. "The ways of the world have been evil, many have lost the path of true faith. We have abandoned the Church of Christ and terror and confusion strikes in our hearts."

He had paused, dramatically letting the echoing sound of his voice die to silence; then he spoke slowly and clearly. "Have you forgotten the words of Jesus of Nazareth himself?" As he uttered the name he bowed his head slightly; then he had thundered, "*On this rock I will build my church and the gates of hell shall not prevail against it.*" Only by prayer and devotion can we have a hope of salvation. Pray to God to give you the strength to accept His divine will. Have trust in He who saves the world.

So thick was the crowd that none could adopt the customary kneeling position and yet despite the enormity of the numbers there was no sound; only the dying echo of his last words from the loudspeakers.

He began his benediction, his hand describing a cross in the air, "*In nomini Patris, et Filius, et Spiritus Sanct . . .* " His words trailed off. Above the opposite rim of the great colonnaded gallery encircling the piazza, the terrifying black bulk of *the ship* slowly appeared.

The carpet below turned black as the heads turned, craning to see the awesome sight. For a few moments, all was still as the unbelievable bulk moved slowly and silently across the sky, across the great piazza, seeming in the end to barely clear the great ornate dome of the basilica. The bright, summer sunlight dimmed until there remained only a ghostly half-light and the warm, balmy air grew cold as a wind sprang up.

Complete and unrestrained panic erupted. People died in their hundreds. Men, women, and children, screaming for succour, crushed and suffocated by the mad struggle to flee. The crowd was so dense, so tightly packed, and the security forces so paralysed by the crushing sight of *the ship* that nothing could be done but let the wild slaughter run its course and extinguish itself.

Eventually the piazza was emptied of people able to stand, the last of the crowd scrambling madly, heedlessly over a carpet of mangled bodies. The Pope, who had remained silent and still, transfixed by the double spectacle, sobbed as he gazed at the sight below. Hundreds of figures lay spread-eagled and distorted in odd postures. The moans and cries of the injured filled the air, many trying to raise themselves in supplication towards him.

He raised his eyes to the black, featureless monstrosity above, quaking, barely able to contain his fear. Clutching the big crucifix that hung from his belt, he raised it shakily above his head, holding it at arms length towards *the ship.* "Out of the depths I cry unto thee, oh Lord. Lord hear my prayer . . .ungh." His words were cut short as two tall, carnival dressed, Swiss Guards rushed out onto the balcony from the room behind, and unceremoniously bundled him back into the building.

He struggled, trying to twist free of their grip, all three tumbling to floor in the process.

"Let me go, leave me alone," he panted as he clambered to his feet, his immaculate gown crumpled and dishevelled.

"But Your Holiness," the Swiss guardsmen replied in unison, shamefaced and helping him to dust himself off and adjust his white, silken robes, "You cannot be permitted to remain outside, it is too dangerous. *The ship* has stopped above the Vatican. It's stationary overhead."

The assembled cardinals in their contrasting red and purple surrounded him. "Holy Father, you must leave this place. There is nothing to be served by remaining here now."

The Pope pushed them back, "And what of those poor creatures out there, they need our help, our support," he indicated the open French window to the balcony and continued breathlessly, "they need absolution, the last rites. Above all they need spiritual guidance if they are not to despair."

Cardinal Giuseppe Melone, tall and slim, urbane in his manner with a pronounced Roman nose and deeply sallow skin, towered over the short stocky figure of the Holy Father. He took him by the arm, "Michael," he said in a soft, cultured voice which betrayed no hint of an accent, "we are already there in large numbers, tending the sick, and dying. We are doing God's work alongside the good people of the security forces. There is no reason for you to expose yourself to unnecessary danger. You must leave the Vatican at once. Provisions have been made for speedy transport to a safe place."

The little Irishman gazed up with his watery, blue eyes into the clear dark orbs of the taller man. "Peppine," he said, "you are one of the wisest men I know and a good and true friend, but this time you are wrong. I know in my heart that I must stay. It is God's will that this terrible thing has come here; here to the very bosom of Mother Church." He turned and walked across the room to a little *prie-dieu* of simple oak that stood against the wall, a huge crucifix above it. "Let us pray for courage and guidance in our hour of need."

He knelt on the velvet step. The cardinals, in unison, faced the figure on the wall, made the sign of the cross and knelt where they had stood. The Swiss guards knelt on one knee but did not bow their heads like the others, instead keeping an alert awareness of what was happening all around.

For a long time there was no sound from those in the room only the faint cries and wails from the dark piazza could be heard through the closed doors to the balcony.

At last the Pope made the sign of the cross and stood up. He turned to the group in the room and said, "It is my conviction that this terrible *ship* has come here for a specific purpose. What that is I cannot imagine, but it is God's will and my duty is to remain here until that purpose is made clear. God, in his own time, will reveal all to us."

He raised his hand, stifling a riposte from the cardinals. "That is an end to it, I shall pray and wait here in this room. The rest of you must go and give spiritual succour to the faithful. Assure them of my good health and ask them to pray for me as I pray for them." He waved them away.

"Dear Peppine," he called to the group as it left, "not you, please remain with me, pray with me."

The tall slim figure turned and smiled, "Of course, Michael, God's will be done."

The two men sat in opposite corners of the room, the Pope near the window next to the crucifix and the cardinal by the door. With some resistance to his wishes, the guardsmen eventually left the room at the insistence of the Holy Father.

Silence gradually descended on the piazza and the queer, dim light slowly faded into darkness. Neither spoke, both communing with their innermost thoughts, fingering the rosary beads in their hands, invisible one to the other in the gloom.

A servant entered without knocking and set a tall candle beside the big crucifix on the wall. The old man, grey and bent with years, moved in complete silence, lighting the candle, opening the prayer book that lay under the big crucifix and kissing the feet of the figure that hung there. Carefully he opened the balcony doors as if afraid to disturb the stillness, letting in the cooler than usual night air; and then, bowing slightly to the praying figures, left the room as silently as he had entered.

The guttering, yellow flame from the candle was all the light in the room, the pallid glow hardly delineating the motionless men and casting dim, formless shadows on the walls. Eventually the cardinal seemed to doze.

The big bells of the Basilica tolled the hours into the night. The sound oddly flat and reflecting emptily from the alien surface above. The world seemed to be waiting.

The last faint echoes of midnight were still hanging in the air when a pale-greenish light began to suffuse the room from the balcony. The Pope started upright in his seat, staring at the open balcony doors. Cardinal Melone seemed to sleep.

A softly glowing, green object drifted silently through from the balcony into the room. It stopped for a moment suspended in mid-air about two metres from the floor. A corona of lambent green surrounded it, halo like. It slowly turned what seemed to be its face towards the startled man in the chair. It was like a featureless man's head wearing a motorcycle crash helmet, glowing with an internal luminescence, green, dusty, silent. It stopped, still, solid, and unwavering in mid-air as if looking at him, waiting.

The Pope swallowed reflexively and slowly made the sign of the cross, carefully touching his forehead, shoulders, and breast. He clasped his hands in front of him and slid to his knees before the unearthly sight, not taking his staring eyes from the eerie object. "God save and protect us," he whispered.

The whispering rustle of his robes, or perhaps it was his sibilant supplication, awoke the cardinal. Melone opened his eyes wide until the whites reflected the phosphorescent green glow. He drank in the scene, rigid with terror, the tendons on his hands knotted as he gripped the arm of the chair.

His Holiness raised his right hand towards the object and trembling, made a slow sign of the cross towards it. *"Benedicat nos omnipotens Deus."*

For a moment nothing happened. Then the green object spoke, "Amen."

Cardinal Melone started so violently that he slipped from the chair and crashed noisily to the floor.

The door burst open and two of the Swiss Guard rushed in, pistols at the ready. Light flickered brightly, nakedly illuminating everything for an instant in a stark, sickly green. The first man's head exploded and the second made a quiet gagging sound as his chest opened like a great mouth. Both bodies crumpled like rag dolls to the beautifully tiled floor. Blood spread in a dark pool and there was a faint stench of burned meat and ozone.

The cardinal repressed an urge to vomit and clutching his rosary got to his knees and laid his hands on the bodies. In a strangled voice he said, "God save your servants and grant them eternal rest."

A hard, unmodulated voice came from the stationary green head. It was not loud but somehow a huge sound which belied the size of the object. The voice, echoing slightly as if speaking from within a large chamber, said in a slow, measured meter, *"Ogni speranza lasciate voi chi entrate."*

The sharp intake of the pontiff's breath could clearly be heard.

Running feet clattered in the passageway outside.

"Fermati, STOP!" the Pope's voice brooked no denial. The corridor fell silent. "Don't come any further, stay where you are," he paused seeming to remember where he was, *"rimanete dove siete."*

He turned his attention to the glowing head, "What are you?" His voice trembled and squeaked, near hysteria. "What do you want?" *What manner of thing kills so unhesitatingly and yet quotes from Dante?* In the name of God what do you want?"

The pale glow around the head began to pulse slightly, dimming and brightening alternately.

"Servant of the Servants of God, listen carefully and do my bidding," the harsh voice seemed over loud in the silence, "I am come to save mankind."

Both men gaped, jaws sagging in astonishment. For a moment they dragged their eyes from the glowing head and looked in wonder at each other and then back to the outlandish object. There was silence for a full minute.

The voice spoke again, somehow commanding in its monotone, "Michael, Keeper of the Keys, you are the chosen one. By this visitation you shall know it, you shall be the tool through which my will be done." A faint beam of luminescence emanated from the object and bathed the Pope's head, looking for the entire world like an emerald halo.

The Pope became transfixed, sweat running from his face, shivering violently, as if in a trance. His eyes stared and his mouth hung open. After some time he seemed to relax, sagging slightly. He slowly bowed his head and said in a whisper, "Thy will be done." The pale beam went out.

Melone stared at him, astonishment clear on his face.

After a moment's pause the voice spoke again, "Mankind has lost the way of truth. Adam has sinned against that which created him in his own likeness; neither Sodom nor Gomorrah can equal the depths of deprivation to which man has sunk. The very garden of creation is despoiled by man's wantonness. This, the most original of sin, shall be purified through me; and through me, man shall again gain the light and the truth. Only through my will shall mankind avoid eternal perdition and everlasting darkness."

The little Irishman trembled visibly and without lifting his head he said faintly, "What is your will? Instruct me in your way."

"All will be made clear to you in time." The green light within the object intensified and the echoing voice grew in size seeming to fill the very stones of the walls. "Bring to this place the leaders of souls and of nations, all who command, and all who teach; the peoples of the *garden* shall gather here before the Basilica. They shall bring their scribes and the world will hear my voice and my will through you, the Chosen One. They shall come in haste for, as of old, I shall await but three days before returning to you."

In the ensuing pause Melone felt the cold, clammy sweat of fear drip from his nose. His guts twisted, his mind raced, confusion filled him, a terror deeper than physical fear gripped him. He slowly bowed his head, his hands shaking.

The pontiff's voice, stronger now, broke the silence, "Thy will be done." He crossed himself.

The light dimmed and the head slowly receded out of the window. The darkness returned, relieved only by the guttering yellow luminosity of the candle.

In the dimness both men seemed carved from obsidian, not moving, not speaking.

Then the pontiff lifted up his head and rising to his full height, straightened his back and strode to the foot of the crucifix on the wall. He laid his hand on the feet of the figure. In the candlelight his face was radiant, his eyes shining. "Peppine, we have heard the word of God, unworthy as we are, we have been visited by his angel, and we have been chosen to do his work."

The cardinal got to his feet, his back bowed, trembling, wringing his hands, "Holy Father how can you be sure, how can we know?"

"We have seen his works, have we not? His might and his power are beyond all nature, beyond all explanation, beyond man. He has conquered distance and time, gravity and the void, the air and the land. Even the very forces of creation, of the atoms themselves are as nothing to him. Yet he comes to us, to the church."

The smaller man reached up to touch the cardinal's shoulder. "Thomas did not believe until he had seen, but you have seen Peppine, you have heard and borne witness to the facts. Apart from the Resurrection even Our Saviour, Jesus Christ, did not work miracles of this order. Do you not understand, do you not see? The second coming is upon us, *Gloria in excelsis Deo.*"

The cardinal's face twisted in his inner agony, "But the deaths, the destruction, surely this is contrary to the teachings

230

of Christ. This might be the work of some alien, unimaginably cruel, life form."

"Do alien life forms go to church? Do they ignore the powers of mankind and choose Christ's representative on earth? Do they quote scriptures? Dante?" The soft irish accent added conviction to the pontiff's words. "Take care that you do not turn your back on the word of God just as the Pharisees did two thousand years ago."

The cardinal wiped the sweat from his brow although he was chittering as if deeply chilled. His voice became barely audible, "May God preserve and protect us." He made the sign of the cross. "This may be the work of the devil, the Antichrist. God doesn't change his mind, alter his teachings."

His face shining with an inner strength, the pontiff's voice had a clarion ring to it, "Doesn't He? You forget that the Lord God Jehovah of the Old Testament had a different testimony. Then there was no teaching of turning the other cheek, the evil were smitten, struck down, and his ways were often harsh . . .an eye for an eye. Mighty was His power against the enemies of Zion. Might this not be the new message from God, a message He has so clearly demonstrated by His own hand? A message for a new age, a new philosophy for mankind. Did not Christ bring a new message from God, change the old order?"

Melone's face was parchment white, greasy with cold sweat, "But a *ship*, a space ship? A machine? How can a machine be the angel of God?"

"Two thousand years ago, Our Saviour came as a man, the son of a poor carpenter to change the world. Why? Why did he choose such a vehicle for his message? Perhaps that was the best, the only way to speak to a pre-technological society. And where did he deliver his message? Not to the military rulers of the world, not to the Romans. No, he spoke to the Scribes and Pharisees, to the leaders of the Jews, an entirely unremarkable tribe of peasants toiling in an arid land. It worked, did it not? The world was changed out of all recognition by his message; by the words of a pauper born in a stable in an obscure and unimportant place."

The muscles of Melone's jaw knotted, "But all those faithful out there, these poor creatures lying here, all those who have died, were they evil? Did they deserve to be struck down?"

The Pope's voice strengthened as if delivering a sermon, "Even the just man sins seven times a day. Who but God can judge the sinner? I tell you Giuseppe, a new age has dawned, a new teaching will be given to us. Is not the world in trouble? Can you honestly say that all is well with mankind? Are we not ready for a new way, a new message? Do we not cry out for succour in this tortured age? I tell you, WE MUST NOT CRUCIFY CHRIST AGAIN!"

Melone stood silent, broken.

The pontiff tenderly laid his hand on the cardinal's arm and his voice softened, "Have faith Peppine, have faith in the hand of God."

The tall man began to weep, big tears ran silently down his cheeks. "I . . . I don't know, I can't come to terms with it. It's too much for me. I am too weak." He turned his face up to the figure on the cross, the candlelight glistening on the wet streaks on his face, "Oh Christ, your hand servant calls to you for guidance. He is unworthy of this task, help him in his hour of need."

"Patience," said the smaller man, "Patience, Peppine all will be made clear in time, but now we must do as we are bid. Go forth and deliver the message to all who might hear. In three days His angel will return and if we are to escape his wrath we must prevail on all."

The cardinal turned to go, still sobbing silently, "What of you Holy Father? What are you going to do?"

The pontiff, his eyes still shining with religious fervour, turned to the crucifix, "I shall pray till morning and seek guidance. Then I will speak to the faithful and bring the glad tidings to the world."

The cardinal stepped over the dead bodies and into the corridor. He signalled silently and a hushed group of men and priests came to the door making the sign of the cross as they looked into the dimly lit room. At the sight of the mutilated bodies, some turned, covering their mouths, others stood in silence.

The Pope knelt on both knees on the floor in front of the crucifix and then prostrated himself on the tiles face down with his arms stretched wide.

CHAPTER 38

Kate sat on the low wall of the stairs that led down to the railway underpass, dangling her legs idly. The early morning air was bright and clear and the sun already warm in the copper blue sky. She liked the railway station at this hour, it reminded her of the sort of place where cowboys waited in western films. The little, low building on one side of the double track and the island platform between them; she tried to remember if there had been an island platform in "High Noon."

On either side of the station the tracks merged into a single line which arrowed straight into the distance in both directions, giving a sort of prairie feel despite the fact that the steep mountain range behind the town was quite close.

Cole and she had often come here to pick up, or bid farewell to visiting guests who had taken the train from Rome. There were many more people than normal that morning. *"Seems to be the case everywhere nowadays,"* she thought. The restrictions on road travel and the omnipresent police checks had made private car travel over any distance nearly impossible.

There was little talk, most people standing apart from one another, uneasy, fidgeting. Kate herself felt the strain, the distrust that permeated the atmosphere. There were even two heavily-armed *carabiniere* at one end of the main platform. She shook her head sadly, she had never seen a policeman in the sleepy little station before.

Looking up, as the lazy, familiar bell began to ring, she strained her eyes to catch a distant glimpse of the approaching locomotive through the already dancing air, her heart beginning to pound. Her relationship with her daughter had been near idyllic, always joyful. Even when motherly discipline had been necessary or teenage independence and rebellion had arisen, there was never a split. They were true friends now, confidants and sharers of life's burdens.

Her joy was tempered, confused, it had been so long since their daughter had been home and now her return somehow signalled final acceptance of the unacceptable. In her mind and heart, her conviction of Cole's continued existence persisted but she knew that she was now playing with fire. If she did not give up her public stance, she ran the risk of being certified as mentally ill, emotionally unstable. The time for sympathy, for understanding her grief had passed. Her friends, the villagers, the doctor, even Susan would have no more of it.

The diesel engine trailing its two little cars pulled up, almost silently, to the platform and the doors opened.

Kate anxiously looked one way and the other searching for her daughter. Her heart leapt, there she was waving, smiling, and clambering down from the rear carriage with a big, soft bag.

Kate stopped in mid-stride, Susan was dressed completely in black. She felt her mouth open, felt a deep sense of guilt sweep over her. Her husband was dead, dead for many days now and it hadn't even occurred to her to wear mourning clothes. Susan's face twisted in grief as she saw the tears well and spill down her mother's face. They ran to each other, embracing, and sobbing loudly.

Outside the station in the modest car park, they endured the close, suspicious, stares of the *carabiniere* as they loaded the big bag into the ridiculously small car. They both stared down at the ground, avoiding any eye contact with the policemen. They had learned already that it was the best thing to do. In the end nothing was said and the tiny motor cranked, wheezingly, into life and they rattled off up the narrow street.

They talked continuously as they wound their way up the steep, twisting road to the village. Consoling, supporting, trying to help each other deal with their new circumstances.

"How on earth did you get permission to travel?" asked Kate as the conversation at last moved away from more emotional areas. "It's nigh impossible to get a travel permit here other than for approved work."

"Compassionate grounds," replied Susan, "I told them that I was going to my father's funeral." She bit off the last of the sentence, clearly regretting the plain language.

Kate tried to ignore it, "But it's so dangerous now. Did you have any problems?"

"Not really, but it was very worrying in the bigger stations, especially *Roma Termini.* There were demonstrations everywhere and violent crime seems to be running amok. I saw several arrests and the police were not very gentle with the suspects. I even caught a glimpse of *the ship* for awhile from the window of the train as it left Rome station. It really is frightening."

They arrived at the main village, slowing down as they passed the piazza. The Sunday bells were ringing loudly and a big crowd milled outside the open doors of the church. Inside they could see the congregation packing the building and a service in full swing.

Kate couldn't resist the crack, "At least Don Giuliano is happy."

There was fresh graffiti on several walls. Susan read it aloud, "*Dio c'e.* God is here. So it's here too?"

"It's like humanity has gone mad," said Kate, "religious fundamentalism is sweeping the world. It won't be long now before they start the killing." She snorted, "Ever since the Pope made his proclamation from the Vatican, he spoke "ex cathedra" you know, even the hardest of agnostics around here have been hourly attendees at Mass, hanging on Don Giuliano's every word. They are all expecting some kind of miraculous happening tomorrow when the heads of state gather in St Peter's."

Leaving the main village they turned right, up a steep and tortuous stretch, soon passing the big house with the green shutters, and continued up to the tiny piazza of the village, chattering continuously. Then Kate stopped talking as she concentrated on steering the little car round a tight, blind rightangle bend and down the impossibly steep and narrow cobbled road to park on the little square of hard pavement standing by the house.

Susan, tall and full figured, unfolded herself from the cramped interior of the car and stretched her full height, languidly soaking in the sun, and shaking out her long dark hair. She unloaded her bag while Kate climbed up the precipitous few metres to the door and pushed it open, going ahead into the dim interior of the house.

The heat was stifling now and the cicadas made a loud, rasping racket in the bright sun.

Kate was already busy with the coffee pot as Susan came in panting from the unfamiliar exertion and the poor footing offered by the rough street. She dropped the bag carelessly on the floor in her usual manner and said, "No, not filter please Kate. It's so long since I've had good, strong, Italian espresso that I have a craving." She reached for the espresso pot, "and what about you?" Susan's tone was gentle, continuing the conversation, "You're a regular church attendee. What about you? Don't you believe the Pope?"

Kate stopped what she was doing. Grim faced and pale she took several deep breaths before speaking, "Susan, I know that we have agreed not to talk about Cole and *the ship*. That it is bad for me, but there is no way that I can associate *that ship* with God. For me it means Cole and that is that." Her tone had become brittle, edgy.

"Okay, Okay, let's change the subject." Susan put her arms around her mother.

Later they sat at the kitchen table and Kate switched on a battered looking television set.

"When did you get that?" Susan got up and examined it. "The screen paled and a snowy picture appeared. She laughed, "Why, it's black and white!"

"Oh, Bene dug it out from one of his dungeons of junk," laughed Kate. "I bet he could find anything you wanted. given time."

"But why? I thought you were all against that sort of stuff." Susan's puzzlement was genuine.

"Oh, that was Cole more than me but in any event, I've just got to keep up with the reports on *the ship*. I have been sitting for hours lately watching the pictures and listening to the reports and discussions."

"Hasn't everyone?" Kate's question was rhetorical and Susan didn't answer.

The picture steadied and gained contrast of a sort. Against a backdrop of the giant *ship* stationary over the Basilica of St Peter's, two men, one dressed in clerical robes, were having a heated discussion. The women drank their coffee in silence listening to the argument rage back and forth, devilish or divine, natural or unnatural.

Kate spoke, "You know it doesn't matter a jot what they say just now. Tomorrow they are all in for a big shock."

"What do you mean?" Susan screwed up her face in a worried, questioning expression.

"They all talk of philosophy, of messages from God, of new ideas. Huh, just wait. We'll see how much 'pie in the sky' they get. We'll see how much room there is for discussion after tomorrow."

"What are you talking about Kate, how can you possibly say any of that?"

Kate faced Susan squarely, " Your father had very clear ideas about certain things. He had great conviction in a particular philosophy, a philosophy for mankind."

She was cut short by Susan, "M-O-T-H-E-R!" she dragged out the word with a warning menace in her voice, that's enough of that."

Kate shrugged slightly and shut up, turning back to the T.V. screen. Without taking her eyes from the picture she stretched her arm across the table, and silently took her daughter's hand.

238

The screen faded and was replaced by a scene which both women immediately recognised as a videotape of the attack on *the ship*. The dramatic sights and sounds of the battle held them spellbound. The confusion of the cameramen as their lenses panned and zoomed, the blinding flashes, and rapidly clouding visibility forcing more and more distant shots. The screaming, almost incoherent descriptions of the commentators heightening the drama until the effects of the titanic struggle rendered all local surface-based observation useless. If anything, the distant shots from the mainland of the huge roiling clouds on the horizon flashing and arcing with fierce light, and the distant concussions rumbling and groaning in the air, gave a greater, a Wagnerian scale to the conflict.

Kate spoke quietly as they watched, "I saw it live, it actually happened while I was watching. In the beginning, no one else had any idea what was happening, for all they knew it was some kind of display. But I knew it was an attack. I didn't need to be told that they had attacked it with rockets and nuclear bombs, I could feel it."

Susan squeezed her mother's hand, "Kate please, give it up, please listen to me. Get away from here and come back with me to Amsterdam."

Kate interrupted, "Wait, Susan give me one more chance. Just one to convince you, to demonstrate to you, that I am not going mad. If I fail and you do not admit that there is something in what I say, then I promise to leave here. Somehow I will find a way to get permission to come to you."

Susan didn't answer for several seconds, seeming to mull the matter over in her mind, "You promise?"

Kate smiled, a cloud seeming to rise from her soul, "I promise, I really do. All I ask is that you listen to what I am going to tell you and then wait to see if my prediction is correct."

She got up and poured them both more coffee. "There is a man I have been talking to, a psychiatrist . . . no, no not that," she cut off Susan's interruption before she could utter it, "an army man, a specialist in psychic phenomena under stress. I have demonstrated to him this feeling, this communication that I have with *the ship,* with Cole. He believes me and has actually tried, unsuccessfully I'm afraid, to convince his superiors that I have predicted some of the actions of *the ship* in advance."

She tipped the frothy milk from the cappuccino machine into the steaming cups of coffee, "I know that you think I'm imagining it but now I have a plan and I am going to risk everything to implement it. With his help and yours, I believe it can work."

"A plan? What sort of plan?" Susan sat back, staring at her mother.

"Oh, don't look at me as if I am mad. I am as sane as you. Just wait and give me my chance, you agreed." Kate waited but Susan said nothing. "Your arrival has gelled the idea in my mind and the timing is perfect. I know that you are incredulous, worried that I am losing my mind. For that reason I will not reveal my intentions until you are convinced of my claims, Okay?"

Kate sensed the over-sweet tone in Susan's voice, the "keep her happy for now" manner.

"Very well, mother," her use of the word was in itself a give-away, "show me, but if you fail to convince me, you promised!"

Kate leaned forward, conspiratorial in her manner, "Tomorrow in front of the world wide news media, there will be a message from God, is that not so?"

Susan nodded, "I am now going to tell you what that message will be."

Susan said in a warning tone, "Mother!"

"It's quite simple." Kate's voice choked, "Tomorrow your father will speak to the entire world."

CHAPTER 39

Cardinal Melone sagged in the simple, upright chair. He was utterly exhausted, even the drugs administered by the Vatican physician failed now to keep him on his feet. He shook his head in wonder at the sight of the Pope, kneeling in fervent prayer before the crucifix, seemingly fresh, alert.

His hand trembled slightly as he accepted the tepid cup of camomile tea proffered by the nun who entered the room at that moment.

"The Holy Father?" she queried.

Melone shook his head and she left quietly, the other cup still steaming on the tray. It had been three days now with no sleep, but today had been the worst. Dignitary after dignitary had arrived; Kings and Presidents shoulder to shoulder with tyrants and dictators, but the religious leaders had been the worst, the most difficult. The lay leaders were plainly afraid, defeated, accepting, but the rag-bag mixture from rabbis to ayatollahs and Mormons to Buddhists were different. All had demanded personal audience, all had challenged or welcomed, all had wished to question, to probe. The pontiff had seemed superhuman, untiring in his response, boundless in his energetic and persuasive communication, uncanny in his effect upon others.

"It's as if he is more than himself, more than the man." thought Melone, *"That in itself borders on the miraculous."*

Even the considerable and vastly experienced resources of the Vatican administration had threatened to collapse under the strain of it all. Media pressure for space, camera access, public relations, and security requirements clashing. It had been a miracle that it happened at all.

"And now there is nothing to do but wait." He muttered to himself, feeling a deep chill grow in his heart. "Suppose nothing happens? It's getting late now, the sun is setting." He got up, walked quietly to the window, and carefully peeked out over the edge of the balcony, trying not to be seen.

Despite the fact that all security forces, media personnel, and private aides had been excluded from the piazza, it seemed to be filled to bursting. Every colour, every language, every creed and political philosophy was represented.

"There indeed is Babel." The Pope's voice came from over the cardinal's shoulder.

Melone turned his pallid, sallow face, eyes sunk in dark holes to face the pontiff who placed a hand gently on his cheek.

"You look exhausted Peppine," he said.

"I am," he replied, "I cannot deny it. I am at the end of my strength."

"Wait and watch with me, Peppine, it won't be much longer now," the Pope's face literally shone.

The two men pulled chairs to the doors of the balcony and sat just inside the room facing out to the piazza, unseen by the crowd below. The already dim light faded quickly and darkness overtook the Basilica. There were no floodlights, no one had considered that there would be a need. Only the normal lamps under the great circular colonnade gave a gentle illumination.

With the sun being excluded by *the ship,* it had been uncharacteristically cold and all of the assembled dignitaries below were well wrapped, but with the coming of darkness it became even colder.

As the bells rang the passing hours the assembled leaders and the world waited. Slowly the tension mounted, a low murmuring gradually growing in the crowd. Some were beginning to complain, to express doubt; others began to pray, calling on their God for guidance. Nothing happened. The darkness of the night deepened and the starless blackness of *the ship* remained fixed, enigmatic above them.

Midnight began to toll.

As the first hollow, echoing note of the bell died to silence, some pointed up to *the ship.*

The second chime sounded, others pointed, nudging their neighbours.

Then the third stroke faded lugubriously. There was no doubt now, *the ship* was beginning to glow, ever so faintly.

As the fourth rang out, some of the people began to cry, "Look, look it's definitely getting brighter."

At the fifth, a low, deep humming started.

By the sixth knell, the glow, pale green in colour, had begun to illuminate the piazza, and the hum to become a low, musical note.

The seventh strike, somehow louder, amplified, brought light strong enough to see by and a depth and strength to the humming sound such that they could feel it resonate in their chest cavities.

The eighth struck, the light was strong enough to read by, the music reverberated from the surrounding colonnade, and the façade of the great church.

The sound of the bell as it struck for the ninth time was hugely amplified and could be heard above the tumultuous standing waves of the sonorous sound.

Ten! Eyes squinted with the brightness and the buildings seemed to shake with the awesome thunder of a hellish chorus.

At the eleventh, a gigantic hammer blow to the bell augmented its voice grotesquely. It seemed to howl out its message like some Gothic nightmare above the shuddering impact of the sound. Fear and awe struck deep into the hearts of the crowd. All stood rooted to the spot, slack jawed and wide-eyed, blinded by the intense light, even through closed eyelids, and deafened by the cliff of noise.

Twelve! The crashing toll seemed less and the withering sound began to slacken, the impossible light to dim. Both began to abate, sliding in sympathy with the fading, dying moan of the great bell; Slipping down, down, ever down, but not to extinction. A phantom remained, a dim green glow from *the ship* and a deep, rich background note like great basso voices echoing dimly from some hellish depths of the earth.

As eyes adjusted, recovered from their trial, all looked up to see the figure of the Pope standing on the balcony and slightly above him and to his right the green head. The ethereal green corona was shining; shining so brightly that the pontiff was silhouetted in the eerie glow, his robes bathed in a clear, limpid, green luminescence.

As one, the entire assembled mass of people gasped.

The figure of the pontiff extended his arms towards the silent, expectant throng. He raised them slightly above shoulder height and turned his palms forward as if in blessing.

He began to speak. His voice seemed enormous, not amplified, but everywhere at once, filling the entire piazza, every corner, every niche overflowing with it, commanding and calm.

CHAPTER 40

In the dim light which spilled from the hallway into the kitchen, Kate and Susan sat on the edge of their seats, gripped by the scenes on the television screen.

The old set was excelling itself, the picture steady and well contrasted as it often was after dark, and the sound crystal in its clarity.

The wide-angle view of Saint Peter's narrowed, the lens zooming in on the brightly lit figure on the balcony. Soon the clear, full-length figure of the Pope was filling the screen. The image tracked upwards but the dazzling object, behind and above the pontiff, lacked any detail, simply washing out the picture as the camera continued to zoom in, trying to examine it.

The picture widened again until the oddly glowing image of the Pope again filled the screen. He had raised his arms, his face shining with an inner strength.

He spoke, but not with his own voice, the sheer volume momentarily overpowering the microphones, distorting the sound for a few seconds.

"I am the way and the light of the world and I am come to save mankind. For man has lost the path of righteousness and distorted the truth of creation. He has sinned and now must make atonement."

The voice stopped, the echoes of the source-less sound rebounding from the underside of *the ship* and folding back again and again until they faded into the rumbling background basso of the choir. Utter silence. No one breathed, much less spoke.

"The gift of life has been given to you but you have forgotten death; this also is a gift. Life is sacred for it comes from God. So also is death, for this also comes from God and without death there can be no life. The garden of creation is made in all its beauty and in all its ugliness, for harmony cannot be without dissonance, as light cannot be without darkness nor justice without injustice. Beware when I say to you in your greed and lust, that you have sought to distort the law, and now the fruit of your loins chokes the garden and withers the tree of knowledge. I give you a new law."

The voice hardened slightly,

"HONOUR DEATH AS YOU HONOUR LIFE."

Susan turned to Kate, pale and shaking, "What does that mean?"

"Wait," said Kate quietly, not taking her eyes from the screen, "wait and listen."

As the echoes folded and faded, the figure of the pontiff slowly lowered its arms to its side, sagging a little.

Then the voice spoke again.

"Atonement shall be bought with the blood of the innocents. For forty days and forty nights let none enter into the garden."

At this, a narrow, parallel shaft of green, spot-lit the Pope from the centre of *the ship* above.

Again the voice, softer,

"You shall know my law through this, the Chosen One."

The corona of the bright object above the Pope dimmed slightly and rose smoothly up into the air, following the path of the light beam, both dimming until they disappeared against the background glow of *the ship* above. Only the sonorous background sound could be heard for half-a-minute. Then the voice boomed, not from all around as before, but from above, "In three days; the temple, in seven; creation, and in forty; JUDGEMENT."

The green glow went out, the tunnel to the bowels of the earth from where the voices had come closed, and darkness and silence returned. A darkness that seemed thicker than before and a silence heavier than lead.

The Pope leaned heavily against the stone balustrade, steadying himself on the parapet.

Below, what had by now become a terror stricken congregation, began to murmur and mutter, all turning to one another, confused, and searching for a lead.

The camera zoomed in closer on the Pope. With what seemed to be great fatigue, he lifted up a flat, thick tablet from behind the balustrade of the balcony. In a normal voice amplified by the public address system, he spoke. His voice shaky and tired, "This has been left to us by God."

As the image of the object filled the screen, it could be seen to have a muddy-brown translucence-like coarse fibreglass texture with dark characters inscribed on it. The Pope with the tears that streaked his face clearly visible, lowered it to waist height and began to read. He read slowly and clearly in English, enunciating each word carefully, and pausing between each sentence.

"Here is the Law." He filled his chest, deepened his voice.

"Honour death as you honour life. Honour death in nature. Honour death in time. Honour death in sickness. Honour death in plague and pestilence. Honour death in birth. Grant death which is willed by the bearer. Grant death which is earned by the sinner. Grant death to that which is yet to live. Impose death that all may live."

The pontiff looked up to the black mass of *the ship*, swayed and dropped the tablet which split in two as it struck the parapet. He slowly crumpled to the floor. Cardinals rushed from the doorway catching his inert body as he fell.

Kate was scribbling furiously on a notepad.

The picture remained fixed, unmoving, unchanging as if the camera had been abandoned. The balcony cleared of activity and soon the empty window was all that could be seen. Still the picture remained fixed. After some time the picture faded and a studio shot of an announcer appeared.

The screen went blank, shrinking to a white dot as Kate hit the remote control switch.

"Well?" she asked calmly.

Susan visibly shaken said, "I, I don't know. It's not very clear, it's all so frightening. I don't understand any of it. I'm afraid."

"Keep calm. Susan, I need for you to keep calm." She reached out and drew Susan's head to her breast, kissing her on the forehead gently.

"Listen carefully to what I am going to say. I am going to try to rephrase slightly, interpret, what we have just heard. Are you ready, are you listening?"

Susan nodded her head in silence.

Kate took a long slow breath and began to read from the pad,

"'Honour death as you honour life.' Oh so much said in so few words. Death should be actively managed in society just as much as life is. We treat life as a sacred thing, something to be respected, and preserved. We should treat death with the same respect, stop denying it, and accept the role of death in the greater scheme of things.

"Honour death in nature." Allow death its natural role. Allow natural drought and famine, disease and disaster to take their toll of life. We interfere beyond reason in the natural order of the world, sending aid and sustenance to people who, since time immemorial, have always died from famine and pestilence and for no better reason than we see them on the TV. What happened in the past before mass communications? Nature dealt out death according to natural law.

"Honour death in time." Abandon life extending research and practices and let life take its natural span. We indulge in absurd efforts to keep alive people reduced to cabbages by old age, terminal diseases, or insupportable pain. We defy the rightful role of death. Society strives to extend life simply as a maxim and not for well-argued reasons.

"Honour Death in sickness." Do not maintain life by gross artificial means. Medicine is wonderful, a true bounty, but we don't know when to stop. With artificial organs, heart, liver, and lung transplants, we are indulging in a grotesque parody of medicine. Unending mechanical ventilation after brain death, enormous efforts to ensure the survival of multiple pregnancies brought about in the first instance by artificial means, it goes on and on.

"Honour death in plague and pestilence." Allow population controlling diseases to play their role. We defy common sense by the enormous expenditure of resources to cure the natural controls such as AIDS and the worldwide diminution in fertility. Who are we to decide these things? In our arrogance we have decided what is best for nature.

"Honour death in birth." Permit only fully viable progeny to survive. Do not maintain life which would not survive naturally. Stop organ transplants for the newborn; blood transfusions for the foetus. Be selective by controlling the quality of the unborn. Should we deny natural infertility by preserving seed and eggs for artificial insemination?

"Grant death which is willed by the bearer." Make the right to death equal with that of life. Make social provision for euthanasia, legalise suicide, respect the wishes of those who wish to die. Allow the individual's right to self-determination in matters concerning his or her wish to live.

"Grant death which is earned by the sinner." Capital punishment for crime. The right to life can, and must, be forfeited by those who offend against the social code. Do not interfere in cases of voluntary drug overdose, or injury caused by indulging in voluntary life threatening activity.

"Grant death to that which is yet to live." Legal and free abortion, contraception, sterilisation; birth control in all its forms.

"Impose death that all may live." Ah yes, this is the big one, managed population reduction; the organised culling of the human race.

Kate looked up from her notes, "Or as your father would say, 'There is only one problem in the world and that is the one-sided interpretation of religious laws. We need to look at both sides of the equation.'"

Susan looked up at her mother, wide-eyed, staring, "OH MY GOD, you're right! Cole, it's COLE." She began to sob.

Kate's smile and shining eyes seemed incongruous against the younger woman's emotional distress, "Yes, Susan, now do you believe me? I have known it all along. Ever since that dream the first night; the feeling has grown. I am convinced that Cole is not dead, at least not in the conventional sense. He lives on in some way in that *ship*."

Susan choked back her tears, controlled her voice, "Yes, yes it's him to a tee. I can hear him now. 'There is only one pollutant . . . mankind. The world is choking in man's fertility. We have already overburdened the system just by existing. We have no future unless the population is reduced by half immediately. We must be mad, nature is trying to tell us something, and we deliberately ignore the message. The only important thing is the continuation of the communal mind, the individual is unimportant.' Oh I can hear his voice, he spouted his bloody philosophy so often that I could recite it from memory. His obsession with the distortion, the "evil" as he put it, of the message of the established religions."

"Ah, but it is oh so ironic, don't you think, that he should choose the churches themselves, especially that of Rome as his vehicle?" Kate seemed almost happy. "It's almost comic the way religion is being made to work reversing the 'damage.' Oh, I bet that if he is alive or at least aware of what is happening, he is laughing. Huh, your father was always too smart for his boots."

Then she stopped, silent for a time and her face saddened, "Oh dear," she said quietly and sighed deeply.

"What's the matter Kate? You've won. you've convinced me."

"You're not pregnant, Susan, are you?"

"No. Whatever made you ask that?"

"The atonement. 'Let none enter in the garden for forty days.' You understand that? No newborn child is to be allowed to live for the next forty days."

"Wha . . . at?"

"As I said yesterday, there will be no room for manoeuvre, for discussion. The law is the law. And don't forget there is to be judgement in forty days. Somehow I don't think delay will be tolerated. This is not Christ, not Allah promising wonders in the life hereafter if we suffer this one. This is a practical god come to save us from ourselves here and now. And mark my words, this is a vengeful god. This is Cole who is no longer human."

Susan's voice was small, almost childlike, "What are you trying to say?"

"I am saying that if these laws are not implemented with sufficient rigour in the forty day time scale, there will be a day of reckoning. We will be brought to account. These laws are radical indeed and I cannot see a rapid implementation. They strike at the very root of our modern day political and social philosophy and as for atonement? Well what do you think?" Kate was still calm, collected, discussive in her tone.

"You're right, of course. The more fundamentalist regimes and individuals might obey immediately, but the majority? In forty days? I don't think so. As for the death of every newborn child, I'm glad I'm not expecting." She shuddered, "So what is your prediction now?"

Kate sat back in her chair, now strong, confident, "It is my belief that if the new laws are not sufficiently rigorously enforced, atonement made, and efficient methods of mass death management introduced within the forty-day time span, he will do it himself. *The ship* will do the job for us, it will destroy half the world population at random."

"Dear God, you can't be serious Kate? How could a single entity be so powerful that it could wipeout half of mankind just like that. It's impossible and in any event, I don't believe that Cole is capable of such a thing."

"You forget, Susan, that gods specialise in the impossible, and this particular god has already demonstrated a number of unpleasant impossibilities. Cole, *the ship* or whatever you want to call it, has already killed thousands of innocent people in Gibraltar and elsewhere."

Her eyes began to brim, "If I am right and he is part of that thing, that *ship*, then he has nothing to lose, nowhere to go." Her voice choked slightly. "He always said that the only important thing was the survival of the species, the continuation of the collective mind, and in the current crisis the individual had no importance. You can be sure that he included himself in that."

Susan put her arm around her mother. "It's so bizarre, a waking nightmare, but there has to be a limit. He cannot be that powerful; half the world's population for God's sake."

"I have no idea of his power, perhaps it has some limit, but I don't think that the human race can stop him. No, WE have to stop him."

Susan's eyes nearly popped out of her head. "US? Stop him? You ARE out of your mind. What can WE do?"

"I have an idea that he is still aware of us, or at least of me. I cannot shake off the sensation of communication. Oh, it's not very precise or clear, but I am convinced that there is a two-way channel between us, at least some of the time. Surely that might give us an opening, a slender hope, that we might influence things." Kate's voice did not sound as if she was very convinced herself.

Susan screwed up her face as if she had eaten something sour. "And how do you propose to make this communication?"

"Using your travel permit I want you to go to Rome and somehow get a permit for me. Jim Crawford should be able to help. I will have to get close to *the ship* and make Cole aware of me."

Susan interrupted, "Kate, you're mad. Whatever makes you think that you can get anywhere near *the ship?* What means do you have of attracting its attention?"

Kate's voice was shrill, "I don't know. But I have to try. Will you help me or not?"

The younger woman looked straight into her mother's eyes for a few seconds, then lowered her own, and nodded silently.

Kate gripped Susan by her shoulders and said firmly, "Good. Now let's get on with it. We've got, what did he say, forty days to work something out."

CHAPTER 41

Siemens and Filshill stood smartly at attention on the runway watching the big jet come to a halt. As the steps were deployed and the door opened, they delivered crisp salutes.

"At ease, this is strictly business, not a parade." Robeson spoke from half-way down the aircraft steps, Borrhim just visible behind his large frame. The President followed behind and in the door of the aircraft could be seen another man, clad in an austere and strangely-styled black suit. Both soldiers knew immediately who he was but both avoided eye contact.

As the President got to the tarmac, he shook each Generals' hand warmly. "How is it going here boys? At least you've still got good weather in Naples." His eyes didn't reflect the jocular tone of his voice. Turning to the tall, slim almost skinny man in the dark suit he said, "High Minister . . . Generals Siemens and Filshill, they have both been closely involved in the 'Coming'."

The man's hard, hawk eyes bored into them, he did not offer a handshake. "Gentlemen, we have much work to do in the service of God."

"Amen, sir," both soldiers replied in unison.

"This way sir, Mister President," Siemens said as he indicated the waiting helicopter a hundred metres away. "The weather's been just fine Mister President, just fine."

The six men spoke little among themselves as they walked, ringed by an double-armed guard of U.S. Marines. They boarded the helicopter, its blades already spinning, as soon as they reached it. A few moments later, it was airborne, climbing rapidly, and banking to the north.

Once inside, Filshill fell silent. As he was the junior of the party, it was not his place to promote discussion and, in any event, the roar of the military craft's engines made conversation difficult.

He gazed out of the window at the patchwork of the countryside as it passed close below them. What was going to happen? The very presence of the high minister made his flesh creep. This was one of the most dangerous men in the civilised world. His powers were almost unlimited. He could make law, remove rights, and ignore any civil ruling almost at will. He was answerable only to the Church Assembly of the American Double Continent. How CAADCON found him, he had no idea but they had certainly chosen well. The President was clearly deferential to him. A chill crept into his bones, *"Even the President is afraid of him?"* he thought.

In half an hour the sound of the helicopter engine changed, the craft turned slightly to port, and slowed to a hover. Filshill reckoned they were over the hills of the Castelli and Frascati areas on the southern fringes of Rome. He could just make out the autostrada a couple of kilometres to the right and below; the gentle hills and valleys were covered in vineyards. *"It won't be long until the vendemmia,"* he thought, *"The grapes of wrath?"*

"There gentlemen, there it is, the 'Ark'." The high minister's tone was filled with awe.

Through the haze of the city, away to the west and slightly north, could be seen the black shape of *the ship*. From this distance and height it seemed that it might be a black hill. It was so low, it was impossible to see daylight or buildings below it.

"You have been blessed with this sight before," the high minister placed his hand on his breast, "but my heart leaps with joy at this privilege. Give thanks to our Saviour that he may spare mankind from extinction and eternal damnation."

The five others responded in unison, "Honour death in life."

"Amen," said the man in black.

Filshill felt a clammy sweat seep down his back. He stole a furtive glance around him, *"Did the others really believe?* Oh God, it was dangerous to even think such thoughts this close to the high minister."* He desperately tried to keep a tremor out of his eyelid.

The helicopter started to move again, but quite slowly. The co-pilot turned, pushing aside his mask, and said, "High minister, gentlemen, please do not be alarmed at our slow progress. We do not have a mechanical problem, we are simply queuing to land."

"So many?" said Borrhim, "What about rebels or unbelievers, we are very low?"

"We are not in danger here, Mister Vice President, so close to Rome and the site of the Ark," said Siemens. "No, the Italian authorities have the situation well in hand."

"Which is more than the Americans can say," the high minister's voice was acid, "or don't you agree, Mister President?"

Albero made no reply, the others sat white faced.

As they approached the outskirts of the city, the ground below became increasingly covered with tents, caravans. and makeshift buildings of all sorts. The roads and lanes increasingly choked with people on foot, all heading towards the city.

"Blessed pilgrims," said the high minister, making a sign of benediction.

Soon they could see the great white mass of the Vittorio Emmanuele Monument clearly. They hovered not much above roof height and watched three other helicopters ahead of them. Each one in turn landed in the open space in front of the monument, disgorged its passengers, and took off before the next was allowed to land.

At last they touched down and clambered from the craft into seeming confusion, ringed by armoured vehicles, and heavily armed soldiers. Senior Italian military personnel greeted the party briefly but with little ceremony. Filshill recognised Comandanté Rocco di Rollo and mouthed a silent greeting to him.

They were rapidly ushered from the area as their helicopter hacked the air and rose, clearing the way for those that followed. They were conducted to the wide avenue adjacent to the piazza where a car waited.

The big limousine swallowed all six men and began to smoothly make its way down the empty avenue towards the huge black cliff of *the ship* towering into the sky ahead. As always, Filshill cowered from the crushing sight.

All were silent, the strain clearly telling on each and every one. Filshill was terrified that someone would address him, he was so shaken that he doubted his ability to control his voice.

Out of the car window he could partly see the monstrous object. He shuddered in his mind, *"What's going to happen? It has been there for forty days, nearly six weeks, silent and unmoving. Not so much as a squeak from it and meanwhile the world has turned upside down. Death and destruction have become the order of the day. Millions have died since that night, just how many no one knows, and no one will ever know,"* he thought darkly.

Every group in the world which had been directly and immediately affected by the new law had rebelled; pregnant mothers, AIDS sufferers, road accident victims, transplant candidates, areas of drought and famine, and on, and on it went. But CAADCON and its sister bodies in Greater Europe, Asia, Australasia, Africa, and Russo-China got their act together quickly. Religious fervour had seen to that. States and governments which had not accepted the new law, had simply vanished, swept away by the tide of religious fanaticism. Dissident voices had been silenced in days. The faithful were myriad and fanatical and they were everywhere. They were unstoppable. God was here and death was His will. Martyrdom had never been so feverishly sought.

Filshill could still not believe how quickly and deeply society changed since that night. A new order had come about; religious fundamentalist states were now the norm.

"Just like the Middle Ages," Filshill remarked one day to one of his aides. He felt the sweat pour from him as the memory came to his mind. Fortunately his pistol had been loaded. Some of the ways the religious police executed you were undignified to say the least.

He glanced furtively at the others, *did they sense his unease, smell his fear?* No one paid any attention to him, all lost in their own thoughts.

He again felt a chill as he recalled how easy it had been to claim that he had executed a heretic.

The car drew to a halt a hundred metres from the entrance to the piazza of Saint Peter's. The six men got out into the dimness and unexpectedly cool air below *the ship's* numbing bulk above. They spoke in low, hushed tones as if in a church.

A tall man, his black robes edged with bright green reaching the ground, bowed low and greeted them in English. "High minister, welcome to the site of the Ark and of the Basilica of Saint Peter."

"Honour death in life," he replied touching his breast and bowing slightly.

"Gentlemen, please follow me, your aides will be shown to the waiting area." Another black-robed priest led the three soldiers away as the high minister, the President and the Vice President followed the first in silent single file down the avenue towards Saint Peter's. They were quickly lost to sight among the files of dignitaries moving in the same direction, many of them chanting.

Robeson and Siemens walked side by side behind Filshill and the priest. To Filshill's eye the cleric seemed very young, perhaps no more than eighteen or nineteen years of age. As they walked, he began to talk in a thick accent. "Did you know sir, that the Chosen One has given some credence to the view that we have been blessed with the return of the Ark of Noah? That the Grand Sasso D'Italia, and not Mount Ararat, is in fact the mountain on which the Ark rested after the flood."

Filshill couldn't decide whether it was a Greek accent or from somewhere further east, "Heaven be praised," he said.

"It is fitting don't you think?" the cleric continued, "that the Lord God who used Noah, his Chosen One, and the Ark to save creation from the wages of man's sin should choose the same Ark and another Chosen One, Michael, to save mankind again?"

Filshill decided that the young man was Greek. "I am but a humble soldier minister, and not worthy of pondering the ways of God. I am glad that the Chosen One and the high ministers lead and instruct us, so that we may follow on the path of righteousness."

They reached a large, ornate gate in the building along the length of which they had been walking. It led through a bend to an inner courtyard, which was so dim that they had difficulty seeing at first. Crossing the cobbled yard, they entered a corridor via a small door and finally a cramped room.

"This, gentlemen, will suffice for your needs I trust?" asked the cleric, bowing ever so slightly. It was clear that it was all they were going to get.

"Thank you, minister, it's fine," said Robeson making it sound as if he was delighted.

The cleric left without another word, closing the door behind him.

Robeson sat down immediately, wiping the sweat from his neck with a handkerchief. He surveyed the room for a few moments and said, "Okay George. It is George, isn't it? Get those TV sets going and find out who or what is on the other end of that telephone."

Within two minutes they were watching the scenes inside the piazza. Both sets showed different pictures, often switching from one camera angle to another.

Filshill spoke briefly on the phone. "It seems that each group in the piazza has a telephone provided and the high minister and the President can connect directly with us. They can speak to us at any time. But while we can make normal calls as we wish, we cannot call the phones in the piazza, naturally."

Just then the phone rang. Filshill stepped back, allowing Siemens to pick it up. "Yes Mister President, I can hear you perfectly and yes we are adequately provided for, thank you Sir and God be with you all." He hung up. "Just checking."

They settled down to watch the TV monitors. Gradually it became completely dark and the continuous arrivals slowed and stopped so that movement in the piazza ceased. Everyone was seated facing the famous balcony in great arcs which fanned out from that point.

There seemed to be two main groupings; the major geographic divides forming wedges radiating from the balcony, and another small group formed by the six church assemblies with the six high ministers and the principal political leaders of the regions in attendance. This group was separated from the main mass by a small railing and were seated directly below the balcony at the focus of the radiating wedges.

One camera concentrated on the church assemblies, giving closeup shots in turn of all present. The members of the CAADCON group were clearly recognisable, the leaders of the South American States and the Canadian Premier, together with Albero and Borrhim seated in a close ring around the high minister. The strain on every face was evident.

In the little room the soldiers paced and fretted as the hours ticked interminably by, marked only by the hollow toll of the big bell of the Basilica. They barely spoke at all, preferring to keep their thoughts to themselves.

At five minutes to midnight the Pope came onto the balcony. In the darkness he was barely visible, only the faint reflection of his white robes from the dim lighting in the piazza picked him out. There was a murmur of the Chosen One and a few seconds of noise as everyone got to their feet before the silence descended once more.

The big bell struck the first toll of midnight. Filshill physically started at the sound, rattling his coffee cup in its saucer. The second hollow echoing, tone rang out and as it died to silence *the ship* began to glow faintly. The third rang out and the glow intensified. There was no sound, no deep sonorous chorus, just silence, and the big bell mournfully measuring the growing brightness. The luminescence grew steadily until on the last stroke of midnight the piazza was bathed in a soft, green light like a misty morning on a Scottish hillside.

As the last echo of the last mournful hammer blow on the bell died to silence, a shaft of light, barely brighter than the diffused General glow, picked out the Chosen One on the balcony. It began to strengthen and as it did so the head-like object could be seen descending the oblique shaft, its brightness growing in harmony with its progress until it stopped, as before, above and to the right of the Chosen One.

The Pope raised his outstretched arms as if in benediction to the crowd. They, as one, raised their arms in response and, as one voice, uttered a great shout, "We honour death as we honour life."

The sound died to silence for nearly half a minute before the Chosen One spoke. It was the same voice as before, strong and evenly filling the huge piazza.

"The laws are given to you. They are the laws of creation. They are the laws of the garden. They are not given in pomp and golden circumstance. They are not convoluted and twisted, full of hidden traps and arguments as are the laws of man. The truths are not distorted and manipulated by liars and false interpreters.

I say to you, BEWARE he who chooses among truths. Twice man has lost the way of truth, choosing among the laws and twice he has been forgiven."

"A Chosen One was given the means to save the righteous among men from the flood of his sin, and yet you have sinned. A second Chosen One was given of death to enlighten the law of life, which is also the law of death, and yet you have forgotten death. Yet a third has been given to bring you the laws, which are ten and all are true but of these the first and the last are the greatest. You may not choose among them. BEWARE, those who seek forgiveness thrice."

The voice grew commanding,

"I am come to enlighten the law of death which is also the law of life."

There followed a gap of a long minute. The last echoes of the great voice had long since died to silence. Not a sound, not a murmur was heard in the piazza.

Then the voice crushed the silence; stern and hard,

"I say to you, the laws have been given, and still you have not weeded the garden. The tree of knowledge still withers."

A thin, keening ululation began to rise from a small segment of the mass of people.

"The law is not mocked and judgement is not set aside." The voice thundered, "I am come in judgement."

"Among the laws, the first shall be last and the last shall be first that the tree may not wither."

Filshill gasped, "Wha . . . at?"

"Among men the first shall be judged that the last may learn from the sins of the first and tend the tree."

Filshill dropped his cup which smashed to smithereens on the floor, "Oh, No . . . NO!"

The shaft of light emanating from *the ship* flared to a dazzling brightness and the head-like object became incandescent, pulsing with a slow cadence. Then, like a star burst, it emitted a thousand, ten thousand, stabbing needles of green brilliance. The scintillating laser-like rays radiated forward, out and down, each lancing again and again among the crowd, flickering hither and thither.

It was over in a matter of seconds. The shaft of light paled and the head-like object returned to its former appearance.

A cliff of sound, of screams, howls of pain and terror filled the air; bodies fell everywhere. Figures scrambled and thrashed, fleeing in utter panic.

The three soldiers, struck dumb by the scenes, remained riveted by the horror on the television.

Then a faint click, more felt than heard, and all the lights went out, the television picture vanished, and the room plunged into darkness.

For a moment nothing happened and then all hell broke loose. From every room in the building and from the courtyard outside, came shouts and crashes, yells and curses, the sound of running feet.

"On the double," roared Robeson, "the piazza."

All three men crashed blindly out of the door in the Stygian blackness and straight into an unseen melé of running and falling men . . . complete chaos.

It was nearly ten minutes before they reached the entry to the piazza. Outside the building the darkness was almost as absolute as inside. It was impossible to see other than by the faint, yellow stabs of light from the few handheld battery torches that some were carrying.

Once they had fought their way through the confusion, they found themselves in a nightmare world of utter darkness and hysteria. There was no way of knowing where they were or whom they were among. Screams and moans mingled with cursing and hysterical supplications, made it impossible to distinguish language, never mind personal identity. The only thing that uniformly pervaded everything was the smell of ozone mingled with that of roasted meat.

The pale, wan light of dawn that filtered in from the edge of *the ship* hours later, allowed the world to see the full extent of the carnage.

CHAPTER 42

Crawford lifted the telephone hand set for the tenth time and then set it back on its rest. He sipped again directly from the bottle of Wild Turkey, the fiery liquid somehow comforted him, letting him push his fear to the back of his mind.

As he set the bottle down on the desk, it caught the edge of the fax machine and nearly fell from his grasp. He tightened his grip and suddenly realised how little remained in the bottle, less than half. It had been unopened when he had first started to make his phone call to Siemens; *how long ago was that?* . . . several hours at least. He looked at the clock on the wall of his sumptuous office, nearly two o'clock. Fuzzily he realised that this was not a good time to phone anyone in Italy. Even these days, meal times were sacred and most offices closed till three or later. He heaved a sigh of relief; he could put off the fateful call for a little while longer.

He took a big swig from the bottle and burped loudly. He realised that he was becoming drunk. "What the hell," he said aloud and took another swig. He looked again at the clock, squinting his eyes slightly, "Two o'clock! God-damn, the train will be here in an hour and a half."

The day was hot and the sun filtered into the room through the slits of the shutters. He relaxed back into the big chair, letting the whiskey warm him, suffuse his mind.

How long ago it all seemed, the days immediately after the arrival of the Ark. *Where had he been?* Gaeta, of course, that sleepy seaside town with its ancient castle dominating the port. Life had been simpler then. It was at that time that he met Kate.

How agitated she had been that day. How courageous, never for a moment admitting the death of her husband. She captured his affections from the first time he met her at that interview in the village when the soldiers brought her down from the mountain.

Was it only six years ago? It seemed much longer, an entire lifetime. The world was a different place now, so much had changed so quickly.

No matter how often he had been back to the village since then, he still felt its peace and beauty. A little smile crept onto his lips as he thought of her. She had accepted him, warmed to him, made a place in her heart for him, even loved him in a way. But he knew that he had never displaced her husband entirely from her soul. Deep down, hidden, Cole still lurked.

Although she almost never spoke of him now, he could feel his presence in her; faint, distant, deep under the surface. Even when they made love, which was often enough, he could sense that she reserved something from him, hid a corner of her mind.

"How difficult all this must be for her," he thought. The new order was harsh and it didn't take kindly to heresy or dissidence. If she had even whispered her belief that Cole was in the Ark, she would have died a lingering and horrible death and probably most of the villagers to boot. Yes the world was hard now and unforgiving.

"I suppose it has treated me well enough though." He smiled ruefully at the thought and looked at his long, three-quarter length, uniform jacket hanging on the coat stand in the corner of the luxuriously appointed room. The jacket had the cross, surmounted by the crescent moon emblazoned in gold on the bright, grass green material with the shattered dagger below it, proclaiming his senior rank in the Army of the Holy Inquiry.

Yes, he was important now. The combination of his skills in psychiatry and his early involvement in the *coming* of the Ark allowed him to manipulate men and situations to his advantage. In time he had risen; clawed, manoeuvred, and lied his way up the ladder of power.

"Was I not chosen by God to be present at the new dawn, the Coming of the Law?" Many a doubting, or obstructive interview had been swept aside with that one.

Siemens too had profited. Still Crawford's boss but now head of the Office of Holy Inquiry, he was a man to be feared indeed; a modern day Torquemada, a powerful friend, close to the Chosen One. Crawford reflexively bowed his head as he thought the words.

His train of thought changed. The Chosen One . . . how he had failed physically. He had become a fragile, wafer thin, old man, bent and withered. His once elfin, eager personality dulled, almost silenced. He was rarely seen now. Indeed his expected broadcast to the faithful was awaited with the added spice that he had not spoken in public for almost a year.

After the Ark left, after it lifted slowly, silently, and majestically straight up, up from the Basilica, up into the clouds, the stratosphere, space, and eventually out of the ken of man; even then, he had still been strong, well in himself.

It had disappeared beyond the scope of man's most powerful devices leaving a world stunned and afraid, looking to the Chosen One and his disciples for a lead and finding it there, strong and clear, a clarion call to righteousness.

But then the visitation. The angel of God had come a last time, had reminded the Chosen One that God had taken six days to make the world, and rested on the seventh; pleased with his efforts. The angel had given "Michael the First" a message.

Man had six years to remake the world and on the seventh, the Ark would come again and man would be judged. If man was not true to the laws, was continuing to choose between them, to distort and manipulate the teaching as before; then there would be no rest until the garden was cleansed. In the seventh year the garden would be remade.

After that "Michael the First" rapidly failed, as if something was taken away. An internal force had faded, gone out of him.

In those six years, man had gone about his task with a will. Gone was compassion and forgiveness. Hard, stark action was all that counted. You were righteous or dead. The world had become a brutal place, violent, full of fear, full of sudden punishment. Suffering was the norm for the great majority. Disease and epidemics swept nations and continents; famine and natural disaster went unchecked. Population was tumbling worldwide and pollution sharply down. Yet it was still not enough. The deep, instinctive drive to breed had not been cowed.

He opened his eyes and indolently picked up a thin report lying on the desk. This was his job, policing the procreation of man. Every day his men spied, and pried into the private lives of the faithful. And every day they turned up illegal conceptions, illegal births, and illegal preservation of life despite the awesome penalties exacted for disobedience to the law. A death always resulted and sometimes the death of all concerned.

Then there were the heretics, the devil doers who refused the law, denied the message of the Ark, and tried at every turn to promote the old decadent ways. There were many who still strove to rekindle the "Life is Sacred" creed.

"No, still not enough has been done," he thought. Crawford shuddered physically and swigged at the bottle again, *"not nearly enough."* In two days it would be the first day of the seventh year since the Ark had left the garden.

His mood deepened and blackened. He pushed a button on the little console on his desk and a sharp click from the door signalled the operation of the security lock. No one could disturb him now. He reached inside his smock-like shirt and carefully pulled out a little golden pendant. It was roughly rectangular in shape with oddly cut facets, an artistic effort to evoke the shape of the Ark. He opened it and gazed at the photograph inside.

Kate's face, tanned and crowned by her dark hair smiled at him. *"What did she really know?"* Her feelings of intimacy with *the ship* had been starkly real way back then, six years ago.

Even now she never seemed to feel troubled or afraid in herself when the subject of the Ark came up. Although she seldom made reference to it these days, he could feel the same old, easy going attitude as of old, in some way pragmatic, unpuzzled by it all. He knew without a shadow of a doubt that she had no belief in the Ark as the messenger of God. For all he knew she still adhered to the old Christianity in secret as many did.

He allowed himself that ever more rare luxury of dropping out of his self-adopted role and thinking freely, "*she must be the key, the only means of avoiding the cull, she might be the saviour of all mankind.*" He trembled with fear at the prospect of what he had in mind. Despite his position and his power, he would die a horrible death if this went wrong.

For years he had carried out his duties with vigour and been an exemplary member of the faithful but in his heart he had never believed the "God crap" and remained a confirmed atheist. But after Filshill's death on the rack through too much loose talk, he had been very, very careful. So many dead, even among the powerful; Albero, Borrhim, and the first High Minister of CAADCON, all swept away. Everywhere new faces, eager, cruel, watching.

A gentle chime sounded. He looked at the clock, "*Show time, time to risk everything.*" The surge of adrenaline sobered him and he lifted the phone. "Try Chief Inquirer Siemens again please." He closed the locket and replaced it under his shirt.

In a few seconds the well-known voice answered, "May you be blessed with death Crawford . . . what is it?"

He consciously controlled his voice, "Thanks be for the gift of death for in death there is life. Sir, I realise that this is bound to be an inopportune moment but I have an extremely important proposal and would appreciate an immediate personal appointment."

"Not now Crawford, you will have to wait. You know as well as I do that this is a momentous time, perhaps in a few days." Siemens sounded strained.

"But sir that will be too late for what I propose. Could you not . . . ?"

Siemens cut across, "Crawford, you'll be seeing a lot of me very soon, but not in private." His voice changed acquiring a slightly choked quality as if his throat constricted, "Joyous news, the Ark has been located, it is returning." There followed a brief pause. "Praise be to the lawmaker."

Crawford felt his bowels turn to ice.

CHAPTER 43

The passengers squeezed and shouldered against each other as they jockeyed for position in the overcrowded train. Kate was used to it now, everywhere crowds, never enough facilities. "Why, oh why, can't the authorities get it right? What is so difficult about providing a public conveyance?" she thought. "They have virtually eliminated road transport and yet they can't upgrade the public services adequately." She invoked that inner control that she had learned very soon after her arrival in Italy, "Pazienza," she almost uttered the words aloud. In Italy patience was an invaluable commodity.

"*Still*," she continued in her now placid detachment from the furore around her, "*at least we have always had the habit of using public transport from time to time. The poor Americans, they must be wretched without their motor cars. I wonder how bad it is over there? I don't think there was much of a transport infrastructure without the road system.*" Her mental meandering was rudely interrupted as the doors opened and she was vomited out onto the platform along with hundreds of others.

She stepped to the side letting the bulk of the press of humanity diminish. The big clock above the concourse of Roma Termini Railway Station said three-thirty. "*At least they still run on time,*" she mused.

It took a little time and not a little effort to fight her way out of the station. She didn't heed her bag, letting it dangle, and be trapped among the pushing and pulling public. There was no stealing now, pickpockets and the like were a thing of the past. Just like virtually all other social crime, it had all but vanished under the death penalty that the least of crimes could now attract.

In the bright afternoon sun in the great piazza outside, the taxis waited in order and the people queued quietly and patiently. *"Is this really Rome?"* she smiled, then immediately wiped the humour from her face as two religious policemen started to walk the length of the queue, staring into each and every face. Their bright green uniforms brought dread to every heart, they looked for an excuse to condemn, to bring death.

She stilled the chill that ran down her back, reminding herself that soon she was going to be in the very heart of their stronghold.

Eventually her turn came to board a taxi and she was mildly pleased at receiving the usual lascivious glance bestowed on all women by Italian men as she clambered into the car. The taxi man had been no exception and had acted in a bright and welcoming manner. He pulled out into the, what was for Rome, absurdly light traffic and turning his head slightly, said, "Greetings sister, where to?"

"The Office of the Holy Inquiry, please." Her words evoked a positive reaction, and a chill damped his brash cheeriness. He drove in silence for the rest of the short journey.

On the way she observed several of the pale grey armoured vans that carried the cross and crescent of the Holy Inquiry. The windows were small and barred, with dark glass, so it was impossible to see inside; but, she could imagine all too well the terror stricken passengers, probably reduced to a state of catatonia by their fear.

She got out of the cab some little distance from the main entrance of the magnificent Renaissance building which housed the Office of the Holy Inquiry. She didn't bother to question the driver as to why he had not dropped her right at the door. Some things didn't need to be said.

In any event she was glad to have yet another few moments to collect her thoughts. *"Why had Jim brought her here, almost summoned her?"* Apart from an isolated incident shortly after his promotion to his current rank when he had brought her to Rome and with pride shown her around his new domain, he had never asked her to come to Rome.

"Something is definitely going on, I wonder if it has anything to do with Cole's return? Could they possibly know and not have made it public? No, she decided it must just be the imminence of the seventh year, something big is planned, and Jim wants me to be a part of it, to share it with him. *Still, why all the secrecy?"* She felt puzzled and worried.

As she ambled in the sun the memory of her dreams came flooding back. *For how long had it been going on now? At least a week,* she decided.

The heavily armed guard brought her sharply back to reality.

"Where do you think you're going?" his tone was coarse, intimidating.

"Oh, I'm sorry, I . . . I," she fumbled in her bag, "I have an appointment."

"Pass?" His tone peremptory; questioning.

Finally she produced from the depths of her laden handbag, an envelope with the Crest of the Holy Inquiry emblazoned on it. The guard opened it, scrutinised it with great car, and then indicated a narrow, picket gate in an internal, massive wooden and elaborately carved double portal. Inside she was met by another soldier, taken to a small room adjacent, and frisked by a female using a metal detector, while a third telephoned Jim's secretary.

At last she stood outside his office while a slim woman announced her arrival. Kate regarded the woman coolly, assessing her possible threat as a rival.

"Kate, it's so good to see you." Jim came out of the room, arms outstretched, and smiling broadly. "Come in, come in, some coffee?" Without waiting on her reply he indicated to the secretary that they would both indulge. They embraced to the point of acceptable decency and went into the big, cool room, redolent of leather and wood polish.

She sat down with a little sigh of relief and kicked off her shoes. "Rome is always too hot at this time of the year." She sank into the deep, cool, cosseting brown leather. They gossiped away for a full half hour, exchanging intimacies and touching a lot, before they inevitably came to the point of the visit.

Jim leant over from the arm of Kate's chair and locked the door to the office from the console on his desk. "Kate" he said and stopped as if unsure how to go on.

"Yes, what is it Jim?" softly, encouraging him.

He got up and started pacing slowly about the room, turning to face her every now and then. She watched him in silence, waiting patiently with understanding. "Kate, this is difficult. I don't know how to say it, what with my position and the way things are."

"Is it the return of *the ship*?" she asked quietly and with a matter of fact attitude.

He started as if she had slapped him. "How... I . . ., what made you say that? Kate, please be careful, don't make facetious remarks or sarcastic quips about the Ark. It's very dangerous, deadly dangerous to speak like that, especially here." He was quite agitated.

"Jim, I'm not being facetious or making light of the Ark. I am simply telling you that it is coming back. It will be here soon."

His eyes opened wide, staring at her in incredulity. Going to his desk, he checked the remote door lock, disconnected his phone from the socket, and then crossed the room to listen at the door. Finally, he sat, or more accurately, sagged, down into one of the armchairs. "Kate, is it possible, can you still feel him, communicate with him to that degree?"

"Then I am right, that's what the problem is. You know the Ark is coming back and there is going to be more trouble. Is that it, am I right?" She was more animated now, sitting on the edge of her seat.

"You might say that, something like that, yes. But how could you know so soon, I only learned about it an hour ago from

273

the Grand Inquirer himself. And I don't think he's known for long. Oh Kate, Kate do you realise how dangerous this is? You could be executed summarily just for saying that you know what the Ark is going to do. I should be denouncing you just for this conversation." He was distraught, "You are uttering a fundamental heresy. Please be careful and do not utter a syllable of this to anyone other than me, and even then, only when we are alone. Will you promise?"

"Yes Jim." Her voice was sad but firm. "I'm not a simpleton, I know the score. God knows, when an inquirer is my lover I would be a fool not to know."

She got up and sat beside him on the arm of his chair. She leant over him and taking his hand in her's, she kissed his head. "Jim, I've known for more than a week."

He looked up at her, long and hard. "A week, my God, how?"

"It was over a week ago. I started to have dreams, vague at first, but always Cole and his friends, those giant creatures, you remember? They were happy, far away, far from the earth but thinking about the planet, about us. Gradually the images got stronger and clearer, each day more enduring until they started to come to me in wakefulness. Now I can almost invoke them at will. There is intent now, they are no longer dreaming, thinking of us. Cole, the giants, *the ship*, the Ark, call it what you like, is definitely coming back. They are already on their way, I believe they will be here in two days on the first day of the seventh year the Ark will return to whence it came."

"Dear Christ, two days."

"And now, I want to know why you brought me here. What it is that is so difficult to say?" She held his hand in her's, clasped it tightly, reassuringly. "Please tell me Jim, what is going to happen? Why does the return of *the ship* trouble you so? Do you think I am in danger, is that it? Or you, are you in danger?"

He took a deep breath as if to steady himself and collect his thoughts. "What you have told me changes everything. I had, like many others, been preparing for some manifestation of the

Ark in the coming months. The Chosen One, as you know, was to speak on the first day of the seventh year, to declare a holy year of renewed effort, a redoubling of will to follow the law."

He spoke as much to himself as to her, "Everyone in a position to know, believes that we are not doing enough, not achieving as we should. In short we are falling short of the law."

"Oh Jim, but how?" Everyone is obeying, death is respected. Why do you say that?" She was genuinely alarmed.

His eyes were cold and impenetrable, "It has been kept very quiet, but there are many dissident voices; many who ignore or deliberately flout the law. Unrighteous life is everywhere. It is like a fungus, it grows in dark, secret places." He paused and looked away from her eyes. "We shall be judged harshly, cast down by the Ark if we cannot improve."

"But why me? Where do I figure in this Jim?"

His face saddened and looking sadly up into her eyes he said, "Oh, it was a grand scheme, dangerous but promising. Kate you know me, know my true beliefs and feelings in these things. I am a hypocrite I know, but I play the game well. I play to the rules and win. I remembered well your predictions in the early days, before all this Ark stuff. Don't you remember why I was first involved? My study of psychic phenomena under stress?" She nodded. "Well, I had hatched the idea that if I could convince Siemens . . ."

"The Grand Inquirer?" she recoiled.

"Yes, yes I knew that it would be terribly dangerous. It would have been like a praying mantis trying to mate and at the same time avoid being eaten. But something had to be done and I believe that deep down, he's not much different than me. His "faith" is a matter of profit and he plays the game, oh so well. If I could get him to accept the idea that you had an inside track on the Ark's movements, on its thinking, then I might have persuaded him to use your knowledge. As a pointer or an advisor, someone who could second-guess the Ark's view of our actions. If we only knew where to concentrate our efforts for maximum effect; perhaps we could survive a judging." He paused, plucking absently at her sleeve, "But if you're right, it's too late, only two days, we are done for."

"Oh . . ." was all she said.

After some time in silent hand holding she asked, , "Can I stay here Jim? Can I stay in Rome until it's over?"

He got up and unlocked the door; she knew it was a dismissal. As he took her hand and accompanied her out of the office, he said quietly, "Very well Kate, if that's what you want."

She pulled the key to his apartment from her bag, opened her hand so that he could see it, and kissing him lightly on the cheek, made her way out of the ominous building and into the afternoon sunshine of the eternal city.

CHAPTER 44

Cardinal Melone called softly, " Si, sono pronto, grazie," to the soft knock on the door of his exquisite but sparsely furnished bedroom. He had been awake long before the servant arrived; indeed he doubted if he had slept at all. He felt terrible, his head thick, and his tongue coated.

With some difficulty he raised himself to a sitting position and called, "Entra."

A young man dressed in a simple, green gown entered with a tray, set it on a small table by the bed, bowed slightly, and exited without uttering a syllable.

The cardinal sighed deeply feeling the weight of his years and the isolation of his position. *"It's true,"* he thought, *"the closer you get to the top of the tree, the fewer the branches. Nowadays they all fear me or envy me."* He leant over, lifted the tray onto his lap, and sipped from the big, flat cup of black tea. *"Perhaps it has always been like this and I was too young and optimistic to notice."* The thought drove him deeper into melancholy.

His mind turned to the Chosen One and his speech to the world scheduled for later that morning. "How he has changed, become weak, and lost that vital spark that once drove him." His inner eye turned to memories of when the Ark had arrived, only six years ago? It seems so much longer. Oh, how the Chosen One had been lit with an inner light that night, a tremendous strength imbued him and he carried all before him. How solid had been his conviction, so simple yet so immutable. Yet now, now it was different; he seemed to vacillate, his indecision pervaded everything. He lost something, some inner force that had driven him to greatness. The cardinal shuddered slightly as if a cold breeze had permeated the room.

He emptied the cup and laid the tray aside, the little biscuit untouched. As he showered and dressed in his magnificent purple robes, he went over in his mind the message the Chosen One would transmit to the world, the message to which they had all agreed.

The earth and mankind were on trial. The very existence of mankind as we knew it was in peril. In sin lay only damnation and suffering. The way of salvation was the way of truth, the way of the law. God was just but also merciful. We had but only to renew our efforts, redouble our energies, to apply and to live by the law to gain redemption.

The more he thought, the more his spirits rallied. *How could he have doubted?* It had all been so clear, so concrete and yet, he had not believed in the beginning. At least he came to believe before it was too late.

Again there was a knock on the door and a tall guard entered at the cardinal's command. "Your grace, the Chosen One requires your immediate attendance."

Melone stilled his immediate sense of unease and followed the brightly garbed soldier from the room.

Michael the First, the Chosen One, was seated on a huge, high backed chair, facing the French windows onto a balcony when the cardinal entered the room. The door afforded a view from three-quarters behind the pontiff, Michael the First, the Chosen One, who slumped like a little, rag doll whose stuffing had been all but lost. At first he seemed to be sleeping and the tall man approached slowly trying not to make any sound.

"I am not sleeping, Peppine, I never sleep now." The voice was thin and ragged. With difficulty the old man rose from the big chair and shuffled to the window. "The time has come, my old friend, the day of judgement has arrived, and I have lived to see it. Oh, that this cup of sorrow would be spared me."

Melone stiffened, "What are you saying, Michael?"

"Come. Come close *carissimo amico*, stand by me in my hour of need." The old man, shrivelled inside his white robe, beckoned with a scrawny, knotted fist.

The cardinal strode the few steps to his side and with a tenderness that spoke of something greater than mere physical love, put his long arm around the smaller man's shoulder. Stifling his curiosity, he stood erect, gazing from the tall window into the great piazza of the Basilica, even now crowded with thousands of pilgrims.

The sun shone brightly from a clear, blue sky bathing the scene with a crystal clarity born of the radical reduction in vehicular and industrial air pollution. From this height a festive quality imbued the crowd, multi-coloured and with many singing.

The old man's parched, paper thin voice spoke again, "Today I had hoped to speak to the faithful of their task, of their need to obey the law. I had hoped to spur them to greater efforts that they might achieve in the coming year that which is necessary to satisfy God's demands of us. We are sinners, all, and God sees our sins. We must make amends." He stopped his inward reverie. "It is too late, Peppine, the Ark returns as we speak." He made the sign of the cross, "God have mercy on us."

The cardinal spoke barely above a whisper, "What is it that you are trying to say, Michael?"

Turning his shrunken face up to gaze at the taller man, his clear blue eyes still with an echo of their past sparkle, the Chosen One spoke slowly and deliberately, "At 2:00 a.m. this morning, I was advised that the Ark has been detected. It is returning to the garden and should have entered the earth's atmosphere a short time ago."

As he spoke the dark heads in the piazza below started to turn pale as some, and soon all, lifted their faces upwards, and started to point frantically to the sky. Both men in the room reached simultaneously and opened the doors onto the balcony.

The pontiff sagged and had to be assisted by the cardinal, who waved away the Swiss Guards rushing into the room followed by a clutch of clergymen and nuns. Slowly and painfully the pontiff inched his way into the open air leaning heavily on the arm of his tall friend. Neither looked up until they stood by the balustrade. No one in the piazza looked their way.

In the clear sky the black shape of *the ship* was already quite large and easily recognisable for what it was. It was directly overhead and not yet obstructing the sun. An eerie silence had descended on the throng below, but as the shape grew inexorably bigger, fear began to spread, a palpable sensation, which welled up like a tidal wave sweeping sense and caution aside. Hysteria flared and total chaos broke out. The black shape began to obliterate the sky, eclipsing the sun, dimming the daylight. Now its terrifying bulk could be discerned, its impossible weight felt. Screams and shouts filled the air as men clawed their way over women and children, the strong climbed over the weak in an effort to flee the square. Every race, every creed, every social and political grouping was there but were all made animals by blind panic. Again they died in their hundreds before the great pillars of the Basilica.

On the balcony the two men knelt in prayer, heads bowed, muttering aloud.

Still the black mountain descended, lower and lower. The lower it came the slower it travelled until, in total silence it came to a complete halt, its slick underside but metres from the pinnacle of the great cupola. Night had all but shut out the day. The two men on the balcony did not look up, but they no longer prayed. The only sounds to be heard were the faint groans of the injured as they lay far below on the pavement slabs of the piazza.

The Pope began to shiver violently as if gripped by an icy cold. "Michael?" whispered the cardinal, gripping him in his arms as if to shield him, "What is the matter?"

At that moment the pale green luminescence returned and moments later the head-like object. Melone looked up, but the

Pope remained bent, head down, eyes closed. Again the all pervading voice, but quiet as if only those on the balcony might hear it, "I come in judgement."

Melone, his heart pounding as if it might crack his rib cage, swallowed hard, "Mercy, oh Lord, have mercy on us sinners, grant us forgiveness."

Again the voice spoke, evenly, in a matter of fact way, "I come in judgement. I bring justice. Mercy and forgiveness are denials of justice. I have come again in the name of the just and yet you have continued to choose among the laws, have sought to twist the ways of the garden. Again I say to you, I come in judgement and justice shall be meted out to all that the garden may flourish. Prepare ye the way of the lord, weed the garden."

The light went out, the head vanished, and Michael the First crumpled to the floor. For a few moments no one moved, then the Swiss Guards strode onto the balcony and bent over the fallen figure of the pontiff. They slowly and with great reverence lifted his dead body and carried it into the room.

CHAPTER 45

Jim Crawford's apartment was all that one might expect of the quarters of an inquirer; one of those historic suites of rooms full of elaborate decoration; an art aficionado's dream. Kate had made coffee in the ultramodern and somehow out of place kitchen in anticipation of Jim's arrival. But now she sat frozen on the edge of the couch, the coffee cooling rapidly, and her eyes glued to the TV screen.

The news broadcast she was watching had abruptly switched to the views of *the ship* as it descended from nowhere to come to rest over the dome of Saint Peter's. Not that she would have needed the television to tell her that it had arrived, the windows of the apartment were directly under the edge of the object. The sheer black cliffs of its side towered into the sky above her head. To her left as she faced the window, all was bright daylight while to her right, darkness stretched away. She felt no fear which was more than could be said for the panic stricken masses in the street below.

She waited for a few more minutes to see if the strange voice of *the ship* would continue but when there was no further sound other than the chatter of the commentator, she got up and went to the window. "*I wonder if every radio and television station in the world received the message?*" she mused. She knew in her heart that it had to be so. Below, the panic slowly subsided and the street became deserted until the pale grey staff car appeared and turned towards the entrance. Jim got out of the car with another in uniform and walked into the building. "Hmm," she muttered, "the sentries have run off."

Jim burst into the apartment his face flushed and breathing heavily as if he had run up the stairs. "You were absolutely correct, you were absolutely correct!" He turned back to face the doorway where a somewhat dishevelled Siemens stood panting.

Kate felt a cold shiver down her back. What was the Grand Enquirer doing here?

"Kate?" he said holding out his hand, "Death be granted to you. I remember you, perhaps you recall our meeting; it seems a long time ago now."

Kate did not know quite what to do, courtesy, bow, or make the sign of benediction. In the end she pulled herself erect and bowed ever so slightly. "Your Eminence, death be with you. I indeed recall the moment of our meeting. I recall it clearly and to this day I regret that you were unable to keep your promise of a return to the mountain to visit the site of the Ark."

The bright steely-light in Siemens eyes made Kate realise that she had overstepped the mark. "I, I apologise for my forward manner Your Eminence. The shock of the return of the Ark has over excited me. It . . ." She stopped short as he waved away her protests.

His voice became cold and hard. Speaking only a little above a whisper so that she had to listen with care to make out all of his words, he said, "Jim has spoken to me of things that are heresy, things that in normal circumstances would have you both caused death with all the due process of the church." Kate recoiled, shrinking into Crawford's arms. "Do not mistake me, either of you, I am prepared to go along with your plan, Jim, but if it fails I will not go down with you."

"What plan Jim, what plan are you talking about?" Kate's voice was small.

Jim held her from him at arms length, "I think you know, Kate. You know what is in my mind. I have spoken to the Grand Enquirer of your strange gift regarding the Ark, I have been frank about your belief that Cole is in some kind of contact with its power."

Kate broke free, "What? My God what have you done? We will both be killed." She spun around to face Siemens and stopped short. He had an automatic pistol in his hand pointed straight at her.

"Keep calm woman. I will not allow even the slightest complication. We will all have to be cool and courageous to have a chance of survival and female histrionics have no place in our plan." He exuded authority. "The plan is simply this. As soon as possible I will attempt to get you into the Basilica, as close as possible to the manifestation of the angel of the Ark. You will attempt to make the contact of which you claim to be capable. You will attempt to dissuade the Ark from its stated intention of judgement." His short sentences delivered in a clipped, military style brooked no interruption. "If you fail, I do not think that I will need to eliminate you but if necessary I will. You will remain here until all has been arranged. You will communicate with no one." With that he turned and left the apartment. Before the door closed, she saw the sentries in the corridor.

"Jim?" her voice querulous, "I'm afraid." She shrank into his arms.

"So am I," he replied.

CHAPTER 46

Darkness had fallen when Siemens returned. He said nothing until they descended the stairs and got into the big car which waited at the entrance to the building. "I can get you into the piazza," he said, "but that's as far as I can go. I hope that it will do." He gazed quizzically at Kate.

She grasped Crawford's arm as she replied, "I don't know, I suppose so."

Siemens waved his hand and the limousine moved off silently down the street and under the bulk of *the ship*. The street lights shone dismally in the unnatural night as the vehicle made its way to the very entrance of the Vatican City. It stopped and the little group got out.

There was a detachment of soldiers wearing the uniform of the enquirer's office and a thin line of Swiss Guards on the edge of the piazza. Siemens signalled to Kate to wait and went forward with Crawford and his men to the line of guardsmen. There followed an animated discussion out of her earshot, but after a few minutes, Siemens turned and signalled for her to come forward.

"This is the best we can do," he was whispering in her ear. "You can enter the piazza but no further. Be discreet if you can. I do not know what you intend to do but try not to make it obvious that you are trying to communicate with the Ark."

She nodded silently and one of the guardsmen unhooked the chain that hung between the bollards that ringed the piazza. She stepped through and soon disappeared into the gloom of the great-unlit circle in front of the Basilica.

She felt very alone in the dark. The strange echoing quality of sound and the lack of stars, moon, or even clouds above unnerved her. Dimly, against the faint light from the perimeter lights of the piazza, she made out the Egyptian obelisk in the centre. She made her way towards it for no other reason than that it provided a marker in the midst of the nothingness. She sat down on the cold stone base and held her head in her hands. *What was she doing here? Nothing could be more dangerous, why had she got herself into this?* At last she turned her thoughts to the Ark, *Cole?*

Time passed and the lugubrious tolling of the big bell echoed her impotence. Nothing happened.

Raising herself up, stiff with cold and having no protection against the night air, she began to wander aimlessly in the General direction of the massive portals of the giant church. She gained the steps, barely visible from the wan lamps that hung high under the roof space above. Her nerves jangled, raw and stretched. A dark figure emerged from the shadows, tall and black. She froze. "Who is it?" The inanity of her remark and the use of English struck her as soon as the words were out.

"What are you doing here my child?" The accented tones of Cardinal Melone were steady, non-threatening.

"I, I, . . ." she realised that there was nothing to say, the game was up; she was facing death and failure.

The tall figure of the cardinal came close, "What are you doing here, my child? Have you come to worship, have you no fear? Do you not fear judgement?"

Kate stood stock-still. *What was she to do? What could she do? Nothing. There was nothing to be done.* She sagged a little as the dark figure turned slightly and beckoned into the darkness. Two guards stepped forward. "Take her."

She jumped back reflexively into the piazza and threw her arms upwards in supplication, "Cole, Cole can you hear me?" A deep green swirl of light flickered for a few seconds on the under surface of the ship.

"Wait!" The cardinal's voice commanded and the guards stopped, standing at attention. "What have you done my child?"

Kate continued to look up, "Cole, oh, Cole can you hear me?"

Again a deep glowing flicker of light roiled on the featureless black. She looked straight at the clergyman, barely visible in his black garb. She made up her mind. "Oh Holy One I have come here because I have been called, chosen by the Ark. The Ark has spoken to me since first it came to save us and now it calls me to this place. You have witnessed the face of God reflect my supplication, have you not?"

The cardinal remained silent, still; then a deep, more felt than heard, rumble echoed around the piazza for a few seconds. The cardinal froze, face ashen, and clasping his hands in a gesture of supplication, fell to his knees, "Yes, yes I have seen it."

Kate knew she had nowhere left to go, she would have to see it through. "Take me to the place of the visitation of the angel of the Ark," she said with a calmness and authority, which astonished her. "No," she said, "take me to the top of the cupola near to the Ark."

The cardinal got up and without a word turned back towards the great door of the church. The Swiss Guard fell in behind Kate as she followed the cardinal. In the portico and before the door, they turned right and followed the curve of the building until they came to a small entrance. The priest signalled and one of the guards stepped forward and opened the wooden door with a key. Inside was the door of an elevator.

"The elevator climbs part of the way and after that the stairs go to the very top of the cupola, close to the blessed Ark." Melone spoke in hushed, reverential tones and stood some distance from Kate. "I cannot accompany you, I am not worthy." With that he reached inside his gown and brought out a small battery-powered torch, which he handed to one of the soldiers who in turn handed it to Kate. She took it and stood for a long time in the gloom struggling inwardly, searching for the courage to begin the ascent.

She entered the little lift and pressed the button. After a short time the elevator stopped and the doors opened. Outside was total darkness. The light from the torch was feeble and the walls of the narrow, ever more tightly turning staircase was almost black in colour. She stumbled often but with every step the feeling of communion with Cole grew. Eventually the stairway became so narrow and steeply twisting that she had some difficulty in maintaining her balance, but in the end she stood at the very topmost level. From the openings in the wall, Rome stretched beyond, delineated only by the street lamps. Great black areas defined the Vatican Gardens and a subtle increase in luminosity, evinced the edge of the ship far away on all sides.

"Cole," she said aloud, looking up to the black surface above. It seemed close enough to touch, "Cole?" she asked again with more force; more conviction. A faint green flickered and settled in the black above her, giving the surface a depth, a three dimensional quality. "Cole?" The green strengthened and became more defined covering a circular area of about five meters in diameter. A shift in the surface suddenly made the material seem to flow like a liquid, making her shrink back. A bump appeared, formless at first but gradually protruding more and more until it formed a stalk with a swelling on the end about the size of a football. The football began to take on a more detailed shape until it had the form of a human head, green and glassy.

"Cole?" she said at a loss for words. The head's features altered and took the likeness of her husband.

The eyes opened, liquidly green and the mouth moved. A deep, dark voice with a gurgling quality, "Kate, is it really you?"

Her heart leapt, her head swam such that she had to grasp the parapet tightly lest she fall. "Yes, yes, Cole it's me."

The gurgling voice followed the movement of the green lips, "Why are you here, what do you wish of me now? You must know that I am changed, am become great. My great work is about to be accomplished."

"Cole, oh Cole, you cannot do this." She felt him close, not as *the ship,* the Ark, but as the man. "Have they hurt you, are you in pain, are you imprisoned?"

The gurgling laugh was so deep it reverberated in her head, "No, no my sweet, I am not imprisoned. I am liberated, I am not in pain but in ecstasy. I am become that which you cannot understand."

She reached out to touch the head-like object. It was cool but not hard, somehow yielding and plastic. She caressed the cheek, "Oh Cole, you have not changed so much that I cannot recognise you, not so much that you cannot remember me. I tell you, you cannot do this thing. The doing of such a thing as you threaten will mean the extinction of Cole. You will indeed be changed by such an act, changed into something you were never meant to be. Your dream of a cleaner world, a world where humanity can survive is under way. It is a harsh world for certain Cole, a place of scant forgiveness and little mercy, but a world on the mend nonetheless. Do not destroy it now, you can have mercy, show compassion, show love."

She stopped.

The green head said nothing for a long time and then it retracted, shrunk back into the green swirl above until no sign remained. Gradually the faint green luminescence faded, the swirls and marks disappeared, the glassy black returned.

"Cole?" she said, but no answer, no sound returned from her querulous voice, darkness reigned. She waited in the cold dark air.

The faintest of hisses, a sighing of the air broke the absolute still. The black receded. *The ship* began to rise, ever upward, ever more distant until she could see its limits. Still it rose in utter silence until the stars shone in all their brilliance; the moon its pallid light bestowed. Suddenly it was gone, disappeared from sight. She felt the hot tears run down her cheeks, the sense of absolute loss invade her soul. She knew he was gone forever.

Turning slowly she fumbled her way down the steep, twisting staircase until at last she stood in the cool, free air in the piazza.

Cardinal Melone approached her and spreading his arms wide called in a great voice that all might hear, "Oh Holiest One." He bent his knees and sinking to the ground lay prostrate before her.

She raised her eyes to the stars, "Oh Cole, what legacy have you left me?"

END?

Lightning Source UK Ltd.
Milton Keynes UK
UKOW041704240413

209686UK00001B/271/P